RAMADAN RAMSEY

RAMADAN RAMSEY

A NOVEL

LOUIS EDWARDS

AMISTAD
— 35 —

An Imprint of HarperCollinsPublishers

"To Zion." Words and Music by Lauryn Hill, Charles Fox, and Norman Gimbel © 2001 Roadli Music, Fox-Gimbel Productions, Inc. and Obverse Creations Music. All rights on behalf of Rodali Music administered by Warner-Tamerlane Publishing Corp. (Contains samples of "And the Feeling's Good" by Charles Fox and Norman Gimbel, Roadli Music.) All rights reserved. Used by permission of Alfred Music.

"To Zion." Written by Lauryn Hill, Charles Fox, and Norman Gimbel Copyright © 1998 Sony Music Publishing LLC, Obverse Creation Music, Rodali Music, and Words West LLC. All rights on behalf of Sony Music Publishing LLC, Obverse Creation Music, and Rodali Music administered by Sony Music Publishing LLC, 424 Church Street, Suite 1200, Nashville, TN 37219. International copyright secured, all rights reserved—contains elements from "And the Feeling's Good" by Charles Fox and Norman Gimbel, published by Rodali Music (administered by Sony Music Publishing LLC) and Words West LLC (P.O. Box 15187, Beverly Hills, CA 90209 USA). Reprinted by permission of Hal Leonard LLC.

HarperCollins books may be purchased for educational, business, or sales promotional use. For information, please email the Special Markets Department at SPsales@harpercollins.com.

FIRST EDITION

Designed by Kyle O'Brien

Library of Congress Cataloging-in-Publication Data has been applied for.

ISBN 978-0-06-301203-5

21 22 23 24 25   LSC   10 9 8 7 6 5 4 3 2 1

To Mama's Mamas

Sarah Lee Metz Lockett

and

"Mom Bert"
Alberta Varnado Lockett Bryant

&

Daddy's Mama

"Momee"
Gessie Carmen Edwards

CONTENTS

AN ABEYANCE

PART III

Istanbul

PART IV

The Other Side of the World

Now let me pray to keep you from
The perils that will surely come.
See, life for you, my prince, has just begun . . .

—Lauryn Hill, "To Zion"

PART I

NEW ORLEANS

THE CREATION OF RAMADAN

Ramadan was blessed. Of course, as with everyone—the blessed and the bewitched alike—he didn't always feel the pleasures of being his natural, divine self. Indeed, he would sometimes become tempestuous and unruly, losing himself and the ability to sense his great fortune even to be alive. And he would stomp around his grandmother's house, gritting his teeth and growling like a madman, or rather like a mad little boy, because at the age of five, say, for the purposes of introduction, and with a scrawniness that made some refer to him as "skinny as a rail," he couldn't really quite pull off madman.

The sight or just the sound of Ramadan tearing through her house at 1216 St. Philip Street in the Tremé neighborhood of New Orleans never failed to crack his grandmother up. "My little bull," an amused Mama Joon mumbled to herself whenever she detected the telltale signs of one of his tantrums beginning in the front room. His pitter-pattering and bovine grunts would echo down the hall to her in the kitchen, and she would snatch a dishrag from her shoulder, extend it in a flapping motion, and wait for the little raging Ramadan to enter the room where she stood, crouched, anticipating his charge. The image of a laughing

Mama Joon waving her dirty towel never failed to seize the child's attention and refocus his mind, like music or motion pictures. That vision of her—combined with the intoxicating smells of whatever she was cooking and the warmth radiating from the stove—would stop him in his manic tracks, returning him to himself. He would again relish the comfort of breathing normally, not snorting, not huffing, his madness becoming, in an instant, play, and the bone-deep longing that fueled his fury would manifest as farce. He would scuff his little Nikes backwards on the old hardwood floor, preparing his advance; wiggle his index-finger horns at his temples (comically disregarding the rigidity of horns); and tilt his head down so that when he made his cushioned leap into Mama Joon's aproned torso he could nestle his neck into the side of her ample belly. She would hug his waist and leverage his forward momentum into an upside-down flip, ending with Ramadan's feet pedaling before her eyes, the vibrations of his sudden, riotous laughter tickling her into a heightened state of amusement as well. Not exactly Abbott and Costello, perhaps. But their interaction had for the players—who were their own audience—the strange allure of low-budget regional theater. Sincere entertainment for a limited constituency. Imagine the quaint production of a classic drama succumbing to too much sentimentality; or being played, somewhere in the suburb of a suburb, unintentionally, for laughs. Not great. Wouldn't travel. But, given the quality of the source material, satisfying nonetheless.

If Ramadan's aunt Clarissa or any of his cousins were around to witness the scene (and they often were because they lived on the other side of Mama Joon's shotgun double and came sniffing and foraging next door anytime they smelled her cooking or wanted to "borrow" some money), their anxieties would be relieved when the dishrag pantomime began, for secretly they felt threatened by Ramadan and his moody ways. In

such moments, their envy, born of their understanding his place of privilege in Mama Joon's heart, would seethe with a bit less passion. They
sensed—quite reasonably—these relatives, these rivals for Mama Joon's
affection and the benefits thereof, that rooted in Ramadan's tempera-
mental nature was a power, a will far superior to their own, and that his
bullishness, were it ever to flourish into its most potent form, a true and
virtuous virility, might somehow be employed to destroy them. That
they implicitly understood there was something in them that might
warrant destruction could be chalked up to the uncanny ability most
folks have, without any specialized training, mind you, to assess accurately their worth (or worthlessness, for that matter), the evidence of a
persistent white noise of truth. Their fear of Ramadan explained why, at
every turn, they stressed the slightness of his form, nudging him about
his boniness (as if accentuating this perceived weakness could truly
prevent his evolution toward strength and maturity), for it was they,
his very kin—whom he loved in spite of their wariness of him—who
were the ones, far more so than the random, chubby playground pal or
the prematurely muscled schoolmate, who called Ramadan, turning a
tease into a taunt, "skinny as a rail."

❦

RAMADAN'S EXTREME LEANNESS was a trait he shared with his father, Mustafa Totah, a Syrian transplanted to New Orleans to help
his uncle Adad run a small but profitable gas station and convenience
store on the corner of North Rampart and Governor Nicholls streets,
just a couple of blocks from Mama Joon's. Ramadan had never met
and perhaps never would meet Mustafa, which of course accounted,
in no small part, for his profound sense of yearning, an impulse so

intense that it sometimes sent him bolting across the borders between species, his being instinctively attempting to substitute a feral closeness to nature for the missing parental bond. Better a wild bull, his psyche had concluded, than an abandoned little boy!

It was in the fall of 1999, less than a year before the birth of Ramadan, when Mustafa had first heard the foreign phrase "skinny as a rail" applied to himself by Alicia Ramsey. A flirtatious and decidedly not "skinny as a rail" New Orleans girl, Alicia had casually offered to cook him a pot of red beans to fatten him up, before leaving him deciphering the simile and her smile. His Arabic ears, preternaturally pricked with suspicion of the American tongue, had heard instead "Skinny Israel." He had thought it curious that a young woman who was plainly coming on to him would call him that. Accurate as it might have been in a strictly geographic sense (true, Israel was a narrow sliver of a country just to the southwest of his own), it wasn't a manner of speaking that one could remotely associate with amorous intent. What, after all, did Israel, skinny or otherwise, have to do with him? Was the girl somehow disrespecting him? Was she an American bigot, prone to Middle Eastern insult without even knowing it? Had he misread her interest altogether? Or was this "Skinny Israel" nonsense some sort of romantic mischief, as when a girl says she hates you but secretly desires you intensely? Yes, he liked this latter rationalization. He liked it very, very much. (Mustafa had a way of turning things around in his head for maximum psychological impact that ultimately accrued to his own benefit—in short, he was a pretty regular guy.) American English wasn't easy, he had learned, and neither, evidently, were American girls.

But, then, Mustafa hadn't really tried very hard to converse with the young women who frequented the store, mostly because his uncle had warned him, before bringing him to New Orleans, not to become involved with the customers. Uncle Adad had taken his favorite nephew for a long walk through Aleppo Park. When they came to the river's edge, he stopped, looked Mustafa in the eyes, and said, "Americans are for the good business. *Money*. Not the bad business."

By "bad business," Adad, with a universal finger-poking gesture, had made it clear just what he meant. "I mean *love*," he had added—though it was obvious to Mustafa and to anyone in the park who might have witnessed his uncle's right index finger darting in and out of the tight, fleshy hole he'd formed with his left fist, that Uncle Adad meant something else.

A few months later, there stood thick-legged, brown-skinned Alicia batting her eyelashes at Mustafa as he squatted in the middle aisle of the store unpacking cartons of Wrigley's gum. "Boy, I need to cook you a pot of red beans." Then she tossed back over her shoulder as she exited with her bag of chips, "Skinny Israel." Mustafa had gulped back his linguistic confusion and physical attraction and quickly returned his attention to restocking the racks with white, green, and yellow packs of Spearmint, Doublemint, and Juicy Fruit.

Lately, he had begun to take this particular task much more seriously, for on a recent afternoon, fascinated by all he did not know about these colorfully designed objects, he had sat at the computer in the store's backroom office and searched "Juicy Fruit." Several mouse clicks later, he found himself transported across the World Wide Web to a place he'd never dreamed of venturing, www.wrigley.com. In retrospect, he thought he must have been searching for the key to the success of a product devoted to idle chewing, trying to solve the mysterious case of the ever-disappearing cases of Wrigley's. He navigated his way through the corporate website and discovered, quite by happenstance, the core principle explaining the surprising necessity for his own employment, the constant need to refill the bins with such a modest and seemingly *unnecessary* commodity. The simple words—which moved Mustafa almost to tears, once he had translated them—were positioned next to the photograph of one William Wrigley, Jr., the great man behind the gum. Yes, Mustafa had decided in an instant Mr. Wrigley was indeed great. Only a great man, a man of rare humility and vision, would dare imagine that something so common, so lowly as chewing gum, something famous for sticking to the bottom of one's shoe, could be the basis of an empire. And—only a great man could be as expressive about the reason for his own greatness. Mr. Wrigley's words had rung through Mustafa's mind as poignantly as the musings of a mystic: *Life and business are rather simple, after all—to make a success of either, you've got to hang on to the knack of putting yourself in the other person's place.*

Mustafa had sat alone in the store office staring at the bulbous Indigo iMac G3 as if it were a burning bush. (He was trying to convince Uncle Adad to buy a sleeker laptop.) Only after the monitor dimmed from inactivity, stirring him, did he blink himself out of his daydream. A tremor of understanding—almost spiritual in nature—had rushed through him, so he had reached into his bag and pulled out the Quran his mother had given him as a going-away present the day he'd left Aleppo. ("It belonged to your father," Rana Totah had said to her only son. "I made the case myself. It will keep you safe in America!" She had pecked his cheeks, adding, "Even though I know you will never sit still long enough to read it. You always want to go, go, go, just like your father, just like right now . . .") Sitting in the office, Mustafa unzipped the silky, gold-colored case, and he thumbed several pages of the Holy Book, which indeed, he never found time to read. The familiarity of the Arabic script soothed him, though, like the memory of the sound of Rana's voice, telling him goodbye. (*Mother tongue*—no wonder they called it that.) Then he tapped the keyboard and brought the monitor back to life, and he let his eyes drift back and forth between Mr. Wrigley's words and Allah's as revealed to the great prophet.

Mustafa hadn't been quite the same after experiencing, in this way, this queer collision of cultures—the digital and the analog; the secular and the religious; the American and the Arab. The store hadn't been the same to him, either. Uncle Adad's little capitalist enterprise began to impress him as a more humane endeavor, for he felt certain this Mr. Wrigley, while special, could not be the only one of his ilk with such forthright compassion. Indeed if, as purported by Sir William, this Gandhi of gum, it was *only* the man who truly understands that people and their feelings are essential to the ability of his products to appeal to the masses, if *only* the empathetic man could truly succeed, then Uncle Adad's store was filled with neatly designed bags and cartons and cans of the evidence of something vital: the inherent power of the people. These products, so the rigorous Mr. Wrigley had affirmed, were popular *because* their makers realized they were *for* the people, and as such, had to be *of* the people. Coca-Cola was, of course, a sterling example of this principle; the proof was in its universal triumph. But so was everything from Planter's Peanuts to Kit Kat candy bars, from Snickers to Campbell's Soup, from Kraft Macaroni & Cheese to StarKist Tuna. They were all splendidly democratic in some distinctly American way. Conversely, any product that failed had had its day in the court of public opinion and, for better or worse, on the grounds of its inability to strengthen or sustain the people, been ruled unconstitutional.

Mustafa accepted and internalized this: Every stick of Wrigley's was redolent of the republic. And for him, America, once as foreign and unthinkable a destination as Mars, once as distant and virtual as www.wrigley.com, acquired a *realness*, as well as some of the specific properties of his favorite product, Wrigley's gum: a familiarity, a fathomable appeal, a surprising and substantive complexity that challenged the showy surfaces of its vibrant packaging—and, yes, a sweetness.

He told no one of his quiet discovery; his uncle and his cousins would have thought he was crazy. America wasn't sweet to them; it was bitter. It was also stony and cold, not to mention potentially dangerous, more like one of those brick cartons of Green Giant chopped spinach in the freezer bin that few of the regular customers bought. (That big grin on the giant's face hid the potential destructiveness of his might—he was a *giant*, after all—beware!) No, you had to boil this place out of its rock-hard state in order to extract and enjoy its nutrients. That was America to his relatives. But, armed with the more flattering implications of his private wisdom, Mustafa began to approach each day's work with a new sense of pride. Now, every time he slid a box cutter through a cardboard case of Wrigley's products to release the bulk of its contents, he felt he was committing an act of civility. The dexterity with which he plucked a fallen five-stick pack of gum back into its carton or stacked fifteen-stick packs onto the end-cap displays acquired a newfound care, a near pianistic tenderness.

It was, of course, these loving and lingering touches he applied to his tasks that had caught Alicia's eye, for if a man cared this much about gum, how much might he, given half a chance, care about a girl? How tenderly might he touch *her*?

During a quiet moment following the after-school rush, a few hours after Alicia had called him "Skinny Israel," Mustafa asked his cousin Malik what he thought she meant.

Malik, bored with the question, was more interested in reading one of his beloved Superman comic books, the latest issue of which was open before him now as he leaned on the side counter. He said cynically,

"I don't know. I think she believes you are the hero who will bring peace to the Middle East."

Jamil, Malik's younger brother, who also worked in the store, shadowboxed and shuffled over to a smirking Mustafa, and jabbed him playfully in the chest. Winking at his brother, he whispered, "Aww, what's wrong, Mustafa? You know, Malik, I do believe our little cousin wishes what the pretty girl really means is that she wants him to bring peace to *her* middle east."

Mustafa had pretended not to find his cousin's vulgarity funny, and when Uncle Adad yelled at them to get back to work, it was easy to disengage from the camaraderie with his cousins, because not only was he still brooding over "Skinny Israel," but he was also thinking about tasting, for the first time, homemade red beans. He stared at the triple-stacked rows of one-pound bags of Camellia beans on a shelf nearby. "Famous New Orleans Red Beans" and "Since 1923," the package with the bright red flower at the top proudly announced, and he guessed these were the beans Alicia had in mind. They *must* be, for patrons, he had observed, bought them with an almost religious weekly rhythm, as if Monday were a leguminous Sabbath.

Hunger would, indeed, play an important role in the relations of Mustafa and Alicia, as it does, metaphorically, in all matters of love and in the activity Uncle Adad had mimed to Mustafa along the bank of the Aleppo River. Two months would pass, and it would be Ramadan— the Muslim season of fasting, of holy hunger—before Mustafa finally resolved to meet Alicia, disobey Uncle Adad's cautionary dictate, and submit to his curiosity; that is, his intellectual craving.

He was in fact starving—in the way that only a slightly irreverent nineteen-year-old male during mid-afternoon on the first day of Ramadan can be—when he came out of the little stockroom from his break.

Looking out the large glass windows toward the street, he saw Alicia reaching into her bag of Lay's Potato Chips, which gleamed bright yellow in the early December sunlight, refracting with the promise of slice after slice of greasy delight, some wondrous blend of populism and pleasure. As he watched this girl who had expressed a complicated desire for him slide a golden chip into her mouth and silently crunch it with satisfaction, the confrontation of his own mode of denial with her casual air of fulfillment empowered him with the will to act, his low-caloric delirium alchemizing into a jolt of energy, a metabolic burst of courage.

He paused at the edge of the checkout counter to look into the mirror near a display of cheap sunglasses. His fresh haircut, a flattering fade, accentuated the best features of his naturally tanned face. The sharp lines of the cut darted at his temples, arrowing toward his marbled eyes, an unprecedented swirl of blues and greens and grays with flecks of white, as if Moneted by Providence in a random act of ocular Impressionism. Uncle Adad was sitting up on his stool behind the cash register waiting on customers, but Mustafa could feel his gaze. From his perch, Adad was aware of every movement in the store. His acute vigilance was all the surveillance system he needed. In his most ecstatic moments of observation, he went from merely seeing to being a *seer*, displaying a near-prophetic ability to predict what was about to happen in the store. During Mustafa's first week at work he had demonstrated his skills by whispering what almost every customer was going to buy or, in more showy moments of predilection, to steal. Malik had the gift as well, and Mustafa sensed that his cousin, who was busy in the back mopping up a puddle of milk, and his uncle were exchanging a rippling, telepathic plea for him to stop primping in the mirror. Primping was necessary only if you were in pursuit of attention, and a particular kind of attention at that. They wanted him, so the tension of their unspoken prudence said to Mustafa, to take two steps *away* from the door, through which the potentially "bad business" girl had just exited, and finish his break *inside*, and then get his butt back to work. But their reticence said something else to Mustafa, for Uncle Adad could have simply dispatched him to the office for a roll of cash register receipt paper or the reading glasses he was always forgetting on his desk. Or Malik could have told him to come mop up the milk. They could have easily stopped him from going after Alicia—but they did not. In their hesitancy, Mustafa read a tacit encouragement. Uncle Adad had his beloved Aunt Zahirah; Malik had Sanaa, the pretty girl from Damascus, whom he was going to marry next year. The older men must have, without even realizing it, actually wanted their young male kin to sample the company of a woman, to test the power of his manliness. Mustafa assumed this to be true (and it was), and he stared out the window with water-lily-eyed want. Alicia had paused at the first island of gas pumps and was looking back at him. As he began walking out to meet her, Uncle Adad's and Malik's eyes lifted from their routine busyness and locked across the room, just in front of Mustafa. Their restraint, a mix of anxiety and permissiveness, held, and Mustafa took another step forward, and then another, moving gracefully through the caution tape of their affection.

Alicia's heart, like most hearts, could rarely be said to race, but what *is* the sudden vision of love approaching, if not an emotional approximation of the thrill of Churchill Downs? There is a galloping swiftness to young love. A loping and a lurching forward. A remarkable velocity of feeling. No wonder we still measure the force of great engines by the accumulated power of horses. We could quantify the pull of passion by it, too. Lust, even. Love—it wants to leave all of its rivals behind. To get there first. To win—and what purse grander than a human heart? Never mind that Alicia and Mustafa were in New Orleans, Louisiana.

That it was December. No matter where you are when it happens, it's as if you are in Louisville, Kentucky—in early May, in a big hat or a bow tie—cheering yourself on to victory.

Alicia knew nothing of the famous Derby or its rituals, including the sipping of mint juleps, but whenever she saw or even thought of the dreamy-eyed foreigner from the Quicky Mart, she knew the sweet intoxication of desire. She knew nothing of saccharined and spearminted bourbon in silver cups. But nineteen and lonely—the existential equivalent of a fresh, fragrant leaf of mint being crushed into sugar—she was particularly vulnerable to the whiskey of romance. And it to her.

Of course, it had been the disinhibiting effects of desire that had pressed Alicia, a somewhat shy girl who had been mostly "raised right," as they say, to flirt with Mustafa in the first place. Red beans? *Red beans!* Where had that come from? She didn't even know how to cook a pot of red beans—or anything else, really. Mama Joon had never been able to keep her in the kitchen long enough to learn how to cut an onion properly. In fact, she associated the smell of raw seasoning vegetables (onions, celery, garlic) with the hours and hours of time and labor it would take to cook whatever it was they were intended to flavor. A gumbo. A stew. Or, yes, a pot of beans. The impatience of her youth was incompatible with such rigors. But her little lie to Mustafa about cooking for him had set something simmering in him; she had seen it brewing in his eyes. As she watched him come out of the store right now, her mind shot through to a time when he would ask her about the meal she'd offered, and she'd have to confess her culinary incompetence. It would occur during some lighthearted, postcoital, pillow-talkish moment that had turned playful. Him: *What! You lied to me?* Her (giggling): *I'm sorry.* Neck nibbles of forgiveness. Penance? A non-negotiable submission to a round two.

But first, here came Mustafa *now*, walking toward her with a gangly gait, emboldened by a catalytic hunger. Here she was chomping on another Lay's potato chip, riveted by the fantasy of what today might do to tomorrow.

The closer he got to her, the wider his grin became, as if she had the power to incite good humor. He stopped abruptly, for fear that if he took another step he would burst into laughter. Yes, he wanted to greet her with a smile, but if he was cackling uncontrollably, he would appear a fool. The pause was just the respite he needed to relax into the winsomeness with which a young charmer should step to a girl, and he bobbed his head back, chinning a handsome hello.

"Hi," she said. "I'm Alicia."

"I know." He had heard someone call her name once, though he had forgotten how to pronounce it. "Hello . . . Alicia," he said, trying out the enunciation for the first time, liking, without even realizing it, the familiar Al-essence on the tip of his tongue, the lingual affiliation of the girl with his god.

"And you are . . . ," she prompted him.

"Who me?" He looked away, up at the $1.15 Regular gas sign, then back at her with an arched, accusatory right eyebrow. "Me . . . I am Skinny Israel."

"Skinny *Who?*" Now it was her turn to grin, mostly with incomprehension.

"That name you call me."

She shook her head. "I never called you any name."

"Yes, yes," he said, stepping a little closer. "You say you want to cook for me—the red beans."

"Right," she said, flinching with guilt.

"Okay—and then you say I am the skinny country of the Jew."

She hunched her shoulders upon hearing what were to her Mustafa's inscrutable words. He was speaking okay English, but they were still going to need an interpreter.

"Skinny Israel . . . *Skinny Israel* . . . ," he repeated. His voice had gone high-pitched, falsetto, mimicking *her* voice, succeeding just enough for her to untangle the last few syllables.

"Oh, God!" She laughed, with the gusto that comes from being *in* on a joke. "No! Skinny . . . *as* . . . a . . . rail. It's just something we say. 'Skinny as a rail.' I don't even know what it really means. All I can think of is like a railroad track, maybe. Or, I don't know, like streetcar tracks. You know, the rails are what the wheels roll on." She put her hand out and sliced it forward through the air of confusion. "A rail is narrow. *Skinny*. Like you!"

Streetcar tracks? He had ridden the St. Charles line one day shortly after coming to town. Poking his head out the window, he had felt like a bad little boy, though the breeze had kissed his face, absolving him of mischief. That is, until the driver had—*Hey, you*—brought him back to the accountability of adulthood. He closed his eyes now and envisioned the long, chugging ride from Canal Street to Audubon Park and back. He saw the heavy, grooved iron wheels nuzzling the tracks; the narrowness of his frame, his profile slight enough, no doubt, to fit snuggly into the metallic embrace of those wheels that transported passengers into and out of the heart of New Orleans. And his head fell back as his laughter, harmonizing with the streetcar clanging in his head, drowned out his embarrassment. When he opened his eyes to Alicia's animated delight, he wished he could have been *more* mortified, if that would have made her laugh harder.

They were both still smiling when he said, "So you don't like the skinny boys?"

"I didn't say—"

"Ah, you say, you say . . ."

His saying "say" was their cue *not* to say anything else, a license to look at each other—and *feel*. Language had distanced them, divided them with its wall of words. Action had brought them together. *Close*.

They were only about a foot apart. Mustafa had never been this close to the brownness of a Black girl's face, unless you counted the way he had sometimes almost touched his nose to a television or a computer screen to inhale the prettiness of the dark-skinned girl in Destiny's Child, having ogled his way past Beyoncé to the relative exotica of Kelly Rowland. That's who Alicia reminded him of. Beyoncé, with her Arabian glow, was too much like the beautiful Syrian women he knew, including his mother, to pique his interest; Kelly's forthright foreignness, on the other hand, had seduced his exploratory impulse, her dark womanhood pointing his desire toward, well, a destination, intensifying his passion to the heights of a masculine quest: wanderlust. For, oh, there was a moment in the music video for their latest song, "Bills, Bills, Bills," near the end, right at the 3:40 mark, where Kelly had a close-up when she said "you" as she pointed both of her index fingers directly at the camera, at you, at *Mustafa*—her lips puckered for as long as you cared to pause the scene on the computer. (No, he didn't always end up going down corporate wormholes when he went exploring on Uncle Adad's iMac.) And another close-up of her at 3:53 saying "think," with one finger tapping her right temple and the other her left cheek in pantomimed pensiveness. The combination of the "you" and the "think" was a blend of sensuousness and contemplativeness he found immensely gratifying, and endlessly rewindable. He couldn't help endowing Alicia with Kelly's alluring complexity, and her proximity to him right now was a wonder, a real-life encounter with American-girl glamor. Only his natural chivalrousness—and a faint paralysis at being so near to her—kept him from reaching up to touch Alicia's smooth brown face.

The silver crucifix she was wearing shined up at him, mercifully giving him a reason to avoid her stare, and he let his eyes angle down at the fortuitously positioned Christ on a chain. A fleur-de-lis adorned each end of the cross, surrounding the martyred saint in a feminine embrace. Mustafa had seen this floral symbol all around New Orleans, and he assumed it held some significance he was unaware of, as did the letters, INRI, engraved above Jesus's drooping head. The mystery of all that, nestled as it was in Alicia's bosom, coalesced for him into something of a sacred lust. He felt helpless, dumb with desire. But what did it all mean? Swooning with hunger from the day's fast and, more so, for her, he heard only one answer—Uncle Adad's warning—*love*.

Is he staring at my breasts? she wondered. *Aww . . .* his first real, if awkward, show of actually wanting her. She pinched the crucifix and twirled it between her fingers. Yes, he was probably just another boy about to run some game on her. Cute accent and comic mangling of the vernacular aside, Mustafa had all the makings of a Creole Don Juan, and she knew one of those when she saw one. She had fallen prey to the Seventh Ward boy/Sixth Ward girl passionfest before (the light-skinned-guy, dark-skinned-chick thing); indeed, it was her pattern, if she had one at all. Anthony Whoever, just last summer, her most recent "boyfriend"; she had mentally blocked his last name, if she had ever known it. Whatchamacallit Francis. It seemed that, somehow or another, they had all been named for saints, and her Catholicism had been her ruin. She'd lost her virginity to a boy named Martin whose mother would never even call him to the phone. It was as if the woman could hear too much melanin in her voice. But she didn't want familial courtesy from this one, this Mr. Skinny Israel, or whatever *his* name was. She just wanted him.

Alicia and Mustafa were meeting at the precise moment when young people stride out of adolescence toward the triumph, or tragedy, that is the fully formed self. Maybe love is only a means, a carrot dangled to insure forward movement. Time had jockeyed them into position; their momentum could not be stopped. The rules they were about to break—only seconds from now—were impossible for them not to break. Like records of speed and fortitude, like hearts, they were made to be broken.

She let go of the crucifix, reached into the bag of Lay's, and took out another potato chip. Mustafa's eyes zoomed in on her hand—his desire converting to actual hunger. When she glanced up, his palpable craving inspired in her something like pity. She paused—instead of crunching into the chip, she extended it to him. A simple act of generosity, it was, in fact, a temptation. Of course, she was unaware of just how much she was complicating his life. He thought *he* knew—but he was wrong. Admirably, he shook his head.

"You sure?"

"I *can't* . . ."

But the way he said "I can't" made her feel how much he wanted the potato chip. She also understood he meant that he *shouldn't*, that eating the potato chip was forbidden. (Then, the darkest thought: What if—if he could deny himself the chip, he could deny himself her? Oh, no, there'd be none of that.) Maybe it was the seriousness of his tone, which conveyed regret, that allowed her to intuit the religious nature of his rejection of the chip. And, too, this hint of sacred denial may have induced her to do what she did—in the manner in which she did it.

As if to prove a point, if only to herself—just because you couldn't cook didn't mean you couldn't feed—she took the chip, wafer-like in its aura and dimensions, and lifted it up halfway between them, as if in offering. All her years of Catholicism—her entire life, really—had endowed her with full knowledge of the authority of this graceful gesture. Only she, since the age of seven, when she had celebrated the sacrament of her First Communion, had always been on the receiving end of this ritual, as the priest raised the metaphoric disk, the symbolic body of Christ, that most blessed of commodities, up to the needy parishioner. It felt as natural as breathing to Alicia, legitimized by centuries of faith and repetition, for her to complete the act and to expect Mustafa to participate in its conclusion.

She didn't even have to tell him to open up. When she brought the potato chip to his mouth, Mustafa's lips parted swiftly, mechanically, like the mouth of one of those notorious vintage metallic banks. In part, it was a gasp, an inhalation of excitement, at the certainty of what was about to occur, at what he was already unable to stop from happening, and the slim opening was all Alicia needed to insert the sliver of crispy, savory sustenance into his mouth and rest it gently onto his welcoming tongue. Her thumb slid slowly against his lower lip as she began to pull her hand away, and the accompanying friction, viscous and sensual, exposed the incipient spindles of saliva already forming in response to his pleasure, lubricating the lazy withdrawal of her finger.

His eyes closed in concert with his lips, and the potato chip melted against the roof of his mouth. Suddenly ravenous in its irreligiousness, his body worked a swift chemistry with the unexpected, intrusive sodium and carbohydrates. Who knew salt could taste so sweet! A digestive dizziness ensued, a swooning at once spiritual and physiological. Mustafa felt both lightheaded and lighthearted, his guilt at breaking the fast of Ramadan blurring with his communion with Alicia. There was something godly in his vertigo. What was the root of dizziness, after all, if not the supplication of an entire planet to a mighty universal force? And if the very ground upon which he stood was vulnerable to the pull of gravity, what chance did he, a mere man, have against the magnetism of a woman? If Earth had the humility to be turned by such force, who was he to deny nature? Not to succumb, if that were possible at all, would have been the real sin. This pronounced rotation of the planet upon its axis, this spinning in his head, felt as necessary as salvation.

Alicia gripped Mustafa's arm, steadying him. "You all right?"

He opened his eyes to her quizzical face. "Me?" he said, before swallowing hard and clearing his throat. "I feel so good!"

The official bad business of feeling good would be consummated two nights later, in the privacy of Alicia's bedroom, with Mama Joon out working her hotel night shift. They would tiptoe around the rules of Islam and Ramadan, which Mustafa would explain to her; they would leap over the hurdles of her religion, which she would outline for him.

"Does this make you a bad girl?" he asked after they had first made love. Alicia was lying on her back, wearing nothing but her crucifix, which he reached over and touched. Rubbing the hard metallic charm between his fingertips accentuated the softness that welcomed his knuckles as, one by one, they dimpled her breasts, forever commingling for Mustafa the two sensations.

"That's what confession is for," she told him. "If no one was bad, the church would go out of business."

"*Right*," he said. Of course, church was business, too! Mustafa liked Alicia's way of thinking. He applied her logic to his religion as well. Would Ramadan be necessary if people were not sinners? Whatever was wrong with his accepting the potato chip from her was the thing at the core of the joy of Ramadan. The necessity for doing penance was a joy. The existence of a cleansing ritual, pointless unless you were dirty, was a joy. The promise of renewal was a joy. Forgiveness was a joy. And the bad business of making love to Alicia, which would persist for the entire season of Ramadan (and beyond), was, too, at least this year, the very *reason* for Mustafa's Ramadan—and, yes, a joy! Every nightly session of passion they shared prepared her for confession and him for the next day of fasting. When, at the outset of the Catholic sacrament of forgiveness, she heard herself say to the priest, as the penitent must, "Bless me father, for I have sinned," she began to hear what was not intended in the overture to contrition. Rather, she heard the demand of the blessing as payment due *for* her sin. Mustafa experienced a similar reversal of meaning with regard to his daily fasting. The hours of daylight would tick by quickly, without his even noticing he had not eaten. Then he would gratefully consume his evening meal—iftar—not because he was starving, but to gain the strength to dine upon Alicia. She had become his real feast. Being without her was the fast he needed to break. When they held each other, enraptured, they felt as though they were reaching the pinnacle of fulfillment—and why shouldn't they—each slaking a hunger that itself had been fed and fattened by faith.

Long after fear and destiny had pulled them apart, this glimmer of religiosity would be for Alicia a means of holding them together, of coupling their spirits as righteously as they had coupled their bodies. Just as Mustafa had heard "Allah" echoed in her first name (her so-called Christian name), she would ultimately hear the Muslim month of fasting—their all-consuming month of love—echoed in her last name.

Their child would eventually be born several weeks early, fully formed and completely healthy, as if his incubation had somehow begun with that first flirtation in the middle aisle of the Quicky Mart. And when the boy arrived, distinguished, to be sure, with the idiosyncrasies of his parents' passion, Alicia would name him for the season of his actual conception—and Ramadan was blessed.

2

THE HOUSE OF RAMSEY

June "Joon" Ramsey was from a long line of single-mother, extended family households, so to her Alicia's out-of-wedlock pregnancy, once revealed, had the sanction of tradition. She did not know who her own father was; her mother, Lola Ramsey, had only told her, on those rare occasions when she'd been bold enough to ask, "Stay out of grown folks' business." Back then, the notion that parentage was not the business of a child had struck June as odd because, really, it seemed more like the *only* business of children. Nevertheless, it was easy for her to respect her mother's decree, because Lola wasn't around much anyway and when she was she avoided June, except to say things like "Go to Mama Gert," "Get me a glass of water," "Do your homework," "Aww, shake it now," and "Pull that skirt down." These commands, which Lola had passed off as mothering, were the essential memories June attached to her, marking the stages of her development: ages four, seven, ten, eleven, and thirteen. She had vowed to press her mother for the truth on her eighteenth birthday, when, in her mind, she would be officially grown. But her mother died the summer June turned seventeen. By then she was already pregnant with Clarissa, and tongue-tied with fathering secrets of her own. But neither the inconsequential relationship she had had with Lola nor the promise of the life growing within her had kept her from sobbing in the front row at the funeral home. You would have thought she had just lost her whole world, instead of a figure who, in the truest sense, was just a "distant" relative. No, what June was really mourning was not the woman up there in the casket. Rather, it was the death of the thing Lola had symbolized most to her—not a mother, but a mystery.

It was June's maternal grandmother, Gertrude Ramsey, who had really raised her, instilling in her an implicit pride in the matriarchal order of things. Gertrude had insisted on being called Mama Gert, employing "Mama" as if it were a title of royalty, and she had a rough-hewn monarchal air about her. In all seasons, she wore a milk-chocolate-color floor-length housecoat of a weighty polyester. Even with its faded hemline unraveling along the lower edges, its pleated bottom swept behind her like the train of a regal robe. June, upon the death of her grandmother, had become "Mama Joon," inheriting the title. There had been no coronation, unless you counted the ring of relatives who, in the wake of Gertrude's passing, had rather unceremoniously begun to circle June looking for consolation, advice, supper, rent money, a cot next door for a few days, for a week, forever.

Mama Joon the First had no castle, no court, no throne. But she had her shotgun double, a front porch, her burgundy leatherette Barcalounger, and the occasional wisdom and fallibility of a questionable queen. When she looked back on things, it was clear that Gertrude had lavished special attention on her and must have secretly selected her, from early on, as Mama successor, heiress to the rickety Ramsey empire. In the end, she hadn't willed June much more than *will*, but that would prove fortune enough.

Mama Gert had nine children by nine different men, and she kept meticulous mental records of each of these absent fathers, which was why June knew that her grandfather was a Haitian named Edgar Toussaint. As a child, she would cuddle with Mama Gert and listen to stories about him. On Sundays, with June in her lap, Mama Gert, in between taking sips of her late afternoon beer, would turn the pages of her scrapbook of men friends, eliciting from her granddaughter the same delight as when, sitting alone, she flipped through her elaborately illustrated edition of *Alice's Adventures in Wonderland*, for her grandmother's cast of characters, in her telling, were as unusual and entertaining as Lewis Carroll's. (Mama Joon had named Alicia in memory of such moments of enchantment, hoping to endow her with a taste for wild escapades— and perhaps in some small way she had.) June's heart would throb as if enlivened with a consciousness of the very blood it was pumping whenever Mama Gert came to the old portrait of Edgar Toussaint. Flecking with age at its upper right edge, it was bifurcated by a horizontal crease just above his belt. Mama Gert would caress this fuzzy picture of the tall, cinnamony, broad-shouldered man with a pencil mustache, whose sensuality radiated through the years, out of the confines of a poorly developed sepia print. Edgar was wearing a cocked fedora and a dark suit, standing in a nondescript doorway, a cigarette pressed between shiny, black, almost three-dimensional lips that were as entrancing as blue eyes. They teased Mama Gert's recollections, and she would say to June, "Chile, when he spoke French, everything he said sounded like 'Open Sesame'!" She would toss her head back and cackle, and June would look up at her and laugh along, not having the faintest idea why they were both so amused. Their interplay infused itself into little June with the clarity of a melody. Every time Mama Gert invited her to sit in her lap and hummed the highlights of her story, it was as if someone were putting a needle to vinyl, tuning a radio to the best station, striking up a band.

"He was Moses, and I was the Red Sea," Mama Gert would add in a voice whose huskiness bore evidence of the cigarettes she smoked incessantly, wielding her Kool Filter Kings with great flair, whether in the company of others or sitting in silence all alone on her back porch. When she lit one up, she could become either the seductress of camaraderie or the slayer of loneliness. Years later, even after June was fully aware of the addictive quality of nicotine, she still thought it was as much the cigarette itself—the thing Mama Gert whisked about at a party with animated gesture, or, when no one was there for her to mesmerize, let sway downward in limp-wristed languor—not the chemical, that made the magic. If this would-be queen had a scepter, it was filtered, full-flavored, scissored between her first and middle fingers and, at its most potent, aflame.

"Why y'all didn't get married?" June had once dared ask her grandmother, who clearly had loved Edgar Toussaint above all the other men. Mama Gert had looked at her incredulously. "Girl, you need to pay attention. I *said* he was Moses, and I was the Red Sea. What that mean? He was just passing through!" Mama Gert had paused at that, before clapping and then hooting some more, all the way to a series of deep coughs—a coda to her carefree past, overture to a cancerous destiny.

Mama Joon had known only one man who wasn't inclined to channel his inner Moses—treating a woman as a passage to be parted, over which to cross, as a means to his own liberation, just before leaving her behind, alone, to pull herself back together. So, when Alicia began to show all the telltale signs of having delivered a man unto himself and, for all she knew, bringing him closer to his God, she knew Alicia had met her first Moses. That was the thing about a pregnancy: it announced a visitation. You didn't have to see him to know he'd been there. At least once. He was gone now, though, and with each passing day, becoming more and more dubious, on the way to irrelevant. Mama Joon wasn't any more interested in the identity of Alicia's Moses than she was in the existence of ghosts. Alicia was her concern. She was there; she was real. Her child, in a short amount of time, would be there, too. Besides, she had been through this sequence of events on numerous occasions with the husbandless Clarissa, who was now comfortably situated next door with the undulating occupancy of her lively brood, five sons who moved in and out of the house depending upon their abilities to meet the demands of girlfriends, probation officers, employers, or Clarissa herself: Clarence ("Crip"); Damon ("Diamond"); Booker T; and the twins, Romeo and Julius. Clarissa had more than a little Mama Gert in her, and her sons' fathers were either dead or otherwise terminally detached from life as Clarissa and her children experienced it. The Ramsey commitment to matriarchy required an appropriately yet ironically Victorian steeliness. What it might have lacked in adherence to societal codes, it more than made up for in familial closeness and an occasionally toxic co-dependency.

Mama Joon had assessed the individual spirits of Clarissa and Alicia long ago and surmised that neither was the proper heir to her minor queendom, such as it was: her position as head of the family, ownership of her mortgage-free house; the substantial savings she had stashed away. Though her daughters were so far apart in age they weren't even in the same generation—almost eighteen years separated them—the deficiencies they held in common disheartened Mama Joon. Neither was artistic, truly industrious, or, most important, wise. The best that could be said of Clarissa was that she could scheme. And the best that could be said of Alicia was that she could love. Such extremities, devilishness and devotion, would get you laid and occasionally paid, but they could not sustain you. Either, without the temperance of wisdom, would endanger the entire household, doom the whole clan. She hadn't suffered through decades of domestic work or endured the lengthy on-again-off-again secret affair with her married former employer—the late, esteemed Judge Emmanuel Dumas—only to have the two daughters she'd quietly borne him mismanage or squander her legacy, or *theirs*, for that matter. Thanks to the largesse of Judge Dumas—albeit a generosity Mama Joon had coaxed from him, beginning while his wife was still alive, with the gentle reminder of the small but revealing cache of love letters he'd ill-advisedly sent her years before—she was, financially speaking at least, very comfortable. She had eventually destroyed most of the letters he'd sent her, his teenaged maid, during the early, most passionate and sat-isfying days of their affair (adultery, like champagne, being at its most effervescent just after the popping of the cork).

One later letter, she'd kept. The one Judge Dumas had written the day Alicia was born back in 1980, ironically enough, on Valentine's Day. Maybe the coincidence of the day had touched something roman-tic in him, mellowed his decidedly judicial air. He had committed his full support of Alicia (and of June), so most of the money had come after that—after Mrs. Dumas had died. Relieved of the sense of his own betrayal (his puritanical reasoning, not Mama Joon's), he had accepted Alicia with a warmth and a propriety Clarissa would never know. In the last two years of his life, he paid off her mortgage on the house, which he'd helped her buy, and gave her, on Alicia's behalf, a thousand dollars each month, and then, just before he died, one last check for fifty thousand dollars. She had never stopped working over the years. The money she made at her hotel housekeeping job more than paid her monthly bills, so she had saved almost all of the money the judge had given her, in an interest-bearing Whitney Bank savings account. She knew she could not will anything of significance to the vulnerably love-lorn Alicia, or to the one-scam-away-from-imprisonment Clarissa. And certainly not to any of Clarissa's criminally confused boys. Not to Crip, who had mistaken recklessness for bravery, so much so that he'd almost died for his cause when, one night three years ago, while still just "Clay," after a fist fight in a barroom with a redbone boy called Rooster, one of his neighborhood drug-dealing rivals with a similar take on things (but evidently with a better aim) had shot Clay in both his right femur and tibia and left him for dead, and with the disability that would hence-forth so crudely brand him. While Clay, reborn as "Crip," survived, less than a month later Rooster was found dead in a burned-out Chevy parked near the lakefront. Mama Joon rarely allowed Crip to visit her house anymore for fear that Rooster's family would retaliate while he was there. She also had no intention of squandering her savings on Damon—though she had a weak spot for him, one that enabled his own weakness. She'd been the first one to call him Diamond, until, for some reason, he'd lost his shine. Now he seemed to think getting high was a spiritual calling, so dedicated was he to maintaining an altered state of consciousness. A near monasticism guided or perhaps had resulted from his marijuana use; she knew where the money she sneaked to him without his mother knowing it was going. He was typically secluded in the back bedroom on Clarissa's side of the house—you smelled the evidence of his presence far more that you saw him—but when you did catch sight of him, he was usually on his way someplace else. "I'ma be right back," was his recurring but rarely kept promise; even when he was *there* he was gone. Conversely, Booker T, mercifully, almost never came home; he had deluded himself into believing itinerancy was ad-venturousness. His swagger said he'd traveled the world. If you could make yourself believe shacking with a stripper in a ratty motel on Chef Menteur Highway one week and with your baby's mother in a Section 8 apartment in Hollygrove the next was a jaunt from one exotic locale to another, you could make yourself believe anything. When Mama Joon looked at him, she saw not Gulliver but gullibility. Romeo and Julius— each identically as handsome as the New Orleans Saints linebacker (a practice squad perennial) who had conceived them during what Mama Joon had to agree really was his "off-season"—true to the unbreakable bond of twins, had colluded in their misunderstanding that, performed properly, promiscuity was a form of philanthropy. Sadly, they had never read the play that had inspired their names. (June *had*—along with any number of other literary classics Judge Dumas had pressed her to read from his extensive library, in between her cooking and cleaning chores and their shared extra-domestic activities, a desultory though fulfilling syllabus that constituted the entirety of her post-tenth-grade education.) But, nevertheless, since puberty Romeo and Julius seemed committed to donating the vast wealth of their romantic charms to anyone who would have them, and evidently to at least one who would not. Mama Joon had given up on the pair completely after they—Clarissa's youngest, while only fourteen, roughly the age of their fictional namesakes—had been arrested for rape. Star-crossed lovers indeed. Their fate was spared when the girl had suddenly dropped the charges, but only after Clarissa, who sometimes played Pitty Pat with the victim's mother, had suspiciously borrowed one thousand dollars from Mama Joon, a likely bribe for the accuser's retraction.

That, Mama Joon was convinced, was how everything she had accumulated would disappear. The money, the house, any promise of Ramsey progress. After she died, in a year or two tops—poof!—it would all be gone, spent on attending to the calming of life's calamities, applying a salve to that which could not be saved. (Calm, calamities; salve, save—she had ingested enough Shakespeare to know the poetic tricks you could employ to infuse meaning and entertainment value into your own pitiful predicament. But "To be or not to be . . ." Really? That wasn't even a damn question!) All would be lost to beating back the encroachment of ordinary life. That seemed a contradiction, but it wasn't. Life was a villain; existence, the damsel in distress. Existence was always on the run from life. To be was not *just* to be. She was very clear about that. Yet she knew that life would not *leave* you be. So she didn't blame her kin, any more than you could blame victims of the Dust Bowl or of a sub-Saharan famine for their plight. Alicia, Clarissa, and those boys hadn't invented the drought of their wisdom, the aridity of their ineptitude. She didn't blame them—but she didn't trust them either, any more than you could trust a big head of cabbage not to be bitter.

She did, however, trust herself. Her reasoning, her judgment. When the right one came along, she would know, the same way Mama Gert had known she was the one. The one you doted on. The one you taught everything you knew. The one to whom you gave the keys to the kingdom of your consciousness and, in time, theirs, because you knew they would know what to do with them, which doors to open and which to leave locked.

What she was craving went beyond the maternal. She had performed the roles of mother and grandmother as proficiently as circumstances demanded, depending on her mood and on her relatives' responsiveness to her offerings. Birthday gifts and bail money were a hit. Cooking lessons and clever quips generally fell flat. Everyone appreciated the house as a place of refuge, but little effort was made to deepen the impression that it was a home.

No, the closest 1216 St. Philip came to seeming a real home to her was when she was there alone, which was not often—but she was no-body's introvert. She longed for the company of someone special. With Mama Gert, more than with anyone else, she had known the sensation of *not* being alone, the sensation of *being*. More than with Judge Dumas. More than with Clarissa or Alicia. More, of course, than with any of her less-than-grand grandsons. Yes, the relationship with her grandmother was the model for the one to which she found herself most open. She had once heard Judge Dumas speak of the idea of "soul mates," and that term, as well as any, explained her feelings for Mama Gert. Oh, Judge Dumas had been talking about him and her. That's what most people meant when they said "soul mates." Lovers. But she and Judge Dumas had not been soul mates. He had just been trying to glorify the affair they had fallen into so haphazardly but that had nevertheless changed both their lives, *created* other lives. He had mistaken their proclivity for mating with each other as proof they were true mates, confused their tender exchanges of consolation for soul. June knew better. For true mates, mating was immaterial. And no, solace wasn't soul. Opportunity wasn't soul. Neither was mere compatibility, though harmoniousness was helpful. Soul was something else. Soul was *song*. Yes—and no one since Mama Gert had made her hear music.

So that morning—*this morning*—when Alicia declined to press her black hoodie into the service of concealing her secret, Mama Joon had looked up at her younger daughter without judgment. Alicia was stand-ing out there in the living room staring, in profile, at the television, at the *Today* show, pouting at an innocuous remark one of the hosts had just made, as if they intended her some personal offense. (Her hormones must have already been setting her nerves on edge.) Yes, Mama Joon had looked up at Alicia and seen not, as some might have, the silhouette of a whore, but the shadow of hope.

3

THE DISAPPEARANCE OF MUSTAFA TOTAH

Where Mama Joon saw hope, Uncle Adad saw mischief. He saw sin. He saw the self-fulfilling prophecy of his own making: *bad business.* And he assumed others—not disinterested bystanders, but Alicia's kin—would see the same. Or worse, rightfully so to his way of thinking, dishonor.

The sun was not yet up, and Adad sat alone at the desk in his office sipping his second cup of tea, brooding over and justifying his decision to send Mustafa back to Syria. It was too late to change his mind now. The boy was already gone. Malik had taken him to the airport yesterday. Adad, treachery in his heart, had not had the will to go along and perform a theatrical goodbye based on a lie. Flight 622 on American Airlines to JFK, then to Istanbul, then home to Aleppo. Safe! Mustafa's mother had conspired with Adad, claiming she was ill; she needed him to come home quickly to take care of her. What nonsense, of course. Rana, Adad's hellion of a sister-in-law, had been a sickly child, but she was now, even in her early fifties, though an avowedly sedentary woman—a seamstress by trade, who read books in her spare time, making her both a professional and a vocational sitter—as healthy as an aerobics instructor, and as demanding and controlling as one as well.

It was late February, and three months had passed since he had become addicted to the vicarious satisfaction of watching from his high stool the seemingly harmless romance between his nephew and the local girl. But his pleasure had turned to panic the day he had noticed the barely perceptible but unmistakable protrusive addition to Alicia's profile. Adad had acquired a fine tailor's eye for detecting the work of thieves; the contours of a customer's body often exposed his or her criminality. A bulbous extra few inches to the butt was not an attractive pulchritudinous bubble, but actually a bag of Nabisco Chips Ahoy or Cheetos squeezed down back. What strained credulity as a newly aroused masculine endowment of stupendous proportions was but, after all, a 22-ounce bottle of Heineken immodestly concealed in some thirsty young man's underpants. And while a girl's swelling tummy could be the measure of her lack of respect for a shopkeeper's property, it could also be a measure of her lack of respect for herself. Or, less harshly put—for Adad was not truly a prudish man—a measure of her resplendence. That was what he had seen on Alicia's face when his eyes had finished their quick scan of her new pooch as she had walked toward him last week, swinging a loaf of Wonder Bread by its tail. No, she was not just resplendent with life in general; she was resplendent with *new* life. He knew that look on her face. That look—and that loaf. Wonders, both! He had smiled at his quiet deduction and at the relief that he would not have to endure another confrontation. No back-and-forth of accusation and denial, before the final, wordless admission of guilt, with a magician's quickness: the unapologetic slap of contraband, a pack of bologna or sliced ham, onto the counter.

Then he had tensed, as it occurred to him—oh, no, Mustafa!—that what he thought didn't matter at all. The girl's family would have the last word. Words like *thief* and *guilty* came to mind. Mustafa, they'd judge, was the one who had taken something that did not belong to *him*. Something far more precious than the makings of a mediocre sandwich. Taken something *priceless* from the girl, which he could not return and for which he would have to pay: her reputation, her good name. *Their* name.

Adad was remembering now how at first it had been *Mustafa's* honor he had feared for, then mourned, before tossing stodginess aside, just letting the courtship play out before him like the coming of spring. As if he couldn't stop it—when of course he could have—preferring instead to whiff the sweet scent of impetuous, youthful romance, like so much flora. Aye-yi-yi, what an idiot he'd been! The boy was his nephew, not a field of wild narcissus. What did he, Adad, care for nature, anyway? He was a man of the town, of the city, of concrete and commerce. There was nothing pastoral that appealed to him at all. He cared not one iota for the country. The outdoors, in general, made him anxious; he was an indoors man, which was why he excelled at his work in the shop. He preferred the smell of incense to honeysuckle, a breeze blowing in through a window while you napped on a cushy cot to a gust that swept up sand and inverted your umbrella. And while the *idea* of an ocean was awesome and seductive, it had nothing on the reality of a warm bath. The worst you could say about him was that he liked a good river. But then rivers always led to towns, anyway. To cities. Great ones. Cities like Aleppo. Cities like this one—New Orleans. The Mississippi River was just over there, straight ahead. If he wanted to, he could skip all the way down Governor Nicholls Street, through the French Quarter, yes, all the way to the Mississippi. The way he used to do, as a boy, skip to and through Saadallah al-Jabiri Square in Aleppo Park on his way to the river at home. He longed to see all the great rivers he'd read about: the Thames, the Volga, the Mekong, the

Seine. Oh, to experience the grand cities the rivers had borne. When he was twenty-five years old, he and Zahirah, newlyweds, had visited Cairo and taken a boat ride on the Nile. The moon had been high that night, not full, but in the shape of a crescent, almost as bright as Zahirah's smile. Or his own. He had never forgotten the lights of the Cairo skyline twinkling, as radiant as the stars, while the boat swept along and the water gushed outward, slicing away like banana peels, like that part of time, of any instant, that didn't matter. Not the meat of the moment. *Them.* Embracing, he and Zahirah had swelled with desire, not just for each other, but for whatever life held. And life itself had never felt so transporting, so capable of delivering them somewhere special or something special unto them.

Gripped by the memory, he reached into the lap drawer of his desk and found the letter Zahirah had sent after he had first arrived in America. He opened the envelope, which also held the photograph a stranger had taken of them as they had stood transfixed under the night sky in Cairo, all those years ago. Adad stared at the picture of himself and his bride for a moment and smiled. *Ah, Zahirah, my love.* Then he reread the letter for the umpteenth time:

Adad, my husband, even though you are the longest distance away from me I can imagine, I feel like you are right here beside me—just like in this picture! Remember this night? Of course you do. May this photograph remind you of me too, your Zahirah. No matter how far apart we are—let it be a symbol of how close we will always be!

Your far, far, faraway wife who awaits your return!

Love,

Zahirah

And, one more thing, Adad. Do not lose this photograph, the way you lose things. It is the only picture left from our special time in Cairo when we knew we would be together forever. That is not the moonlight sparkling in my eyes. That is you!

Yes, Zahirah, like Mustafa's girl, had been resplendent, Adad thought, sliding the letter and photograph into the envelope, and tucking the memento from his youth back into the drawer. He remembered how, after the stranger had handed them their camera and walked away, he had held Zahirah close and they had kissed and cried—and then . . . gone on to build their whole life together on that moment, on the flow of things, on submitting to the romance of movement and time, on the Nile.

So, of course, he liked rivers. Loved them. That was the worst you could say about him when it came to being susceptible to the sentimental charms of nature. But no—he wouldn't be caught dead by a stream! A babbling brook? He shuddered. There was something vaguely untrustworthy about a ripple. A sinister quality to its tone, its presentation, as if it were hiding something. Or merely teasing you, baiting you to trust its "natural" gentility—right before the jaws of a shark or, here, in these remnants of a swamp, an alligator lurched up to chomp off your arm. No. Damn a ripple! He had enough subterfuge in his life, what with the myriad of ways inventory could be hidden and removed from one's possession without recompense. Give him a river. Give him the lap of a wave, courtesy of a tugboat, barge, or cruise liner coming into port. Or the *whoosh* of the figurative wave of humanity that rushed in and out of his store every day, frank about its inclination to challenge his propriety, or that *swooshed* by in buses and cars and SUVs up and down North Rampart Street outside his shop window, or, in his memory, along the busier streets of his beloved Aleppo.

And yet last December, winter and her bleakness must have turned him wistful for spring, the season that made even a metropolis vulnerable to the trappings of the bucolic, of things that blossom: flowers, prosperity, love. That was all he could think—winter had weakened him. Some sentimental wish for the season to come, combined with the fasting of Ramadan and the distance from his Zahirah, had softened his heart.

Oh, how he had almost fallen off his stool that day when he looked over the top of his cash register and saw Mustafa outside opening his mouth and letting that temptress have her way with him. A potato chip! Why was he so surprised? Eve had used an apple. What next, beef jerky? No, he had no illusions about the chastity of that Alicia. She had bought condoms from him in the past and at least one pregnancy test kit. Oh, she was no Virgin Mary, that girl. But then, he thought, who was in this age? Or in any age, for that matter. "The Virgin Mary." The very phrase was a puzzle to him. What about her celibate husband? "The Virgin Joseph" was just as astonishing a reality. Joseph, he knew, had been accorded some sort of backhanded sainthood, but why wasn't this man of admirable restraint a more prominent part of Christian doctrine? There was a double standard at play. A reverse chauvinism. "The Virgin Joseph," if enshrined as a heroic figure, might have proven an important role model for young men. He could have been instructive, saved lives, or at least spared favorite nephews their ruin. But then, if "The Virgin Mary" hadn't stopped Alicia from purchasing and presumably using Trojans and Lifestyles (upon further reflection, if only she'd employed them more—how else to put it?—*religiously*), then how could Adad expect "The Virgin Joseph" to save Mustafa?

It was only his panic for his nephew's security that was firing his fantasies of a more virtuous world being a safer one—the same panic that had forced him to act, in effect, to deport the poor boy. He had feared not for the well-being of Mustafa's soul, but for his physical well-being, for Adad was quite aware that Alicia had numerous thuggish cousins or nephews. They frequented his store, though they also disappeared for many months at a time, away in jail or prison for various crimes, some involving drugs and guns. Anyone who read the newspaper or watched the evening news knew about them, and Adad had witnessed their petty thievery for years. The one called Crip limped like a veteran of the war that was his rough-and-tumble life. Crip, who bought Marlboro Lights but stole roll after roll of five-flavor Life Savers. Adad, having once glimpsed a pistol poking out of Crip's side like a dagger, had thought it unwise to interrupt his misdeeds. His stealing seemed to Adad a vaguely legitimate tax for doing business on this gritty little corner, a tax that in the end he accounted for by charging the pilfering patron an extra fifty cents for every pack of cigarettes. (Adad's various dealings with taxes had led to his most playful, if corny, manipulation of English, vacillating from outrage to acceptance, resulting in vapid, aphoristic pith and bumper-sticker-ready sloganism: "Every tax has a cost." "No tax is free." "Tax now, pay later." "To tax is to ax.") The first time he had quoted Crip the cigarette upcharge, the two had exchanged knowing looks, and the thief had flashed an extra-wide, gold-toothed smile of respect at the merchant. This, they tacitly agreed, was how, from then on, they would do business. Still, mutual adherence to codes of manhood aside, or maybe *because* of Crip's clear-eyed agreement to such rules of common-law retribution, Adad assumed that, in defense of Alicia's honor, he might one day seek vengeance upon his nephew. Bad business would always be accounted for, one way or another. Hot blood bred bad blood. His own brother, Mustafa's father, had learned that brutal lesson and paid the highest price. In the end, *The ledger of lust is almost always in the red*. All right, that one was too long and too preachy for a bumper sticker, he had to admit, but he admired it nonetheless.

Adad sighed, allowing this last conclusion to help validate his having undone Mustafa and Alicia's affair. He sipped the dregs of his tea, which had gone as tepid as the rationalization of his zealotry. Discomfort had sneaked up on him with the bitterness of the final caffeine-laden slurp. A gurgle, he gathered now with a harsh truth snapping up at him, possessed an alarming relationship to a ripple. Yes, he had feared for Mustafa's safety. That was fundamental to what he had done. But there was something else slithering below the surface of the truth; his actions had not been so pure. The relationship between Alicia and his nephew was an open secret in the neighborhood, or at least within the store. Of course, they had hidden the more provocative aspects of their friendship, their kisses and their et cetera, et cetera. But people knew they were a couple. Malik knew. Jamil knew. Adad *knew*. Surely, someone in her family knew—and did not object. No, there was something else, something Adad was being forced to admit to himself now, two cups of oversteeped tea into his morning quiet time. No need to be coy, with Allah watching, awaiting your admission of guilt. He had let his mind dance around it with the little fugue of river worship and city mongering and love along the Nile. *This*: his own unbearable loneliness. That's what had played no small part in his willful separation of Mustafa and Alicia. If Mustafa went away, Adad, thousands of miles from Zahirah, would not have to witness—and be devastated by—on a daily basis, no less, Mustafa and Alicia's romance. Such tenderness, sordid as it was, was enviable nonetheless. All the pretend "goodbyes" that weren't "goodbyes" but actually "good nights" or "good evenings" or "see you this afternoons" or "see you tonight when nobody's watching and the moon, in crescent form or in any configuration, casts its shadow on your bedroom wall while our kisses blossom in the season of our love, which is always some-how, even in December, spring!" That was "goodbye"? Hah! That was not "goodbye." "Goodbye" was arid. "Goodbye" was June. "Goodbye" was the Aleppo International Airport kiss that lingered on your lips only till the middle of July, when the New Orleans heat starched the last blush of it away and left you reaching across the counter for ChapStick, balm of the dehydrated and the as-of-late unkissed. Cherry-flavored soothed Adad best, its feminine fruitiness a waxy approximation of his wife's moist sweetness.

At first, watching Mustafa and Alicia had excited him, reminded him of himself and Zahirah, and he had indulged, wickedly perhaps, in the way his blood rushed when he saw the lovers courting outside the store, plotting their next not-so-secret tryst. (Mustafa's primping had grown constant, and he was tiptoeing out of the house almost every night—or offering to close up, and not coming home until who knew when.) Exactly when Adad's envy had displaced his admiration, he couldn't say. He was barely admitting it now, and as soon as the caffeine overdose began to dissipate, so would the severity of his self-critique. He was beginning to come down already. The sinking back into the basic, less authentic him had begun; he was dimming into simply the doting uncle, the protective surrogate father, not the bit-ter lonely husband who, because in part he couldn't bear to witness love pantomimed on his doorstep every day—*Mustafa and Alicia: The Ballet*—and because he had the power to stop it, had done just that, under the guise of goodness. Well, goodbye to all that. Goodbye to goodbyes that weren't goodbyes! This was the trouble with vicari-ousness. It feigned admiration, but deep down it was just selfishness. Amorality, however minor. What else could it be, taking pleasure in someone else's pleasure? Taking something that did not belong to you!

(The weight of his guilt was already decreasing, its eradication made possible by the misdemeanor of overreaching empathy.) Adad, too, had been a thief—and he had put a stop to his own larceny. There. He had done the right thing, really. For himself, for Mustafa, for everyone involved. The boy was safe in Syria. The girl would be fine. Adad would do what he could for her, if she needed anything, if she asked anything of him—anything except that he bring Mustafa back to her. And the child? Well, time, Father Time, as it were, would adopt him or her, parent the kid with tough love just as he did everyone else.

The awful reality of Adad's jealousy, which had racked his nerves a moment ago, *for* a moment, was only faint now. Only its luster remained, refracting back to the more satisfactory rationalization for deporting Mustafa, whose journey would end in irony—home would be exile. Adad again took refuge in the color of loss. You could blame it all on bad business, he reasoned. Yes, in the end, *The ledger of lust is almost always in the red*. Actually, if you printed it small enough on a bumper sticker, you could make it fit.

❧

IF THE COLOR of lust, as Adad imagined, was in the final accounting red, then the color of love was black. At least for Alicia, who found herself writhing in darkness. The net of love was depression; its dividend, despair. She had received only a brief note from Mustafa, left in the mailbox here at the house, explaining his hasty departure:

> Dear Alicia,
>   My mother is very sick and she need me. I must to go to her today. I do not know when I will return. I hope you think about me. I hope

you do not find another man when I am away. No one have more hungry for you than Mustafa. Do not feed no other man. But if you do, do not like it like you like to feed me. I sin for you. You sin for me. This is love.

Skinny Israel

The letter didn't seem real to her when she had sat in bed reading last night. It was as if she were standing over a stranger's shoulder eavesdropping on some other girl's devastation. From the vantage point of a movie director's well-placed, downwardly angled camera, the actress's trembling shoulder blocking the letter's lower right edge, the part that read *This is love.* But then you'd hear that anyway, read in a voice-over by some actor with a Mustafa-sounding accent, right before the camera, like Alicia's vision, zoomed in on the last thing the lover wrote, the most private thing they would ever share, the soul of their rapport: *Skinny Israel.* And that's when the screen, in deference to the girl's numbness, would go black.

Until now, she hadn't really understood how emotionally attached she was to Mustafa. His absence was as tangible as his presence—she could feel it, like cold or heat, or like the sensation he had referenced in his note, *their* sensation, hunger. Feeling love, it turned out, was nothing compared to feeling the *loss* of love. Love was child's play. Loss was for women. Not sex, not love, not impregnation, even, had made her feel like this. Like a woman. Holding hands and kissing, doing naughty things with boys while your mama was at work—all that was sugar and spice. This—heartache—was a blade that sliced away your emotional baby fat. (The way she'd once seen Mama Joon trim the lardy excess from the bottom of a brisket.) Here she was, left with the meaty core of herself. A finer cut, perhaps. Or a more muscular one maybe. Who knew? But, an incipient rigidity of spirit accompanied this loss. Or maybe that was pretense, the illusion of fortitude, as temporary as the instinctual clinching of her fists. The pain of the severing was wrenching and oddly embarrassing, and she had wrapped her arms around her waist to withstand the achy shame of it all, the punch of her pride jabbing affectingly at a sore spot near her ribs. She had squeezed herself tighter, trying to wring out every drop of naïveté. That's what was forming in the corners of her eyes—the last residue of childishness, of girlish gullibility—pooling there, like sap from a pine. Sap from a pine! Was this why they called anything overly sentimental "sappy"? Why if you ached for someone you were said to be "pining"? She despised her anguish, even as she wallowed in it. What were tears if not acknowledgment of an awful truth you were simply too foolish not to have anticipated? He would leave. Of course he would leave. What was she thinking? Nothing lasted forever. One day, Mustafa had shown her how he stocked items on the shelves in the store, describing a system she had been too trusting to imagine. "Old stuff always up front," he had told her, stopping her from buying an almost out-of-date can of peaches. "Reach in back for the fresh one." No, nothing lasted forever. Not life. Not boyfriends. Not canned fruit. Everything had an expiration date. Forever, like the hoax of "nonperishable" goods, was for unvigilant shoppers. Sooner or later, the truth would come out, impose itself. Like Santa Claus and fairy tales, forever was for children. The world could not sustain the lie of eternal anything, especially "happily ever after." Love was as perishable as peaches. Yes, she was a woman now, fermented into maturity, almost instantly, by the acidity of grief.

That was last night. Last night she had gone to bed a woman—but she woke up this morning feeling like a bitch.

Her entire body, lean from loss, ached with anger. She had dreamed of rushing out of the house and going straight to the Quicky Mart to see Adad. Mustafa had told her his uncle, despite his stiffness, had a soft heart; she also knew that in the Totah family, he was in charge. Mustafa's father had been stabbed in a fight in Aleppo and died before Mustafa was born. Uncle Adad had always been like a father to him. She would confront him—no, put her bitchiness aside—*confide* in him, tell him the truth: she was pregnant. She hadn't told anyone yet, not even Mustafa! (Hadn't he guessed it? Hadn't he noticed her bump? No. Boys were so stupid. Even the smart ones. And so blind. Even the ones like Mustafa with 20/20 vision and mystical-looking eyes.) She hadn't even told Mama Joon. But she would tell Adad, because he and he alone could bring Mustafa back. She would tell him about the child. Tell him how much she and Mustafa were in love. Touch the tender spot in Adad that Mustafa had assured her existed behind his dispassionate façade. Then he would help her. Wouldn't he? Yes. Love, even in its perishability, was remarkably persuasive. Just look what it had made her and Mustafa do!

She grabbed the black hoodie she'd been wearing ever since she realized she was pregnant and slid into its camouflaging comfort. Only this morning, she didn't bother to zip it up all the way. This morning she would let the change in her show. If Mama Joon was in the hall or the living room, Alicia would saunter past her, and give her a good look, not flaunting her state, but introducing the news, prepromoting it for later, like they did on the *Today* show, which she heard blasting from the television in the front of the house when she opened her bedroom door and walked down the hall.

"And when we return," a woman's voice was saying, "we'll have an exclusive interview with the man behind the mystery that everybody's talking about. Back in a moment . . . this is *Today*."

There was, Alicia found, always something on television that mirrored what was happening in your life, if you bothered to notice. Any channel, at any given moment, could startle you with knowing. A football player might score a touchdown just as you finally solved an algebra problem (which had happened for her one Sunday afternoon a couple of years ago when she was struggling to complete some homework), and all of the loud cheering that ensued would blare down the hallway into your bedroom and make you feel like it was for you. "A ninety-nine-yard pass from Pythagoras to Alicia Ramsey!" She had jumped off her bed and, wearing slippery socks, almost fell on the hardwood floor. Or a snippet of a song playing in the background might capture what you were thinking or feeling. That, too, had happened to her not long ago. She had been watching the movie *Dead Presidents* on cable, last October, around the time she'd found the courage to flirt with Mustafa. It was the scene where Chris Tucker, having come back from the Vietnam War a drug-addicted nut, died from a heroin overdose, with Al Green's "Tired of Being Alone" playing in the background. That's what had gotten to her. The Al Green and her own loneliness and the idea that, if you weren't careful, you could end up like that. But that wasn't even the craziest part. The song wasn't just playing, like on the soundtrack or even on a radio in the room. When the cops burst into Chris Tucker's apartment to arrest him for that messed-up robbery he had been a part of and find him with that needle sticking out of his arm and his head tossed back, eyes wide open and blank with death, they also find Al Green in there wearing a big fuzzy hat cocked real cool to the side, coming out of the television, on *Soul Train* singing "Tired of Being Alone," like a preacher or like anybody with some good advice, because, in case you didn't realize it, if you're not careful, you really can die of loneliness. Or certainly alone. Or both! At least that's the way Alicia had taken it. She hadn't had a boyfriend in a long time—within a week, she was flirting with Mustafa. You never knew when something, like that needle coming out of Chris Tucker's arm, might stick *you*.

On her way out, she was relieved Mama Joon wasn't in the living room relaxing in her recliner. But then her mother's voice emerged above a loud commercial for Tide. "Where you going?"

She stopped without turning to face the kitchen, where Mama Joon was. The question almost doused her bravery. But she stuck her chin out and yelled back over her shoulder, in the undeniable tone of a woman, sounding more like Clarissa than herself, "To the store. I'll be right back."

"Bring me back some eggs," Mama Joon said. Then, without pause, as if eggs were a medium, as if hens proffered little Rosetta Stones that bridged the linguistic gap between generations, and you could dispatch someone to buy them from the corner store, she added, "We need to talk."

Alicia slammed the door behind her, wondering what she would say to Adad, whom she really didn't know. With each step, she gained more and more confidence, along with the sense that from now on, the thing growing in her would inspire her voice. Wasn't she already in communication with it? She hated biology, but she'd picked up enough to know that cells were rapidly dividing inside her uterus. *Cells*. A woman with child was her own cellular network. She would do the talking for it, for her or him. And in its strange and powerful way—it had already shut down her period, reason enough to admire its savvy—it would help her figure out what to say to Adad. But how would she figure everything else out? Was there something in the biology classes she had skipped or dozed through that could have explained it all to her? In high school, she had concentrated on the basics, English and math. But rhetoric and grammar weren't offering up any answers. There was no conjunction that would connect you to where you needed to be now. *And? Or?* Not helping. No preposition, even: *Over, across, beyond.* Words that sure made you feel like they should be able to prop you up, carry you through, get you there, but they couldn't. Not now. Not once you were pregnant with a vanished Syrian's child, and you were suddenly all alone. Well, almost all alone. (She rubbed up and down the orb of her stomach.) Maybe math could help you calculate where you were, what was left, who you were now. Was there an algebraic formula that could reveal the new you, the X that equaled you minus him, the one you'd lost, divided by you plus the one inside you?

$$X = \frac{YOU - HIM}{YOU + 1}$$

Yes, she saw the problem clearly in her mind, but she could not solve it.

ALICIA STOOD OUTSIDE the Quicky Mart waiting for Adad to look up. She could tell he knew she was out there, though he hadn't yet acknowledged her presence. When he finished with a third or fourth customer, he finally raised his head. Their eyes met between the intermittent spaces of the glowing red, white, and blue neon Bud Light logo hanging in the store window, right through the middle of the capital U in BUD. It was as if that letter were shining an accusatory beam onto each of them, reading, as it did, the same in each direction, an electronic palindrome of incrimination. "You!" it said for Adad, who wanted the girl and her polluted, potato chip seduction never to have happened. "You!" it countered for Alicia. Thanks to Adad's prolonged pretense of her invisibility (he saw *everything*—anybody who frequented his store knew that), and to the scorn he was transmitting through the "BUD," she was now certain of his complicity in Mustafa's departure. Just like that, as the *Today* host had promised, "the man behind the mystery everybody's talking about" was revealed.

She watched him motion to someone at the back of the store to come and take his place at the register. He was animated and appeared to be angry, further confirming, for Alicia, his guilt.

"What's wrong?" Malik asked his father, as he climbed up to the checkout platform, but Adad rushed past him without speaking and headed out the door.

He had operated his store for seven years with a necessary mix of fairness and greed, courage and fear. His judgment about when to be kind and tolerant and when to be firm and confrontational had always been right. The man who said "I don't want any trouble" was already in trouble, so he never said that, though this instance—a visibly anxious young woman recently impregnated by your kin, with gun-toting relatives only blocks away, showing up at your place of business, not coming in to buy something, just standing outside staring you down, eyeing you with suspicion, calling you out—was surely a moment when it might be prudent to retreat, to assume a defensive posture, find the humility within, deign to be trite and just say it: "I don't want any trouble." Which was true. He didn't. He could maybe even thicken his accent. "I dun't want no trouble," he could say, groveling with the imperfections of an immigrant's tongue, pandering with the obsequiousness of a wretched inferiority he knew he did not possess. He could not stand his ground because, really, it wasn't his ground anyway, this uneasy but *ideal*

American corner that he rented—he thanked Allah for it every day—roamed by Black men with a territorial swagger Adad quietly respected and admired. Yes, something could be trite *and* true—"I don't want any trouble"—but that was not his style. He preferred to be tough and true, and that's what he'd be right now. Not mean, but firm, immovable. Oh, he would make the girl understand that there was nothing here for her. He would present her with the obstinacy of an ATM given the wrong PIN. Presenting himself as a mechanical man, that's what had made him successful in a place that barely acknowledged his existence and that he sensed might reject him if it did. In fact, he was like the opposite of an ATM to most of his customers. They walked up to him—to *the It*, positioned up there behind the cash register, the anti-ATM, the Almighty Taking Man, surely that's what he was to some of them—and gave him their money. *He* was invisible to them. The *He* who had the beautiful wife, Zahirah. The *He* who had two sons, the very evidence of his humanity, working right here with him, looking just like younger, more attractive versions of his flesh-and-blood self, if anyone cared to notice. The *He* who had pumping through his heart the sweet memory of a moonlit night in Cairo on the Nile, an affection for rivers (including their own Mississippi), and yes, an occasional ill-advised sympathy for the irrationality of young love. No, most of the people he encountered every day, all day, did not even really see him. Not him. They saw the anti-ATM who smiled on cue and who without fail, indeed with the precision of a machine, though he took and took and took, gave them their change.

Alicia wasn't the worst of them. At least she knew he was a man, not a machine. Now. Now she knew. Mustafa was a man—Adad was Mustafa's uncle, so he had to be a man, too. Alicia knew. That's why she had come to the store this morning and was standing there staring at him, for the first time, at *him*. You didn't ask a machine "What happened?" with your eyes. You didn't come to see a machine about your problems. You came to see a man! His nephew, if he had done nothing else by conquering this woman, had gotten that done. He had made someone here *feel* the realness of Adad Totah! Of the entire Totah family. Made someone realize they were here. Planted the Totah seed in this fertile, foreign, *American* soil. Yes! Like a tree. Like a flag. Like their Stars and Stripes on the moon!

So then, yes, there was pride in Adad's toughness. Alicia had gotten herself into trouble, not him. She had tempted Mustafa, and she had tempted fate. One of those seductions had worked out for her just fine, in the short term—she'd had her little affair; the other, in the long run, so the frustration on her face said now, had not. Next time she'd think twice about whose mouth she fouled with food during the fast. And Mustafa? Well, next time Mustafa would *think*. He would be back at home now, probably just having arrived, beginning to understand that he'd been banished from America because of his irresponsible ways. No, his mother was not sick. "But, Mama, you look fine," he would say when she and Zahirah, not their neighbor Hasim, showed up at the airport to greet him, as his uncle had said. And Rana would be glaring at him, almost through him—when his sister-in-law was mad her hijab seemed to pulse from the heat of her anger—and Mustafa would know he was in trouble. "What did you do with that girl?" she would ask him. "Give me your passport! Give me your visa!" And she would rip up his papers right in front of him, right there in the airport. That's what she'd told Adad she would do. And he knew she would. Rana applied her formidable gifts as a seamstress to everything she did in life. If she didn't like something, the way it was made, she would tear it apart at the seams. Then she would put it in her work pile and later, when she found the time, at her leisure, she would sew it back together, better—the way she thought it should be. "I'll fix him!" she had yelled, when he had called to tell her of Mustafa's predicament. "I'll fix him good!"

Channeling Rana's rage, Adad looked Alicia in the eyes. He allowed his own convenient contempt for her moral failing to tighten his tongue.

"Mustafa is gone!" he said, louder than he'd intended. Alicia flinched, almost as much from his forcefulness as from the truth of his words. Two boys walking on the sidewalk rolling a bicycle between them turned their heads in unison toward Adad's shout, where they saw nothing unusual, nothing but Alicia and the man who sold them snacks. It was as if they thought they had heard the call of an exotic bird but looked up to see only a couple of pigeons, and they moved along without breaking stride.

"I know!" Alicia had recovered, drawing strength from her misery.

"Then why are you here? Why do you come to my store and look at me through the window? What do you want from me?"

"I don't know!" She wanted to say she knew he was somehow the reason Mustafa had left, that she knew he had something to do with breaking them up. But what good would that do? Adad's brow had pressed forward, shading his eyes, dehumanizing him. If she could see his eyes, she might know what to say to make him help her. But he wasn't giving her anything to work with. He was only a stiff, yelling, masculine figure that could walk and flap its hands, pause to pull up its khakis by the belt (exposing faded, grayish white socks, melting from their fraying elasticity, puddling at the ankles of pale, hairy legs), and shout a few things if you pulled his strings: "Mustafa is gone!" "Why are you here?" "What do you want from me?" He reminded her of a life-size doll, only one that, in its middle-aged duress, had lost all of its cuddle appeal.

"I guess . . . I thought you would tell me what to do," she said.

"About what?"

"I am going to have his baby."

Adad's hands rose up and covered his face, as if to shield him from a blast. Though he already knew it, Alicia's truth felt like a desert gust. As he slid his hands down, they wiped away moisture from the corners of his eyes.

"Well . . . a baby is a blessing." Then he sniffed away his feelings, and hardened his heart to the situation, before adding with a brutal finality, "Even one with no father."

"Why do you say that?" she asked. Adad's sniffle cast itself upon Alicia with the contagion of a yawn. Her shoulders trembled as she tried to stop herself from crying. "Mustafa's not coming back, is he? That's what you mean."

"I don't know what I mean."

"He doesn't know about the baby. If I write to him and tell him, he will come back."

"He will not come back."

"How do you know?" She was crying now.

"I know." He wanted to do something to console her, but he restrained himself. She might cry for hours—right here in front of pump number 2—if he permitted his storefront to be turned into a haven for heartbroken women.

"There is nothing I can do for you. You should go home now. May All— May God be with you."

Alicia heard mostly Adad's tone, which was tapping into its lower regions, and that was, as it turned out, soothing enough. The key words, each sobering if inscrutable, registered. *Nothing. Home. God.* The nouns. Maybe language, not just math, would help her after all. Her tears had mostly evaporated by the time she managed to shake loose her hoodie and cover her head. Then she moved past Adad, not walking homeward, but toward the store.

He turned around, confused by her defiance. "Where are you going? Where are you going?"

She stopped to answer him, but she did not look back. "We need eggs."

⚜

SOMEWHERE DOWN THERE, Mustafa thought, looking out his airplane window, amusing himself, *somewhere down there is the real Skinny Israel.* That sacred place between the Jordan River and the Mediterranean Sea. The country that had given him a nickname and a girl. It was truly, for him, the Holy Land now.

Beyond that, Syria. Aleppo. He was almost home.

Skinny Israel. As effortlessly as jet engines propelled this aircraft through the Judeo-Arabian skies, his heart, aflutter at the memory of his and Alicia's private joke, was spiriting him across the landscape of their romance.

He looked down at the empty middle seat next to him and saw his Quran, which he had pulled out an hour ago when the plane had hit a rough patch of turbulence. Touching the beautiful silk cover his mother had made, he wondered, *Am I a bad son?* He was hardly thinking about his mother's well-being at all. (Well, he *was* thinking about Rana—mainly about how upset she would be if she ever found out about Alicia.) Why wasn't he more concerned about her? Maybe because of what Malik had said yesterday while driving him to the airport in New Orleans. "Cheer up, Mustafa. Don't worry—at least not about Aunt Rana. *She* will be fine."

"What? Did Uncle Adad hear some good news?"

"Him and his news. He sees everything. He hears everything. But he only tells the news that is good for him. Don't you know that? One day maybe he will tell what is good for someone else. But that day is not today."

Then, when Malik dropped him near the entrance to the American Airlines check-in area, he had said, "Remember, don't worry. You will be fine, too."

Of course he would be fine—he had Alicia! Would his mother see that on his face? Would she see Alicia in his eyes? The evidence of her imprinted on his lips, swollen as they were by American kisses? His image mirrored back at him in the window, and he watched his phantom finger rub the ridges of his lower lip. He closed his eyes and pretended his finger was hers. (Alicia inserting things into his mouth—bite-sized pieces of food, morsels of herself—remained the essence of their bond.) When he felt the tip of his nail graze his teeth, he thrummed an onanistic moan. Ah, their trysts. Their touches. Their stares that, since the day they'd met, defied translation. The silences made the kisses possible. All those kisses, which they had realized soon enough, were the most articulate means of expression anyway. He was stiltedly bilingual, but that didn't matter. They were beyond lingual. Their tongues *were* their tongue.

But they'd also had moments when the heat of intimacy had ignited language, when pillow talk itself, at least briefly, had surpassed the eloquence of sensuality. Just last week, while massaging his back, she had asked, "Do you miss Syria?"

"When I first came here, yes. All the time."

"What did you miss?"

"My mother. Playing soccer with my friends. Aunt Zahirah's cooking. Aleppo at night. The lights. The Citadel. So beautiful it can make you feel like you live in the best place in the world!"

"Hmph . . . that's the same way we feel around here."

"I know. And now I am agree with you. I say is true. You and me, we live in the best place in the world. For us."

"Really?" she asked.

"Yes." He looked over his shoulder to see why she had stopped tracing her fingers down his spine.

She frowned and shook her head.

"Not New Orleans," he said. "That's not where we live. You don't live here, and I don't live in Aleppo. We live together . . . in Skinny Israel!"

He had rolled over while she was still straddling him. His slender hips nuzzled perfectly between her thighs, she had leaned forward, and he watched her crucifix dangle hypnotically, from one breast to the other. She sank into him, sealing the necklace between their chests, cupping her hands behind his head. Her lips and tongue moved against his ear as she whispered, "The love of my life . . . the love of my life." Then, marveling at his own prowess, he stroked her giggle into gasps of ecstasy.

Mustafa sighed now, opening his eyes and staring out at streaks of clouds against a pale blue sky. He pressed his lower back deeper into the seat cushions and stretched his legs, making room in his jeans for the bodily consequences of his nostalgia.

Since being with Alicia, he had a newfound, athletic grace. In her presence, it manifested as friskiness combined with a purposeful daring. (He thought of it, with pride, as masculinity, though in reality it owed to his heightened self-assurance, a genderless confidence of being.) But his enhanced physicality was even more pronounced when he was not with her. Jamil had stopped wanting to shadowbox and wrestle with him in the backyard of the little house Uncle Adad rented on the edge of St. Bernard Parish, close to New Orleans. One day, after Mustafa had penned him to the ground in record time, Jamil had grunted a surrender and, rising, dusting off his jeans, still crouching, asked, "What is she *doing* to you?"

"Alicia? Nothing. I am still the same."

"No. Everything is different. The way you talk—so much more English, my brother. And the way you act—now you fight like Muhammad Ali!"

That had sounded absurd to Mustafa, if funny and flattering. That is, until less than a week later, when a shabbily dressed man, possibly homeless, had come into the store and started waving a knife at Uncle Adad. Though he was husky (a borderline heavyweight), without hesitating, Mustafa had sneaked up behind him and punched him in the back of his head with such force the man collapsed without knowing what or who hit him. For Mustafa, who had never struck anyone into unconsciousness, the shock of watching the man fall was matched only by the thrill of knowing he had made it happen. He had never had such urgent cause to defend himself or his family. But wrong was wrong and right was right. An intense satisfaction at his first taste of triumph surged through him. Part of him wanted to be challenged again, immediately, if only so he could crush the enemy once more (as he was clearly capable of doing), and feel *this*, the joy of winning. The blade of the man's knife, when it had pinged against the tile floor, was a bell tolling the news of his victory.

The only thing he knew about Muhammad Ali was the general fame of his name. But Jamil's comment and his own accidental knockout blow had piqued his curiosity, in the same way the constant need to restock Wrigley's gum had. So, at the first opportunity, there he was again, sitting at Adad's computer exploring the World Wide Web, discovering that, yes, Ali was a great boxer—and, as indeed his name indicated, a Muslim. But he had not always practiced Islam, and he had not always been "Muhammed Ali." One photograph—they were countless in number but this one was the earliest picture of him—was dated 1954, when he was twelve years old. Only twelve. But apparently already well-known enough to be photographed shirtless, wearing only trunks and laced-up leather boxing shoes, posed like a real fighter. According to the caption, he was "Cassius Clay" and was about to box on a television program called *Tomorrow's Champions* in his hometown, Louisville, Kentucky. His eyes expressed hope, but his face was a mask of uncertainty; the kid was, after all, skinny as a rail. Mustafa searched the black-and-white image of this scrawny preteen for traces of the legend to be, but all he could see was a boy. No—something even less developed than that, so vastly different was this child from the man in later photographs of the cultural titan—the Olympic champion, the Hajj pilgrim at Mecca, the Heavyweight Champion of the World. Looking at the twelve-year-old Cassius Clay, he felt as if he were looking at the embryo of Muhammad Ali, a giant in gestation.

Mustafa had kept clicking, wondering if, as with Mr. Wrigley, he might find something to explain Ali's rise to such prominence. He began to suspect he might, when he noted that in addition to being celebrated for the things he'd done, Muhammad Ali was also renowned for the things he'd said. He linked to quotes about religion, boxing, love. Oddly, the most praise was reserved for something boastful and pithy the champ, in a poetic mood, had once said about a pair of alliterative insects. But then, having surfed his way to some obscure website called Warrior Wisdom that appeared to be based in Saudi Arabia, Mustafa had sat up—for here it was! Written in Arabic, these more profound words might also have been inspired by Ali's meditation on the same floating and buzzing inhabitants of the garden: *The man who has no imagination has no wings.* So, Mustafa had concluded, the boy had seen his future, and he had taken flight.

The plane glided ahead reassuringly. Staring out at *its* wings, Mustafa thought, Men can actually fly, soar! He felt this miraculous means of transport stimulating his own ambition, aiding his reverie. From Ali to Alicia, as close for him now as their names in a dictionary. From Israel to Skinny Israel, geographical neighbors on the map of his enigmatic self.

If Skinny Israel wasn't as real as the country below, then how could the mere thought of it do this to him? How could it make him, after only a day away, already ache to return there? No. *Their* Skinny Israel, his and Alicia's, was *real*. An island maybe. Except they weren't that remote. They weren't Cuba. They weren't Madagascar. Their families touched parts of them—the Totahs on one side, the Ramseys on the other. Skinny Israel was a peninsula, perhaps. A tiny nation of two. It had only a brief history and one supreme rule of law—it was a colony founded on passion. Like all great romances, it was a democracy, of course. In this case, one whose constituents voted with desire. Unless he and Alicia were together, it wouldn't exist. So was it real? Were they? Right now, with her in America and him in this vessel bolting farther away by the second, it was starting to feel like just a fantasy, a utopia of their own imagining.

The PA speakers crackled. "Ladies and gentlemen, we're beginning our descent into Aleppo . . . ," the pilot began. When Mustafa heard "descent," he squirmed. As long as he was aloft, everything was still somehow *now*. As long as everything was *now*, America was not the past. Alicia was not the past, and not what being away from her would turn her into, a memory. But no—no need to panic (the back of his neck was prickling with warmth and dampness)—this separation was only temporary. He would be going back soon. Back to the homeland of their love. A real place—not make-believe. Strange. To be without your lover was to be in exile. He laughed to himself, *at* himself, as overwrought with emotion as a character in one of those cartoon books Malik was always reading. No wonder they called them comics! Okay, okay. Be strong, Mustafa. As long as you are without her, you'll just have to be a solitary man—a comic book hero—staggering about the earth trying to get back home. Your superpowers are in jeopardy, dwindling by the hour. (Knife-wielding maniacs, the planet could be yours!) You will lose access to the Force forever, without the girl, without the kisses. Until you get back, you will know the struggle of all who have been cast out of their native land. You will be Mustafa the Wanderer. Mustafa of Palestine. Mustafa the Jew! You are daunted by the challenge: to take back and defend your rightful place in the world. You didn't ask for all this responsibility—but there's no turning back now. You know you will have to *fight, fight, fight* for you and yours. You might be, you *must* be, the Muhammad Ali of Love!

AFTER RETRIEVING HIS two suitcases from the baggage claim area in the Aleppo airport, Mustafa turned and saw, instead of Hasim, Aunt Zahirah standing near an exit, calling to him. Her face was welcoming but tremulous, which he took to mean she had missed him and was overwhelmed that he was home at last. He lumbered over to her and put his bags down. "I know," he said, hugging her. "I am happy to see you, too."

"Oh, *Mustafa* . . ." Her voice had always sounded to him like an instrument tuned to express glad tidings. She could say a simple "hello" or "good morning" on an average day and make you think she'd said "Eid Mubarak!" as if your presence marked the end of her having to abstain from you any longer, as if *you* were a cause for celebration. So her whispering his name this way—unnecessarily comforting, far from cheerful—alarmed him. Had Malik contrived his optimism to hide the truth?

As they separated, he asked, "What's wrong? Where is Hasim? Why are you alone? What is happening? Mama . . . is she . . . ?"

Zahirah was looking up at him, tight-faced and teary-eyed, and Mustafa thought: *My mother is dead.* That's what happens when you spend your entire Ramadan sinning, cavorting with Christians, letting America have its way with you. That's what happens while you are casually cruising on a plane—barely thinking about your sick mother at all—relishing your transgressions, fidgeting indecently in your seat at the memory of it all, converting to Judaism in jest. Your mother dies. He'd sacrificed her for potato chips and gum, for phony superpowers, for the affections of a convincing stand-in for a lesser member of Destiny's Child. (But, no, only Alicia could make losing Rana bearable. He couldn't let the fear of his mother dying indict their love. Loving Alicia had been his greatest act of bravery. He wouldn't deny her and commit his greatest act of cowardice. Rana herself had raised him better than that. So just like that—saved by his finest rationalization—he recommitted to life's irony, which he and Alicia had discovered together, the oath of their love: your sin could be your salvation.)

Zahirah's hand gripped his wrist, confirming, he felt, that she thought he needed consolation. He would mourn his mother with a double dose of grief. She could have her sorrow, plus the sorrow his father's eternal absence had denied him. Absence was not death, just its own brand of nothingness. Being fatherless was all he'd ever known; it had been impossible to grieve oblivion, though he had tried. This despite Uncle Adad, who had always shielded Mustafa beneath the umbrella of his paternity, offering him manly teachings and security from the physical dangers of the world. But once, when he was five years old, Mustafa had gone wandering on the outskirts of their neighborhood and gotten lost. He kept trying to trace his steps, but every turn, down one narrow cobblestone street and up another, led him to increasingly less familiar environs. Then, dusk nearing, a scruffy vagrant had darted out of an alley and chased him for a couple of blocks. He'd somehow escaped and eventually made it home safely but, traumatized, he didn't leave the house alone for weeks. Late at night during that unforgettable phase, he would tiptoe into his mother's room, because he couldn't sleep for weeks either. Not to crawl into bed with her for a sense of security, which he desperately wanted to do. Rana would have told him no—*had* told him the first time he tried—and sent him back to the room he shared with his cousins. "Be strong, Mustafa!" Instead of cuddling, he would settle for picking up the framed picture of his father that she kept on her dressing table near the window. His eyes would dart from the Uncle Adad look-alike to his mother's slumbering bundle reflected in her vanity mirror. But the most intriguing vision was the one beyond the black lace curtains of Rana's own design. He would stare at the rooftops and the maze of streets and, in spite of the panic he relived when he remembered being chased—or maybe because of it—something in him, in defiance of his own fears, longed to be back out in the streets of Aleppo, getting lost. Those unfamiliar streets. Those alleys. Alone, but alive with anxiety. Breathless with vulnerability. Running for his life. His anguish—usually barely felt whenever he sat holding his father's photograph—suddenly animated. Of course, he had the rest of his family: his mother, Uncle Adad, Aunt Zahirah. But not—not now, *never*—his father. Being lost had felt strangely natural to him, in accord with who he was. It felt like *being*.

For even if he searched every corner of Aleppo—was this why he'd gone wandering in the first place?—even if he could travel the world, this man in his hands was nowhere to be found.

"Aunt Zahirah," he said now. Was his mother really dead? Did his aunt's speechlessness augur this reality? Something definitively dark—*the end of something*—was in her eyes.

"Please tell me the truth, Aunt Zahirah. You always tell the truth!"

He could tell she wanted to say it. She wanted to soften the blow of this thing that was going to break his heart. Her sympathy-drenched eyes widened, angling upward, to his right shoulder, as if the source of his agony, like a chip, rested there. Her lips parted. But the response to his plea did not come from her; rather, for more than one reason, it seemed to issue from a ghost.

"And I do not always tell the truth?"

Befuddled, he stiffened with surprise at the disembodied voice. Where had it come from? He knew who it was pretending to be, but who had *really* spoken it? And why? And if it was actually her, *how?* He was just about to turn around—the voice must have come from behind him—and confront the mystery when the punch, as forceful as the one he'd thrown to fell the madman, struck him in the back of the head. Aunt Zahirah yelped and made a languid attempt to catch him, but the momentum of his collapse was more than she could handle. He braced himself for the landing, and as his face smacked the floor, he saw the toe of her black slipper edge out below the hem of her voluminous blue dress. She knelt beside him and shook his shoulders, trying to revive him, though he was still conscious. Then she tried to roll him over, but he declined, exaggerating his weight, wanting gravity to have its way with him, treat him as if he were dead. Rana, it was now clear, was not. He could hear her raging from above.

"*Are you crazy? Do you want to die?*" She saw in him the same thing he had seen in the man threatening Adad at the store: lunacy, danger.

"I will tell you this truth. Yes, you are crazy! Yes, you want to die! The family of this American girl. Do you know these people? No! Adad says there are killers in that house! Do you want to end up like your father? I never told you why he was killed in that bar. He wasn't killed by just any man. He was killed by someone's husband. There, that is your truth. Is that what you want? To be like your father? To be like Muhammad Totah? I see now you *are* just like him. Wanting a woman you should not have. But this woman—whoever she is—I tell you right now, you *will not* have!"

Mustafa, sucker-punched but not necessarily down for the count, wanted to get up and go another round. When his mother had attacked him, he wasn't even ready. (In retrospect, in fairness—he realized it now, lying here, so unjustly defeated—maybe he should have called out to the madman before striking. Maybe he could have talked him down. There were, he admitted, reasons for rules of engagement.) Round One with his mother had been a bust. He wanted to pick himself up—but the embarrassment of it all was too much to bear. (The feet of a security guard were scurrying their way.) He sighed and let his head sink into Zahirah's thigh. "Bae-bae," she kept saying. Her fingers, moving through his hair, strummed his body into a state of peace. "Bae-bae . . ." His mother was still screaming, pointlessly. She'd already won; she was just piling on. No, he didn't want to be Muhammad Totah. He wished he had the strength to tell her, if only to silence her. *There are other Muhammads, Mama—millions of them. All over the world. I'll imagine myself one of them. I already have!* As surely as he was rejecting the idea of his father, he was also resigning himself to the improbability of ever again having Alicia. It was much more likely—his mother's rantings proposed no more pleasant an alternative—that he would remain in exile forever, never to return to Skinny Israel. Of course, he could try not to give up. If he could withstand the pressure of holding out in fruitless desperation, he could live his life as one long cliffhanger. A comic book character who keeps unsuspecting readers like Malik turning pages in vain. Then, at the end, the hero—Mustafa the Dreamer, Mustafa the Fool—never sees her again. Never holds her again. Never regains the superpower of which she is the only source. Yes, he could fake his way through years of convincing himself hopelessness was hope. But Aunt Zahirah, still rubbing his head, had stroked him down to a more conclusive truth: he wouldn't get to be the Muhammad Ali of Love after all. He would have to be the Muhammad Ali of something else.

4

BEHOLD—RAMADAN RAMSEY!

Mama Joon had been thinking the child should be named Pamela if she was a girl or Tristram if he was boy. Clarissa's name had come from the same section of books in Judge Dumas's home office, where they had so often met behind locked doors while his wife was out shopping on a Saturday or visiting her mother after church on a Sunday. (His collection of Elizabethan plays was in a case to the right of his volumes of eighteenth-century English literature, and that was where she had decided, while dusting one afternoon, that Romeo and Juliet would be original names for twins. When Clarissa had given birth to two boys instead of a boy and a girl as expected, she had insisted on bestowing upon them a masculinized version of her idea—and Romeo and Julius were born.) Her baby-naming mojo hadn't met with many beneficial results. Those she had attempted to endow with a literary flourish had mostly proved mockeries of their antecedents.

So she wasn't the least bit upset when Alicia handed her the new baby boy on the afternoon of Friday, August 4, 2000, and, ignoring her mother's suggestion, said, "His name is Ramadan. Ramadan Ramsey."

Yes, of course, it was. Just like his father's name was Abdullah or whoever that boy she had been running around with was. She couldn't remember his name, though she thought she would recognize it if she ever heard it again. She had been in the Quicky Mart one time when another worker had called out to him—the same good-looking, narrow-tailed young man she had once seen hurriedly kissing Alicia goodbye on the front porch before dashing away when she had opened the door, not to run him off, but just to say, "Hello. How are you? Would you like to come in?" That was the only time she had seen them together. Kashif—no, *that* wasn't it—had stopped coming around not too long after that, so Mama Joon had thought the baby's father could also have been one of Alicia's other secret lovers, a throwback maybe. But now she knew better. Alicia was making a statement when she said, "His name is Ramadan. Ramadan Ramsey." No mistake about it—this was Mos Def's child.

"Hello, Ramadan!" Mama Joon beamed down at the boy. Beaming was her thing. When she was eight years old she had begun occasionally spelling "June" as "Joon" because she had felt, deeply, that she was closer to the moon than to any month, even the month of her own birth, which connoted warmth, another of the essential qualities she felt emanating from herself. But it was the light of the moon, which had warmth in it, too, that she sensed was more indicative of her whole spirit. And the visual rhyme of "Joon," while technically superficial, had the advantage of those double o's, whose shapes mimicked that of the changeable and mysterious celestial body she was claiming as her muse. Those vowels ogled duplicitously like eyes, the body parts most capable of emitting your beam, assuming you had one.

Ramadan's own eyes were closed now, but it was Mama Joon, looking down at the radiant boy, who was momentarily blinded. His brightness matched and perhaps surpassed the light of love she felt swelling in her. She blinked a few times and tried to bring him into focus. A fuzziness remained, but she could see him plainly now, and gradually she smiled her way back to 20/20. There had not been anything mystical about the boy's luminescence at all, just a Black grandmother—a dark brown one anyway—going sightless with surprise at the pallor of her minutes-old grandbaby. Under the harsh incandescence of the Charity Hospital delivery room, he had left her squinting in search of his negritude. It was there, she finally noted with relief, at the tips of his ears, in the curvy line of his lower lip, which was reminiscent of Alicia's and her own, and even—well, *maybe*—in the curly, if wispy, nap of his black hair. Her sense of unquestionable ownership returned. That moment of doubt, followed by the sudden affirmation that he was theirs, *hers*, made Mama Joon draw Ramadan even closer to her. It was as if, during the first thirty seconds of their meeting, she had *had* him, then *lost* him, then *found* him again. The lilt of that contracted mini-drama of suspense—reminiscent of the elusive, rhythmic phenomenon dubbed "swing"—sealed their bond. (Yes, she could *feel* it—"Ah!" she said—here it was, the music she was after!) The *had him, lost him, found him* ordained them not just grandmother and grandson, but also inseparable companions, soul mates—irrevocably conjoining not just their spirits but their destinies.

5

RAMADAN'S FIRST ADVENTURE

Perhaps only one such affinity can exist at any juncture, for Alicia found it impossible to forge a bond with Ramadan rivaling his and Mama Joon's. Instead of nursing him, she busied herself attending to the thing she had birthed along with him, as if a twin, a demanding little bundle of gloom. It had begun its incubation right around the time of Mustafa's departure, though its origins must have lain deep inside her all along, some dark ovum of delirium waiting to be seeded not by a spasm of love but of loss, waiting to be inseminated by pain. While Mama Joon rocked Ramadan in her arms, Alicia lay in bed mothering her melancholy as if it were an alternate, more intimate newborn. One who wanted and needed her in a way Ramadan did not. Whenever Ramadan was hungry or irritable, Mama Joon was there to comfort him with a bottle and a lullaby. But this other one wanted to be pampered by only Alicia. Only she could meet his demands to be held so tightly he could feel her heartbeat (as if his own had not fully developed, if it ever would), subsisting as well on her thoughts, even as he murmured things back to her with a strange precocity. His neediness registered as abject loyalty, a loyalty that, unlike Ramadan's, was exclusive and unconditional, placing his "brother" in an unflattering light.

Nevertheless, Ramadan was eight months old the day Alicia—aching to connect with him, all that was left of Mustafa—strapped him into his stroller for a trip to the river. Unlike on some days, this April morning her depression did not render her immobile or housebound. With an effort that presented itself as grace, on good days like today, she could change Ramadan's diapers, give him a bottle, burp him, rock him to sleep. Her movements were noticeably slower, but if you didn't know her before she'd given birth, you would have thought she was just more naturally deliberate than most. Even those who did know her chalked up the difference to the arduousness of childbirth and a rough transition to motherhood, which was, after all, quite a job.

Clarissa came out onto the porch and saw Alicia on the sidewalk grappling with Ramadan and the stroller. "Strap him in good. Boys always wanna get away."

She wasn't just remembering the experience of placing one of her own boys into a stroller. She was thinking more about the relative ease with which she had performed this same act with Alicia, a sibling so much younger that she was more like a daughter. Looking at her baby sister tussling with her own infant aged Clarissa and made her nostalgic for an innocence that had long since perished. She had been eighteen and still a virgin the first time she had held Alicia in her arms. Mama Joon had guessed it and pronounced her "a late bloomer." Something in the way Clarissa literally refused to let her hair down back then, insisting upon wearing a schoolmarmish bun until a few months after Alicia was born. Late bloomer—the phrase had hurt her at first, harmonizing with the other deficiencies Mama Joon, under the guise of motivating her, had charged her with possessing: tardiness, laziness, stubbornness, slowness to laughter, all of which were true. But when she had finally bloomed, it had been with an azalean flourish. Less than three months after Alicia's arrival, the bun came down. That was when she had let Leo Walls take her to a motel room on Airline Highway, where he had abruptly stopped kissing her neck, spun her around, and pulled out the three bobby pins that had so long triangulated the bun into place. Then he had raked his fingers through her hair, tousling it free. In that moment, she wasn't sure if she was in for sex or a shampoo—which, in retrospect, she would not have minded one bit, water whooshing from a faucet, setting her whole head a-tingle, cooling the entire orb of her scalp, the anticipation of a bubbly rub, a sensuousness that left you, in the end, clean and fully intact, the one who beneath it all you always were, only better. But then Leo's hands had moved so fast from her head to her breasts that Clarissa's whole body was drenched in wetness anyway, awash with his warmth and surprising humidity. His touches, manly and manic, lathered her up. And she wasn't her ordinary self anymore but some long-haired alternative-universe Clarissa—something at once beautiful and strange, perfect and horrifying—a Rapunzel in waiting, the Cousin Itt of herself, who had always, without ever knowing it, been in need of this: a good conditioning. Later, while Leo enjoyed the nap he'd earned, she had gotten out of bed and looked at herself in the bathroom mirror, hair all over her head, not hanging from a window or from head to toe as on a freak, but sticking up and out, as wild as a bush. That's when she had again heard Mama Joon's "late bloomer" jab and seen herself anew in the dim motel room, head adorned with tufts and curls that looked like blossoms, some new living, breathing variety of rhododendron. In sex she had found a way to counter all the shortcomings "late bloomer" re-indicted her with, the laziness and stubbornness, the lack of a comic sensibility. She had found a way to avoid being marked tardy or absent ever again—as Mama Joon would have it. A way to be diligent; to be not obstinate, but fully compliant; to respond, quickly and properly—with gusto and good humor—to something vitally amusing in life. She had watched her shoulders hunch themselves in the mirror, and smiled *inwardly* at the smile that was reflecting back at her, and then she hugged herself, the one who she was literally, at that moment, holding in higher esteem.

Thereafter, every act of sensuality would be for her an act of self-improvement, an aspiration to a better self, to the spring of herself. Her boys were blooms, too—arriving in quick succession, faster than perennials—as duplicitous as roses, beautiful but thorny as all get-out; bruised, prom-night corsages from season after season of self-actualization.

But still, when it came to mothering, Crip wasn't her first; Alicia was. Alicia had been the baby whose smile gaped with the vulnerability of a buttercup, inspiring Clarissa's own flowering. Even now, her femininity on parade down there on the sidewalk, Alicia effortlessly contradicted Clarissa's conceit about her boys. They weren't blooms at all—maybe some roadside wild things, technically weeds, which occasionally pressed forth some pale triplet of leaves that might, to an inexpert horticulturalist or a desperate bee, pass for petals.

When had their bond been broken, hers and Alicia's? It must have been not long after Clarissa had had Clarence, her real first. *Hers.* Oh, but no—she knew when. Exactly when. Yes, it had been one day when she was taking care of them both. (Seeing Alicia down there fumbling with Ramadan was bringing it all back—a memory she'd willed into meaninglessness. But here it was, as alive and fidgety as Ramadan, as undeniable as Mama Joon's affection for him.) Alicia had been a year and a half old, crying in her crib, while Clarence, only a few months old, was sleeping soundly on Mama Joon's bed. Hearing her sister in diaper distress, Clarissa went down the hall to the bedroom, where Alicia, ready to be rescued, stopped crying and struck the "pick me up" pose of damp-bottomed toddlers and landlocked angels. But two steps into the room, Clarissa stopped. Alicia hummed a few puffs of anxiety at the delay of her deliverance, and then she followed her sister's gaze to where Clarence lay, resting peacefully and dry, or if not, oblivious to his wetness, so *not* in conscious need. Still, Clarissa had moved to her right, away from Alicia, toward the bed, toward Clarence, *hers*.

Alicia had cried out, not a *cry*, but the word she knew best. "No!"

Clarissa had heard her, but she could not stop herself. Call it hormones, love, or the inclination to do wrong when no one is watching—but she did it. She rushed past her crying baby sister, whose "no" warbled into a wail. In her hurry to get to Clarence and leave the room, the scene of her crime (a stroke of incivility that even to its perpetrator felt felonious), Clarissa had swooped her baby up with such force she woke him. Startled into unwanted consciousness, he also began to cry.

"There, there," Clarissa had whispered to him, pressing him to her breast, soothing him, trying to soothe herself. "Did she wake you up with all her damn crying?" As she was carrying him out of the room, she paused, looked down at Alicia and said, "See what you did."

In the hallway, she had heard Alicia's shrieks growing louder and louder, even though Clarissa was moving farther away, defying the laws of physics. How was that possible? It was a riddle for a genius, something a latter-day Einstein might puzzle over for decades before finally solving, positing some perfect relationship between decibels and deception. Guilt had gripped Clarissa. A fear of being found out seized her as well (if science could sort out sound, couldn't it sort out sin!), and she had called back over her shoulder, "I'm coming back. I promise. I'm coming back." She had meant it, too. Sitting in Mama Joon's chair in the living room, she had rocked Clarence to sleep as fast as she could and

laid him on the sofa. Then she had run back to the bedroom. Alicia, dis-
trust in her eyes, was there waiting with her arms up, like one of those
statuary angels, stuck in stone.

Now, years later, the vestiges of her sister's betrayal fueling the rejection of her advice about strapping Ramadan in tight, Alicia called up to
Clarissa, "I got him."

"Booker jumped out on me one time before he was one. That was
how I knew he could walk. No, run. Ran clean across the street before I
could catch him. People looking at me like I'm crazy. Letting a baby run
across Rampart Street."

"I said I got him, Clara."

"Where y'all going?"

"Just for a walk."

Ramadan, sensing an adventure, smiled up at his mother and began
pumping his arms up and down. The moving would happen soon. *When
Mama Joon put him in like this and the blue was up there and everything
flipped upside down, the moving was about to happen, the awayness, the
gone. But there was nothing like the moving. Not until you got to the gone.
Getting to the gone was—*

Alicia's silver crucifix, dangling from the chain around her neck,
caught Ramadan's eye, and he reached up and gripped it for a couple of
cheery fist pumps before releasing it into a gentle pendulous swing.

"Just like your daddy." Alicia leaned down farther, smiling back at
him, remembering how Mustafa, in the afterglow, liked to play with
her crucifix, rubbing it so much she sometimes thought he was less
interested in her body than her soul.

Thinking of Mustafa, she felt a promising twinge of intimacy, inspiring her to pull the little blue blanket in the carriage over Ramadan's exposed arms. Maybe he was feeling the chill of the morning breeze. She

was, and she snuggled her oversized gray cardigan around her sundress. As she was rising, still relishing these moments of caring for Ramadan (they were rare), having found the strength to take this stroll with him, the initiative to adjust his blanket, she looked down and saw him frowning, maybe not cold after all. (She really had no idea what he wanted.) He shoved the blanket down and began stretching and wriggling his arms ecstatically, writhing with a freedom of his own design. And with those defiant movements, an innocent rejection of his mother's attempt at attentiveness, he effortlessly dashed all her hope away.

WITH THE NEGLIGENCE of the dispirited, Alicia pushed Ramadan through morning traffic into the French Quarter, heading for the river. The driver of a passing St. Claude Avenue bus honked a warning at her back, but she exuded a carefree air, the horn barely penetrating the inebriation of her malaise.

But her pretense of ease was soon exposed when, three blocks away, at the corner of Bourbon and St. Philip, outside Lafitte's Blacksmith bar, she tripped and tumbled to the ground. The cracking sidewalk had dipped, its failing design presenting the need to navigate an undulation, to surf the stony, unforgiving little shard of a wave, and the toe of her sneaker caught on the last lapping inch of its jagged crest. Her balance shifted to the left, toward the street, and she reached out to try to grab the left handle of the stroller—partly to keep herself from falling too hard, partly in an ill-conceived effort to protect Ramadan from rolling into traffic. Luckily the tip of her finger only tapped the handle and slid away. Had she succeeded, she would have overturned the stroller, hurling Ramadan into the middle of Bourbon Street. Instead, the little carriage wobbled from side to side, tenuously at first, threatening to topple over before steadying itself. Then it rolled and bounded to a stop on the sidewalk, its front right wheel wedging into a gap in the crumbling brick of the centuries' old bar on the corner.

Inside, Ramadan gripped the blanket he had earlier rejected, and it was bunched at his waist, cushioning his hip against the rigid inner frame. Though motionless, he was swept upon a curious current, basking in some vague impression of the womb, the elegant negation of being. But it was a turbulent nostalgia, competing with the here and now—*which meant*: this bright blue sky above that at once beckoned to him *and* pressed down with a weighty discomfort; the cloth of his little cotton T-shirt that felt good one moment but irritated him the next; the pungency of the French Quarter air (whatever its source) that he needed to survive, but that also stung his nostrils, hurting him even as it sustained him. That breeze Alicia had tried to protect him from with the blanket—but that he had wanted to feel flowing over his skin, arms, neck, chin, lips, nose, and then finally to take in, in, in!—that breeze was not all bliss. He could have cried (and crankiness would have been a fair reaction to one's first instance of real disillusionment), but there was too much pleasure in the sweet memory of the unbreezy wherever he had come from, and too much promise in his stark awareness that where he was now had enough of that place in it to remind him, from time to time, if not always—but now, yes, *right now*—of that before-feeling. So you could cling to the brightness of the blue and the memory of the bliss. (Were they the same thing?) The blue and the bliss—and the breeze, of course, even laced with this stench of impurity. Could you live on that? On this! Could you? His heaving chest, his thumping heartbeat said he could. Yes, yes, he could! And so, there on the sidewalk outside Lafitte's Blacksmith, the eighteenth-century barroom named for a pirate, a structure that appeared to want to cave in on itself but apparently would not—a building in the throes of an architectural existential crisis that matched Ramadan's own—an optimist was born. No wonder the tantrums he would throw a few years from now—that moodiness Mama Joon could tame with a rag—would always give way to giggles.

As Alicia fell into St. Philip Street, she watched an old rusting pickup truck come chugging down Bourbon Street. Its bright red body was crudely adorned with colorful handwritten words that, in the blur of her tumble, were illegible. The truck looked like an out-of-season Mardi Gras float as it glided past, and its wheels rolled over the spot where she might have flung Ramadan. She closed her eyes in anticipation of pain, but her sundress billowed like a parachute, and she could have been touching down in a meadow somewhere, her palms flattening not against grainy concrete but thatches of summer grass. Her chin bumped into her wrist, and she heard the springs of the old pickup squeak. Looking up, she saw the front bumper, angled out of its rightful position. On the faded red-and-black front door and the side of the slow-passing vehicle, she read a scrawl of yellow and white words: ORANGES and AVOCADOS and COLLARDS and BELL PEPPER and SWEET CORN. The truck bed was loaded with cardboard cases presumably filled with the fruits and vegetables advertised on the body of the truck. Then she heard an old man's muffled but amplified voice, thickened with the most local of accents, calling to her (and anyone within its range), as the vehicle creaked farther away, "I got unyun . . . I got collyflowuh . . ."

The driver's raspy cries and the odd spectacle of his produce-hauling contraption—a market on wheels—magnified for Alicia the purity of the man's entrepreneurial impulse. On the ground with embarrassment and fascination, she thought of Adad, the Syrian merchant with his strangely relevant little storefront, who somehow had helped shove her down in this street. He and the vegetable man were kin, peddling what they had accumulated to those who could not be bothered to gather things for themselves, entrusting their welfare to the whims and desires of others. They were as vulnerable as she was, as Ramadan was. Cast by chance into the world from the soft center of some woman not unlike herself. Seeded there with the randomness that had produced the passing vendor's tomatoes and cabbages. By a force as potent and invisible as Mustafa! It was all entirely preposterous, really—but, okay, somehow wonderful. She got it. It was the Mustafa part that made it wonderful. Otherwise the absurdity of it all would have doomed the entire enterprise.

She could have lain in the street much longer musing about her fall, her safe if bittersweet landing, but—

"You all r-i-uht?" a balding, red-faced man with a salt-and-pepper mustache was asking as he bent down and extended a ring-laden left hand. His right hand held a clear plastic cup of sloshing beer, and an ash-tipped cigarette was wiggling between his lips as he spoke, like the baton of a sluggish conductor, guiding the rhythm of his speech with a millisecond's delay. A lazy musicality distinguished his tone. Alicia couldn't tell if his accent owed more to the drawl of his Southernness or insobriety.

She nodded that she was fine, though her left leg was stinging. When she looked down, she saw a dark, grit-speckled contusion forming on her shin. The man helped her up, extending his beer away from his body with a ballroom-dancing flair that cost him a swallow or two of frothy beverage. Standing, she was about to thank him, but gratitude morphed into a gasp of delayed concern for Ramadan.

She rushed over to the stroller and peeked under the canopy, where Ramadan appeared wide-eyed and smiling, like a kid after a roller-coaster ride, flapping his arms up and down. Alicia sighed and dusted off her knees.

"Honey, you better be more careful out here," her rescuer warned. "These streets will *kill* you!"

She flinched. Had her clumsiness betrayed her? Revealed a wish so apparent that any tipsy streetwalker could see it—her not-so-secret desire *to lie down*. Clarissa hadn't seen it, but she wasn't observant and, anyway, she was probably too busy hiding her own wish for Alicia to fall, to fail. But then she saw a twinkle in the man's blue eyes and realized he meant something else. *These streets will kill you!* had more to do with him than her. When he resumed walking down Bourbon Street, he lifted his splattering cup in one hand and his cigarette in the other. Then he looked back and said through hoarse laughter, "*Believe* me!"

MINUTES LATER, AS she was concentrating on crossing Decatur Street, a glint of gold flashed in the corner of her eye. The sun was reflecting off the hind legs of a horse suspended about ten or twelve feet in the air. A miracle, this golden horse, levitating way up there? But no, once she moved closer and the branches of the crape myrtle tree that had been obstructing her view parted, she saw the tall stone base upon which the gleaming animal was posed in mid prance, and her eyes traced the lines of the statue. Perched atop the golden horse was a golden girl, her scarf sweeping backwards and her long hair hanging down her back with an enviable thickness, like a wondrous weave. She circled the statue while pushing Ramadan, and he gurgled with contentment, admiring the flecks of gilt flickering in the irises of his mother's awakened eyes. Up close, Alicia could see that the literally statuesque girl riding the horse wore a tight suit of armor, and her feet pointed straight down into stirrups on either side of her steed. She raised a flag high above her head triumphantly, and even before Alicia read the engraving on the base of the statue, she knew she was looking at the warrior saint:

JOAN OF ARC

MAID OF ORLEANS

1412–1431

That was all. You were expected to know who she was and why she was here. What little Alicia knew about Joan she had learned one Sunday years ago from the homily a priest visiting from France had delivered at St. Augustine Catholic Church. She couldn't quite remember his specific theme. Something to do with being virtuous, the ideal of standing up for something maybe, fighting for what is right. No, that wasn't it. But he said he had been to see this very statue, and it had moved him to tell the congregation—well, whatever it was he told them that day.

She stared up at the memorial with its tombstone-like engraving and wondered what it really meant, what those few words and dates celebrating Joan's existence didn't say. Yes, her name was Joan. And, what, she was from someplace named Arc? Or was she just a distant relative of Noah's? Who wasn't? So that didn't make any sense; the "Arc" meant something else. She was a maid? Not like Mama Joon, of course. Joan didn't clean houses or hotel rooms; she was a soldier. No, she was a different kind of maid, as in maiden, as in an unmarried young woman, like Alicia, though, *unlike* Alicia, pure. Famously pure. "Poor and *pure*," the priest had said, inspired by his subject to seek poetry in a foreign tongue. Alicia could see that in Joan's sculpted face now, the determination and the purity, her eyes wide open, peering straight ahead and focused on saving France. You couldn't save a nation if you were too busy flirting with guys, looking back to see if a certain hot young Syrian was staring at your butt. "Of Orleans." From *Orleans*. *Old* Orleans as opposed to *New* Orleans. Which explained why someone decided to put her in Decatur Street, thousands of miles away from home, far from where she'd had her divine visions and her triumphs, before martyrdom, before sainthood. That much, Father what's-his-name had made clear. "They burn chère Joan—how you say—at dee stake . . . *at dee stake*." He had been vague about the exact details. (You could cut an icon some slack when it came to the particulars.) Legendary was legendary. That was why all they had bothered to etch into the stone was her name, birthplace, marital status, and birth and death dates. That was all you needed to know, Alicia thought. Joan was enshrined on an island in the middle of the street ("Drive around my majesty, please!) in a strange country almost six hundred years after her horrible death. All because she had *believed* in something. That was it! That's what the sermon had been about. *Faith.* Joan had believed in God and in her visions. You have to believe, the priest had said. You have to believe.

Alicia read Joan's dates again. 1412–1431. As she was wont to do, she did the math. Nineteen! Joan was just nineteen when she died. The same age she was when she met Mustafa! But if Joan of Arc were alive and she tried to buy a drink in the Quarter, they would card her and deny the saint a daiquiri!

You have to believe. Was that really true? Maybe you could do something small, or nothing at all (while believing only a little or not at all), and then die a quiet death—not *at dee stake*—and be perfectly happy not ever knowing what it feels like to be Joan. But if you wanted to wind up like Joan, immortalized in gold, sitting high above tourists and lonely girls to make them feel good about themselves for a few minutes, then it probably *was* true. But even then, believe in what?

As if in search of an answer, she began moving the stroller again, heading toward the river, putting her hand out to the oncoming traffic. The driver of a Ford F-150 skidded to a halt, though he had the green light, and she pushed Ramadan bumpily to the other side of the street.

THE MOMENT THEY passed the French Market shops, the scent of the river rushed them. Ramadan writhed with excitement, rocking the stroller with his movements. Without realizing it, Alicia pushed him faster. When she reached four steps leading up to the levee, she stopped. The front wheels of the stroller hit the bottom step, and Ramadan's head lifted from his pillow and landed with a poof. Confused, he clinched his fists and would have cried if Alicia hadn't scooped him up. His head rested on her shoulder; the sky, which he knew so well from his travels in the stroller, dominated the scene. But there, below that sky, was this quivering thing that he would forever connect to the wet wind whipping his face, seeping into his mouth like the last wispy sips from a bottle, the part that always made you want more. Behind him Alicia was struggling with the stroller. Finally, she decided just to drag it as she backed up the steps.

Once at the top of the landing, she resumed her quicker pace, jerking the carriage over wheel-averse railroad tracks. The Crescent City Connection, spanning the river, caught her eye. Even though from this distance it appeared toylike in scale, the bridge emphasized the Mississippi's breadth. Ramadan, sensing he was missing something, wriggled around so that he was facing the river again. As she moved them closer to it, the waterway seemed to summon their presence and herald their arrival. Determined, she let the wheels of the stroller thump against the next set of steps as she lugged it carelessly behind her. With the river revealing its true dimensions as she ascended, she felt on the verge of a Joan-like vision of her own. Could the eyes of the defiled witness the divine? Well, yes, apparently—for there it was!

The river dazzled Ramadan, too, and now, understanding its absolute liquidity, he wanted it with a fetal intensity. He wanted to be in it, to be *of it*. *Again*. Yes, again! His tongue, as if a prehensile appendage, stuck itself out of his mouth, desiring the water, desiring to be watered. He seemed to have arrived at the source—the Mother of Mothers—*which meant*: maybe he was on his way back to where he had been before there was any need for a bottle or a nipple or the fraudulence of a binky. Before the embarrassment of hunger, which had sealed his fate, his banishment. How the need to suckle had humiliated him with this *hereness*! In a display of frustration—his first real episode of Ramadanian alienation, his first tantrum—he began to beat his fists against Alicia's chest, wanting it not to be true. But there was no way back; he understood this now. He *knew*. No way home, whatever and wherever that was. Just this place that for some reason wanted to make you forget about the better place—and sometimes did—that tried to make you feel like you were in the better place when, really, you were just *gone*. So he banged his mother's chest. Somehow she had done this to him; she was complicit in his capture. She had helped push him out of the water and into all this. Forced him to forsake everything—which was nothing. The supreme comfort of not being here. The joy of not being. Blue skies and buggy rides—upon further consideration—what a crock!

Alicia endured Ramadan's flailing as best she could, struggling to hold him in her arms. His little fists pounding into her served only to remind her how little they had in common, how little he liked her, how little she liked him. He wanted something she could not give him; that was clear. And she wanted Mustafa. Not this declension of their love. This fraction of their fervor. Not Ramadan—who would always want something she could not provide. He wanted Mama Joon more than he wanted her. She accepted this completely now, as Mama Joon was in every way a more substantial version of motherhood than she was. Any child could see that. Even hers. Earlier this morning she and Ramadan had had a chance to come together, to come *back* together. (Not long ago, they had been one.) But that was before he had pushed the blanket away. Then again, maybe they'd still had a chance at Bourbon Street, after her fall. If only he would have cried out for her. If only. But he hadn't. He had chosen the roller coaster, the thrill of life over her, over needing her. Anything but her, *even danger*, was what he wanted! And now here he was hitting her, each thud of his fists thumping her chest in an arrhythmic pattern counter to the beating of her heart, his life force so fundamentally out of sync with hers. So, no, they had no chance. Not now. Not with him wanting something else so badly, something other than her, and with her knowing now, so irrefutably, that he did.

Compelled to let him know she knew, she yelled, "What do you want, Ramadan?"

He kept staring at the river, banging his fists and squirming in her arms.

"What do you want?" she asked again, following his eyes, deducing the approximate truth. "Do you want the river? Is that what you want?"

Leaving the stroller behind, she started to climb down the rocky decline of the levee toward the muddy bank of the Mississippi. Ramadan's gyrations stopped, and Alicia felt emboldened. Finally, she had figured him out.

It was only about thirty feet to the long flat strip of land that formed the river's edge, a mix of dark sludge and patchy grass. The sloping landscape was not steep, and the large chunks of beige and gray stones were no more treacherous than the buckling French Quarter sidewalks that had tripped her up earlier. She wedged her sneakers into the spaces between stones and tiptoed her way down. A city girl who had never set foot on a hill, she thought, "So this is hiking." A helpful gust whipped up, keeping them from leaning too far forward. Another strong blast blew from a slightly different direction, and she followed its force, too, listing to the right for the next few steps. Was this what you called "riding the wind"? Or was that just something you did when you sailed or took flight? Out of her element, she staggered ahead, aware that whatever else she was doing, she was definitely throwing caution to the wind.

The focus required to scale the levee had calmed her anger at Ramadan. With her last two strides, she set her feet close together on a dry-looking patch of dirt, and she looked up at the climb she would have to get back home. Then, Ramadan holding still in her arms, she turned and faced the Mississippi.

"Okay, there it is," she said. "There's your river."

He remained quiet and calm. He could feel Alicia's heart beating against his chest, pulsing from her exertions, as accusatory to him as his hammering fists had been to her. He blinked at the river and its curious vibrations. The sun had risen higher, and its mirroring on the surface of the water hurt his eyes. He looked up at his mother's relatively soothing face.

"There's your river," she said to him again. "There it is—and you can't have it!"

Ramadan didn't know the meaning of her words, of course, but she had spoken them with authority, as if speaking some absolute truth. She saw his face turn contemplative and knowing, the way babies look when processing new language, the look of enlightenment. Yes, he knew, again. He couldn't really have the thing he wanted anyway. That was lost. This was as close as you could get. You couldn't ever truly have the bliss again, could you? That glare on the water had dispelled the myth that this thing was the Mother of Mothers. It was the thing that hurt your eyes just as you were about to repossess the thing you missed the most. He turned back to the river, ready to resign himself to the disappointment of being. But then—the light was already softening, and if he let his head bob a little, up and down, or tilted it from side to side, it didn't hurt his eyes at all. He had discovered a way to make the glare disappear. *Could* you have it, then? If you put yourself in just the right position, just the right place *in this place*, could you have it back— whatever *it* really was?

"Ah!" he said. It was a wordless projection of the affirmative, all his preverbal self could muster. *Ah!*

"Ouch!" Alicia screamed, not in response to Ramadan's *Ah!* but to the pain from the mosquito feasting upon her ankle. She bent down and slapped it, staining her palm with the splat of her own blood and the gray wings of her attacker. She tensed with revulsion at the sight of the foul, ruddy splotch, and as she tried to flick it away, Ramadan fell from her arms, rolled into the mud, and landed facedown. The water was rippling toward the shore, edging its way toward him, licking his toes.

"Oh," she said, posed in a stiff crouch, unsure if she should first rinse her hand in the river or pick up Ramadan before he started wailing.

But then he lifted his head, and he had that same smile she'd seen when she rushed to him outside the barroom on Bourbon Street. His chin was painted with a goatee of Mississippi goo, and he sort of looked like a pirate, one of whom had given that old watering hole its name.

Then he rolled over, as amused as he'd been back at the bar. Instead of crying like a baby, he was laughing like a Lafitte.

❧

ONE MONTH LATER, as Alicia lay dying, she knew it was the mosquito. The doctors couldn't say for sure. Through the fog of her illness, it wasn't clear if they had even diagnosed the virus. Maybe they had, but either way, they couldn't do anything to save her. Whatever—it was the mosquito.

The sin of feeding Mustafa during his fast had come back, almost literally, to bite her. You couldn't trick God with your excuses. Oh, the blithe irreverence of youth; the impetuosity of love. Sin was sin. She had seduced Mustafa out of his holiness with that damned potato chip—and she did mean damned. God had not forgotten or forgiven her transgression. An eye for an eye? No! More like a tooth for a tooth! She had fed him indiscriminately and, in return, she had been fed upon. Fatally. Besides, the world survived on juicy stories like hers. It ate them up. Her death was but a digestion.

Yes, her fate had been determined the moment she tempted Mustafa—whose destiny suddenly struck her as also likely imperiled by his weakness. Where was he now? After the incident with Adad, she had never gone back to his store. Adad had made his contempt for her clear that day, and she couldn't bring herself to beg him for anything. She would have had as much luck penetrating his implacable spirit as she would have had in asking him to return an opened box of Cheerios. To him, *she* was damaged goods. So those eggs had been the last things she ever bought from him. Whenever she needed groceries, she took her business elsewhere, walking the few extra blocks to Matassa's in the Quarter or riding with Crip or Booker T to Winn Dixie. Unlike at Adad's, you could get a decent steak at those stores, plus you didn't have to endure a stare that made you feel *in*decent, a piece of meat gone bad. No, she didn't want Adad to see her growing bigger and bigger each day, swelling with longing for Mustafa. And after Ramadan was born, she had not wanted to give Adad the opportunity to reject him again, this time in person, so she had denied him Ramadan altogether.

Where was Mustafa now? she wondered again. Lying somewhere far across the world dying like her, being consumed, eaten alive by, if nothing else, a ravenous guilt? Did he even know he had a son? Surely not. Even if Adad had broken down and told him about her being pregnant, Mustafa would have no way of knowing whether she'd had a girl or a boy. So no, he did not know he had a son. Only now on her deathbed, thinking of Mustafa on his, did she really regret not conquering her pride, not being stronger, and confronting Adad with the reality of his kin. There must have been something of Mustafa in Adad, something that would have made Adad care for her, *love* her. She should have boldly rolled Ramadan into the Quicky Mart every day. She should have looked Adad in his all-seeing eyes and given him something truly to behold—Ramadan! She should have taken bundle after bundle of Pampers without paying and dared Adad to charge her. Couldn't she have worn down his defenses? Couldn't she have defeated him? If only she had had that vision. If only she had seen Joan of Arc while there was still time. She might have been inspired, realized that even a girl like her, single and poor, could change the world, *her* world. A woman could be a warrior! At least then there would have been a chance for Mustafa to know about Ramadan. But not now. Now it was too late.

And what was to become of Ramadan, the boy she'd dared to brand with *the occasion* of their sin? In naming him, she had felt she was committing a sacred act, not sacrilege, like going to confession. You had to tell what you had done in order to be redeemed. She had meant Ramadan's name to be, in part, an apology—no more, penance. But God had not accepted her offering, she knew now—and her punishment was this death. Was Ramadan, then, also doomed to be devoured too soon, like a calf, a duckling, a lamb? No. The mosquito had landed on *her*. Ramadan was safe. Maybe she was the sacrifice that would afford her son some divine absolution. Any mother would die for that—to save her child. (On the last day she had been able to speak, she asked Mama Joon to make sure to give Ramadan her crucifix. She had a fond memory of how he had grabbed it the day they had gone to the river; he liked it as much as his father.) So yes, she was ready now. She had discovered her cause, without even knowing she needed one, a reason to die: Ramadan!

She was fading in and out of consciousness in her hospital room, so drowsy and bleary-eyed she couldn't tell if anyone was here with her. Maybe that was Mama Joon or Clarissa in a chair near the door, which opened to what must be the hall. She saw a pale rectangle of light that ghostly figures drifted through from time to time. Nurses, not angels—no wings. But maybe that was just a blanket with a pillow propped up vertically on the chair, and the whole assemblage had acquired the rumpled slouch of a worried relative. The television was on, but she didn't have the energy to analyze its radiance for meaning. A *Law and Order* with a murderer named Mr. Muss Kito, maybe. Better still, an old *ER* in which nobody can solve the riddle of this young woman's severe headaches and fever until someone, a pretty internist trying to flirt with a hot, hunky doctor, makes a bad insect joke in the cafeteria about how maybe the patient just has a bug, and then George Clooney's face mimes "Eureka!"

"*What'd you say?*" he asks.

"I said, 'a bug.'"

"That's it! That's it!"

And Clooney drops his tray—a spray of mashed potatoes and gravy and pellets of green peas splatter against the lower legs of Julianna Margulies's scrubs—and he dashes off to save the girl in the nick of time. In the medicine closet he rummages through boxes of bottles until he finds the last remaining vial containing the serum to counteract this disease, which occurred mainly in the remote jungles of South America or in Madagascar maybe—and that, yes, was transmitted by mosquitoes!

"Yes!" Alicia yelled, not as herself, really. Her voice bellowed out from the depths of her achy chest, going Clooneyesque, attempting to embody the essence of the actor playing the doctor who, in her delirious mind, was holding the glass tube of precious serum up to the light and shaking it with admiration and gratitude, this elixir that would save his patient's life—*Alicia's* life—doubly grateful that he had chosen this career, not as a doctor, but as an actor with the privilege of playing a doctor. And even if this scene wasn't real, he was still a man honoring with his art a man who saved lives. (Her "Yes!"—her last word—had all of this in it, an overdose of empathy, adrenaline laced with hope.)

"What did you say?" The blanket and the pillow propped up in the chair called out to Alicia in the voice of a weary Mama Joon. "Did you say something, baby?"

Alicia hallucinated her mother's pillow-head and torso seamlessly adjoined to a blanket of legs, a centaur of sympathy. Then she closed her eyes and sank into the last layer of consciousness. All of the pain she had felt for weeks, headaches and severe neck and muscle soreness that medication had dulled but not alleviated, was now leaving, blown away by the breeze of her retreat. The anxiety, too, was flaking away like ash, all of the worry that, had she the focus to experience it, would have traumatized her. One day, before her mind faltered, she had overheard the doctor say "meningitis" to Mama Joon. She had been drifting in and out of sleep, but she had heard enough in his tone to detect that he feared the worst. The paralysis that had already started to grip her body had saved her from suffering the full impact of that blow. Weakness had given her the strength to endure it. But that day she had begun to live with this thought: *I am going to die.* If she had been depressed before—and, of course, she had (for what but depression was Ramadan's twin, the one who had declined birth, the dark one who Mustafa's absence had impregnated her with as surely as his presence had inseminated her with the light of Ramadan?)—this reality, this majestic flow of death, at once imminent *and* eminent, had purified her blood with an intravenous efficacy. It was as if one of the plastic bags hanging beside her bed was tubing, needling, and dripping into her veins potent, intermittent hits of *I am going to die.* Evidently, one pleasing side effect of this drug was its ability to abort the insidious progeny of gloom. For Alicia, the threat of mortality was a menstruation, cleansing her of that thing incapable and unworthy of achieving humanity.

Her room was dark when it finally came for her, when the world purged itself of *her.* It wasn't so bad, being unborn, being unalive, not being, being been. It was as natural as putting one foot in front of the other, as natural as the way she had experienced—that day Mustafa had started walking toward her at the Quicky Mart—the approach of love. Was death love? Was death life? The rationality of it subsumed her. To pronounce it drowning would have diminished its swiftness, the clarity of its truth. This was absolute. Proof of something. This—death—was the answer!

And just like that, she saw her unsolved equation, the mathematical means of quantifying who she would be after losing Mustafa but gaining Ramadan:

$$X = \frac{YOU - HIM}{YOU + 1}$$

And, too, just like that—she knew the answer! It was the *You – Him* numerator that gave it to her. She knew now that for her (and she was the *X*), *You – Him* = 0. From there it was easy! Every third-grader knew that 0 divided by any number (other than zero) equals 0.

Therefore:

$$X = 0$$

Even the addition of Ramadan to her life (*You + 1*) was not enough to recalculate the immutable mathematical result of losing Mustafa. Without death and its unique authority on the matters of nullification—and this was almost her last sensation—she would never have known that. People were always questioning what good algebra was. Middle school kids everywhere famously whined while struggling with Pythagoras, "I'm never going to need this stuff to get through life." Well, it sure had come in handy for her while trying to get through death! If she'd had the strength to crawl out of bed, she would have. She would have staggered across the room, thrown open a window, and shouted out to the city, to the world, "Learn your algebra! It could save your soul!"

Alicia felt triumphant, as if by puzzling out her equation, she had conquered the riddle of herself. She thought of Joan of Arc again, golden and high up on her horse. Joan had triumphed and then she had died, crowned the Maid of Orleans. Alicia knew she hadn't saved the world or even her city (why anyone would need to save New Orleans was beyond her), but she had just saved herself. It was better that she had not wasted the strength Joan had given her on trying to win over Adad, because she needed all of her strength now. She needed the will to die.

In her last breath, she was settling for something less grand than Joan's achievement, yet somehow just as momentous. How strange that being zeroed out to nothingness by mathematical deduction and by death could bring her to such a conclusion, to such *wholeness*: I am the Maid of Me!

PART II

EVACUATIONS

6

THE STORM

Alicia's dying thoughts may have seemed random but they would prove, so she might have insisted, as prophetic as television. Especially her fleeting acknowledgment of the inability to save her city. For soon, on that quintessentially Ramadanian day—during which the five-year-old Ramadan is transformed from a charging bull back into a giggling boy by the *deus ex machina* magic that is a grandmother's love—on that very day, the most consequential of storms was heading straight for New Orleans.

It was early afternoon on Saturday, August 27, 2005—less than two full days before landfall—and Mama Joon, intent on prepping a pot roast for Sunday dinner, had not paid much attention to the news of the tropics. She and Ramadan were in the kitchen, basking in the bounty of their affection. (Husbands and wives have bedrooms. Grandmothers and grandchildren? Kitchens. Where else, to the envy of all other relations, under the guise of making a meal, to make love?) Ramadan was skipping around the kitchen munching on the carrot stick Mama Joon had let him swipe off the counter from the bunch she was going to chop up and toss into the bottom of the roasting pan. They didn't know it then, but it was to be the last day—for two months, at least—of such routine. The last day when you knew what was going to happen next, when the biggest question was whether to slow-cook a roast at 300 degrees, which would mean rising early tomorrow morning, or to go with 350 and sleep in; whether to bite the pointed end of a carrot stick or the fat end first.

When the phone rang, Mama Joon picked up the cordless handset and checked the caller ID. *Clarissa*. She pressed the TALK button and, defying its command, hummed instead. "Mmm hmm . . ."

"Mama, they're saying this hurricane is really coming!"

Hunched at the kitchen counter slicing through onions on her chopping board, unmoved by Clarissa's breathlessness, she asked calmly, "What you want me to do about it? Do I look like Nash Roberts to you?"

She wasn't even sure if Clarissa remembered the beloved retired local weatherman, but she wanted to disarm her with a wisecrack. Whatever amount of money she was about to ask for would require negotiating. Lately, Clarissa was working off and on as an unlicensed beautician, but she didn't have any steady income. She was forty-two years old now, so it was clear to Mama Joon she never would. With her, every crisis had budgetary implications. The use of "Mama" and "hurricane" in the same sentence was a loan inquiry; or more likely an application for an unrestricted grant. One of Clarissa's better submissions, in fact. But she wasn't fooling anybody by leaving out the "Joon." Just saying "Mama" emphasized their blood relationship, prioritizing her funding request. She knew her daughter—Clarissa was leaving nothing to chance today. No mere mother figure or friend affiliation would do. *Mama* . . . hmph. More like MAMA. Like FEMA, an acronym: the Motherhood and Money Administration.

Indeed, Clarissa had no clue who Nash Roberts was, but she knew Mama Joon was joking, and that to help her case she needed to play along. So she laughed uneasily and mellowed her side of the exchange. "No. Really, it looks kinda serious. Things are happening fast. Every channel is saying we probably need to evacuate. I just finished talking to Crip and Booker T on three-way. We're going to Baton Rouge."

"Mmm hmm." If she started the roast now, it would be done in plenty of time. When the lights went out, she and Ramadan would have something better than cold cuts for sandwiches.

She listened as Clarissa rambled on about some girlfriend of Booker T's with a big house near Southern University. "A college professor!" she said, not impressing Mama Joon with her son's ability to seduce even the most proper of conquests.

"Sounds nice."

"There's plenty of space for all of us. We have two cars. Crip and Booker T. You and Ramadan should come."

Clarissa knew better. The last time Mama Joon had been in a car driven by one of her grandsons was a couple of years ago, after she'd started having severe abdominal pains. Damon, forsaking his high, had picked her up and carried her to the backseat of the Cadillac that Crip had parked in front of the house to take her to the hospital for what turned out to be an emergency appendectomy. They were zooming along when the cops pulled them over on Basin Street near Canal. Not for speeding, as it turned out—the car had been reported as stolen. But with Mama Joon screaming from the pain and the hospital only a few blocks away, the cops, who actually recognized Crip as a neighborhood criminal of some renown, had been compassionate enough to let him drop his grandmother off at the emergency room before arresting him.

"Ha!" Mama Joon said to Clarissa's proposal. "I'd rather swim."

She meant that, too. She was thinking of 1965. Hurricane Betsy. Recalling how she, with a two-year-old Clarissa perched on one shoulder and her overnight bag and pocketbook on the other, had waded through the rising waters to the Lafitte Housing Project and the safety of her friend Margaret's second-floor apartment there. That's what you did in those days when a hurricane was coming, if you were lucky enough to know someone living in the sturdy brick structures that had once deigned to mitigate poverty with comfortable, affordable housing in a central location. None of this evacuation madness. Cars jammed up on the interstate inching along at the pace of a much lesser species—the most recent exodus, which had proven unnecessary, had reduced the entire Greater Metro Area to a community of slugs. No. She really would rather swim. After hustling Clarissa off the phone with a minimal amount of haggling, she went back to prepping her roast and, as best she could, herself . . .

Ah, Betsy! What Mama Joon remembered of that storm was not the destruction of property but the destruction of pretense, of the false sense that everything was so wonderful before the storm, of the lie that complacency was happiness—but, conversely, also the destruction of the gloom that comes with the conscious acknowledgment of that pretense, a measure of relatively *real* contentment with the idea of life as, well, *fun.* She had been renting this same house back then, before she had gotten enough money from Judge Dumas to buy it. What a shock the water had been to her ankles when she had stepped off the porch into the shallow stream that had formed on St. Philip. Then, a few blocks away as she waded around a corner—what an audacious, lapping sensation the water had given her (at her knees, along her inner thighs) when she had sunk unexpectedly into a pothole hidden by the flood and filled with sludge. She had yelped from the surprise and from the secret delight at being licked so intimately in the middle of North Villere Street. Nature was nasty! If her hands hadn't been so busy holding up Clarissa and their belongings, she would have slapped at the surface of the water as if it were the back of a man's head and told it, with great disingenuousness, to stop it. The rain had begun again just as she arrived at the edge of the Lafitte Project, and she pulled Clarissa to her chest and covered the child's head with her chin. When they ducked into the hallway leading to Margaret's apartment, she was laughing as she climbed the stairs. Clarissa, who had begun to cry when the rain started to pelt her, quieted down, less from the relief of their having found shelter than from curiosity at her mother's mood. Tromping up the stairs to Margaret's, Mama Joon felt alive, released. She would spend several of the best days of her life waiting for the storm to pass and, in the aftermath, for the conveniences of daily life to return: electrical power and, yes, that complicated complacency that rooted you to routine. In the meantime, the camaraderie with Margaret and her neighbors had set the tone of adventure. Beer from well-stocked coolers had flowed, as had conversation and a newfound esprit de corps. A man named Rufus had set up a grill on the balcony across from Margaret's—which was where the best card games happened—so there was always something hot to eat: chicken, ribs, baked beans.

When it was time to go home, she had left with a sense of dread, a fear of returning to the drudgery that attended being safe and sound, day after day. As she had walked along Claiborne Avenue, the street as dry as a desert now, watching enthusiastic workmen sweep up broken tree limbs and storm debris, she had begun to cry: it was over. The break from the ordinary. No more Miller High Life, no more close communal hum. She had paused in the middle of the street, coughed, and gathered herself. "Stop it!" she had said out loud—trying to remember the way the water had felt her up—sniffling and forcing a smile for Clarissa, who had been enjoying the walk until her mother had inexplicably grown sad. Then she had looked back at the projects (part port-in-a-storm, part French Riviera), and promised never to forget the thrill of it all, her escape from the ravages of Betsy and her little respite from the clutches of the quotidian. But she hadn't thought about it in a long time, really. It had all come back to her now, though, forty years later, with another big storm looming, one that might possess the ironic duality of Betsy, of all life-threatening tragedy—both the strength to kill and the power to make folks feel more alive.

⚬✴⚬

LATER THAT EVENING, as she and Ramadan sat in the living room watching the news of the hurricane on television, Clarissa came to collect the three hundred dollars Mama Joon had whittled her down to from the five hundred she wanted.

The garlic-stuffed roast was in the oven, and it smelled good enough to smother the scent of municipal anxiety seeping in through the gaps of the window frames with the alarming specificity of natural gas. Clarissa was reeking of it when she entered the room, a full-fledged gust of worry.

Mama Joon picked up the envelope from the coffee table and handed it to her without taking her eyes off the television. Clarissa thumbed the cash while repeating the Baton Rouge offer. Mama Joon ignored her.

"Well, do you at least have all of your important papers together?"

"What papers?" Mama Joon asked, glancing up with an insouciance that she leered into suspicion.

"You know, insurance and stuff."

Mama Joon sighed. She knew her family assumed (correctly, of course) that she had a stash of funds someplace, plus a valuable life insurance policy. Though she never discussed her finances in any detail, her prosperity was evident in her careful and quiet largesse. She could always come up with money when necessary, say for a new roof or for an emergency with one of Clarissa's boys. Sometimes she even spent money on things that weren't vital at all, like the expensive toys and clothes she lavished on Ramadan. After her appendix scare, she had indeed gotten most of her affairs in order. That was nobody's business. But with the strange mix of vapors colliding chaotically and noxiously in her living room, smothering the aromas of the roast—Clarissa's gaseous greed, the city's pheromones of fear—this was as good a time as any to clear the air.

"All I know is, you better hope nothing don't happen to me. Everything I got is going to Ramadan, and that's that."

Ramadan was sitting on the floor watching the coverage of the storm as if it were one nonstop cartoon. The swirling satellite images and animated newscasters and meteorologists were almost as entertaining as *SpongeBob SquarePants*. He didn't quite know what was going on, but there was suspense. Something was going to happen. The people were talking like they wanted to keep it from happening. But they kept showing the bright red-and-green moving pictures of it happening. And whatever was going to happen was beyond their control. He could tell it was just a story. Like watching a movie on DVD. Or like they were reading from a storybook. Didn't they know you could just fast-forward? Didn't they know you could just turn to the last page and know how things turn out? It was right there, right before you saw "The End." Good or bad. Happy or sad. You couldn't change the end of a movie. You couldn't change what was already written in a book.

But when he heard Mama Joon say his name, he turned away from the hurricane coverage to look at her. "If you want to be helpful to him"—she was staring at Clarissa but pointing at Ramadan, unaware that he was now looking at her—"and to yourself, just make sure the attorneys at Mason and Dumas, up on Baronne Street, know you're taking care of Ramadan, and you'll be taken care of, too. Otherwise he'll probably wind up in a foster home somewhere with a big bank account waiting on him to turn eighteen. And you'll wind up somewhere with nothing—here, I guess, maybe, that is, if you can figure out how to pay Ramadan rent." She raised an eyebrow at Clarissa. "Any questions?"

"Well—just so long as you got it all figured out."

"Mmm hmm."

Clarissa folded the envelope and stuffed it into her bra, and she was almost out the door when she decided to stop and ask the question ("any questions?"—hell, yes, as a matter of fact, she did have one) that she had always wanted to ask. The tension of the money wedged against her left breast squeezed the words out of her chest like a moan of pleasure but she was, in fact, voicing her fundamental pain.

"Mama Joon—*why do you hate me so much?*"

"Why do you hate yourself?"

Clarissa didn't respond. But she knew, as brutal as it was, it was a valid question. She stood still while Mama Joon, slicing through her with a stare, said, "Maybe it's something you did. Maybe it's something *I* did. Maybe it's something you didn't do. Maybe it's something *I* didn't do. Maybe it's something you're *going* to do. I don't know the answer. I really don't."

If these were the options, then Clarissa *did* know, after all. She gloated with superiority and was half-smiling through her anger when she fired back, "All of the above!"

Ramadan watched and listened to this exchange without truly understanding the ramifications, but he knew it was an ugly confrontation.

And he knew the tension had something to do with him. He wanted it to end—and knew how to make it stop.

"Mama Joon," he said, tugging at the sleeve of her white cotton duster.

"What, child?"

"The roast," he said.

Mama Joon sniffed the air, and then she jumped up from her chair and hurried down the hall to the kitchen.

Ramadan looked up at Clarissa, who shot him an accusatory glare. He shrugged and said, "I ain't did nothing."

"Oh, everybody's so innocent!" Clarissa spat at him. "Well, I ain't did nothing either. I mean, look at me."

Ramadan followed her directive, starting with his aunt's wide feet, which edged out over the front, sides, and heels of her gold Daniel Green slippers. Then he scanned up to her ashy knees; the frayed lacy hem of her short hot-pink dress; and the pooch of her stomach with its doorbell of a navel. He had reached her bosom, bulging unnaturally with Mama Joon's money, when she said, "No, boy! Don't look at me!" You could sometimes forget he was just a child. Like when his little slick ass played the diplomat and stopped an argument by reminding people to go check on a roast.

"I mean, take me for an example," Clarissa said. "What did I ever do to her? I'm as innocent as the next person."

But she flinched and pulled her tight traveling dress down—she didn't feel innocent. She looked at Ramadan and thought about how she had left Alicia crying in her crib that day and picked up her own sleeping baby instead. So what if selfishness was an essential part of who she was. It saddened her, sort of, to know it, to accept it, but there it was.

"If only your mama hadn't died," she said, as if to beg forgiveness or to offer condolences to Ramadan, when she was really thinking that if

Alicia were alive then maybe Mama Joon would have willed both her daughters her estate, would not have felt compelled to cut her out in order to insure Ramadan's well-being. "If only you had a daddy."

"I ain't got no daddy," Ramadan said.

"That's not what I mean. And of course you have a daddy."

"I do?"

"Everybody's got a daddy, Ramadan." Then she mumbled, "Lord, this house . . ."

"Who he is?" It was the first time he had asked anyone this question.

"Hmph? Some A-rab from around the corner your mama was sleeping with."

"He's around the corner?"

"Nooo . . . not anymore. But his people—"

"Where he at?"

"The other side of the world, boy. After your mama got pregnant with you, his people sent him back home faster than you can say abracadabra!"

"Abracadabra!"

"Mmm hmm. That fast. I shouldn't even be telling you this." She arched her neck toward the kitchen, peeking for Mama Joon.

"Why?" he asked her.

"Cuz it's none of your business."

"I want my daddy!"

"Now here you go—shut your lil skinny ass up!"

"I want my daddy! I want my daddy!"

Clarissa got nervous when she heard Mama Joon clanging a pan in the kitchen, and she said, "Well, you can't have him! I gotta go."

She slammed the door behind her and jogged down the porch steps. Climbing into the front seat of the car parked out front, she grumbled to Crip, "Get me the hell outta here."

"What's wrong, Mama?" Crip asked.

As they sped off, she glared back at the house and thought: *What if the hurricane blew the whole damn house away? What if it blew them both away, Mama Joon and Ramadan? Then what? Any questions?*

⁂

AFTER CLARISSA RUSHED out, having articulated for Ramadan what no one ever had—his unspoken well of longing—he turned back to the television and saw the red swirl of the hurricane roaring toward New Orleans. His pulse and breathing quickened with every rotation of the storm's development. The images matched the torrents of heat rising in him. The jagged red ball slicing angrily through the Gulf of Mexico was the very picture of his fury. *"It's clearly getting stronger,"* the weather lady said, pointing at her maps. It was as if the satellites and radars were tracking his volatility. He couldn't read all the words he saw, but he understood the big WARNING! that kept flashing on the screen. Another word, *depression*, even with *tropical* in front of it, felt applicable to him. As he listened to the newscasters try to explain the situation, he knew something they did not: The hurricane was lonely!

"The pressure is dropping—that's not a good thing."

His rage surging, Ramadan closed his eyes, gritted his teeth, and stomped on the living room floor. As if chanting a mantra, he repeated, *"I want my daddy . . . I want my daddy . . . I want my daddy . . ."* Then he began to run around the coffee table. After his third orbit, he slapped the basket of plastic fruit from the table across the room. An apple flew toward the side window and tapped a pane. A banana grazed the television, hitting the weather lady's chin. *"This is the big one!"*

In the kitchen, Mama Joon heard the commotion, and she shoved the roasting pan back into the oven, splashing gravy on her towel in the rush to minimize the damage of Hurricane Ramadan. She had been wondering if all the commotion about the storm would set him off. Standing at the kitchen island, she looked down the hall and saw, as suspected, Ramadan jumping up and down, pitching one of his fits. Then she watched him bestow literal meaning upon the object he was manhandling—he threw a throw pillow. Judging from the direction of his aim and the ensuing thwack and crash, it had landed against the already dented drum shade covering that cheap floor lamp in the far corner, toppling it over. She had bought it on sale at Walmart, Ramadan-ready, priced for disposability. She sighed with satisfaction—it's wonderful when things, even like this, work out the way you planned. From where she stood, she couldn't see what had become of the lamp, but in her mind's eye the pillow had wedged into the shade, disengaging it from the harp. The long black metal pole was probably angled over the edge of her lounge chair, like a fishing rod. The cracked bulb would be dangling and baiting in vain a darkness it would never again defeat. Such was the fate of light—and the elusiveness of darkness. Bulbs break. Even the stars, they would have you believe, disputing your own eyes, have already burned out.

There were those days when Mama Joon, an aging life force herself, felt as if her own light was starting to fade. But she knew if she slid the rag from her shoulder and started waving it, Ramadan, roiling in his anger, would look up, see something flickering in the distance, and be beckoned by what was left of her glow. So here she stood (while she still could), calling to that fiery one down the hall, the key to any hope she had of enduring, of continuing to shine, like a star, even after she was gone, summoning him and all of his crazy energy—an energy that would never have existed without her own—to come dive back into her and recharge her spirit.

Ramadan had just picked up the April 2005 issue of *Ebony* magazine from the coffee table and was about to rip through its Kanye West cover, when Mama Joon's flapping, gravy-encrusted dishrag caught his eye. In his fitful state, she did not register as his grandmother, but rather as where he needed to be: *a place*. Like the ferocious red blob twirling on television, which wouldn't stop until it slammed into somewhere— maybe into New Orleans—he was going to crash into the coast of Mama Joon. He was going to the place calling out to him, the place that was ready to catch him. In its unconditional willingness to receive him, it might as well be called "home." That's where he was going, so that must be where the lonely hurricane that was on TV acting bad like him was going, too. The hurricane was going home.

He flung the *Ebony* behind him, and as its pages fluttered through the air, he began pedaling his little legs down the hallway. The mechanics of running, purposeful and exhilarating, aided the recovery of his self-control, animosity succumbing to animation. His muscles redirected his blood to their use, away from the tumult of his frustration. With every stride, he became less like a tempest and more just a being in motion. The bull-boy emerged, teased out by his toreador-grandma. But halfway to the kitchen, something happened.

The bull-boy knew he was *not* a bull-boy. Had the storm done this to him? Made him see himself? Pinpointed the eye of his emotions, somewhere deep inside? No—it wasn't the storm. *Everybody's got a daddy, Ramadan.* It was Clarissa!

By the time he was ten feet away from Mama Joon, he could have stopped running altogether and just stood still in the hallway and said, "No!" Because everything had changed. But, obeying the commands of inertia and affection, he kept running.

And this time, as he leaped into Mama Joon's arms, he was only pretending he was the boy who was pretending to be a bull. It would be his last such performance. Because flying through the air as himself was a whole lot more fun. It was *he* who had taken flight. Why be a bull when you can be a boy who can fly! Always trying to bring him down for some reason, Clarissa had set him soaring.

By the time the *Ebony* had tapped the ceiling fan chain in the living room and sent it swinging, and hit the mirror before ricocheting onto the ottoman; by the time the weather lady was pointing at yet another satellite image and saying, *"Look at the strength of this one!"*; by the time he landed in Mama Joon's midsection and the two of them started laughing—Ramadan was Ramadan.

ANY QUESTIONS?

Mama Joon heard her bitchy retort to Clarissa come whizzing back like a boomerang of retribution. The next night, with the hurricane churning into town, as she sat straight up in her uncomfortable seat in the Superdome, arms around a sleeping Ramadan, she had *many* questions. All for herself, and all of which amounted to one: *What the hell was I thinking?*

Why had she let nostalgia, her memories of surviving Hurricane Betsy, endanger her and Ramadan? How could she be the head of a family so dysfunctional that she couldn't trust them to transport her to someplace better than this dubious "shelter of last resort"? Why hadn't she checked at the Ritz-Carlton, where she'd worked for the past couple of years, to see if they had any vacancies? Maybe not—but she hadn't even made the call! What would it have cost to charter a private jet? What good was hoarding money if you didn't use it to take care of yourself, to keep you and yours safe?

She and Ramadan were perched in the Plaza, the first section up from the artificial grassy expanse of the football field, and she was staring out at the 40-yard line. Great seats, if they were here to watch a Saints game. Next to them, a large woman named Cassandra with a leopard-print scarf loosely tied around her head had taken over most of the seats in the row with her three youngsters and their belongings. Friendly but noisy, she kept dialing numbers on her cell phone, but it wasn't working. At least she *had* a cell phone. Question: *Why don't I have a cell phone?*

And why didn't she own a car? Why didn't she know how to drive? She and Ramadan had walked to the Dome. It wasn't that far from the house, but still—*what the hell was she thinking?* After the mayor issued that mandatory evacuation, she knew they had to make a move. It was too late to catch a ride out of town, so she had settled for the Superdome. She had been inside the venue only a few times, for a football game, a concert, the circus. It had always struck her as welcoming, the most natural place in the city for thousands of people to gather for a special event. The powers that be must have felt the same way. A big-ass storm is coming. Yes, of course, let's go to the Dome. Didn't they know that the productions that thrived in this place took months, if not years, of planning? She didn't know anything about anything, but even she knew that. What kind of Mickey Rooney–Mickey Mouse governance was this mess? This was a municipal emergency, not a time to just put on a show!

She huffed, more at herself than at politicians and bureaucrats. If you wanted to be forgiving and not count the decades of warnings, then technically they had had only a few days to figure out what to do about people who didn't have anyplace else to go. But she'd had her whole life to devise a better plan for herself. She was damn near sixty years old and, quiet as it was kept, a woman of means, but still here she sat in the middle of this storm, in this colossal arena, helplessly sheltering in a structure designed for entertainment. She felt as if she'd been situated upon this massive stage, having stupidly accepted a role for which she was ill-prepared, unrehearsed. Or part of a ragtag pickup squad of thousands, none of whom knew any plays, and someone was about to yell, "Hut!" The sheer scale of the building suddenly struck her as indicative of its awesome vulnerability. Before finally drifting off to sleep, like most of the others nearby, her last thoughts were, "*Titanic* sank . . . Goliath fell."

⚜

"OH, BUT JUST wait—I'ma beat his lil ass!"

Mama Joon had lost count of how many times Cassandra, during the last week, had threatened that assault (or a more gruesome one) upon her son Ricky, who, on the night of the storm's arrival, had gone missing in the Superdome—along with Ramadan.

At the moment, the two women were sitting side-by-side on cots in a makeshift evacuation center inside the Astrodome in Houston.

Then Cassandra got up and said, "I'll be right back, Miss June. I need to go see if they charged my phone yet." She pointed to her two children asleep on another cot and said, "Would you watch them for me, please?"

"Oh, sure, honey."

Cassandra's cell phone hadn't worked since the night the hurricane hit. At first her cell service wasn't connecting. Then she had kept trying to use it so much she had drained the battery dry. Her dialing had been as insistent as it was futile—family, friends, 911, New Orleans Police Department Central Lockup (a number she had committed to memory),

Charity Hospital. With every number she punched on the handset, she seemed to be taking a poke at a different part of Ricky's body. Back in the Superdome, when they had both awakened to the sounds of the storm passing and realized the boys were gone, Cassandra had vowed to Mama Joon (and to all within earshot) that she was going to "wear that lil mutha-fucka out." Outside the Dome waiting for the buses that would take them away from the heat, funk, and stench of catastrophe emanating from the oceanic remains of New Orleans, she had said, "I'ma tear that lil fool a new asshole." And along I-10, as their bus had cruised through Beaumont: "Baby, his lil ass is mine!" Just before admitting the truth—she wasn't hot with anger, but ablaze with anxiety. "Got my nerves on fire!"

A less vocal, emotional inferno herself, Mama Joon would have sep-arated from Cassandra and suffered alone in silence but she felt bound to this stranger by mutual loss and by the same hope of being made whole again. It was too much of a coincidence for her son and Ramadan to have gone missing at the same time, from the same place, and not have been somewhere together—wherever they were. If and when they turned up, maybe they would still be together—*and safe*. Besides, this woman with the authoritative touch of an Antebellum overseer had an incongruously delicate confectioner's flair. Mama Joon had reluctantly accepted the praline Cassandra had offered her shortly after the two of them had introduced themselves and first begun to fret about the whereabouts of Ricky and Ramadan. She rarely ate anything other than her own food, and she didn't have much of a sweet tooth. But it was only neighborly to accept Cassandra's "made 'em myself" offering. ("Every-body say mines is the best. Thinking 'bout startin' a bizniss.") As the sweet, buttery, impossibly moist candy had dissolved in her mouth, al-most granule by granule, it liquefied into a deliciousness that soothed her worries with the potency of an antidepressant. Cassandra had been muttering something under her breath about Ricky having raided her stash of treats, and said, "I'ma *choke* his lil ass"—then, without pause, jovially soliciting Mama Joon's review of her candy—"not bad, huh?"

In spite of Cassandra's causticness about Ricky, and because of the coupling of all that professed viciousness with the humility, *the innocence,* of her question about her, really, for all intents and purposes, perfect confection, Mama Joon had no choice but to betray her own pacifistic nature. She had smiled and *mmm*-ed her hearty approval. *Yes, beat his ass!* she might have been saying. This woman was the Betty Crocker of brutality. The mix of culinary acumen whipped together with torturous intent was an oil-and-water concoction to Mama Joon. Cooking, for her, had always been linked to compassion and care. She made her best meals when she was in a good mood and thinking about serving what she was making to her family. Yes, even to her disappointing brood. Wasn't there always the chance, she had wondered, adding a bay leaf to a pot of beans or sprinkling slivers of an extra clove of garlic and more basil into a tomato sauce, that the perfect balance of spices, hitting a devilish tongue, might set even the most no-count Negro straight? And she had never cooked more lovingly and successfully than since her darling, her last grandbaby, the one who should be here with her now, had started eating table food. The delight on Ramadan's face after tasting his first spoonful of her gumbo is what inspired her to conjure it again and again. And it was that same vision she would take to the grave, as it was the thing, more than breathing itself, that made her feel alive. When she had swallowed the last of the praline, she had almost shed a tear, for the sublime delicacy, for her complicity in Cassandra's abusiveness, for the return of despair, which surged through her heart at the precise rate with which the sweetness in her mouth dissipated.

Mama Joon had never hit Ramadan and never would. But since

Monday—when she had discovered she had lost him—she had bludgeoned herself with blame. On some level, she had always known she would lose him. That moment at the hospital the day he was born. At first, he was all hers. But then as she glanced down, for a second he looked like one of those maternity-ward mix-ups. For one frightful instant, the baby boy she thought was hers, wasn't. Her own face had felt as tight and pale—and foreign—as his had looked. In that flash of doubt, *she* wasn't even hers. But then something shifted, and there it was. The resemblance. Just enough of an *ourness* to bring him back to her—and to bring her back to herself.

That was the first time she had lost Ramadan. Quick—and it was over. This time, though, days in duration, the loss had taken its toll. She was a mess. Her gums were sore from grinding her teeth to withstand the self-inflicted pain. Her neck ached, she was having back spasms, and she had noticed a strange bruise the shape and color of a medium-sized eggplant on her right thigh. The muscle and joint issues could have been the result of tossing and turning on this Red Cross cot, but what was that weird mark on her leg? Was she whacking it with her fist as she slept? Submitting subconsciously, *unconsciously*, to a corporal punishment consistent with the mental abuse she was inflicting upon herself? Most disturbing, the last time she had gone to the bathroom, she had seen evidence of her psychic torment achieving a more intimate physiological expression. After wiping herself, she had gulped when she looked down and saw red stains on the tissue. No, she wasn't the least bit afraid anything was seriously wrong. She knew it was all because she had lost Ramadan—a personal crisis as dire as the municipal one. The city wasn't prepared for its struggle and neither was she. (The images on the television monitors in this shelter kept showing the flooded streets of New Orleans on every channel, although when she had seen her neighborhood the other night on CNN, she had quietly rejoiced at the sight of her relatively dry block.) Yes, the splotches on the toilet tissue had shocked her, though not because she was looking at her own blood. She just didn't know the body could do that. And, no, she didn't need a doctor to diagnose the problem: her heart was leaking! First the levees, she had thought before flushing—now this.

She could have sat in silence in the Astrodome pining for Ramadan in the abstract until she died for committing the sin of having lost him. The notion of death—oh, God, Alicia! She was experiencing the loss of a child all over again, in a different way. All she could do was pray; she hadn't prayed yet. And she didn't need just any prayer. Not an Our Father. Not the Apostle's Creed. Paternalism and a masculine sensibility would not soothe her broken heart. Like leaving the levees to the Army Corps of Engineers—she'd seen only men on the news. They were dropping sandbags from helicopters to plug some breaches, she had overheard a man say, shaking his head in disbelief. No. Stemming the tide of all that would gush out of her if Ramadan was gone was not to be attended to by men, heavenly or otherwise. This was woman's work. Nesting. Bleeding, bleeding, bleeding, until you achieved an incubation. Midwifery and wailing. This was about having nurtured a male child only to have him get away from you—as somehow you always knew he would—and the world having its way with him. Your divine boy! Only a woman could come to her aid now. Only a woman who had suffered such a loss. She needed one prayer, one prayer only. No, she thought, as she looked around at the hundreds surrounding her, slouching on their cots in various poses of discontent—she needed two.

She dug around in her purse until she found the old rosary buried deep at the bottom of an inner pocket where it had settled during its many months of disuse. As she lifted the black-and-gold strand, it flickered to life in the Astrodome light. Then she bunched it into the fist of her free hand. Without bothering to find the single bead representing the prayer of her choice, she closed her eyes and said:

Hail Mary, full of grace. The Lord is with thee. Blessed art thou among women, and blessed is the fruit of thy womb, Jesus. Holy Mary, Mother of God, pray for us sinners, now and at the hour of our death, Amen.

Then, without stopping:

Hail, holy Queen, Mother of mercy, our life, our sweetness and our hope. To thee do we cry, poor banished children of Eve: to thee do we send up our sighs, mourning and weeping in this valley of tears. Turn then, most gracious Advocate, thine eyes of mercy toward us, and after this our exile, show unto us the blessed fruit of thy womb, Jesus. O clement, O loving, O sweet Virgin Mary!

She sat on her cot saying the Hail Mary and Hail Holy Queen over and over again. The magnanimousness of the prayers—the "us" and "our"—brought the other evacuees into focus, and she was grateful to be pulled out of her singular sadness.

". . . and after this our exile," she was praying again, when—

"Miss June! Miss June!"

She heard the world calling her out of the spiritual realm with a rough approximation of who it thought she was, pulling her back into its grand tedium. She opened her eyes and saw, across the field of cots of humanity that lined the Astrodome floor, Cassandra yelling and waving her cell phone in her right hand.

"They found them! They found them!"

Mama Joon didn't know who the "they" were, but she knew the "them." Cassandra kissed her phone, making three loud smacking noises. "MMMwah! MMMwah! MMMwah!"

In response, Mama Joon pumped her hands in the air and rejoiced at a distance with the woman whose pronouncements of violence toward her missing son had blossomed into this silly bit of public foreplay with a telecommunications device, and not a particularly fancy one at that. Mama Joon gripped her rosary, and just as reflexively, overwhelmed that Ramadan was coming back to her, that her pleas had been heard, she lifted the fistful of cheap religious jewelry and smashed it into her lips. A couple of the plastic beads scratched her front teeth, and she winced at the way grace, believe it or not, could grate. The sentimentalist in her gave way to the pragmatist. Mary might have been a conduit to God, but Cassandra's cell phone had messaged the answer to her prayers. Whatever miracles the world had left in it—and she wasn't cynical enough to think only a few remained—would owe both to God and to that little instrument upon which Cassandra was lavishing an embarrassing display of affection.

In the way that trauma can sometimes leave one vulnerable to the oddest of devotions, Mama Joon found herself transformed from an occasional Catholic and a haphazard Luddite into a woman of prayer and an early adopter.

"I WANT MY daddy! I want my daddy!"

A week later, Mama Joon was awakening—yet again—to the voice-over of Ramadan's nightmare. She moaned as she propped herself up on the edge of her twin bed in their little motel room in Southwest Houston. Then she crept over to Ramadan and rubbed his back until he recessed into silence—"I want . . . I want . . . I . . . I . . ."—back into some semblance of soundness.

But she was so flustered by his cries tonight that she couldn't go back to sleep. Ramadan's uncensored desire echoed throughout the small cave of a room. She decided to take a shower, if only to blot out the boy's shouts, which she couldn't help feel were a commentary on some deficiency of her own. Stepping into the splattering wetness, she thought about how she had raised two daughters, not particularly well—she'd be the first to admit it. Still, she had known how to do that. But here was Ramadan calling out to the world, or at least to her, that he wanted more than her. Her grandson was out there squirming in a strange bed, crying out for someone, a stranger, to give him something she apparently could not. What was that? Protection? A different kind of love? Harder hugs than she could muster? A manly projection of his little boy self? Someone hairier, more muscular, *taller*—someone quite literally to look up to! Yes, yes, yes to all of that, no doubt. Oh, God—the limitations of matriarchy!

She couldn't even remember the Arab-sounding name of the young man she'd seen with Alicia. Even if she could, there was no telling what might have happened to him in the storm, assuming he was even still in New Orleans. Then, as the water splashed her face, hiding her tears— saying another Hail Mary, *now and at the hour of our death . . . our*—she heard a sound, repeated, that seemed to toll with meaning. A word. *Our.* Maybe it was nothing—but it felt like something. Maybe—it *was* something.

When she and Ramadan had been packing to evacuate to the Super-dome, she realized she needed a loaf of bread. Having slaved over that roast, there was no way she was going to leave it or throw it out. And, of course, she couldn't bring it with them whole, so she was determined to make sandwiches. Instead of going all the way to Matassa's, she and Ramadan had made the short walk to the Quicky Mart, which she rarely went to, thinking it less a grocery store than a filling station. She knew Alicia used to shop there, but she couldn't bring herself to do it. Buying food where people pumped gas was an unpalatable proposition. The smell of petroleum nauseated her. In fact, the idea of gas *gave* her gas. But that day, with the city a-twitter and in full evacuation mode, she had held her breath and tromped into the place that, in that moment at least, was the very essence of itself—a convenience store. As she was checking out and paying the man behind the counter, Ramadan had heard someone blowing a trumpet and run outside toward Rampart Street. "A parade!" he had yelled.

"Boy, that's not a parade. Git your butt—" But he was gone, bolting as fast as he had down the hall earlier.

The man had started to give her her change, but she pulled her hand away. The quarter, a dime, and three pennies hit the counter and fell onto the floor as she rushed out.

"Ramadan!" she had yelled, trying to catch him before he got to the street.

When Adad heard her say, "Ramadan!" he was gathering the scattering coins, and he paused while pinching the metallic embossment of George Washington's neck and his ribboned ponytail, thinking, What an odd name for a New Orleans boy. *Then, as he continued picking up the rest of the change, he began adding things together as naturally and absentmindedly as he counted money. It was only as he was picking up the last penny that the sum of the truth came clear—the thirty-eight cents in his hand was a pot of gold. Looking down at the coins, he read the words* IN GOD WE TRUST, *and he whispered to himself, "Allahu Akbar." Then he clasped his fist tight, kissed his fingers, and rushed out to bring the woman her change—and to have a better look at the child (yes, he was sure of it) who was a part of his family's fortune.*

By the time he reached Mama Joon, she had Ramadan in her grasp.

"How many times do I have to tell you?" she was saying. "You can't just run outside every time you hear a horn blow. You wanna mess around and get killed?"

Adad was breathing heavily, only in part from the sprint. He let her finish schooling the boy, and then he went to her and put the change in her left hand. For a second, he just stood there smiling. With only one quick glance at Ramadan, Adad saw a miniature version of his own nose, Mustafa's jawline, and that unmistakable, ancient Totah-esque pearliness roiling, less turbulently but there, in the boy's eyes, with an American gleam or his youth, which may have been the same thing. Then he looked back at the woman—old enough to be the boy's grandmother, he thought—and extended his hand to shake hers, proposing a union of sorts.

She had had to undrape her arm from around Ramadan's shoulder to accommodate the greeting from the man, who had even laid his second hand over hers in a warm, if inappropriate, show of emotion. She had chalked it up to some kind of foreigner's hurricane fever, an inability to maintain his composure in the midst of the mania happening all around him as the city panicked. And then he'd said it:

Take good care of our boy!

Our boy? It hadn't sounded so odd at the time. People tended to get all communal in a crisis, didn't they? She had witnessed that during other storms, and she was counting on it again. That was one of the reasons she was heading to the Superdome in the first place,

tempted to experience once more the fellowship she had known decades before during Hurricane Betsy—the impassioned consensus
to survive. When everyone was feeling all *we* and *us*, the mutually
possessive *our* was understandable. *Our boy.* Okay. Whatever. Surely
it was the same even in—wherever this shopkeeper was from. The
fumes from the gas pumps were starting to make her swoon. Maybe
they were playing with his head, too. At any rate, he looked uncomfortable. Something awkward in his posture spoke of an indoorish
nature. He was stooped over, almost bowing to her and Ramadan, as
if he felt the sky was lower than the ceiling in his store and therefore
more threatening.

"Of course," she had said, starting to walk away from the pumps,
wanting to breathe the less fumy, pre-hurricane air, which, though it did
not smell toxic, had a pungency all its own. "He's my baby."

*Adad wanted to add, "Yes . . . mine, too." But instead, he merely said,
"Please come back again."*

Mama Joon had told him goodbye, and she and Ramadan went
home, fixed the sandwiches, and joined the spotty procession to the
Dome.

But now, in the shower hiding from Ramadan's adamant pleas, she
couldn't help but reconsider the meaning of the man's two-fisted hand-
shake and his *our*.

The next morning, while Ramadan was taking a bath, she called
Clarissa in Baton Rouge.

"That was Adad," Clarissa told her. "He owns the place. And of
course he came running after y'all. He figured out Ramadan is his
people."

"How do you know that?"

"Haven't you ever taken a good look at Ramadan, Mama Joon? He ain't nothing but a little Quicky Mart kid. Probably not the only one, neither. His daddy was the tall one. Adad's son or his nephew. The one named Mustafa."

"Yes!" Mama Joon said. "Mustafa!" That was it. She knew she would know the name when she heard it again. *Mustafa*—not Mos Def! "But how do *you* know him?"

"I didn't *know* him. But I know Alicia was in love with him, or whatever. I used to hear them going at it through the walls while you were at work. He stopped coming around not too long after she got pregnant. You know how that goes . . ."

And so she did.

After she hung up with Clarissa, all she could think about was this mysterious Mustafa, less mysterious now that she knew his name. When she finished dressing Ramadan and pulling herself together, it was early afternoon, so they headed out for lunch. There was a Popeyes fried chicken restaurant near the motel, and she decided it would have to suffice. Without a kitchen of her own and no transportation in this sprawling if hospitable Texas town, she didn't have many choices. Besides, Popeyes, as much as any fast food could, tasted like home. Before they even rounded the corner, Ramadan looked up, saw the orange, red, and white sign out front, and shouted, "Popeyes!"

Inside, as she watched him bite into a drumstick, her thoughts of Mustafa faded. No, she wasn't thinking about Ramadan's daddy at all. Seeing him sitting across the table breathing and eating—*alive*—sent a tremor of Alicia's being through her body. Overcome, she moaned. Ramadan paused mid-bite and looked at his grandmother.

"What?"

"Nothing," she said. "You just like your mama, boy."

"I am?"

"Mmm hmm." Mama Joon shook her head and smiled. "She sure did like greasy-crunchy. Just like you."

It felt good to be thinking and reminiscing about Alicia. Maybe talking about her—which they rarely did—the lost soul who connected her and Ramadan, would help pull him out of his funk.

But then Ramadan, lips glistening, took another bite of his drumstick, narrowed his eyes, and said, "I bet my daddy like greasy-crunchy, too."

7

RAMADAN AT THE WINDOW

After two months in Houston, Mama Joon had had enough of fast food and the slow torture that is exile. Clarissa had driven to New Orleans a few weeks earlier to check on the neighborhood and reported that the house had not flooded, or been damaged or vandalized; she even had the utilities turned back on.

"Everything's good. But we like Baton Rouge," she had said, calling Mama Joon from her brand-new cell phone. "At least for now."

Sure they did. As long as the FEMA gravy train was rolling—money, food stamps, free apartments. It all felt like some kind of backhanded, day-late-dollar-short attempt at reparations to Mama Joon. Well, so be it. Better America's tit than hers!

As for her and Ramadan, it was time to go home. She was too old to let go of the past, her life in New Orleans, and he was too young to imagine a future anywhere else. Especially since, as he reminded her every day, if not with words, then with his increasingly mannish behavior, home was where the search for his father, now that he knew he existed, would begin. She wanted him to meet his father, too, as well as his other relatives, who apparently had been right around the corner from their house all along. With Alicia gone, with Clarissa being Clarissa, with her sons being who they were, and, most critically, with the blood that was reappearing however occasionally in her stool, Mama Joon thought Ramadan might need his paternal family. Besides, locating his father, who Clarissa called . . . Mu-stafa—oh crap, was that even it?—might be as easy as walking over to the Quicky Mart, shaking hands again with that Adad, and formally introducing him to the little boy they both knew was his kin.

So then, on their first day back in New Orleans, Mama Joon, still standing in her musty, unlived-in living room, surrounded by their luggage, didn't resist Ramadan's tug of her arm; she knew where he wanted to go. He had gotten everything but Mustafa's name out of her—mainly because she still wasn't sure she had it right. But also, she didn't want to make him too real to Ramadan. What if Clarissa's information about all of this business was as untrustworthy as she was?

On this sunny late October afternoon, Mama Joon found herself trudging to the Quicky Mart, trying to keep up with the boy as they passed mostly populated if quiet-looking homes. She saw open storm shutters, shadows moving past windows, garbage cans overflowing at the curb. The cabbie who had driven them from the airport had said, "In the daytime things ain't so strange . . . in some places, like where you live at. But at night—it's a whole lot darker everywhere." Well, so far he was right. She was tired and looking forward to sleeping her way through their first night home in the comfort of her own bed. For that, the darker, the better.

But unlike the rest of the neighborhood, Adad's store was still shuttered. Large planks of plywood covered the big windows facing Rampart Street, as though no one had returned since the storm's passing. Mama Joon held Ramadan's hand, and they walked slowly past the now odorless gas pumps. The window on the Governor Nicholls Street side of the building was not boarded up. A hodgepodge of posters— BEER, SOFT DRINKS, SANDWICHES, BEST PRICES—blocked a clear view into the store, but someone a foot taller than Mama Joon would have been able to peek in at Adad, seated behind his cash register—*were he there.*

A man walking by on the opposite side of the street saw Mama Joon craning her neck to see inside and yelled, "Don't look like they coming back!"

His voice startled her. She felt as if she were trespassing—or had just been caught being nosy, which was somehow worse.

"Somebody said them boys got deported. Some kinda Nine-Eleven, hurricane mix-up. Nice people, too. I hear they still ain't found the old man."

Pretending to be satisfied with this information, Mama Joon began to walk away. But Ramadan stood his ground, grabbing her wrist and jerking her to a stop.

"What?" she said.

"I want to see." He was pointing up at the window.

She looked warily to the left and right. The gossipy passerby was gone and she didn't see anyone else. With the store closed, whatever vitality this corner once had, at least for now, was lost.

She faced the window and the wall of posters and said, "It's too high."

Ramadan took two steps toward the building and began jumping up and down. "Pick me up! Pick me up!"

"All right, all right—don't be making no scene! Not out here. Time for you to grow up, anyway."

She tossed her purse to the ground. Then she bent down and came up behind Ramadan quickly, putting her hands around his waist and lifting him over her head. He stretched his legs out straight, parallel to the ground, pressed his hands down on her shoulders, and, with the balance of a gymnast mounting a pommel horse, he lowered his body. In a flash, he had wishboned himself into place. His thighs rested on her shoulders, his crotch nestled against the nape of her neck, and he secured the position by clasping his calves under her armpits. Each had surprised the other—and themselves—with their dexterity, impressed that their well-practiced kitchen choreography transferred admirably to other locales.

She had seen people hoisting children in this way, but she had never done it herself. The sharp pain in her neck told her it was a masculine move. But maybe this was what would be required, if Ramadan was to quell his fever dreams. (Just last night she had massaged him out of another of his recurring nightmares.) Muscle. Testosterone. Balls. Things she had in little or no supply. She was grunting just from holding up his little bitty butt right now, as light as he was. From the looks of this deserted storefront, the chances of finding this Mustafa were about as slim as Ramadan's frame. If his zeal to find his father persisted, in the end he would be mostly on his own. She could give him a nudge and some encouragement. But that was about it. With her back, she just wasn't cut out for this crap.

Ramadan had watched, with envy, kids being lifted like this at parades, but no one had ever done it to him. So this was what he had missed! Up here, you could see the tops of things. Off to his right, the graffiti on top of a big red metal garbage bin read "S-P-L-A-T!" He sounded it out the way Mama Joon had taught him to do. *Spuh-lat-tuh . . . Spuh-lat . . . Splat!* He didn't know what it meant, but he was pretty sure he was pronouncing it right. Pointing, he said, "Splat!"

She arched her neck to see over the crest of his jeans-covered thigh.

"What that mean?"

"It means you better hold on tight, boy, that's what it means." Shuffling toward the window, she added, "Got me out here playing G.I. Joe."

Ramadan saw his own face, reflected in the pane, enlarging with each shaky step Mama Joon took.

"Don't know what you think you gonna find in there anyway. You heard the man. They're gone."

With no room to inch any closer, she stopped. Her breath misted the glass. "Hurry up. I feel like a camel."

Ramadan leaned forward, imprinting the dusty windowpane with his fingers and palms. Then he pressed his face to the window, and his nose, lips, and chin flattened into a peculiar new visage, a sort of Basquiat boy, youthful and yearning, *Ramadan at the Window*. Peering out of his mushed face into the gloomy interior, he struggled to detect anything helpful, any evidence of his father, his family. Once replete with the necessities of daily life, the shelves, except for a few stray items scattered here and there, were empty. A sliver of sunlight caught dull patches of color here and there, but mostly he saw shadowy nothingness.

Mama Joon's right calf started to cramp. "Ramadan . . ."

He recognized the tone. Impatience. With him.

"Wait," he pleaded, but he could feel her start to wobble.

"Boy, my leg is killing me. Hold on."

Without any notion of how to bring him safely to the ground, she reached for his waist and let out a loud groan. Now her shoulder was tightening up, too. This child was just going to have to do another one of his fancy Nadia Comăneci moves and improvise his own damned dismount.

As he descended about six inches, the sunlight his head had been blocking flooded the interior of the store. Mama Joon's slumping was bringing him down to where the posters would be blocking his view, but his eyes, frantically probing, found the open door leading to Adad's office. The back room caught just enough light to reveal the edge of a wooden desk; the curved arm of an office chair; a scatter of papers; and, resting atop the desk, the glint of something metallic or maybe just reflective.

"Ah!" he said.

But he had no time to process what he'd just seen, as Mama Joon, needing to attend to her leg, flung him from her neck and sent him flipping skyward.

His rotating, topsy-turvy perspective tickled the fear of falling out of him. Mama Joon's head whacked against the window, cracking but not shattering it, only a thin, vertical line forming on the glass. After one full somersault, Ramadan drifted toward the ground in a crouch, feet and hands prepared for the landing, which he accomplished gracefully. He looked up at Mama Joon, who had not fared as well. She was holding her head with both hands and trying to regain her balance.

"Mama Joon!"

When she turned to face him, her forehead and hands were splotched with blood.

"Mama Joon!" He was stricken with the sudden premonition and terror of his grandmother's death, flushed for the first time with the understanding, the certainty, that he would one day have to live without her. And this specific incident—*his* having knocked her over—convinced him that her death would somehow be his fault. In a fit of guilt and grief, he grabbed her around the waist. "Mama Joon . . . Mama Joon!"

"I'm all right," she said. She would have patted his head, but she didn't want to stain him with her blood. "I'm all right. It's just a scratch."

A glance at her reflection in the window told her it wasn't so bad. Only a wet patch and a trickle of blood remained on her forehead. She held her palms up to keep them away from Ramadan, who was still wailing and calling out her name.

"Hush up now," she said. "Hush up!"

Personally, she wasn't squeamish about seeing the liquid of life spill out, even her own. She had drained more blood from a fresh fryer. If anything, seeing this red on her hands gave her comfort, hope. She was still here, capable of bearing witness to this accidental flow, evidence of her existence. For a woman of somewhat questionable health, holding your life in your hands like this was a blessing, a cause for celebration. And what color! This blaze of cherry popping against the boring, even *lifeless*, neutrals of skin. This was life!

Ramadan was still sobbing into her stomach, so she said again, "I'm all right!"

He loosened his grip, and she dabbed her forehead with one of her sleeves.

"Okay. Come on now. Let's go. Go pick up Mama Joon's purse for me."

Wanting to atone, he picked up the bag, dusted it off, and carried it for her.

As they walked home, neither knew they had each just seen the way forward. But that slit on Mama Joon's forehead was a crack in the doorway to her exit; her flowing blood, the ray of life, pointing to an enlightened ending. Ramadan had seen her ending, too—but its darkness had been punctured by that other vision—sunlight spilling into the office at the store. And that had impressed him as a *beginning*, a pathway to *his* blood.

❧

THAT NIGHT AT about ten o'clock, determined to return to the Quicky Mart, Ramadan crept down the hall and peeked into Mama Joon's bedroom. She was asleep, with a towel on her forehead. He tiptoed to her and removed the damp compress, placing it on the bedside table. The bump on her head was no longer bleeding. As she moaned and turned over, she appeared to smile. Comforted by her comfort, he slipped quietly from the room.

Outside, none of the streetlamps were on, and the porch lights seemed dimmer than they used to be; Mama Joon's wasn't working at all. When he jumped off the porch, he felt the night envelop him. His path illuminated mostly by moonlight and hope, he made a left onto St. Claude. Then he crossed Ursulines Street and came to St. Augustine, one of the three churches he had attended with Mama Joon, along with St. Jude's and St. Louis Cathedral. He wondered less about the infrequency of their churchgoing than the itinerary.

"How come we came all the way over here?" he asked Mama Joon last Easter after they had made the longer walk to St. Jude's.

"Every church is different," she said. "Sometimes you need the Father, sometimes you need the Son, and Lord *knows* sometimes you need the Holy Spirit. It's up to you to figure out which one you need and where to go get."

He had frowned with confusion.

"Don't worry," she had said. "One day you'll figure it out for yourself."

But so far, he hadn't. Sitting in any church he would wonder which part of the Holy Trinity he needed the most. The Holy Spirit? No—too ghostly. The Son? Wasn't *he* a son? That left The Father. This heroic figure—even before Clarissa's revelation—seemed closest to what he needed. *Our Father. Bless me, Father. Forgive me, Father. Almighty Father!* These all rang out as mellifluous as bells. But what resounded for the masses as song and salvation always left Ramadan feeling unfulfilled.

As he turned right onto Governor Nicholls Street, the moon cast the shadow of the cross from St. Augustine's steeple onto the street in front of him. Sparks of irreverence, play, and a suspension of belief inspired his quick hop over the sacred T, and he scampered toward the store, which was just ahead at the end of the block.

Instead of going back to the spot where he and Mama Joon had broken the window—which he did not care to revisit—Ramadan ducked into a narrow alley jungled with overgrown weeds and strewn with cardboard boxes, milk crates, and old, rotting two-by-fours. To his right was a chain-link fence dividing the back of the store from a vacant lot. He made his way down the dark path, feeling the crunch of an aluminum can beneath his sneaker with one step, the slippery spin of a bottle with another. When he was about twenty feet in, a stray cat screeched and leaped up at him. One of its paws bounded off his left shoulder, and it launched itself onto the top of the fence. Ramadan clasped his hand on his shoulder and fell backwards, banging the side of the same red garbage container that a few hours earlier had taught him the word *splat*. The bin boomed once timpanically from the impact of his body and a second time when the back of his head thumped it. From his crumpled position on the ground, he looked up and saw the cat prowling along the upper line of the fence. Its silhouette strode in front of the moon before it dove into the darkness of the yard next door.

Rubbing his hand over the curls at the back of his head to soothe the throb of his minor injury, he looked up at a patch of starlit sky, and the blue-black night and the energy of the cat settled him. He rose, dusted himself off, and, more cautiously now, approached the back of the building, where he saw a closed door and a high, wood-framed, six-paned window. He went over and tried the rusting gold-plated knob, but it wouldn't turn. He jerked it front to back and side to side, without success, and overcome with fury, rammed his shoulder into the door four or five times. Pain encouraged reason, and he remembered the milk crates in the alley. After a couple of trips, he had stacked four crates, in twos, side by side below the window.

"Yes!" he said, pausing to admire his work and catch his breath.

He hopped backwards on top of his makeshift platform and, once seated, scooted and rotated his body. Then he gripped the window-sill and leveraged himself to a standing position. Gazing through the lower middle pane into the back room, he was wide-eyed and searching. *Ramadan at the Window (# 2)*.

The room was, of course, darker than the front of the store during the day, but the moon was helping. Remembering how he had seen the cracked door only after moving his head, he shifted to the left, and sure enough, moonlight poured into the room. He saw papers scattered about the floor, the whole back of the chair, and there on the desk, the thing that had glinted just as he toppled from Mama Joon's shoulders: a laptop computer.

The room was the picture of desertion: yellowing newspapers, an elongated ashtray with the nub of a stick of incense, a brown-leafed bro-meliad near the window, its spent, pale pinkish bloom slouching with decay. Ramadan fixated upon the laptop, the lone prize. Nothing else promised life. It wasn't metallic, but white and plastic. In the moonlight, it didn't shine at all, though it had a luster about it, hinting that it could be—and was maybe waiting to be—resuscitated.

If anyone had seen him smashing the window with the two-by-four he retrieved from the alley, breaking the panes and the wooden frame, lining the glass-chipped lower ledge with flattened cardboard boxes, and crawling into the store, they would have reasonably branded him a burglar. If they had seen him rifling through the lap drawer of Adad's desk, searching feverishly for clues to his father's identity, finding there only one thing, perhaps, of any significance, extending halfway out of the pages of a faded Superman comic book, an envelope addressed, in a decidedly feminine hand, to ADAD TOTAH at 1199 N. RAMPART STREET, NEW ORLEANS. 70116 U.S.A. with a return address on the back that he couldn't decipher, except for ALEPPO, SURIYE, shoving the envelope into his right front pants pocket, they would have thought him a scavenger or a thief.

And if they had witnessed him exiting the alley with Adad's Apple iBook G4 tucked under his arm, sloppily wrapped between pages of the August 29, 2005, *Times-Picayune* he found on the desk—the "Ground Zero" hurricane headline facing out and the laptop power cord trailing behind him like the cat's tail his furtive efforts had earned him—they would have labeled him a belated looter.

But Ramadan felt he had just performed a rescue, or taken possession of something that belonged to him. As he hurried home, the moon, which had aided him tonight, seemed to absolve him, too, its paleness casting him in the most innocent of lights. Trotting along, he played the childhood game of attempting to catch up to his shadow, to dissolve into it, and, finally, to be made whole. He couldn't do it, of course, but about halfway home, he vowed never to stop trying.

Slinking inside, he made it all the way down the hall to his bedroom, but as he pushed the door open, its century-old hinges creaked the news of his return.

"Ramadan!" He couldn't tell from her voice, which was phlegmy but firm, if she had just awakened or not. It was sharp with accusation, though, stiffening his pose.

"What you up to out there, boy?"

"Nothing. I'm just going in my room. You all right?"

"Oh, I'm fine. I just had a bad dream, that's all. It was all about how you went out without me knowing about it and how then you almost made it back in without getting caught—and then that's when I woke up."

"Oh," he said, not budging. She was almost done—but not quite.

"Next time I have a dream like that, somebody else around here gonna think they having a nightmare. Now good night."

"Good night."

He stepped into his bedroom and closed the treacherous door behind him. Sliding the laptop from the folds of old newspaper, he laid it on the bed. As he was whisking the paper out of the way, he remembered the letter, and removed it from his pocket, tossing it carelessly on the bed next to the computer. Then he plugged the power cord into an electrical outlet behind the bedside table. When he stood back up, he heard a faint hum and saw a green dot of light blink near where the cord was attached to the laptop.

"Ah!" he said softly.

There was no computer of any kind in the entire house, either on Mama Joon's or Clarissa's side of the double, so even though he knew what the laptop was, he had no idea how to operate one. First, he tried to pry it open at one of its corners, like a book. When that didn't work, he tugged at its seams. After jerking for a while, he tossed it back on the bed. Part of him wanted to smash it on the floor in frustration. How could the series of difficult, even criminal, actions he had performed to acquire the laptop be easier than just opening the thing?

He closed his eyes and took a deep breath. His head drooped, and he realized how exhausted he was from the long day of skulking around: climbing Mama Joon like a tree and seeing her bleed; sneaking out in the middle of the night; smashing the store window, breaking in, breaking laws. He crawled into bed and rolled over onto his side; his head hit the pillow, and his body relaxed. Then he reached down for the laptop and slid it near his face. When he gave it one last admiring look before falling asleep, he was staring directly at a silver sliver embedded in the white plastic casing: the latch. He pressed it with his thumb, and the lid began to rise. Owing to either the Macintosh propensity for the magical or his drowsiness, it was unclear to him whether the lid continued to lift on its own, forcing his hand to levitate, or if he was aiding the process. With heavy-lidded wonder, he sat up on one elbow and perused the white keyboard of alphabet and symbols, all neatly arranged but not in an order that made sense to his linear, preschool, ABC mind. He slid his fingers over the row of numbers, counting along. Then he rubbed the large trackpad; still nothing. The darkness of the screen reflected the restive state his body was craving, and only a few moments passed before he, too, was asleep, recharging his own battery.

Hours went by as the sleeping Ramadan lay next to the sleeping iBook. At some point, as he relived the day in his dreams, his hand slid down the monitor, and his fingers rubbed the upper edge of the keyboard. When his index finger nestled into a circular indentation—the inconspicuous "on" button—the laptop awoke with the Mac's signature opening chord, the auditory approximation of dawn. In his unconscious state, he heard a lullaby, a call to retreat into a deeper sleep. So as the Apple logo appeared in its homage to nourishment, knowledge, and original sin, he moved toward innocence and inner inquiry, asking the same question that had consumed him for months—"Where is my father?"

As sometimes happens while one is not listening, indeed while one snores, the world posits answers. As he slept, the computer was solving the riddle of his life, for a background picture filled the screen with a panoramic aerial view of a great distant city—a postcard photograph of

Mustafa's hometown. A breathtaking evening shot of the old Citadel, the man-made flat-topped hill that looked exactly like the fortress it was intended to be, with the ancient Syrian city glittering in every direction. Any casual admirer of the landmarks and wonders of the Middle East would have recognized it immediately, rendering the title in the lower right corner unnecessary: "The Love of Aleppo."

But, only moments later—awakened by the light—Ramadan found the words informative. Especially the last one.

"A-lepp-o!" he sounded it out.

Then, feeling a distinct twinge of recognition, he began scrounging around in his bedsheets in search of the envelope he'd taken from the desk drawer at the store. When he didn't immediately find it, he stood up and started flapping the bedspread so wildly he almost knocked the laptop off the bed. He was nudging it back to a safer spot when, out of the corner of his eye, he saw the letter at the foot of the bed, wedged between the mattress and the footboard. The back of the envelope was facing him, and he saw what had made him start scrambling for it. There it was, the same word—the same place—on the computer screen: *Aleppo*.

Opening the envelope, he took out the letter, which was written in a script that was to him inscrutable. A faded old photograph of a man and woman fell out, and he picked it up and studied it. The couple's emotions required no translation: they were in love. Who were they? Friends of his father's? Relatives? Something in the man's face looked very familiar. Just what, he couldn't quite say. What he *could* say, looking back at the envelope and the screen, was this: *Aleppo*.

This time when he said the word, it roller-coastered its way through the tunnel of his mouth, from the back of his throat, to the tip of his tongue, to the propulsive final pop of his lips. *Aleppo!* And he said it again and again and again . . .

cW

BY THE TIME Ramadan was seven, he understood that there was a sto-ried country in the Middle East called Syria and that one of its most important cities was called Aleppo. By the age of nine, he would know the map of the entire region better than he knew the map of the United States. Because the contents of the computer were password-protected, he was never able to search it beyond the background screensaver photograph of Aleppo. It was as if this powerful machine's sole computational purpose was to orient the compass of his heart. He secreted it away in the back of his closet (with the letter sealed between its keyboard and screen) under an old quilt. At first, every few days, he would take the laptop out and boot it up—just to stare at "The Love of Aleppo."

Over time, weeks would pass, then months, then years, before he would pull the computer out again to remind himself of how intensely he had once felt about going someplace he would probably never visit and of how passionately he had once felt about finding someone who, so the passage of time would begin to suggest, he would never know. A resignation befell him, a dormancy of desire.

Then, in early 2011, not long before he turned eleven, when he began to see news reports about the political upheaval in Syria and about its subsequent escalation to war, he made a special trip to St. Augustine Church and lit a candle for the return of peace to the place where, he imagined, his father had lived as a boy, and where, perhaps, he lived now as a man. And, like that candle, his old yearning began to flicker. As with the uprising, something within him, too, began to rise. When he watched the people marching and chanting through the Syrian streets on television and the internet, they reminded him of himself and the tantrums he used to throw. "The Arab Spring," they called it. Even though his days of rage were long gone, his inner Arab—these were his people—channeled their passion. Not politically, of course, as he had no idea what they wanted specifically. But personally, *privately*, he understood. He still wanted, as he could see they did, *something else, something more.* Deep down, he knew he had a real problem with the powers that be.

8

RAMADAN AND MAMA JOON GET PASSPORTS TO THE OTHER SIDE OF THE WORLD

Ramadan sat with Mama Joon in a rear pew in St. Louis Cathedral at nine o'clock mass, and he was about to take a selfie with the latest gift from his ever-doting grandmother: a brand-new iPhone. She'd told him it was a birthday present, though he wouldn't turn twelve for another two months. Just as she was now a weekly churchgoer, she had also kept the vow she made while watching Cassandra kiss the cell phone that heralded the return of their boys. She and Ramadan were still staying at the motel in Houston when she bought their first phones. He had sat on the edge of his bed pressing the keys on the little Motorola flip phone. "Mama Joon, why you got me this?"

"Because God can't bother with being the only one who knows where your lil narrow behind is at any given minute," she had said. "He must get sick and tired of people always begging Him to find other people for them. Lost children. Wayward husbands. Suckers who owe them money. I'm exhausted for Him."

Fiddling with his phone, Ramadan had slapped her with an out-of-the-mouths-of-babes "You do seem kinda tired."

A grandmother's child, he had already mastered the tone of sympathetic old soul. She had cut her eyes at him, her face tight from the insult at first, before surrendering to comic admiration.

"Anyway," she said, "maybe that's why God gave us these things. Maybe every cell phone is a miracle."

That flip phone hadn't felt miraculous. Within a couple of days, he had broken it in two. Did miracles do that? Come unhinged? But this iPhone was different. Like the treasured bit of contraband stashed in his closet—the Aleppo-revealing iBook—it was branded with the Apple logo, so in his mind it was anointed by association.

The priest was delivering his homily, and he kept saying "curiosity." His voice conveyed a sense of otherworldliness, as if he had acquired, from years of proximity, the sonic moodiness of an organ. But Ramadan was too distracted with his phone to process the sermon. Looking down at it now in selfie mode, he saw his face mirroring up at him. He smiled as his contentment doubled, knowing the *feeling* of his grin and the pleasure of seeing it reflecting back to him. Then he scrunched his face, stuck out his tongue, pursed his lips, and crossed his eyes until he couldn't really see himself at all—all in avoidance of looking at the same old him. If you didn't know any better, you would think he was no different from any other beige American boy who came from tawny American parents, and for whom Providence had reserved a brown American life. The faint streaks of blue in his amber-colored eyes and the dense merengue of dark curls that refused to grow beyond the three inches piled on his head hinted at atypical infusions but not at the specifics of his roots. And certainly not at any extraordinary destiny, which was essentially what he was trying to impose upon his face, upon himself.

The priest was saying:

"A little girl, I tell you . . . a little girl from Kansas—where else, of course . . . a Dorothy called Clara—she is the one who named it: Curiosity! So when the rover Curiosity lands this summer on that famous planet, more famous perhaps than our own Earth, when you think about it, a hundred million miles away . . . all right, not that far, but millions of miles . . . it may as well be a hundred million . . . we will all know why that little girl understood the majesty of 'curiosity.' And why we must all reach for the moon, the Mars within, for there resides the soul. The soul is what makes each of us worth exploring. The soul is what makes each of us extraterrestrial. Not merely of the Earth, but beyond it. Above it. The soul is what makes each of us a star!"

As the priest said this, Ramadan accidentally switched the lens direction and touched the shutter on his phone. The flash lit up their row. His body tensed and, awaiting Mama Joon's admonishment, he held his breath. When no "shush" or slap on the hand came, he glanced up and saw she wasn't the least bit disturbed by him. She was staring straight ahead, her body as stiff as his—only not with apprehension, but rapture.

A woman turned to glare at him, and the priest had paused, too. He smiled and then used Ramadan's interruption to support his thesis.

"Yes, we are all stars—as bright and seemingly as fleeting as a flash. Little twinkling lights in the constellation of humanity—while we last!"

Ramadan looked at Mama Joon, whose mouth opened just enough to say "Ah!"

Ah!? Had he gotten it from her, or had she gotten it from him?

He went back to tinkering with his phone. Now he wanted a picture of him and Mama Joon, with her going *Ah!* Tapping the reverse perspective on the camera, he disabled the flash.

"For, let's face it, we do not, in the current state, shine forever—though, ultimately, shine forever we shall!"

Ramadan's hands were shaking as he rushed to frame the shot. The screen was filled with a blurred image of the cathedral ceiling. Then, just him and the marble statue of an angel hovering over his shoulder holding a vessel of holy water.

"And thus, in our current state, we must cling, like Clara, to our curiosity. We must try, as best we can, to explore the secrets of our souls. Therein lies the secret to our light and to life! To everlasting life!"

"Ah!" Mama Joon said again. Ramadan leaned to his right, touching his shoulder to hers, and guided the camera's eye until the iPhone displayed them both. There! He tapped the shutter three times, hoping at least one shot would be well lit and in focus.

"This is why we go to the moon, why we go to Mars, why we go to Maui! Curiosity! We go in search of signs of life and Life! Little l and big L. Of course, we are really searching for an even bigger L. LOVE. And what is the means of our exploration? It isn't, as they say, rocket science, dear friends! We don't need NASA. We don't need a jet engine. No microchip. No code. We simply need Christ."

When he heard this, Ramadan stopped looking at his phone, and he tugged at the crucifix around his neck, his mother's, which Mama Joon had given him when he turned seven and celebrated his First Communion.

"Christ is our rover. He is the one who will help us discover—should we be curious enough—what is there under the dust of ourselves, for surely we are dust. We are, each of us, an unknowable planet—but not to Christ. He shines the light on what quakes beneath the rock-hard surface of humanity, the DNA of life: love. In exposing love, he shows us that indeed there was, is, and always will be life on Mars. Eternal life."

He watched Mama Joon mouth *Ah!* again.

"Let us pray . . . the Profession of Faith."

She closed her eyes in prayer and rose from the pew. Others stood as well, but Ramadan returned to communing with his phone. He saw that in every picture he'd just taken, positioned over his and Mama Joon's shoulders, the angel was still there.

"Ah!" he said, turning to look at the actual statue. Mama Joon, now stirred by his movements, opened her eyes. Patting the back of his head, she motioned that it was time to stand up and pray.

AFTER MASS THEY stepped into the New Orleans summer sun, which though a famed oppressor—its downward look upon its subjects, its power to wilt the spirit—today lit Jackson Square in a way that liberated its beauty. The heat had sanitized the square, and the sunlight was having its way with the city scene—dappling the original art easeled against the park fence with a vibrancy the artists could not achieve on their own; embellishing the sweaty spots on the polo shirts and khaki shorts of brunch-seeking tourists, their armpits and crotches, with a suggestive humor they'd never have tolerated at home. The slate and cobblestone walkways were clean and dry, as if the sun had sizzled away the residue of an early morning rain—Nature's own eco-friendly power-washing, an admission of Her complicity in modernity, Her genuine care for the urban landscape.

As always upon exiting the cathedral, Mama Joon focused straight ahead, on the park. There—what a surprise!—she saw, lining the iron fence, the bright green leaves of the banana plants finally regenerating from the storm; they'd been in tatters for years. She hadn't been here in several months, and seeing the healthy-looking stalks rising high, set against the sky, so full of strength, growth, *life*, she felt there was hope. In the throes of her own persistent, post-storm ailments, she dared to consider that the long-awaited rejuvenation of the banana trees, and her ability to *notice* it, might be some kind of a sign that she, too, was entering a recuperative phase. Couldn't life—the signs of *more* life, that is—be like that? First an uplifting sermon. Then the leaves of fruit trees reaching for the heavens. Omens! Yes. Salvation, if you could count on it at all, would be delivered as *this*: a sunny Sunday morning in June!

As she and Ramadan strolled through the square, they came to a paisley-cloth-draped table behind which sat a stoic fortune-teller, the implements of her craft laid out before her. Tarot cards, crosses, crystals, other stones. Beside her stood a baroquely chalked sandwich-board sign: BEATRICE "MISS BEA"—SERVANT OF THE SECRET ARTS. TAROT. PALM READING. SPIRITUAL ADVICE. Oracular and ageless—was she sixty or a hundred?—Beatrice was looking away, exuding the confidence of the soft sell, as if the mere aura of her mastery was the only solicitousness necessary. Indeed it was her aloofness that spoke to Mama Joon. *Look at my back, the edge of my profile,* her detachment said, *and intuit for yourself the reason you are staring at me in the first place: you want me to turn and look at you, to see you whole.* (Later, after her reading, Mama Joon would wonder if Miss Bea had intentionally avoided making eye contact with her, hoping she would take her business elsewhere, not wanting to be the bearer of such news.)

With a nudge to Ramadan, Mama Joon indicated her wish to sit in the two wood-slatted folding chairs in front of Beatrice's station. He followed her lead, and they each settled in opposite the woman and her cards. With a look of absolute composure and quiet anticipation, the woman greeted them with upraised palms. Her ruby-red scarf was embroidered with swirling threadwork that complimented her large gold-spangled earrings, whose cutouts of stars and crescent moons twisted and rotated with her every movement, like miniature Calder mobiles. Her earlobes drooped low, stretched by the weight of the jewelry, but also, perhaps, elongated by time, decades of close listening, of straining to hear things whispered on the wind. Her blue eyes twinkled at Mama Joon and Ramadan, revealing nothing of what they beheld, only the promise that they were, indeed, capable of seeing something others could not.

"Who is first?" she asked. "Mama or the boy?"

Her voice was vaguely European, or maybe merely theatrical. Though Mama Joon had never seen *The Treasure of the Sierra Madre*, for some reason the title, the melody of the phrase, popped into her head when Beatrice spoke; the impenetrable accent sounded like what Humphrey Bogart and his scruffy companions must have been after. Ramadan heard simply what the woman wanted him to hear, the tone of enchantment.

"Oh, no . . ." Mama Joon paused, looking at the sign. "Beatrice—"

"Call me 'Miss Bea.'"

"Well, Miss Bea, I'm June. And this here's Ramadan. But it's just me. For the reading, I mean. Just me."

Miss Bea shrugged. "As you wish." Then she added, "But nothing is just you. We are all connected."

She paused before clarifying, "All right, maybe not me. I stand alone—mostly sit, to tell you the truth. Out here or at home. Me and my cats. Ha!"

Then she pointed her finger, moving it from side to side, grandmother to grandson, tracing an invisible line. "But you two—*you* are connected."

Ramadan and Mama Joon enjoyed this weird moment, the odd

satisfaction of having a strange stranger affirm their attachment—the central emotion of their lives—which they had never articulated for themselves. It almost wouldn't matter what Miss Bea said after that. She had already earned her fee. Was this how they worked? Mama Joon wondered. She had never seriously considered stopping at one of these tarot tables; the suspension of disbelief necessary to sustain her own faith had proven quite enough for one sinful citizen of the Catholic world. Now here she sat, carried away by the prettiness of the day and the sprightliness of foliage, looking for a miracle in a deck of cards. Right. *But you two, you are connected.* Was this how all this mystical mess with people like Miss Bea worked? They identified a silent if obvious truth, these types; they'd spot a vulnerability, a weakness, a thing you showed up with as plain as a weight problem or a hand-covered smile—or, say, a beloved grandson, arm-in-arm, almost as if you were a couple, but who you had to lean into a bit too heavily on a smooth bricked path, to keep your balance, to blunt a sharp pain. They squinted out the goodness in that, what they felt you could take, and then they served that palliative part of your predicament up to you sweetly, with an air of certainty and authenticity, leaving you charmed with the fresh knowledge of something you already knew. The best part of it, the beloved, arm-in-arm, *connected* part, not the lean.

Miss Bea offered a red deck of cards to Mama Joon. "Now—"

Mama Joon interrupted. "Yes—I want to know what's going to happen *now.*"

Miss Bea smiled. "Nothing is just about now. Like people, time is connected. The past, the present, the future. I am here every day looking up at the cathedral, so I am always staring at this truth. Look at it!" She pointed up at the church with her left hand, which was holding her deck of cards.

Mama Joon and Ramadan turned their heads and looked over their shoulders.

"See high up there," she said. "Three!" The church's triumvirate of slate-tiled spires jutted up into the azure sky. "To some people—the Father, the Son, and the Holy Spirit. But not to me. To me they are the past, the present, and the future. That is *my* Holy Trinity."

"Which one is which?" Ramadan asked.

"That is for me to know, and for you to find out for yourself. Maybe it depends on where you are in your life, or *who* you are."

Pointing at the tallest spire, the one in the middle, topped with a cross, Ramadan said, "The big one is the future!"

"Well, let's find out."

Mama Joon accepted the cards from Miss Bea and shuffled them slowly. Then she put them in the middle of the table, and Miss Bea instructed her to cut the deck into three stacks—presumably the symbolic present, past, and future, but she didn't elaborate. Then, again as directed, Mama Joon placed one stack on top of another and handed the cards back to Miss Bea, who paused before she began to turn over one card at a time. When she was done, she had formed a cross with six cards. She was about to flip another card, but she stopped, sighed, and glanced knowingly at Mama Joon.

"I see. I see . . ."

An understanding passed between them, and Mama Joon sighed, too. Her shoulders went slack, but she pressed her chin up in a show of strength. Staring at the park, she said, "I thought maybe the bananas, the trees . . . they look so alive."

Miss Bea arched an eyebrow. Without looking at the trees, she said, "You can't trust bananas. A lot of people make that mistake. Plantains! Now, that's another story."

Mama Joon hummed agnostically. She dug a ten-dollar bill out of her purse and handed it to Miss Bea, who swiped it away so quickly that it vanished without Mama Joon knowing where she put it.

Through a half-chuckle, Mama Joon said, "Another story would be nice." She was rising to leave, when Miss Bea reached out and touched her hand.

"And another story is what you're going to get!"

Miss Bea's expressive eyes posed a question as she pointed at Ramadan, who was preoccupied with his phone. She winked at Mama Joon, who mouthed, "Okay."

Miss Bea said, "Okay, Ramadan. Mr. Big Future. Now it's your turn!"

She reassembled the deck and slid it across the table to him. He put his phone down and turned to Mama Joon for approval. She smiled an enthusiastic *yes*.

Yes—because this would be the easiest reading Miss Bea ever gave. Whatever she would tell Ramadan would help prepare him for what Mama Joon's reading had just portended, a truth she had somehow divulged to this oddly observant woman. Ramadan's future would be foretold to be as bright as this day. That was the deal. It was in Miss Bea's wink—and in the cards, however they landed. This deck was stacked.

Ramadan picked up the tarot cards. They felt cool and smooth in his palms, almost slippery. Just as he had seen Mama Joon do, he began to shuffle. The hard, waxy coating on the surface of each card let them slide over and under one another in his hands with a surprising ease, and he found the unusual combination of the kinetic and the tactile hypnotic. Controlling this series of potentially never-ending motions felt so empowering that he didn't want to stop.

Mama Joon said, "Ramadan, if you want to know what happens, you have to let go."

Her words lifted him from his reverie. When he started neatening the deck, a single card flew out, flipped beyond the edge of the table, caught a breeze, and began fluttering to the ground.

"Catch it!" Miss Bea's voice was filled with urgency, as if not retrieving the card before it landed would imperil the reading, if not something more crucial.

Ramadan didn't really need her encouragement. He had already reached out his long, sinewy left arm and, with the lowest edge of the card only an inch from the ground, pinched the corner pointing at him like the quill of a feather. This rogue, would-be sliver of his fate shined against a background of worn slate-gray stones, which had been trod upon by millions of ghosts. If the tallest spire of the cathedral was his future, that hard, dull ground looked like so many destinies already done. It was all make-believe, of course, but in rescuing the card, he felt a rush of success, the thrill of saving himself from an imaginary demise.

"I got it!" he yelled.

"Well done!" she said, sighing with relief. "Now . . . place it here, facedown."

Without looking at the card, he put it on the table next to his phone. Then Miss Bea guided him through the rituals—his cutting the cards, her turning some of them over slowly, building the suspense of an impending answer to an unspoken question. As she revealed each card, she reacted with exaggerated delight, giving a convincing performance. And what wasn't there to believe? Even to a layman, the first few cards would have predicted prosperity for Ramadan: the Sun, the High Priestess, the Chariot, the Wheel of Fortune.

"Yes!" Miss Bea said.

"What?" Ramadan asked, breathless.

"Thanks to a great lady, you will go far in life, Ramadan." Her eyes angled up from the High Priestess to Mama Joon, who, mulling over Miss Bea's tip, dialed back her smile.

"I will?"

"Yes. And you will go *very, very far!*" She tapped the Chariot.

"I knew it!"

"And you will have luck in your travels." She stroked the Wheel of Fortune.

"Yes!" Ramadan yelled. "Tell me more!"

But then Miss Bea placed a fifth card at the top of the cross, breaking the streak of symbols so easily interpreted for good. As she released the corner of the card, it slapped against the tabletop with an ominous, amplified snap: Death.

She swallowed, and Mama Joon looked away, ashamed, as if her mortality were a moral failing.

Ramadan, eyeing their anxiety, said to Miss Bea, "What does it mean?"

She ignored him and turned a sixth card: the Ace of Swords.

"Yes!" she said.

"What does it mean, Miss Bea?" Ramadan begged.

She stared into his eyes and said, "You will slay the dragon!"

He was too old to believe in dragons, but he was just the right age to begin to appreciate a good metaphor. A dragon could be anything: a problem, a person, a weakness. Miss Bea looked at him as if trying to instill in him the fortitude she was predicting. He took a deep breath, wanting to ingest her faith, and his head went a little dizzy, as he found himself beginning to believe in her powers, to believe in Miss Bea.

Oh, the Death card had momentarily shaken Beatrice's faith in herself, but now she, too, felt flushed—telling the boy's story was the kind of challenge she lived for!—with a renewed confidence in her ability to read whatever the cards foretold. Reassured of her gift, she pointed to the card Ramadan had caught just before it hit the ground. "Now turn that one over—your mystery card!"

He flipped the card, and its message hit Miss Bea first—she yelped, threw her head back, and raised her hands. Then Mama Joon held her face in both her hands, but Ramadan couldn't tell if she was laughing or crying. When he picked up the card to figure out why they were so over-come, he saw the illustration of a man wearing a red robe draped over a white garment. His left hand was pointing down, but his right hand was holding up a scepter or a wand. A symbol of infinity hovered over his head like a halo, as he stood behind a table, on top of which rested a golden chalice, a sword, a long staff, and a disk imprinted with a five-pointed star. Surrounding the man and his instruments and weaponry were a cascading archway and a bed of leafy roses and lilies. This im-agery was so captivating that the last thing Ramadan noticed was the name of this card which had so enthralled Miss Bea, Mama Joon, and yes, now him: the Magician.

INVIGORATED BY RAMADAN'S reading, if not her own, Mama Joon sug-gested they take the short walk to the riverfront. He had undergone a growth spurt within the last few months and was almost as tall as she was. With his new stature and the ongoing development of the phys-ical poise he had always had, he could be mistaken for a lanky teen, maybe even a diminutive young man. He was no prizefighter, but no one had called him "skinny as a rail" for some time either. Holding her grandson's arm and leaning into his shoulder as they dodged Decatur Street traffic, Mama Joon let herself feel girlish and glamorous, as if she were Audrey Hepburn traipsing up Fifth Avenue with George Peppard circa 1960. Some fifty-plus years and fifty-plus pounds ago, she had seen *Breakfast at Tiffany's* when it had premiered. An impressionable sixteen at the time, she had made a personal heroine of Holly Golightly. In many ways, her long affair with Judge Dumas had been imaginable only because Audrey Hepburn had made Holly's daring, flirtatious dreamer so believable for June. An essentially good girl could take risks, be wild, screw up—*have secrets*—but still have things work out. No, not quite as you planned, of course. But still, here she was after all these years, even with all of her issues, on the arm of a handsome young fellow, in the middle of a fine American city, with money in the bank, on her way to the real Moon River, capable of pretending everything was just *marvelous.*

When they stepped onto the curb in front of Café du Monde, Ramadan realized he was strong enough to help lift his grandmother the few inches to the sidewalk. The warm river breeze moistened his face, as he blushed with pride. They were a couple as filled with romance as the city itself. Years from now, remembering their final weeks together, Ramadan would think of Mama Joon as his first great love, just as she realized at this moment, with absolute certainty, that he was her last.

They walked to the top of the levee, where they sat on a bench watching the water and its traffic flow.

"Mama Joon, did you know you and me, we both say *Ah!?*" Little-boy grammar was one of the last vestiges of childhood, which he could sense being devoured by time. So he indulged in it as a means of self-preservation. If you could pick your wobbly grandmother up, maybe things were moving too fast. A weak tongue told the world maybe you weren't quite ready. No one, not even you really, had to know your language was a lie.

"You and *me*, Ramadan? Really, son? I didn't teach you how to read my own damn self and I don't pay good money for you to go to that fancy school to have you walk around talking like that."

"My school is free."

"Boy, nothing is free. I pay my taxes, don't I? And they pay for that magnet school."

"Okay, you and *I* . . . Did you ever notice how we both say *Ah!*? Whenever we see or hear something special, like a surprise, we go *Ah!* What's *up* with that?"

"I never noticed," she said, telling a half-lie.

"You *didn't*?" he asked, doubtful that he was more perceptive than she.

"Well, I know *you* do it," she said.

"You did it today in church."

"I did?"

"Mmm hmm. While Father was giving his sermon. Look . . ." He pulled out his phone and showed her one of the photographs.

"Oh, yes! Jesus!" Her head fell back, as she replayed the priest's words, which had seemed meant especially for her. *The body doesn't last forever.* No—that wasn't it. Not "the body." He hadn't been that blunt. What was it? She brought her head down, opened her eyes, and the river jogged her memory. *The current state!* That's how he had phrased it. Well, hell, he had been pretty prosaic after all, only now that she was looking at the river flow, his words acquired a bit of poetry. The current state—that's what didn't last forever. *The current state!*

"Ah!" she said, to concede Ramadan's point.

"See—there!" he said. "Just like that! Where does that come from?"

"I must get it from you."

"That's what I was thinking! But how? You ever heard of something called 'evolution'?"

"Boy."

"Well, we learned in class that evolution works the other way around. You're my ancestor, right?"

She looked at her grandson, who was almost eye to eye with her on the bench. "Hmph. Pretty much."

"So then I'm supposed to get stuff from you."

"Well . . . Mr. Darwin didn't know everything. Life is a back-and-forth between people. Just like this conversation we're having. I'm getting stuff from you and you're getting stuff from me. I'm saying things to you without even saying them."

She had said that because she knew she would never be able to say what she wanted to tell him—about the impermanence of the current state and all. She would have to find another way. "Are you paying attention to me?" she asked.

"Yes, ma'am."

"All I know is . . . I never said *Ah!* before I met you."

"You probably did. You just don't remember."

"Nope. Never did."

She put her arm around Ramadan and said, "Look at all those boats and ships."

"Where do you think they're going?" he asked. It was his turn to lean into her a little, not for physical support, but for intimacy.

Thank you, Lord! she thought. He would make it easy for her. "That's a great question," she said. "I think they're going wherever it is they're supposed to be. Some are coming in . . . and some are going out."

Ramadan scanned all of the river within view. "I like the ones going out."

"You know what? I do too." She sighed and said, "Sooner or later, we've all gotta go somewhere."

"I know. Like after the storm, when we went to Texas."

"Exactly."

"Let's go somewhere together!" he said, bouncing up and down once on the bench. "Not the whole city this time—just you and me."

She laughed, and they cuddled. Maybe they could take a little trip someplace. The doctor she had finally forced herself to visit the week before last had told her she might have two or three decent months. She thought of Ramadan without her, and powerlessness seized her. There was no way to console from the grave. Or maybe there was—who knew? But you couldn't count on the long shot that was divine intervention. Surely God had his hands full managing the mounting dead. The living were likely on their own. What were people thinking! She'd have to do for Ramadan what she could *now*. Compassion made her say, "Okay, let's go. Just you and me. *Before* the storm this time."

"What storm?"

She just squeezed him and said, "So where should we go?"

"Somewhere far, far away. Like Miss Bea said. The other side of the world!"

"Ramadan—" she cut him off. She hadn't heard him use that phrase in a long time, but she knew what he meant. That damned Clarissa! She had done this to him. Whatever she had said to the boy in some hissy fit of jealously and greed had put this insidious father fixation in him. Daddy lust! Wasn't a woman's passion for a man enough trouble for this world? Did a child really need to become psychologically entangled with a creature as deft at distancing himself from such relations as he was at creating them? Hadn't Clarissa's own life taught her anything about the male menace? *Menace*. There they were: reflected in a word capturing them at their all-too-prevalent worst. Oh, there was no short-age of other incidental descriptors: *maniacal, mendacious, malevolent.* Clarissa's violation of the matriarchal code was unforgivable. And now Ramadan was cursed to pine for something as unreliable, mysterious, elusive—*invisible*—as a man! All because Clarissa wanted things she couldn't have: Mama Joon's money; the deed to the house; the affection her mother lavished upon her sister's son. Oh, but if Clarissa only knew what her own father had thought of her, she might not have been so cav-alier about unsettling their mama-centric household. Mama Joon had never been so cruel as to subject Clarissa to Judge Dumas's harsh con-clusion about how her origins had tainted her very existence. (It was in that Valentine's Day letter—the one he'd signed *Love, Manny*—a mis-sive as forceful in its repudiation of Clarissa as it was in its glorification of Alicia.) But the proof of his indictment seemed to rest in the apparent darkness of Clarissa's nature.

"You know I don't know where your daddy is," Mama Joon said.

"I know," Ramadan said. "But Aleppo is just six thousand, seven hundred and twenty-two miles from New Orleans."

"*Aleppo?* How do you know that?"

He held up his iPhone.

"Hmm . . . Syria. You know, there's a war going on over there, boy? Did your phone tell you that?"

"Yes, ma'am." He pouted. "Okay . . . then let's go as close as we can get to Syria."

"And where would that be?"

"Turkey. It's right next to Syria."

"Turkey? Ha—You say 'turkey' to me and I start preheating the oven!"

"Mama Joon!"

"Three hundred and fifty degrees . . ."

"No. Turkey! Like, the Ottoman Empire."

"You say 'ottoman' to me and I wanna put my feet up!" She leaned back on the bench and stretched her legs straight out. They laughed until she started coughing.

"But seriously—Istanbul is just six thousand, one hundred and seventy-five miles away!"

"Really? That'll save us a whole, what, six hundred miles off that Aleppo trip."

"Almost—five hundred and forty-seven," he corrected her. "Your math is not what it used to be."

"Oh, no, mister?"

"I mean, three hundred and fifty degrees to bake a turkey, Mama Joon? I thought three twenty-five was better."

"Well, it is—if you got that kinda time."

"Right. Three twenty-five takes longer."

"Exactly."

"I guess it all just depends on how hungry you are."

"Everything depends on how hungry you are, Ramadan. Remember that."

He looked at her and said, "Okay. I will."

"And you are hungry for Turkey," she said. "Well, we'll see about all this."

"We need passports," Ramadan said firmly.

Mama Joon let the mood of metaphor that had settled upon them hold sway. Anything could be something else. The cathedral's tallest spire was a boy's future. A country was a holiday feast. A leg rest could conjure the majesty of an empire. She could tell Ramadan what was happening without actually telling him. On some level, he would know.

Maybe already knew. The impermanence of the current state. A boat moving downstream, she was one of the ones heading out. She didn't have time to slow-cook a Butter Ball!

"I'll get you your passport, Ramadan," she said. Then she added with resignation, "I already have mine."

❧

AS MAMA JOON was in the last phase of going out, Ramadan stood alone beside her hospital bed looking down at her as she slept. He saw no bloody forehead this time, felt no shock that one day she would die. During the six weeks of her decline, he had conceded that certainty. The day was here. No, no blood now. But still, he had ridden her too hard, put too much weight on her, until she had bent over and banged against something harder than glass. And this time *she* had cracked.

"I killed you," he murmured.

On some level he knew better, but now that he had spoken the words, they rang true. So he said them again. "I killed you."

Suddenly Mama Joon's eyes opened wide, and he jumped back. "Ah!"

She smiled at his reaction, and with wonder—she was yet alive.

"If you killed me, then how come I'm still here?" She had no idea what had made him say what he'd said, but he needed consoling. "Come here."

As he moved closer, his guilt begin to fade. She always had this effect on him, had always helped him escape his demons. Her embrace had been his refuge, a womb in the world. Now she was straining to open her arms to him, and he took two quick steps and fell onto the bed, sinking, one last time, into what was left of her. She moaned from the impact to her sternum, which, having gone to gristle, practically contoured to the shape of Ramadan's head. She was full of enough medication that the dull ache from being pillowed in this way was to her just another indication she was really leaving. The laughter she used to feel rippling out of him and into her when she tickled away his fears was sobbing this time. But, as if in testament to all that had ever passed between them, Ramadan's rhythmic heaving massaged her, placating the last of her pain. Surely she was entering another realm, transforming, because she could feel him, but not his emotion. Twin angels, the morphine and the morphing, were ushering her onward, telling her what to whisper to numb Ramadan's anguish and aid *his* transformation.

"Don't be afraid. It's going to be all right. You will be big and strong. But remember this, the world is stronger than you are. If you know a storm is coming, *leave*. Evacuate! Don't do like I did for the big storm. You and I, we almost lost each other. Don't you lose yourself."

Ramadan, eyes moistening, tried to speak. "I—"

But she wasn't in a listening mood; she didn't have time. "The next time a storm is coming—and believe me a storm is gonna come—you get on the first thing smoking and worry 'bout the rest later, you hear me?"

"Yes, ma'am."

"Mama Joon is leaving you enough money to go wherever you want to, and then come back when the coast is clear. Or—or never! Or just whenever you good and ready. You *hear* me, baby?"

"Yes, ma'am."

"Oh, and let me tell you, Mr. Ramadan, you are going places! You are going to go places. You understand me?"

His tears kept coming. Not because he was going anywhere—but because Mama Joon was.

"You are going to go far. In life. That's what I mean. Just like Miss Bea said—and when you get to Istanbul, I'll be there with you."

She let out a loud laugh, and he raised his head and stopped crying.

"What?" he asked, staring into her aura, all that was really left.

The jokes she had made when they had sat by the river talking about taking a trip together came back to them, and they both said, "Turkey!"

Their last laugh together subsided quickly. He fluffed her pillows, she closed her eyes, and her head fell back. In her mind, she saw herself, Ramadan, a Thanksgiving banquet, and a great big ottoman in the sky.

⚘

IT WAS TOO late now—but something was bothering Mama Joon as she lay dying. Something she had left undone. Something for Ramadan. Something important. And she had done so much to prepare the way forward. Spent hours and hours with him in the kitchen teaching him how to cook, so that he could feed himself when she was gone. Secreted away the money. Willed him the house.

The attorney managing her affairs would take care of any legal or financial issues that came up. Wilfred Dumas. Yes, Judge Dumas's son, his one legitimate child. Little Willie knew nothing of his extended family, his half sisters, the dead Alicia and the deadened Clarissa, but Mama Joon had practically raised him, too. After his mother had died when he was eight years old, he had latched on to her. She had been the beneficiary of his need to exercise his motherless muscles. His extreme animalism had fascinated her, so different from Clarissa, who was just a couple of years older than Willie. But his affection, as it grew about her, also had the suppleness of tendrils. Their attachment, while not biological, acquired a botanical quality. His hugs dug into her more deeply, as if he was seeking to reconnect with the very taproot of life itself, searching for the nutrients he needed to survive and to grow. It was Willie who had turned her into a cliché, an "earth mother." It was Willie who had made her long to nurture a boy of her own—Willie who had tilled her for Ramadan.

He had taken to calling her "Mama." Not "June." Not "Mama Joon." Just "Mama." Which, coming out of the mouth of a little white boy, sometimes startled even her. (When she had first shown up, unannounced, at his small but swanky office downtown on Baronne Street a few years ago and was confronted by his receptionist with a heavy dose of "you need an appointment" attitude, Willie had swung in through the front door on his way back from lunch, thrown his arms open to her, and yelled, "Mama!" The rude young woman had gulped and, much to Mama Joon's satisfaction, spilled the bottle of pink nail polish she'd been dipping into.) Willie was the only person who called her that. The only one she allowed to. She had resisted it at first. But he had been so lonely, and she harbored such guilt about her affair with his father and their betrayal of his actual mother that she had acquiesced. With her family, and anyone else, for that matter, she insisted on the "Joon," in an attempt to keep herself whole. To be specific, not generic. Not homogenized. To be just "Mama" was a diminishment. But with Willie, it felt like retribution. Every time he called her "Mama," it felt like she was paying an installment on a debt.

Yes, Willie had set up everything for Ramadan—both emotionally all those years ago, and now administratively. He had written her will, and notarized it. Ramadan would inherit everything. Everything. Clarissa would technically be his guardian, and in exchange for that, she could live like the queen of her half of the double. Free to reign there for the rest of her pitiable life. But not free to reign *over* Ramadan.

"You understand?" she had asked Willie. "Everything belongs to Ramadan."

"I understand."

He had made all the financial arrangements, created some kind of a "trust." She loved the sound of that. And he had gotten Ramadan an American Express card for his living expenses, which Willie would pay off monthly, as needed.

"Ramadan can use this for anything he wants, anything—and for emergencies."

"Yes!" Mama Joon was looking at the stylish green card Willie had placed in her hand. Seeing "Ramadan Ramsey" embossed in the lower left-hand corner and the roman warrior in profile in the middle of the card made her smile.

"A gladiator," she said.

"Yeah, it's a good logo," Willie said, organizing some papers for her signature.

And last month, Willie had gotten Ramadan the passport she had promised him, but that she would not live to see him use. Willie had insisted on getting her one, too—ha! She hadn't told him how sick she really was. He had assumed she was just planning ahead. If she had been half as diligent about attending to her health as she had become about securing Ramadan's future, she might have lived another twenty years.

Too late now. Too late . . .

When had she lost it, the impulse to go charging on, the zest for it all? When? She had always loved living. She had been adored by a grandmother. She had had a great, if imperfect, love. She had developed a conscious philosophy of being: motherhood as power. In her own way, she was an artist: a master of cooking. Yes, for most of her life, she had loved living. Absolutely *loved* it! She wasn't sure most people did. Not the way she had. To the contrary, she suspected most people actually wanted out—the way she did now. The way she had for some time. But since when? When had she become normal, run-of-the-mill, un–Holly Golightly, ready to retire, inclined to recline, as now, more desirous of rest than recreation? *Any questions?* Still so many. Here at the end, you'd think there'd be answers. But no. Not yet . . .

And now again—that *other* question: What had she forgotten? *The letter!*

"The letter," she mumbled aloud.

"The letter?" asked Ramadan, standing nearby. Did she mean the letter he had found in the store? But how would she even know about that? Plus, except for a few words on the envelope written in English, he couldn't even read it. So, of course, Mama Joon couldn't either. What could the letter matter to her? What did it matter at all? Backing away from her bedside and settling into the chair in the corner of the hospital room, he sighed, tearing up at the inscrutability of everything: Arabic; Mama Joon's improbable last word; his strange lack of fear.

The letter, she thought. Yes, that was it. An answer—not a good one. She'd meant to destroy it. It was useless to anyone, even to her, after all these years. She had held on to it because it was her last letter from Judge Dumas. *Love, Manny.* The only time anyone had signed a letter to her that way. It was a celebration of Alicia's birth and their love—of course she'd kept it. But it was the letter's darkness that did not need to see the light of day.

What if? she wondered. What if the judge had felt about Clarissa the way he felt about Alicia? (Light-skinned and shrewd, Clarissa was actually much more like him than her sister, who looked and loved like June.) Would Clarissa have been a different person? Better? Would her boys have been different, better? Oh, God—that day her appendix had burst and Damon had picked her up without anyone asking, picked his grandmother up and carried *her* like a baby to the car and then into the emergency room—*Don't worry, Mama Joon . . . I got you!*—she'd seen it in him, again. That sparkle—the beauty, strength, and pricelessness— that had made her once call him Diamond. It could have been him. With just a little more luck, a little more love, he could have been her first Ramadan—she could have had *two*. Would even she, June Ramsey, have been a better person if the judge had treasured his firstborn? Oh, well, even if Clarissa found the letter, it would only mean she'd know something about her father. (Her lifetime lack of curiosity about him was, to Mama Joon, her greatest charm.) So, then, so what if she found it? So what! What, would it make her any more bitter than she already was? That seemed hardly possible. Nothing would gall her more than not getting her hands on Mama Joon's money.

Besides, the truth did not always come out. If anything, the truth *rarely* came out. People say that what's done in the dark always comes into the light. Nonsense! Again, the opposite was closer to the real truth. Everybody eventually learned this, as she was learning it now. Everybody felt it in their bones, as she was feeling now: What's done in the light, like say, *life*, recedes into darkness—death. Always. Now that was certainly true. Name the biggest unknown you could name, the biggest thing hidden in darkness: *Who is God?* No one would ever know that. Ever. Moses had stared right into His radiance and asked Him, and all he got was "I am that I am." Really? A truth that big was just a riddle? Well, maybe that was all it could be. The riddle of being. Sensing sin in her inquiry, she twitched, losing a few precious seconds' worth of her fast-dwindling strength, and she said a quick Hail Mary in penance, rushing through a ragged, silent recitation, racing to finish before it was too late: *Holy Mary, Mother of God, pray for us sinners, now and at the hour of our death! Amen.*

Whew! The fear of every praying Catholic, not making it to the end, *at the end*, of this one perfect prayer, when you need it most. Now—and at the hour. *Right now.* But she'd made it.

Religion was right: Eternal life was real! Only not as they imagined it. It—*this*—would always be true. Eternally. There was no stopping *this* truth. There was no taking her life away from her now. Strangely, only the end of it made this so. Only this finish gave life its power. The darkness *was* the light. Made the light visible. That was what those people who had "died" and lived to tell about it had seen and nearly walked into. Black enlightenment.

She got it now. All those stars that lit up the sky *were* dying. Would we even have their light without their deaths? Our own sun even, the source of it all, was dying. We were all living on death. The moon—her precious moon—but a reflection of that dying sun, yes, just a shadow of a deathly thing, was light! In the end—she knew this now—it was Death that had made her do everything. (Ah! Alicia's death—that was when she'd lost it, the will to live fully. That was when she had lost her Holly Golightly! And Alicia's death had given her Ramadan, all to herself. But Ramadan could not bring Holly back. Even Ramadan was not enough.) Death had made her prepare for *It*. Death had forced her to put her things in order. Death had forced her to teach Ramadan how to cook, so that he could eat and grow—survive! Death had got Ramadan his passport to the other side of the world; Death *was* hers. Death had fired her up, empowered her, *powered* her. People think it numbs you. But no! Death charges you. Death is electric! They think it's all about darkness. But no—Death lights the way!

And Death would take care of Ramadan, too. It already had. It would again, she sensed. It would have to. First Alicia. Now her. Who was next? She couldn't say. But someone else would have to die for Ramadan. She saw it plainly. The three steeples of St. Louis Cathedral. Ramadan's big future up there high in the middle. There was always a trinity. The past, present, and future. The tarot card lady's connectedness. Mama Joon felt she was but the second in a trinity of death. Yes, someone else would die for her boy. Maybe already had, and she just didn't know who it was. So be it! Death would keep him alive. Death would save Ramadan. But then, Death saved everyone, she thought. Death was the deliverer. *Ah!* Of course—this was why the story of Christ rang so true! A man up on a cross being crucified! Lord have mercy, for real. How in hell could a death so vile make the world rejoice! And she realized now something she must have known all along, something she must have *believed* all along, as she had allowed herself to die, as she had let cancer crucify *her.* Now she knew who she was—a savior! Now she knew what her life was about, what her *death* was about: the Redemption of Ramadan.

Alicia flitted through her mind again, and she flinched—a near-final, near-fatal physical sensation. Had her child died too young to find meaning in life? Too young to find a truth for herself that would make everything all right? Maybe she had. *No*—she hadn't! She was smarter than Clarissa, smarter than her mother. Besides—and Mama Joon accepted this and let go, finally, of the agony of having lost Alicia—dying, as the priest had said of soul searching, wasn't rocket science! It wasn't physics or advanced math. (Even Clarissa would die well, she concluded, though not for some time. Hers was not the third death that would save Ramadan. That much she was sure of. "The good die young" was the saying. Nobody dared to say anything so pithy about "the bad." They didn't write songs about how the bad live long. Maybe it was too offensive a thought, too ugly an irony, to acknowledge—but that didn't make it untrue. No, Clarissa had years and years of crassness and laziness and greed ahead of her. She would die old. Oh, well . . . the French had coined a phrase for the general acceptance of cruel truth, and there was never a more appropriate moment to be reminded of it than this one: *C'est la vie!*) Anyone could die perfectly. Everyone was born knowing how. Everyone, when the time came, did it flawlessly, as she was doing right now.

And she thought this, felt it fully at the last (in homage to Moses and his meeting with the Maker on the mount), with the absolute understanding that her mark, however modest, was indelible—her life was over; her existence, everlasting—*I was that I was!*

9

INHERITANCE TAXES

'm the mama now!" Clarissa had burst into Ramadan's bedroom as if conquering long-disputed territory.

Arms akimbo and brow furrowed, she scowled down at her nephew, who was lying on his bed staring at a French workbook, even though the start of the new school year was still three weeks away. Her main intention was simply to make a good show of appearing strong, assertive, and borderline mean. Such theatrics, combined with snippets of vulgarity and a bit of physical force, had usually worked with her own sons, whom she had watched grow from playful pups into full-grown pit bulls in what, looking back on it, seemed the same flash of time required to complete the actual canine progression. Now, hearing them call each other "dog" or "dawg," in the urban male-to-male parlance of the day, she was glad she had been quick-tempered with them whenever her once lovable little beings had turned defiant, if not downright deviant. (The question of whether her sons' referring to themselves as a lesser life-form owed to their being treated or behaving as such did not confound Clarissa; she wasn't that inquisitive or cynical. That accepting them as "dogs" made her a "bitch" was vaguely appalling to her. But there were days when she needed to be a bitch, anyway—a big one—just to maintain her sanity. The disgust she sometimes felt about it all was a small price to pay for order and survival. When her boys had become less and less responsive to her verbal admonishments, she gave them the occasional slap on the backside. Later, as they grew bigger, stronger, and wilder, she resorted, on an as-needed basis, to outright violence, employing the last-resort disciplinary implements of ghetto motherhood: a belt, an extension cord, an airborne shoe, both ends of a broom. She had tamed them— thank goodness—so that any danger they posed (a significant amount, if their rap sheets were to be trusted), as they did battle with a world so ruthlessly and inventively opposed to them, did not extend to her. Maintaining the balance of her own preservation with theirs had always been tricky, but with guile, threats, rib shots, Advil, and a succession of forgivable micro-loans from Mama Joon, she had managed. Crip, Booker T, Damon, Romeo and Julius, the hulking men who surrounded her, all of whom, on occasion, had been jailed—caged, as it were—recognized her as part mama, part master. Sure, she had meted out punishment, sometimes harsh, when they had gotten out of line. But she had also fed them, *un*caged them when necessary (a.k.a. bailed them out), and rewarded them when they did as she commanded.

Admittedly, her quest to dominate Ramadan was beginning somewhat late in his development. But he had none of her boys' natural aggression anyway. He was a totally different breed—a collie or a lab or, at worst (she was remembering his early years), a yappy terrier. Whatever methods Mama Joon had employed to rid him of his madness—all that lovey-dovey, spoil-him-rotten crap—had actually worked. If there was any doubt in Clarissa's mind that he would ultimately bend to her authority, it had something to do with his braininess, with whatever he was acquiring in those books he was always studying, and with that dormant streak of passion he used to flash without warning. At any rate, she had decided it was best to catch him off guard, thunder into his room unannounced and, not having combed her hair, show him her best Medusa.

Ramadan, though, looked up from his French textbook and saw not the imposing figure Clarissa had meant to project, but a comic one. Maybe it was that he was conjugating the verb *rire*—as in, "to laugh." Or maybe it was that *rire* was pronounced "rear," and his aunt's butt was wide enough for him to see its outer edges trembling behind her even as she faced him. Tautly stretching her blue-and-white floral-print dress, her backside quivered with the fright she hoped to elicit from him. He considered hiding behind the mask of preadolescence and faking fear, but his intellect betrayed him. He had to stifle a chuckle. Putting his head down, he pretended he was laughing at what he was reading, which in a way he was.

"You can laugh all you want, but things about to change around here. I don't care what Mr. Lawyer Man said. You can't just be a child, all unsupervised, living up in here like a king. The world does not work like that. No, sir, it does not. Mama Joon musta been outta her everlasting mind!"

"Ever-*loving*," Ramadan corrected her.

"Ever-*what?*"

"Nothing." He looked down at his workbook again.

"That's right," she said. "Go on back to your books. You don't need to be worried about none of this mess anyway. I'll take care of everything. Everything's gonna be all right."

"I know," Ramadan said.

"Up in here living like a king," she muttered on her way out.

After the door slammed, he heard Clarissa trudging down the hall, toward the back of the house. Whatever humor there was in the situation left the room with her. Mama Joon had told him she was leaving him in a position to take care of himself. Mr. Dumas—"*Call me Mr. Willie*"—had reassured him as well, even coming by the house once already since the funeral to check on him. Until now, he had had no reason to question his security, and so he had given no thought to the idea of anyone stepping into Mama Joon's role. Besides, there was only one Mama Joon. Only one person had held him like he was a part of her she had lost and that only he allowed her to touch, to *feel* again. No one would ever love him that much. He wondered if his aunt even *liked* him. So, then, what was to become of him if, as Clarissa had just proclaimed, she really *was* the mama now?

⚜

CLARISSA FLUNG OPEN Mama Joon's bedroom door as forcefully as she had Ramadan's. The same conquistador spirit consumed her now, pressing her forward with a Cortésian glee. Her Montezuma was no more, and what was left behind rightfully belonged to her. She wanted what every looter wants. Loot, of course—on the low end, anything of value; on the high, something precious, unexpected, unknown. Without hesitation or strategy, she proceeded: rifling through dresser drawers; crouching on her hands and knees to check under the bed; lifting the mattress; swinging open the closet door; tossing blouses and dresses wildly over her shoulder.

After a solid fifteen minutes of effort—resulting in knee bruises and a brief, uncontrollable, dust-induced fit of sneezing—she had unearthed remarkably little of value. The first letdown: a single quarter found in the back corner of the bottom dresser drawer under the lacy edge of an old, stretched-out pair of Mama Joon's panties. When a lift of the mattress revealed a crisp twenty-dollar bill, she had flipped the entire queen-size cushion over and shoved it against the wall. But nothing else green was sprouting there. The dozen or so retired purses she discovered under the bed also looked promising at first. But each, once opened, turned upside down, shaken loose of even lint, had proven improbably penniless.

The closet, of course, had the vastness of a vault. The instant she began raiding it, the disappointment she was feeling from not having made a quick, big strike faded. Every hanging garment had the rough silhouette of her mother. Maybe she needed to hack her way through this phalanx of Mama Joon phantoms, as shady as the slights she'd endured her entire life. Maybe that would clear a pathway to the recompense she had earned for suffering through decades of not being told, *but somehow still knowing*, that she was not truly cherished. Forging ahead, she felt as if she were peeling away layer after layer of Mama Joon from the premises. *Yes!* she thought, committing to the task, lifting weighty bunches of clothes all at one time. She would have to put some muscle into moving Mama Joon out of the way, so that she could find her true reward. Of course—to arrive at what belonged to her, the thing that would reveal her true worth, maybe her true self, she would have to go *through* Mama Joon. Somewhere in here, hidden under all this stuff, was the real treasure: *her*. Yes, the only way to uncover the mother lode would be to remove the mother load! As Clarissa tossed aside armfuls of JCPenney, floral, poly-blend Mama Joons, more and more light flooded the closet, filling her with hope. Sure, the physical nature of what she was doing—the squatting, bending, pulling, throwing—was partly responsible for the adrenal surge. (Plundering, however petty, was still work.) But the real cardio workout for Clarissa was the release of a lifetime of pent-up Mama Joon emotion.

The unshakable sense that she was insignificant in her mother's eyes had been debilitating. She had scant evidence of any real difference between how Mama Joon had treated her and her sister, but wasn't the proof in her lack of self-worth? If Alicia had outshined her—and Clarissa was convinced she had—it was because their mother had stroked and polished her with pride. If she had had any doubts about her suspicions, Ramadan's anointing dashed them away. She had produced five—five!—handsome, if complicated, boys. (Of course they were complicated—she had passed her disillusionment on to them like a cleft chin.) Any one of them could have been Mama Joon's number-one guy. Clarissa could have lived on that—and *off* it—both emotionally and financially. Crip and Booker T had each looked the part of a prince. But, okay, maybe Clarissa, insecure and already growing bitter, had clung to them too much. Plus, Mama Joon had just had Alicia. In retrospect Damon, her middle son, had probably had the best shot at royalty. Mama Joon had even dubbed him "Diamond," only days after he was born. But he was barely walking when he stopped putting a sparkle in her eyes. Alicia, only three years older than her newest nephew, was already the fairy princess by then, anyway—that lil wench could rock a tutu. Watching her prance around in lace-encased splendor, scepter in hand, at her fourth birthday party, Clarissa had felt a warmth rising in her chest, her own inner Tinker Bell almost reviving. Meanwhile, where was Damon? At the table spilling his punch on the cake, wetting the candle wicks before they'd been lit, dousing dreams. Mama Joon had quickly downgraded the would-be gem to a rhinestone. The twins never really had a chance—not that they deserved one. Even Clarissa would admit that. As adorable as their professional football player father—a memorable one-night stand—they were also just as self-centered and ruthless. If she could have traded them through free agency, she would have listened to offers, let them go at a loss for the sake of the franchise. But family was a team for life. Against the world, you had to field the players drafted by fate. You could bench them, but not release them. The only game changer was death.

Fate? Yes, she had considered the possibility it was all preordained.

Maybe she was meant to be shoved aside, relegated to a life on the other side of the shotgun double, separated from Mama Joon by walls, however thin, from the source of real power, away from the money, away from the action, away from the—she could say it now that Mama Joon wasn't here to deny it to her—away from the love. Maybe her lot in life was not to be loved in a way that made her feel like a winner. Maybe she was a born loser.

But no, now the game *had* changed for Team Ramsey. Mama Joon's death had combined with Alicia's to reposition Clarissa. She was no longer sidelined, a lesser sister, a ne'er-do-well daughter. Maybe her destiny was not to be doomed, after all, not to be worthless but to be—at last— endowed. She was the one who was alive. Not Alicia. Not Mama Joon. As fate would have it, she was the last bitch standing.

When she had cleared the closet of Mama Joon's clothes, all that remained were countless rows and columns of shoeboxes stacked against the back wall. The cardboard cases, all lidded, rose up to her waist. If the jungle of clothes had given her the impression of camouflaging something, this neatly arranged cache looked capable of doing the opposite: revealing. She stepped toward the boxes, so meticulously aligned they might have been an architectural detail, wainscoting or tile. As she lifted the lid off the first box, bulging and misshapen with envelopes, she felt as if she were performing an excavation. Forcing out one envelope at a time, she registered confusion at first, then anguish—then utter disappointment. She didn't even have to pull them completely out to know what they were. A logo branded every return address. AT&T. COX. ENTERGY. STATE FARM. SEWERAGE AND WATER BOARD. VERIZON. She opened an Entergy envelope. Along with an invoice dated February 20, 2012 (only a few months ago), for $147.33, she found Mama Joon's canceled check for the same amount. Bills! And no—not just bills. Also the documentation of payment. Then she began randomly removing a single envelope from a box here, a box there, and found that Mama Joon had been filing away these payments for years, if not decades. A Cox Communications cable bill from August 14, 2010. A Tulane University Medical Center bill from September 3, 2001, which must have been a payment for Alicia's hospital stay. A Macy's credit card bill from March 1998! Frustration mounting, Clarissa lifted lid after lid, ripping out more envelopes in the hope that somewhere beneath this monument to Mama Joon's debt-free life was something that did not indict her own entire existence as being in arrears. But there was nothing. Every proof of payment was another charge against her personal account with the planet, a line of credit she hadn't, until now, acknowledged she'd ever opened. In her agitation she began thrashing at the boxes, toppling them, tossing up fistfuls of envelopes that fluttered around in the closet before landing with a feathery lightness, a near weightlessness indicative, certainly to her, of the sum of their parts.

A familiar emptiness invaded Clarissa, the sensation that *she* was nothing, and yet, in tears, she sank to the floor with a mighty thud, an ironic density of self-doubt. She looked down and realized she was still clinching the Entergy envelope. A message in bright red letters warned: KEEP YOUR DISTANCE. STAY AWAY FROM POWER LINES. When a teardrop landed on the envelope, dampening DISTANCE, she irrationally twitched, as if the liquid of her emotions, striking this electrically charged advice, were capable of conducting a shock. She whisked the envelope away, onto the heap her frenzied actions had created. Sobbing, she crawled blindly out of the closet and dragged herself onto the bed, where she fell back on the hard box spring. Her head bounced a few times to the rhythm of her deep shudders, before her body settled there, trembling with shame. Even in her absence, Mama Joon had found a way to humiliate her.

Clarissa wallowed there until she felt embalmed with the vice her mother's blatant efficiency showcased in her: sloth. If only to counter the accusation of sluggishness and immobility, she bolted upright and stared at the mess she had made. Cleaning it up would be her first task, a rebuttal to Mama Joon's now posthumous charge that she was lazy. It's all trash, she thought. She was being trashed by trash. A dead woman's debtlessness. What could be more worthless than that! She would bundle it all up and throw it away. But then what? She didn't know. One thing at a time. The important thing was to *do something.* Surely doing something, *anything,* was the only way to defeat the legacy of Mama Joon.

As she sat there trying to will herself to move—but not moving—the box spring began to irritate her. When she reached down to rub away some of the discomfort, her hand, instead of touching the synthetic fabric of her dress, slid across the sharp edge of a folded sheet of paper.

"Ow!" she yelled with surprise and pain, for the paper had cut her middle finger like a blade.

Looking down, she saw a red droplet ballooning at the tip of her finger, and she brought it to her mouth and sucked away the blood. Then she rolled over a little onto her left hip and dislodged the offending object.

Upon closer inspection, she saw there were in fact three pages of old copy paper folded together. They must have been pure white once, but they had darkened, grayed, perhaps on their way to acquiring the taupe of the mattresses they had been sandwiched between for who knew how long. She unfolded the pages and flattened their creases. Then she read the date at the top of the first page—*February 14, 1980*—which chilled her, for it was a date she had envied since the world had ticked it into being. Alicia's birthday. Valentine's Day. Even love was her birthright. The offending date, like the rest of the letter—it was obviously a letter, not some ultra-important financial document that warranted concealment, say a big bank statement or a deed—was inked in blue in an authoritative, masculine script. Though written in a hand unknown to her, its meaning streamed forth to Clarissa with a remarkable lucidity, lending it an air of inevitability and the veneer of truth.

My Dearest June:

She is even more beautiful than I dreamed she would be. I did not believe I could ever know such happiness, such joy, such hope! What is it about a daughter that gives a father such a feeling of completeness? I've been contemplating that all evening. I suppose he feels the possibility that all of his inadequacies might be refuted by her perfection. All of his filth might be expunged by her relative purity. I think a man looks upon a daughter and senses that the scales of his life, so imbalanced by the weight of masculine imperfection, might be righted by the gravity of her feminine grace. It's the judge in me talking, perhaps. It seems the only poetry I can muster is rank with the prose of my profession—but there it is. We are who we are. A boy can't give a father that. Only a daughter. And I love my boy. You know I do. But this one, this one, whom you say you'll call Alicia, after the girl in Wonderland, will lighten the load of my life, and of yours, too, I suspect. She will make everything all right. We must cherish her. Lavish her with comfort. A fine home. Everything she needs. I will see to that, for in some way, my life depends upon it. Upon her. Whatever salvation there is for me, for you, too—for us!—shall somehow pass through her. Because of her, the grave looks less grave.

Do you know what I mean? The other one—she could not do that for us. Conceived while Martha was still alive, while you and I were conspiring to deceive, committing crimes we thought would have no punishment, the spiritual felony of infidelity—she was not marked with grace, could not be. If anything, she was destined to bear the stain of our betrayal. She was the scar of our treachery. The embodiment of our unfaithfulness—unholiness. You and I both knew that—even if we were powerless to stop ourselves. As a result, she is shrouded in darkness. How could I ever embrace that? How could you ever, really? We're not those kinds of people. We're better than that. To embrace that child fully would have been to cling to what was wrong with our love, to submit to its darker implications—to accept our transgression, celebrate our sin.

Is that just the judge in me being judgmental? Maybe so, but I always knew instinctively she would be as tainted as the circumstances of her creation. And the proof is in the person. Just look at her. Her selfishness, her gluttony. The daughter of desire—illicit desire—she will always want things she should not have. Things that rightfully belong to others. Things that make her fat. Things that make her mean. In the end, maybe no crime goes unpunished, even a crime of the heart. Maybe she is our punishment. I must say, to look at her, the few times I have, has been to feel indicted. To feel on trial. To feel pronounced guilty as charged. To feel imprisoned by regret. Your bravery and generosity in raising her have only strengthened my admiration for you. I could not have endured the constant presence of my accuser. I could not have fed my prosecutor. I could not have nurtured the judge, jury, and jailor of my soul! (Bless you, June, for your sacrifice. No doubt, for this you shall be rewarded.)

Which makes the birth of Alicia all the more important! I have found that when in life, as in a court of law, one is presented with compelling evidence, it's important to acknowledge it and to let it guide you to the truth. It is as if, upon appeal, the original verdict in our case—Dumas and Ramsey v. The United States of Passion—has at long last been overturned. In Alicia—born on this sweet day, as if a sign of her meaning—we have a tribute to our love, not a symbol of our sin. As evidence goes, the date is perhaps circumstantial, but Alicia's being is direct; she is the absolute proof of our love. Love absolves! Love expunges! Alicia is the proclamation of our innocence!

And, of course, I have you to thank for her—you, who might have lived a different life, a far better life than you've probably admitted to yourself, but for being tasked with loving the likes of me. Thank you! Thank you! Thank you! Today, for the first time in many years, I feel clean, I feel just, I feel free!

Love,

Manny

It was as if Clarissa, at the age of forty-nine, was staring into a mirror and seeing, for the very first time, its true response to her. Before, what she'd seen had been misted with secrecy. Her real reflection—she knew this now for sure—had been obscured behind the fog of all she didn't know about herself. Oh, the outline of her face, the outline of *her*, had been there and, looking at only a shadowy likeness, she had even been able to pretend she didn't feel ugly inside. Maybe, she had sometimes told herself, the *her* she didn't know was actually beautiful. Maybe what was hidden from her and the world was a beauty. Maybe one day that would be revealed to her, ridding her of self-doubt. But every line of the letter was like the swipe of a hand removing mist from the mirror. Now she saw herself whole, her silhouette filled in with the textures of specificity, the garish colors and jagged edges of the truth. As she had madly searched through her mother's things, mere greed had seemed her motivation, but she had really been looking for her own beauty, for "evidence," to use her father's word, of her own worth. What she had found instead was her singularity, the thing that made her special. But no—it wasn't pretty; neither was she. Yet there she was. There *it* was: the portrait of someone too grisly to look at—or, so it was written, to love. Not who she was necessarily meant to be, but the improbably horrid thing that had been made of her.

"Okay," she mumbled, folding the letter and tossing it back where she'd found it, thinking that as good a place as any for it to remain buried. *Fine!* If beauty and love were Alicia's birthright, then ugliness and hatred would be hers.

Charged with the acceptance of her fate, she got up and muscled the top mattress back onto the bed. After hastily and sloppily making the bed, she gathered the clothes, bills, and boxes, flung and shoved them all into the closet, and shut the door. As she was walking out of the room, she stepped on the twenty-dollar bill she had found under the mattress. She picked it up and casually fanned her face with it. This simple, wristy motion engendered in her the illusion of composure, softening for the moment her hardened heart. Heading down the hall on her way out, she could almost be said to have been sauntering. Sustaining this act, she opened Ramadan's door, flounced into his room, and extended the twenty to him.

"Here you go," she said sweetly.

"What's that for?" he asked.

"I found it in Mama Joon's room. I'm sure she'd want you to have it."

Ramadan shook his head and went back to his studies. Clarissa dropped the money at the foot of his bed and hurried out. He glanced at the bill and saw the portrait of a frizzy-haired Andrew Jackson. Picking it up, he noticed a striking resemblance between the warrior president and the heavy-breathing Clarissa. The chaotic masses of hair swirling wildly on both their heads were remarkably similar. But the brooding brows were more concerning, poignant even, framing a sadness in their eyes as they stared off at something troubling or frightening only they could see. They both looked like they needed a hug.

When Clarissa had given the money to Ramadan, it reminded her of the time she had not picked up the crying Alicia, but then went back later to console her. Here she was doing it again, not being the bad person her instincts sometimes begged her to be, someone who would deny care but then give it, someone who intended to take what she could from its rightful owner, actually taking it—but then giving it back, correcting the error of her ways. When push came to shove, she could sometimes give the world what it wanted from her, what it wanted from itself, really, the pretense of goodness.

She did feel bad, of course. But by the time she exited the front door, she had recovered, regained her fury, and was feeling bad—but in a good way. As in *bad-ass*. When family let you down, rejected you, you had to get in where you fit in. If her boys, like millions of other afterthoughts, could find their humanity in the hound and be self-proclaimed, forthright dawgs, then she could be a bad-ass bitch in what must be a long line of bad-ass bitches. Some ancient lineage, a mongrelized Amazonian race of wounded, castaway women forced to make a way when there wasn't one.

They took everything from her, now something's gotta give!
She had to lose it all before she learned how to win!
She's a bad mother—shut your mouth!

So *what* if the climax of her life story was just a pithy Blaxploitation tagline. So what! If somebody was going to play you in a movie, you could do a whole lot worse than Pam Grier. At least Clarissa was still here. Mama Joon wasn't. Alicia wasn't. Her ever-*hating* daddy, whoever he was, *wasn't*, and he never had been here! Not for her, anyway. *She* was here, planted in this place, in this time, knee-deep in the mess that was her life. Her existence counted for something, and she was determined to make the most of it. Everybody else would just have to get over themselves—and they'd better watch their backs.

A propulsive instrumental buoyed her thoughts. Okay, so no—maybe she *wasn't* the mama now. Maybe she never would be. Maybe she wasn't cut out to be a mother at all. What was motherhood, anyway, if Mama Joon was the measure? Mama Joon, who most people considered the mother of their dreams—but who had made of Clarissa this nightmare.

No, she thought. *I'm not the mama now. Just like my no-count daddy never was the daddy. I'm the bitch who bred a bunch of dawgs. I'm not the mama. But I'm a bad muthafucka!*

She stood on the porch and closed her eyes to the vision of her new self, a woman whose father had written her off, but whose name was now—she could see it—writ large:

10

THE DISAPPEARANCE OF RAMADAN RAMSEY

When it happened, only a week later, Ramadan was on the front porch in the same spot where hopelessness had electrified Clarissa into an action-movie heroine in her mind. Some sites, by design or destiny, which may be the same thing, solicit arrows of energy, torrents of it, like lightning rods or any place nicknamed "Tornado Alley." Suffice it to say, when fortune, good or bad, ordinary or outrageous, sets its sights on you and/or the place you're standing, there's no eluding its aim.

The sound of a brass band coming down St. Philip Street drew Ramadan and his cousins out of the house.

"It's that second line for Mr. Rock," Damon said when they first heard the trilling and thumping of various instruments, as he, Romeo, Julius, and Ramadan all sat in the living room playing video games.

Mr. Rock was a beloved neighborhood tuba player who had recently died. A huge, round man, whose silver horn fit him snugly, like a suit of armor or a metallic hoodie, he would walk up and down St. Philip Street, going back and forth between his house and Jackson Square, where he busked. Mama Joon had liked him, and Ramadan thought about how, if she were alive, she would have cooked something and brought it around the corner to Miss Eunice, his wife, for the repast. She used to joke about his rotundity. "Big as a boulder, really. But 'Mr. Boulder' ain't got no kinda ring to it." So Mr. Rock it was. Had been.

"Let's go, y'all!" Damon said, when they heard the music getting closer. "Come on, Ramadan. You know you like second lines. We can watch from the porch."

Damon led the way, followed by Romeo and Julius. None of them usually moved very fast, especially when, as now, they were puffing on marijuana.

"Damn!" Romeo said, rising, his head dipping into a smoky shroud of his own making. "Already? This nonsense 'bout to blow my high before it's even a high." As he moved toward the door, he passed the joint behind him to his identical twin like a baton in a relay.

"Say, dawg," Julius said. "At least you got a hit." Without breaking stride, he expertly pinched the joint, elbowed it up to his purplish, puckered lips, and inhaled deeply. Before taking a step, he released a spasm of coughs. Ramadan smiled as he watched their comic interplay. They were fifteen years his senior and should have been more like uncles to him than cousins. But no. Lean and naturally muscular, they looked and behaved like terminal teenagers. Ramadan, maturing quickly in every way, felt like their contemporary.

Romeo and Julius—as bound together in real life as their namesakes were in fiction. Ramadan had rarely seen one without the other, which was always like seeing double. They wore the same clothes and sported the same haircuts at all times. Lately, tight, nappy twists all over their heads; black T-shirts and jeans, attire that flattered their burnished gold skin. There was something romantic about their alliance. They were as committed to each other as any married couple, as if they had whispered an in utero vow they were powerless to break. Their routine matching silhouettes were like silent soliloquies, daily professions of solidarity. True soul mates, they were linked by one of the few things more passionate than poetry, more powerful than story—genetics. Shakespeare would have approved: a pair whose destiny was more indelible than any even he could compose, for it was written in the blood. And like his star-crossed lovers, they, too, would have died for each other. Unlike them, perhaps, they would have also killed.

Witnessing their rapport, Ramadan wondered what that was like. Always having someone to help balance things out, have your back, pass you the joint. It was clear to him that his twin cousins, who had had years to welcome him into their inner circle, would never do so. He even resembled them. He had the same dark hair (but his would probably never dread). Plus his skin was just a shade lighter—he was wearing a white T-shirt tonight, but he also looked great in all black. Far from begrudgingly accepting him as their cousin, shouldn't they really have embraced him as their little brother?

Damon stopped abruptly at the door, and the twins, attending to their highs, kept moving forward and bumped into him. "Damn, D, sorry," Romeo said. Julius mumbled a similar apology.

"Don't be sorry. Just wake up and stop being stupid! And open your droopy-ass eyes, if you know what's good for you."

Ramadan watched the impromptu huddle, which seemed to have turned more serious than necessary. The twins made exaggerated efforts to raise their eyelids.

"We good, D," Romeo said.

"Yeah, we good," Julius said.

"Y'all better be," Damon said. "Now let's roll. No—hold up." He

smiled at Ramadan, looked at Romeo, who had the joint, and indicated
that he should pass it to their little cousin.

Romeo took a quick puff and extended his hand through a patch of
cumulus. The generosity took Ramadan by surprise, and he said, to no
one in particular, "Me?"

"Yeah, you," Damon said. "Live a little!"

As Ramadan reached for the joint, the long-awaited thrill of being
invited into the Ramsey fraternity flushed through him, and he saw what
looked like pride come over his cousins as he brought the damp tip of
the joint to his lips and inhaled the way he had seen them do so many
times. The smell of burning herb, generated for the first time by his
force, and closer to his face than ever before, was warmer and sweeter
than usual. More intoxicating, too, of course—but not as intoxicating
as the feeling that he was, at last, being initiated into his own family.
In the rising swoon, the headiness of that first hit, he reveled in the
suspension of his loneliness. He held the smoke a full five seconds, not
wanting to release it, preferring to asphyxiate on the vapors of acceptance, for he was afraid that when he exhaled, this kinship might end.

When he finally blew the smoke out, he was laughing, as were his
cousins. He couldn't tell if they were laughing with him or at him, but
with his high ascending, it didn't really matter.

Damon took the joint, and then he flipped up the porch light
switch, setting the pale, yellow curtains on the front window aglow.
He opened the front door to the celebratory sounds of the brass band
and the mass of second liners dancing up the street. Romeo and Julius
went out first, shuffling their way to the far left, Clarissa's side of the
porch. Damon stepped to the right and held the screen door open for
Ramadan.

The light from the naked bulb above the doorway, set against the blackness of the night, momentarily blinded Ramadan, who was also adjusting to the effects of the marijuana. He closed his eyes to relieve the harshness of the glare, but the music, more seductive than ever, was his guide. Drumbeats came to him as a pulse, as if the parade were something large and incarnate. He was always a little afraid at first, but then he let it take him by the hand. And he stepped forward, ushered into the presence of this living, breathing thing that promised, as always, to feed his spirit by devouring him whole.

He would later recall, in nightmares that replayed the memory, the shots that rang out sounding like some off-kilter, syncopated drum riff. Not truly sinister. But somehow indicative of a mood change—things going from brightness and revelry to darkness and menace, the rhythmic equivalent of a minor chord. You could have danced to this weird cadence, if the rat-a-tat-tats had followed more of a pattern, if they had repeated themselves with any predictability, if they made sense—and if they hadn't ultimately turned *him* into a cymbal or a snare, the thing that gets hit to create the big finish.

Stepping onto the porch, Ramadan had just raised his arms to strut to the funked-up version of "Lil Liza Jane" the band was playing as it reached the front of the house surrounded by more than a hundred people bouncing along, all for Mr. Rock. But before he could snap his fingers, he felt the sharp sting of the bullet piercing his left arm, its heat burrowing into his flesh near the top of his shoulder.

The surprise and force of the shot spun him around and, surely, to a few who saw him he must have looked like a boy dancing to the music with a balletic flair. The bulb streaked down on him like a spotlight, adding showmanship to his freakish pirouette. But his jerky motions didn't look anything like choreography to most—certainly not to anyone near the dark alley next to the abandoned, vine-suffocated house across the street from which the gunshots had rung out. And not to anyone who recognized the telltale sounds of run-of-the-mill, run-for-your-life street violence, those who knew the difference between avant-garde music and mayhem. To them, Ramadan's gyrations looked like exactly what they were: a slow drag with death.

The crowd began shrieking and scattering in waves. Those far enough from the band to make out the sound of gunfire had started yelling and running first. Seconds later, the chain reaction of fear spread to the next layer of revelers, whose retreat prompted those in front of them and so on. In less than fifteen seconds, the entire street had cleared. The thrum of escaping masses, huffing and chatter, whistling and scared laughter, echoed through the neighborhood with a musicality of its own, a choir, a Ghetto Chorus, improvising a denouement to disaster. The whining counterpoint of police sirens blew in, pianissimo at first but building fast. Finally, the whole moody, operatic composition introduced its diva, as Clarissa thundered onto the porch with a dramatic, what's-all-this-commotion-about air, almost slamming her screen door into the twins. Then she took a couple of steps through droplets of her nephew's blood. She nearly slipped and fell, but Damon caught her—and she looked down and saw Ramadan splayed across the steps. His left foot was hanging over the edge of the bottom step, toes an inch from the ground. He was lying on his stomach, and his wound was seeping, soaking his white T-shirt with rivulets of red.

"Ramadaaaaan!!!" Clarissa screamed. "Ramadaaaaan!!!"

Romeo and Julius rushed from their corner toward the steps.

"Don't touch him!" she yelled, thrusting her arms out, clotheslining the twins back against the house. "Don't touch that baby!"

And she screamed his name again.

Some of the second liners, the threat of imminent danger having passed, crept back to the scene. A caravan of police cars glided down St. Philip Street, streaking the night sky with red and blue flashes of lightning, like the approach of a wicked storm or an otherworldly dawn.

Through his withering consciousness, Ramadan heard Clarissa's cries. He managed to open his eyes, and the last thing he saw was his upturned left palm pooling with his own blood. As his eyelids shut, he strained to make a fist, thinking, irrationally perhaps, that if he could keep his blood clinched there, he would somehow save his life.

Later, in the emergency room, when one of the nurses pried his hand open while prepping him for surgery, the fistful of blood was still there, only now it was as thick as Mama Joon's roux.

⚶

"AS LONG AS he alive, we gon' be dead broke."

Two weeks later, Ramadan was lying on the living room sofa waking up from a nap. His recovery would be quick, the doctors had said. *You're a lucky boy. When this is over, you'll be a brand-new you. You'll see. Just take your meds.* Antibiotics, painkillers. The latter always put him to sleep. Whenever he woke up, as now, he was never quite sure he wasn't still dreaming.

"I know."

"I know you know."

Two similar voices penetrated his grogginess. Where were they coming from? The other side of whatever divided slumber from consciousness, or from the other side of the living room wall?

"I think we gotta wait awhile before we try again."

No, he wasn't dreaming—and the voices, he realized, belonged to Romeo and Julius, who were out on the front porch. In actual distance, only a couple of feet away. He propped himself up on his good arm and leaned toward the window.

"How come? Let's just get it over with. Wait awhile? Nigga, we broke *now!*"

"Say, dawg, just think for a second. Dude git shot at a second line, that's normal. Happens all the time. Nothing strange about it. Dude git shot, then what, git shot *again*, or you know, just up and disappears. Niggas got bad luck, but not *that* bad. Now what's that gon' look like?"

"Straight-up foul play!"

"Foul play? I'm talkin' *flagrant* foul."

"Mmm, hmm. A upon-further-review, big-ass-fine-from-the-commissioner *flagrant-ass foul!*"

"Thank you!"

The voices joined in a round of laughter.

When that subsided, Ramadan heard the hiss of a long inhalation, and he knew his cousins were sharing a joint as they plotted his murder. Getting high as they sank to a new low.

"How long we gotta wait, then?"

"I'ma say . . . a few months."

"A few months? Fool, last time I checked, your pockets was empty as mine. We got a whole gotdam ATM machine right here on the premises, and the PIN number is real simple: P-O-W . . . *pow!*"

Through a giggling high, the other voice said, "Okay, then not a few months. Call it, like, I don't know, three."

"What, three ain't a few no mo'? When that happened?"

"Bruh, four and five is a few."

"Four and five is several, muthafucka! Three is a few!"

"Aw, shit. I think you right."

"I *am* right. We don't need to wait nothing but a couple of months anyway."

"Right, right . . . and a couple . . ."

". . . is *two!*"

"True dat. Like me and you. Two months. Perfect."

"Two."

"Let's go tell Mama we figured it out."

"Nah, nah. She say she don't want to know nothing about it this time. Just get it done, and she'll take care of everything else."

"Ah!" Ramadan gasped. During his crisis, Clarissa had assiduously, *earnestly*, so he thought, played the mama role: screaming out on the porch; holding his head until the ambulance arrived; staying with him at the hospital; setting him up at home; bringing his meals (including, last week, a little store-bought chocolate cake for the gloomiest birthday he'd ever had); making sure he took his meds; changing his bandages; *telling him everything was going to be all right!* His aunt Clarissa? His caregiver? As the montage of kindly acts flickered through his mind, what he'd just heard pierced his being, as if he'd been shot again, by a bullet with a better aim.

"No!" he said.

"What was that?" one twin asked.

"What was *what?*" asked the other.

Ramadan clasped his hands over his mouth. The muscles in his still healing left shoulder ached from the sudden movement, and he grimaced. He slid his right hand from his mouth and massaged his wound. Quieting his hurt, his hurts, he buried his whimpers in the back of his throat.

"I thought I heard something."

"Uh, maybe it was just the wind blowing some damn money your way. You ain't heard that in so long your stupid ass forgot what it sounds like!"

He heard the twins laughing again. "Two months," one of them said.

"Two," the other responded. "Like me and you."

Ramadan pressed his face into the sofa cushions, wrapped his arms around himself, and wept in silence, trembling with disbelief.

"Let the countdown begin."

"Let the countdown begin..."

THAT NIGHT, SLEEP anesthetized him from his aches and anxiety. He dreamed of his tarot card, the red-robed magician surrounded by weapons of survival. He didn't believe in the supernatural, and Mama Joon's death had shaken his faith in religion. (Never mind that as he slept, he rubbed his mother's crucifix.) Mama Joon had prayed; she had died. *He* had prayed; she had died. But when he thought back to the encounter with Miss Bea, he felt drawn to her way with the truth, however dark. He remembered the subtleties of Mama Joon's reading, which he knew now had acknowledged her sickness. Maybe some progressions of events—like cards turning over in a certain succession on a fortune-teller's table—set things in motion. Or tell you what will happen—*unless* something else happens. Unless you do something. Like catch your lucky card before it hits the ground. No amount of praying would stop his family. He would have to *do* something, something as different from prayer as he could imagine. His slumber was a mix of rest, deliberation, and resolve. The next morning, he didn't have all the answers but, armed with a supreme confidence—maybe you could call it faith, after all—he woke up believing he could save himself.

Like many citizens of the stupendously vulnerable community in which he lived, Ramadan was wired with a particular kind of survival instinct. It did not, primarily, involve the police or authorities of any kind. Besides, if he called the police, what would he tell them? He had no evidence. Muted voices heard through his drug-induced haze. And if the police did for some reason believe him and could find proof to his claim, what would happen to his family? He didn't really want to hurt Romeo and Julius, or his aunt Clarissa, for that matter. He had always felt a complicated affection for them. Much more complicated now. He wanted a solution that, instead of dooming them, would somehow save them, too. From their recklessness. From themselves.

Mama Joon's words came back to him now . . .

The next time a storm is coming—and believe me a storm is gonna come—you get on the first thing smoking and worry 'bout the rest later, you hear me? . . . and then come back when the coast is clear. Or—or never!

And he knew what he had to do—an evacuation was in order.

He pulled the small black suitcase Mama Joon had bought him from under his bed and began picking through the clothes in his closet and dresser. With evacuations, you never knew how long you'd be gone. Could be a day. Could be a week. Could be longer. Some people had *never* come back after the storm. But the optimist in him said, "Pack light." He folded two pairs of jeans, one blue, one black, and tossed them into the suitcase, along with about a week's worth of white briefs, T-shirts, and socks.

While on his knees in his closet rummaging through his sneakers, he came across the old laptop he had taken years ago from the Quicky

Mart. He hadn't touched it since before Mama Joon died, but today he couldn't resist. Snapping it open, he revealed the letter tucked inside; he'd forgotten it was in there. Moments later, staring at the screen, at Aleppo, his old boyhood passion flared up again. He liked to tell himself he wasn't that little kid anymore, the one crazed with longing. But with Mama Joon gone, and his only known relatives out to get him, he felt his heart regressing, aching with boyish need. He picked up the envelope, looking at the front first, and then at the return address on the back. Aleppo: 6,722 miles away.

He remembered talking to Mama Joon about going there. Yes, there was a war going on in Syria. Damascus, certainly. But not Aleppo yet. Still, it was clear from the news that the country, except for the mad or the brave, was off limits.

But . . . Istanbul wasn't. Only 6,175 miles away.

Turkey? Ha—You say "turkey" to me and I start preheating the oven!

She was whispering through his memory, nudging him out of his duress, just the two of them watching the ships come in and head out.

No. Like the Ottoman Empire, he had told her.

You say "ottoman" to me and I wanna put my feet up!

Soon he was stretched out on his closet floor, writhing with laughter on a bed of Reeboks and Nikes.

Only after he composed himself did he realize that, like the Magician, he had everything he needed. Money. A passport. An iPhone. An idea . . .

Everything he needed to make himself disappear.

Two months, he had heard his cousins conclude, was the time required to deflect suspicion of their intended crime. Ramadan started a countdown of his own. As advance warnings go, two months was an eternity. He would need only two days.

AS HE GOOGLED, clicked, and white-lied his way to and through the Delta Airlines online ticket-purchasing process—there were, indeed, no flights to Syria, so Istanbul it was—he learned that, because of his age, he would need the assistance of an adult. Someone would have to show up with him at the airport, according to the information posted under the airline's "Unaccompanied Minor Program." Pretending to be fifteen years old allowed him to buy the tickets (New Orleans to Atlanta, from there to Istanbul) with his American Express card, but if anyone at the airport bothered to read the birth date on his passport, he would be exposed as underage. He needed an adult to check him in and send him on his way. Of course, that wasn't Clarissa or any other Ramsey. Mr. Willie, the lawyer in charge of his finances, would never agree to his leaving the city alone, much less the country—plus he would ask too many questions anyway. Ramadan's independence would become as endangered as his life. Mama Joon's secession plan, as messy and tenuous as it had proven, had given him the thrill of autonomy. His entire life was one magnificent "Unaccompanied Minor Program"—and he was not willing to relinquish that, at least not without testing the limits of his freedom. He would probably wind up a regular kid again, once Mr. Willie saw the credit card bill next month. But by then he would be long gone. Maybe already back. Or maybe—who knew—gone for good.

No—there was only one person he could think of who would understand the wild adventure he was envisioning. Only one person he knew who believed he had both the imagination and the power to do whatever he wanted to do. Only one *adult* who would encourage him and maybe help him go through with it.

Just after six thirty that evening, he tucked his packed suitcase under his bed and left the house. Standing on the porch, he paused. He hadn't been out here since returning home from the hospital. Looking down at the place where two weeks before he had lain injured, unaware of having been betrayed, he took a deep breath. Then he tiptoed down the right edge of the first steps avoiding the illusory outline of his own crumpled form. But then, thinking better of this careful descent, which struck him as cowardly, he decided to skip the three lowest steps altogether and leaped to the ground. The landing jolted him a bit, but being airborne had felt like a little prelude to tomorrow—flight. He gathered his footing and jogged into the French Quarter.

At the St. Ann Street corner of Jackson Square, spent from eight blocks of running, he leaned against a lamppost in the shade of the Presbytère building, letting his pulse settle. The cathedral bells intoned the three-quarter hour, and his body relaxed into that moment's dual feeling of calm and anticipation, his ambitions synchronizing with the most sacred sounds of the city.

When he stepped into the square, Miss Bea's back was to him. Her day's work was coming to an end, and he watched her through the shadowy movements of the passersby as she gathered her things—a block of amethyst, two small votive candles, and her cards. She placed these items in a black canvas tote bag, whose side was adorned with a golden winged lion holding a book, and the word *Venezia*. When she picked the bag up and placed it in her chair to finish her load-out, Ramadan recognized the building depicted on the other side of the tote. Even if *Roma* hadn't been printed below it, he would have known it was the Colosseum. Seeing her bag emblazoned as it was with the markings of travel made him think she might be more sympathetic to his cause than he'd dare hope. Encouraged, he walked toward her, dodging a hand-holding, middle-aged couple in matching Alabama Crimson Tide football gear, tipsy with a tourism to which he aspired.

Still not facing him, Miss Bea was about to remove the cloth draping her little folding table, when she suddenly stopped moving. Maybe it was the breeze rustling the banana leaves that alerted her. Or maybe some inexplicably keener sense of smell, or hearing, or *knowing*. Are there logical explanations for mysticism? Is all magic—like the perplexity of life itself—just a science the world has yet to decode? Whatever the mechanism of her divination, the fortune-teller was compelled to stop what she was doing and then, after a pause, stand up straight, her spine stiffening as Ramadan got nearer. He was only a few feet from her when, with a flourish, she whirled around.

"I've been waiting for you!" she said. "I knew you'd come back to me."

She removed the bag from her chair, sat down, and waved him over with both hands. Ramadan had not known what he would say to her, but Miss Bea's greeting him this way relaxed him. He rushed to the table and sat down. "You knew?"

Her smile melted and her eyes went moist, as if she'd been spritzed like an orchid. "How's your shoulder?"

"Oh, it's—" He stopped and gave her a quizzical look. "How'd you . . . ?"

She reached into her tote bag, pulled out the front-page coverage of his shooting, and placed it on the table. 12-YEAR-OLD SHOT AT PARADE, the headline reported. "You're the only Ramadan I know," she said.

Touching the newspaper with her finger, she said, "This thing tells the past. I tell the future. Not to judge—we all have a job to do."

"I wasn't twelve yet," he corrected the headline, rubbing his shoulder even though it wasn't hurting him. "But now I am." After a pause, he said, "Mama Joon is gone."

"Yes, well . . . not really," Miss Bea said. "I bet you hear her voice all the time."

Remembering sitting with her in his closet last night, he smiled.

"See!" Miss Bea said. "Just as I suspected."

He pulled out his phone and looked at the background image, the photo he had taken of them in the cathedral. "So I'll always have her with me?"

"Of course."

"I believe you. But the problem is, I don't think she can help me now."

Miss Bea said, "Help? You need help?"

He looked away but immediately felt the fortune-teller's hand on his chin guiding his face back to her. She leaned in, and Ramadan blinked from the pressure of her stare. Then she released him and leaned back in her chair. "So—this is all about what happened to you, isn't it?"

"Mmm hmm."

"Do you want to tell me about it?"

"Yeah. But I—" He couldn't tell her what he knew about his shooting any more than he could tell the cops. He'd have to implicate his family. His telling wouldn't be as dishonorable as what they'd done to him—and were still planning to do—but he didn't like the way even thinking about tattling made him feel. Then he looked back at the big middle steeple of the cathedral, and he felt certain there was no future in that either. He scrunched his face. For a few agonized seconds, he considered Miss Bea's powers and, turning back to her, he asked, "Can't you guess, Miss Bea?"

She looked at the newspaper headline haunting her table, then into his eyes, and she spoke his truth, as, for a seasoned soothsayer, reading this twelve-year-old's mind was simply child's play.

"You're afraid it's going to happen again."

"Yes!" he yelled. "Yes!" Miss Bea was now a prophet—it wouldn't have surprised him if she had proceeded to call Romeo and Julius by their names. Maybe it was his youth that left him so vulnerable to her charms, or maybe just desperation.

She sighed, basking in the fruits of her grand empathy. He needn't know her secrets. The real trick of her trade. He hadn't yet learned—most never do—that if you care enough about people, you can read the human heart.

"It *is* going to happen again," he said. "Unless . . ."

She sighed and leaned toward him again. "What kind of help do you need?"

"I have to get away. It's dangerous here."

"It's dangerous everywhere, Ramadan—but you already know that."

"Yes. But when you know a storm is coming, you have to evacuate."

Miss Bea raised her hands up and said, "Preach!"

Ramadan picked up his phone and showed his itinerary to Miss Bea, explaining what he needed her to do. When he was finished, she looked at him and said, "That's it?"

"That's it."

"It's so easy. Anyone could do it, really. Just . . . *leave*." Her tone had turned wistful. Was Miss Bea, he wondered, filled with some longing of her own? Was, as she had just implied, everyone?

He asked, "Do you—do you want to come with me?"

"Oh, no! My traveling days are over. Besides, who would feed my cats? No, I have to stay here. That way, you'll know you have someone waiting for you when you come back home."

"Miss Bea, *will* I come back home?"

"You know, Ramadan, I'm not so sure we ever *really* leave."

Dear Aunt Clarissa,

I know everything.

I'm not afraid but I'm going away for a while. Far away. Please bring in the mail. If you see a letter from school, open it. If I miss the beginning of school, make up an excuse for me. Tell them I'm still recovering. Something like that. That really is the truth. If they call, cover up for me. Cry to make sure they believe you. You know how to do that. If Mr. Willie asks about me, tell him I am ok. Lie. You know how to do that too.

I think my phone will work. Mama Joon always knew I would travel. She took care of everything. Almost. But don't call me. When I get back, you and ~~me~~ I will talk.

Now I have something to tell you. Something I never told you. Something I never told anybody. Not even Mama Joon. She knew. But not like this. I still remember the day you told me about my daddy. Remember that? The day before the storm. That was a big day for me. I'm sorry about the way I acted when you told me. I threw a big fit. Remember? I wasn't mad at you. I was mad at the world. Mad at not knowing who my daddy was. Who he is. But I was happy at the same time because all of sudden it was like I knew he was real. I guess I knew he was before then, but crazy as it seems, I didn't really know. It's hard to explain. I mean, do you know your daddy? Anyway, half of me was kind of dead before that day. Dead as whoever shot me wanted me to be. But when you told me about my daddy, the dead part of me woke up. To tell you the truth, I don't have too many memories before that day. That's why I had a fit. I was like a newborn baby. You know how they come out crying. Mad *at the world because it's strange. But happy to be out of the dark. That was me that day.*

Nobody had ever told me about my daddy. But you did. You. And I never thanked you for that. So THANK YOU! Thank you for making me feel alive!

Love,
Ramadan

He was folding the note and writing Clarissa's name on the outside when it occurred to him he had something important to ask her. He unfolded the note and wrote:

P.S. When you get this, text me my daddy's name. Just that. If you don't know it, then don't send me anything.

❧

IT WAS ALMOST five a.m. when Ramadan turned off the porch light and crept out of his front door. He was clutching his suitcase and strapped with his backpack, which was filled with a few toiletries, an extra T-shirt, and the letter from Aleppo. He tiptoed to Clarissa's side of the house and placed the note in her mailbox. To avoid the risk of waking anyone up, he had told Miss Bea to pick him up a block and a half away, at the corner of St. Philip and Rampart. He could see the intersection from the porch, and when he spotted the old red Volvo station wagon she had described coast by and veer to the right, he jumped off the porch and ran down the street. He almost turned to look back at the house, just in case he never made it home, but he decided what was in front of him was more captivating.

"Good morning, Ramadan!" Miss Bea said as he scooted into the front seat. "You got everything?"

"I think so." He didn't bother to remove his backpack, and he slid his suitcase onto his lap.

She was about to tell him he could put his gear on the backseat, but she could see having his belongings in his possession was giving him a sense of security. "Okay, here we go," she said, pulling off.

They rode along the quiet streets listening to National Public Radio's *Morning Edition*. Miss Bea shook her head and sucked her teeth, as the show offered updates on the big news story of the day, the Syrian Civil War, detailing casualties and the mounting chaos in Damascus. Thinking Ramadan, still so close to his own episode, would be agitated by hearing about violence and bloodshed, she reached for the dial. "Maybe some music would be better."

"No!" Ramadan yelled. "It's about my people."

"Your people?"

"My father is from there."

"From Syria?"

"Yes."

They looped onto the interstate, cruising to the airport. Her eyes darted from the road to Ramadan, sneaking glances at him listening to the stories of rebellion and roadside bombs. When a reporter said, "*Yesterday another fifteen hundred Syrians fled their homeland. Seeking refuge, they crossed the border into Turkey on foot,*" she said, "I see."

So now she understood Ramadan's venture more fully: he wasn't just running away from something—he was running *toward* something. How had she not figured that out? Ramadan had made his spiritual inclinations clear the first day they met, when he had pronounced the big steeple of St. Louis Cathedral as the future. Though she looked up at that central conical, architectural wonder every day, she had never drawn that conclusion. If anything, like most people, ensnared by the here and now, she thought it was the mighty present. But Ramadan knew better—at least for himself. She knew this much: a boy who could look up at the highest point of a church and see his future was blessed. *Ramadan was blessed.* There. She'd said it. If nobody else knew it, she did. Yes, this was the reason she knew everything was going to be okay. Sometimes messages came to her like this, from wherever—she couldn't help it. In the past tense. As if written somewhere long ago. Already recorded. There was no taking it away, no making it untrue: *Ramadan was blessed.*

And now, with her help, he was about to jet into his tomorrow. She gripped the steering wheel tighter and sped toward Louis Armstrong International, hitting almost eighty miles an hour, her aging Volvo wagon trembling in its eagerness to satisfy an urgency rarely demanded of it. Focused and determined, Miss Bea drove as if, without her best effort, a prophesy would go unfulfilled.

⚜

AT THE AIRPORT, as she watched Ramadan walk up to the kiosk in the Delta terminal and print out his ticket, she found herself repeating, in amazement, the same thing she had said to him yesterday when he presented his plan: *It's so easy.* Then again, when the helpful, unsuspecting Delta agents assisted her with filling out the "Unaccompanied Minor Program" form authorizing Ramadan to travel alone. *It's so easy.*

"'Scuse me, ma'am?" one asked.

"Nothing," she responded. "Nothing at all."

She was a woman who in many ways believed in magic, yet she had never witnessed anything more convincing than watching this child tap his phone and press buttons on the freestanding machine that spat out his boarding passes. She had never felt the power of the pen she experienced when the inky scribble of her own signature on the authorization form liberated Ramadan from the shackles of childhood. (She was so thrilled with her participation in his escape that she slipped the Delta Airlines pen she'd used into her purse as a memento.)

As she escorted Ramadan down the long corridor to his gate, another airline rule, she again mumbled. *It's so easy.*

"Good morning, ladies and gentlemen, we're now ready to begin boarding Flight 799 to Atlanta," the agent at the gate announced only about ten minutes after they had checked in and sat down.

Ramadan, holding his suitcase, stood up. Miss Bea rose as well and said for the last time, "It's so easy."

"Special needs passengers and children traveling alone may now proceed to the boarding area."

Reaching into her purse, Miss Bea said, "I have something for you. Unaccompanied minor—hah!"

Extending her hand, she said, "Take this." With a snap of her fingers, she flicked into view the tarot card that had flown from the deck during his reading: the Magician. She wasn't about to be outdone by smartphones, touch-screen ticketing units, and the lax authority of the adult world that was, all around her, passing for magic.

"But, Miss Bea, it's yours," Ramadan said.

"No—it's *yours.* Take it. That way you will not be what they call 'unaccompanied.' And—there is nothing, absolutely *nothing,* 'minor' about you."

Ramadan took the Magician and inserted it between the cover and first page of his passport, face-to-face with his own photograph. Then he embraced Miss Bea with a tenderness he had only ever bestowed upon Mama Joon.

"Thank you!" he said, his breath warming her cheek and neck.

Miss Bea had known many satisfied customers who had shown their appreciation in a variety of ways, but she had no experience with such a physical expression of gratitude. People had shaken her hand and even high-fived her. Some had tipped her hundreds of dollars for her kind of compassion. Many had written letters of praise, warming her as if she'd been held. *As if.* But Ramadan's show of affection was not *as if.* It was. He was not a customer, not anymore, if he had ever been at all. She lived alone with three cats—Dante; Faith, a nutty Siamese; and Sam, the jet-black, yellowed-eyed captain of the ship. All of her years of cuddling these fine creatures, touches she had built her life on, unspooled into the ether, the emotional safety net of her entire existence unraveling in an instant. Like a crocheted afghan undone by a mischievous claw, her security blanket was reduced to a pile of yarn. On some level, she had always suspected the truth, *and this was the trouble with cats*—far from liberating you from the need for serious human attachments, they rendered you even more susceptible. With one hug, Ramadan, however unintentionally, had ruined her.

When they separated, Miss Bea, implausibly grateful for her own devastation, rubbed the side of Ramadan's face and said, "Go!"

He did as she commanded, turning and walking away. Just as when he had left the house, he refrained from looking back.

But then she called out to him. "Ramadan!"

He turned to see a look of panic on her face. And she *was* panicked, stricken with the fear that she might never have that feeling again, Ramadan's embrace. Dante had run off once, gone missing for three days. His absence—and the suspension of the nighttime nuzzling he preferred and to which she'd become accustomed—had frazzled her nerves. She had been unable to sleep; lost her appetite; made a useless, embarrassing, teary phone call to the police. When, late one Sunday afternoon, he slinked back into her apartment through the French doors that opened onto her private courtyard, purring at her feet as she stood at the kitchen sink washing dishes, she had broken a glass, cut her hand, bled with relief. Cats come back. But what about kids? She couldn't see the answer. She had no idea what was going to happen to Ramadan or, if he didn't come back, to her.

Draining as much worry from her voice as she could, she said, "*Are you coming back?*"

Ramadan didn't know, either. Even though he could see she wanted him to say yes, all he could do was shrug. She sighed with understanding, and he turned and gave the agent his boarding pass.

As he walked through the portal toward the plane, he heard Miss Bea's mantra humming in his head, and he wondered if she had kept saying it to reassure him as he continued moving forward, alone. *It's so easy . . . It's so easy . . . It's so easy . . .*

Cozying into his seat on the plane, he smiled about how easy it was indeed, and how important it was not to look back. That's what had made his escape possible: sneaking out of the house, jumping off the porch over the steps, jogging to the corner to meet Miss Bea. He hadn't looked back then, only a couple of hours ago, and he wouldn't look back now. *Don't think about them. Think about you. Don't think about then. Think about now. No—think next.*

In this moment, he found his own command easy to follow. He had a window seat, and the morning sunlight was kissing his face "Good morning!" with the sort of old-soul affection that had always brought him the greatest comfort. His instinct was to press into its warmth as if it were the soft, cushy body of a caring old woman. His eyes closed, he leaned his head sideways, and his forehead banged against the windowpane. He relaxed there, his body slumping against the frame of the plane.

The head bump wasn't that hard, but it knocked something out of him, the last bit of get-up-and-go. He could no longer maintain the suspension of his fatigue, which seemed equal to the sum of a whole life's worth of depletions, and he collapsed into a peaceful sleep. It was as if he had been punched unconscious, delivered a necessary blow, a concussion of convalescence.

AN ABEYANCE

TAKING FLIGHT

Have you ever been to Rome? Have you ever set out for Paris? Ever jetted off to any foreign land, to fulfill a dream or escape a nightmare—or like Ramadan, thrillingly, to do both at once?

If so, then you have an idea what taking flight incites in him. How a continental shift can promote a constitutional one. You know the change that being set in motion can, well, set in motion. You know how motion can precipitate emotion. Moving is *moving*. You may not have devised—who has?—a method for calculating the degree to which kinetics stimulates the intellect, physics modifies psychology, but you know all too well that the distance between where you disembark and where you land is only crudely measurable in miles or kilometers, and more accurately mapped in feelings and revelations.

And if you haven't been anywhere, well—*what the hell are you waiting for?* A hurricane? A war? A literal shot in the arm? A cure for the plague that is fear? An invitation?

Birth is your invite! Breath, your passport! Bravery, your visa!

In a way, the notion of birth, earthly or otherwise, is precisely the point. Home is a womb. It nurtures. But imagine never pushing forth into the world, your growth inhibited by habitat, the comfy confines of your mother's accommodating girth. Wouldn't persistent satiation feed a need? Wouldn't nourishment, without growth, nurture a longing? Create, in effect, an appetite for hunger? Thus, your stasis, replete with life's essential nutrients, would equal starvation. Feast would become famine. With the usual dire consequences. To remain fetal would be fatal.

Oh, to be Ramadan, who, parallel to this pause, is plunging headfirst (with a tender spot on his forehead from that bump against the airplane window to prove it) into another world. Him today, you tomorrow—*why not?* What's a bruise on the noggin, or any other part of the body, when the trade-off is a balm for the soul? You pack for the trip, of course—clothes, toiletries, a snack or two—but really, your only carry-on is you. Though you may be toting a suitcase or haversack, you leave behind your real baggage—your life—like old, dead skin. Travel is an exfoliation. What emerges, as you move forward, buffed to the surface—by merely going *there*—is a shiny new you!

You become the you you are in Barcelona. Your Amsterdam you. The you you're meant to be . . . in Berlin. The you of São Paulo. Who are you in Tokyo? What's your heart rate in Brussels? Will anyone recognize you in Dakar? Will you even recognize yourself? There's only one way to find out . . .

In short, you are reborn. There—it's been said. This is about *rebirth*. What is "rebirth" anyway but seeing visions, hearing strange voices, breathing different air, walking a new path—*arriving at a new place in life?*

Well, to arrive . . . one must first depart!

Once there—wherever you've had the daring to roam—your senses will awaken to the wonders of your new world. You will see something new. Hear something new. Taste and smell something new. Oh, you are really feeling yourself right now. You realize that you *believe* in this new you. (Yes, this little suspension of the suspension of disbelief, this abeyance, is also about *belief*.) This new you, you discover, is real. How can this *not* be? For here you are saying "Spasibo" in St. Petersburg. That wasn't Marcello Mastroianni who just said "Buongiorno" in Venice, it was you! For it not to be you but to be, say, Salma Hayek, she would have to have acquired the familiar silhouette, the profile and posture, inherited from your mother, the one you see reflected, out of the corner of your eye, in a hotel lobby mirror in Mexico City, mouthing, in an admittedly ear-splitting accent, "Donde esta el desanuyo?"

Yes, you will find yourself speaking in tongues!

The far-off place to which you've submitted—the ground zero of your rebirth—becomes your redeemer, the deliverer of the new you. As a new you, as *this* new you, this new believer, you may find yourself a disciple of your destination. And, as happens with many a convert, you will become quite evangelistic. Oh yes, you will become a proselytizer for Prague, a missionary for Mumbai. Your passion for the land to which you've traveled, which has made you you, made you *anew*, may consume you entirely. If it does—and the machinations of faith predict it will—you will make a movement out of movement.

You will find yourself wondering, "Might my zealotry for the world *save* the world?" Well, yes, quite frankly, it might.

But, oh, you say, *I can't afford to go to Sydney! I have no way of getting to Timbuktu!*

Ramadan—you protest—*is blessed! He can go wherever he likes. Istanbul? No problem . . . He had a Mama Joon!*

Well—what if the truth is that Mama Joon is but a figment of the imagination? Okay, it's a big what-if, but *what if*? What if someone told you she was just dreamed up for the purposes of Ramadan's daring escape? What if she isn't real at all! Of course, you wouldn't believe that (and why should you—she's so real that even though she's gone we think she's still here). But it *could* be true. She might be just a fantasy, a *falsity*, so necessary to the existence and survival of Ramadan that she simply appeared in a flash, as spontaneously as a captured culprit's lie. But okay, settle down, there'll be none of that pouting—all right, all right, she's real. But still . . . if you're really honest with yourself, you'll admit that you can *imagine* a scenario in which she is not. *Ah!*—as Ramadan would say.

Imagine. Imagination. Imagine/Imagination. Which came first, the verb or the noun? It's a chicken-egg kind of thing. Does time fuse the action and the act? Does travel blur the doing and what's done? Who cares! The point is: Should you need a Mama Joon, there she is. At least you can imagine that she is. Or—and here's the zinger—maybe your imagination *is* your Mama Joon. The ticket to your ticket. The imagination. That's where all fantastic beings come from anyway. *Beings.* Not just persons or creatures, but *existences.* All great *ways* of being owe to imaginative flourishes. Yes, let's speak the cliché and in this context, in this Ramadanian moment, make *it* anew. All great modes of living spring from this: *flights of fancy!*

And if your imagination fails you, then you can always just let a chosen child—the blessed boy—show you how it's done! Now boarding . . . *Air Ramadan!*

Miss Bea was right: *It's so easy.*

As easy as tapping a few hotlinks on a smartphone. *It's so easy.*

As easy as rising from your chair and heading out the door. *It's so easy.*

As easy as turning a page . . .

PART III

ISTANBUL

11

EATING CHICKEN IN TURKEY

Ramadan was the first passenger off the plane. Back in Atlanta, on his connecting flight, a sympathetic attendant had relocated him to a vacant front-row seat.

"Plenty of room up here," Debbie had said. His ears were so ready to try to decipher a foreign language that he heard the nuances of her drawl. *Plenny-a-room appear.* Buckling him in, she winked and said, "Plus this way oggin keep an eye on ya."

As he exited the plane now with his suitcase and backpack, he waved goodbye. Debbie's outstretched arm and wiggling fingers stiffened into an arrow, and she looked like a directional signpost. But then her unsuspecting Georgia charm humanized her in a way no customer-service seminar could have. "I'm sure your daddy's right out there waitin' on ya, sweetheart." You can't train "sweetheart."

He wanted to believe the lie he and Miss Bea invented: his father, a Mr. John Ramsey, would be meeting him at the gate. Yesterday's version of the same lie he'd been telling himself for years. Or was that the day before yesterday? He had no idea what day or time it was. When he pulled out his cell phone, its blank face reminded him it had been off since Atlanta. Pausing to power it on, he stepped aside and leaned against the wall, as other passengers rushed by.

The phone hummed to life, displaying 3:58, *Tuesday, August 14* above the photo of him and Mama Joon. *And when you get to Istanbul, I'll be there with you.* He liked knowing that with one tap he could hold her in his hand. Pressing ahead, he merged into the stream of people hurrying off the plane. He almost tripped over the rolling luggage of the man in front of him, and a woman bumped into his back. "Okay?" she asked, playfully hitting his backpack.

"Okay," he said, congratulating himself on speaking his first, and mercifully universal, word in Turkish.

Entering the airport terminal, he wondered what it would be like if his father really was out there about to welcome him with the passion of a man who had been waiting for this moment his whole life. Indeed, his vigilance for the one who was *not* there alerted him to someone who was, an officious-looking steward, scrutinizing the exiting passengers. The man's eyes angled down, searching, it seemed, for someone with the generic height of a child. A certain "Unaccompanied Minor," perhaps? Yes—specifically, *him*. When a passenger pointing to the Departures/Arrivals monitors asked the man for assistance, Ramadan ducked behind a couple of French-speaking travelers and slipped by undetected.

"*C'est bon, n'est-ce pas?*"

Recognizing the phrase, he almost blurted out, in celebration of his maneuver, "*Oui, c'est si bon!*"

A safe distance from the gate, he darted behind a floor-to-ceiling stainless-steel pillar marked with a "Welcome to Istanbul" sign. Poking his head around the edge of the post, he saw the steward, back at his station now, pick up a microphone; his lips moved in sync with the words booming throughout the terminal: *Passenger Ramadan Ramsey . . . please report to Gate Number Two Zero. Passenger Ramadan Ramsey . . . Gate Number Two Zero . . .*

Ramadan gasped when he heard his name broadcast, echoing for everyone to hear. He hid behind the column again, clinging to it for cover and fortification. Was he on the verge of being discovered already, deported before even being admitted?

After a moment's grace of PA silence, he decided to hazard another glance, and he saw the steward busy at his work, studying the computer screen and fingering his keyboard, determined to find this missing Ramadan Ramsey—*him*.

But then the man looked up from his monitor, and Ramadan watched relief register on his face. Following the man's line of vision, he saw a father and son at the far end of the gate's seating area. The father was kneeling to tie the youngster's shoelaces, and he and the steward exchanged tentative greetings. There was enough distance between them to blur ambiguity into confirmation, and the steward gave the man a thumbs-up.

Initially comforted, Ramadan sighed. Then the father, having jerked the boy's shoelaces into two smart bows, reached up and tousled his son's hair, and Ramadan felt a pang of regret at benefiting from their intimacy. As they walked away holding hands, his remorse darkened into self-pity. In the last vestige of his tantrums, he brushed his suitcase against the post hiding him from the steward but not from himself. His left shoulder, pressed to the column, bore most of his weight, and he noticed, much to his surprise, it no longer hurt. Still, he reached up and rubbed it, massaging the phantom ache, as if to soothe a deeper wound, one that might never really heal.

He closed his eyes for a few seconds and, relieved of the burden of sight, his head tilted up. When he opened his eyes, he was looking at a sign: PASAPORT KONTROL. No English translation necessary, though one appeared below. And hadn't he heard something on the plane about needing a twenty-dollar visa as well? He pulled out his passport and stared at the back cover, which, blank and navy-blue dull, hardly projected the power to grant him passage out his front door, much less through the gates of a foreign metropolis. But then he flipped it over and his confidence swelled when he saw the golden PASSPORT at the top, UNITED STATES OF AMERICA at the bottom, and the intimidating seal of an elaborately winged bald eagle in the middle. The Magician card jutted out, and he opened the booklet to its lemon-colored flash. Opposite that, his own little portrait smiled at him, and he felt dually validated: his passport documented his existence, his realness; the Magician, his dreams. Without either, he could not have made it here. But he *was* here. He was!

He gathered his backpack and suitcase and set off, and moving through the airport, he began to feel more comfortable. Many of the people were dressed like him, in jeans and a T-shirt. But even those who weren't—men here and there in long cream-colored robes, women with scarves draped over their heads—exuded a casual vacation idleness or a business-trip swagger. And for Ramadan, a boy who was anxious about his status as a low-level fugitive, the best thing about these strangers was the way they seemed to find him as unremarkable as he found them. Far from being conspicuous, he fit right in.

Wanting to hold on to the feeling of being just another anonymous member of the crowd, he decided not to rush to the passport and visa lines. Instead, he spent a few minutes drifting, strolling by gates that looked familiar, shops that did not. This quick detour left him feeling both connected and disconnected, so he was about to turn around to go check in when he saw three teenage boys jostling one another as they went up an escalator. Swayed by their wily spirits, their youth and his, he decided to flow along a little longer. He hopped onto the escalator, which ascended to a colorfully lit mezzanine.

Did he smell it first? Or was it the familiar orange-and-white logo of the fried-chicken chain restaurant at the upper landing that roused the full-on assault of his senses? POPEYES. Ramadan had known the sign's meaning and its call since before he could actually read it. In New Orleans, where this famous fast food had originated, its signposts were as iconic as live oaks. Whenever he and Mama Joon had eaten at the Popeyes in Houston after the storm, they had almost felt like they were at home. "Ah!" he said, because seeing the sign felt like a sign.

Hunger, not even a suggestion before, was now a command. Out of the corner of his eye, he saw the other boys dash off to a Sbarro for pizza, and he released the notion of companionship he had quietly harbored. In just this way, taste—say, the penchant for deep-fried poultry over cheesy bread—may have doomed countless would-be alliances. But a consensus of the fundamental urge had forged consequential unions as well. *Alicia Ramsey and Mustafa Totah.* That one potato chip, impetuously shared years ago in New Orleans, should lead to *this*! A boy in Istanbul, breathlessly overordering. Buying four pieces of chicken, instead of two. Spicy. *Yes, please, a Coke, a large.* Rushing off to a table in a quiet corner. Content to be alone with his thoughts and feelings, mostly gratitude and quivers of pleasure. As he was nibbling the crusty edge of a wing, the pointy, gristly end nobody knew what to do with other than to pierce it with the cuspids, to savor and suck and marvel that it was there for you, he paused. The wing tip pinched between his tongue and upper front teeth, some tiny drop of ambrosia leaking from inside the bird's defining feature and dissolving onto one of his more sensitive buds, he was overcome with carnivorous delight—and with something more. *Who knew salt could taste so sweet!* It was as if his humble, greasy origins—the potato chip transferring from his mother's hand to his father's mouth—had finally caught up with him. But he wasn't feverous with understanding. What *was* this wetness he was wiping from the corners of his eyes? What were these sniffles? Too much spice? Had he inhaled some stray flecks of pepper while devouring the food? The real surprise seemed to be that though he had eaten only a drumstick and half of this wing—he would wrap up the breast and thigh and put them in his backpack for later—he was already satisfied. Mama Joon had taught him to appreciate a good meal. *Everything depends on how hungry you are, Ramadan. Remember that.* So he simply attributed the power of the moment to the supremacy of sustenance. As he dropped the remains of the wing into the paper serving tray and sighed, with what felt a little like fatigue, he was aware for the first time how realizing that you are no longer hungry, that you indeed are *full*, can be an emotional experience.

PURCHASING THE TWENTY-DOLLAR visa, which looked like an expensive postage stamp the security officer glued inside his passport, went smoothly, as did checking in at passport control. But as he was walking near the baggage claim carousels, he realized he had only his backpack. *No suitcase!* And he knew immediately where he'd left it. Popeyes. . . Feeling so at home, he'd forgotten he wasn't. But his disappointment passed quickly—he hadn't lost anything he couldn't replace. He still had his identification, his credit card, some cash, and he could get more at an ATM if necessary. Besides, he wasn't sure how long he'd

be here anyway. Maybe losing his suitcase meant that he wasn't supposed to stay more than a day. Just go outside. Find transportation into
the city. See Istanbul. Look across the Bosphorus, to the east. Feel his
father's homeland up close, smell the winds of Syria, and let it all go.
Then—maybe he would just turn around and go back.

But after he had stood in the fast-moving cab line—TAKSi, the
signs on the vehicle rooftops read—and hopped into the yellow car
idling at the curb, he accepted that he was not going home today. The
welcoming backseat settled the matter. There was always another mode
of transport waiting for you if you looked for it and followed the signs.
His own legs. Miss Bea's car. The first plane. Another plane. This cab.
What was next? A boat? Who knew? Just keep going! No—he would
not go home until he ran out of money or ideas, or until commanded to
leave by a force stronger than himself.

The cabbie was sweating—from the August heat, it seemed—and
dabbing at his face with an already drenched blue towel when Ramadan
slid across the backseat. Even the back of his head, scalp peeking through
a closely cropped haircut, was glistening with moisture. As best Ramadan
could tell, he was also irritated by the swelter and, without turning to look
at his passenger, he asked gruffly, "Hotel?"

"Hotel?" Ramadan said, stalling. *Oh, yes, a hotel!* he thought.

"Hotel!" the man said again, impatience rising in his voice. He turned
to Ramadan, his round, bearded face pleading for more than an answer
to his question. His look softened. "You no man. You boy. American?"

"Yes."

"Where you family?"

"I don't know. I mean . . ." Ramadan paused, figuring he would have
to lie. But then, taking a leap of faith, he uttered the claim that had sustained many a sinner before him—"I . . . I am meeting my father later."

"Okay. Where you go *now*, son? Hotel?"

"Okay, yes, hotel." Ramadan heard Mama Joon's voice in his head as clearly as he heard the cabbie's now. Once, when they were walking together on Canal Street going to buy him some new sneakers, she had escorted him inside her workplace and showed him the vast, ornate public areas. *It's an old building, boy, but the hotel is young, almost the same age as you!* While she went into a back office and visited her co-workers, she had left him alone in the lobby, and he bounced around from one cushy chair to the next. "Let's stay here!" he said when she came back. She had laughed as they left to finish their shopping. *Maybe one day. The name sure sounds just like what it is, doesn't it?* Then she said it—as he was about to—only with more conviction. Unsure if there was such a place in Istanbul, if his response would even make sense, he said, "The Ritz?"

"Okay," the cabbie responded, and he turned around and drove off.

Ramadan pulled out his phone, thumbed it to life, and smiled at Mama Joon.

It's so easy!

As the cab left the airport, he stared out the window, saying a good-bye to the place where he had touched down safely, here on the other side of the world. The whole experience felt intergalactic, and Ataturk International looked like a space station. Home base in a strange land. Then he heard the cab driver sigh and say, "Oh, Ramazan!"

Pulled out of his alienation by what sounded like the calling of his name, he answered warily, "Yes?"

"What?" the confused-looking cabbie, wiping his brow, asked. Their eyes met in the rearview mirror.

"You said 'Ramadan.'"

"Yes."

"How—how did you know . . . ?"

"Know *what?*" The cabbie moaned with mild frustration and looked back at the road. "My English . . . no good."

"I mean, you said—"

"No . . . I say 'Ramazan.'" The cabbie was speaking quickly, and Ramadan again heard his name.

"Yes!"

"No . . . I mean *yes!*" He moaned again. "I no think so good now."

Ramadan muttered under his breath, "You did say 'Ramadan.'"

"I hear what you say, Mister Boy."

"What is going on?" Ramadan asked rhetorically.

But the cabbie answered, "*Ramadan!* You understand when I say in English? You know Ramadan?"

"Do I know *what?*" Ramadan asked.

"Oh!" the driver cried out, this time as if in actual physical pain. He threw his arms up, and the car swerved sharply to the right. In the backseat, Ramadan was tossed against the door to his left, and his backpack tumbled onto the floor, spilling some of its contents. The driver grasped the steering wheel with both hands and regained control of the vehicle, setting the cab back on a straight path.

"So sorry," he said, with sincerity. "Sorry, sorry . . ."

They had moved along only a short distance more when the cabbie began sniffing the air, moving his head from side to side in short, jerky motions, and, with a marked note of distress, asked, "What is this *smell?*"

Ramadan, picking up his backpack, noticed that the bag of leftover Popeyes had fallen out, and its aromas were beginning to pervade the cab. He held up the savory-smelling package, thrusting it forward so the driver could get a good whiff and understand that it was only food.

"Fried chicken! You want some?"

"Oh, no! You try to kill me, boy!"

"No!" As Ramadan shoved the bag into his backpack, he read the nameplate on the back of the driver's seat: EMIR ADEM. "No, Mr. Emir, I'm not trying to kill you."

"I no eat . . . I no eat . . . Ramadan, oh, Ramadan . . ."

Ramadan was about to answer to his name again when—*Mr. Emir . . . no eat . . . no eat . . . Ramadan!*

"Ah!" he said. "It *is* Ramadan!"

"Yes!" the driver yelled back.

"Mr. Emir!"

"What, boy?"

"Mr. Emir . . ." Ramadan patted his chest twice and, with a pride he had never quite experienced while stating his identity, said, "I *am* Ramadan!"

"What?" Emir asked, clearly not understanding his young passenger and plainly in the throes of hypoglycemic agitation. "What you say, boy? Speak English!"

"My name . . . my *name* is Ramadan!"

"What? Your name Ramadan?" Emir shook his head. "I no eat. I no think good. Am I *dream?*"

"No—you no dream," Ramadan said, mimicking Emir's grammar and his accent.

Emir side-eyed Ramadan, as if sensing insult. Then he smiled. "You Muslim?"

"No."

"Christian."

Ramadan was unsure of how to answer. "I . . . I *used* to be," he said, hoping to end a conversation he wasn't prepared to have.

"Used to be? What are you now?"

"I don't know."

"Well, Mr. Ramadan, with Jesus around your neck, when you find out, tell me!"

Ramadan grabbed his crucifix and tucked it inside his T-shirt. "Okay."

"American boy name Ramadan—the world is change," Emir said with resignation. "The world is change." He wiped his brow again. "I tell my wife, Yonca, when I go home. *Oof*—if I no die before dinner."

As the car sped toward the center of Istanbul, Emir adjusted the air-conditioning and rolled up the windows. After a few minutes he said, "Ramadan . . ."

Preoccupied with looking out at the city and used to Emir calling out his name but meaning something else, Ramadan didn't respond.

"*Ramadan!*" Emir repeated.

"Oh, me?"

"Yes, you. Where is your luggage? You have just this fried chicken bag?"

"Oh—I forgot it in the airport. But I don't need it."

"Your father, he is bring you more things?"

"I hope. One day."

"Tomorrow?"

"Uh . . . no, sir," Ramadan answered, enjoying being honest, however vaguely.

Emir shook his head, giving Ramadan the impression he might turn the cab around and head back to the airport. Instead, he asked, "You have reservation at hotel?"

"No, sir."

Emir peered at Ramadan in the rearview mirror. "How you pay, boy?"

Ramadan removed a wad of bills and his American Express card from his pocket and showed them to Emir, who said, reading the card, "Ramadan . . ."

"Ramsey," Ramadan said.

Then Emir shrugged, handed him back the card, and said, "Okay."

A couple of minutes later, Emir said, practically singing, "Ramadaaaan . . ."

This time Ramadan met the cabbie's stare in the mirror. "Yes, sir?"

"How long you stay here, boy, with no reservation, no clothes, and with father who come maybe tomorrow, maybe never?"

Looking out the window in search of an answer, Ramadan said, "I've been wondering about that myself." The modern buildings of downtown Istanbul reminded him of downtown New Orleans and downtown Houston. The little boy in him, the fantasizer who had brought him all the way to this distant land, asked: If Istanbul is just another city, why can't I just stay forever? But the little man in him, the one who was noticing how everything was actually different here, even things that seemed the same—the Popeyes chicken, for instance, hadn't really tasted the way it tasted in America at all—secretly wanted to find his way back home and conquer his own corner of the world. Through the two visions, he saw mosques doming out of the landscape, thrusting up as organically as mushrooms, minarets sprouting like blades of grass. He felt the naturalness of everything—however the same, however different—sweeping him forward, wising him up. His probing, maturity-inducing gaze rewarded him with the inkling of an idea. It had something to do with the convergence of two things: the auspicious timing of his arrival in this new place and the arrival of a new him.

"Mr. Emir, when does Ramadan end?"

"Saturday is the last day. Only five more days." Then he added with a grimace, followed by a laugh, "Allah, give me strength!"

Five days. Maybe that was how long before he would be ready to go home. Maybe. He laughed along with Emir. Then he closed his eyes and heard himself asking Allah, or any god who was listening, really, to bestow upon him the same blessing Emir had just requested.

⚜

WHEN THEY ARRIVED at the Ritz, Emir honked at the burly security guard posted in the driveway kiosk, and the man waved them through. He drove past the entrance and parked at the curb. Ramadan watched him lean forward and grip the steering wheel, his head bowed, as if in prayer. "Are you okay, Mr. Emir?"

Emir turned and said, "I ask you the same, Mr. Ramadan. Are *you* okay?"

Ramadan looked at the glass doors leading to the hotel lobby and the uniformed bellmen standing there. "I . . . think so."

"You think so?" Emir cocked his head to the side. "I think I need to help you."

"But why?"

"I have son like you. Young like you. Mehmet. He like to go places with no tell me. He think I no know. But I know. He go everywhere, all over town. Sometime with friends. Alone, sometime too. Just like you come here to Istanbul. But he good boy. You good boy? Yes, yes, I see you good boy. Not like Ahmet, my big boy. No, he is a man now. Is hard to be a good boy when you is a man. Ahmet want to go away. To the war. I don't know why. He need to stay in school. Finish study to be something. I worry. He watch the war on the TV, on the computer, and he think it is just a movie, like the silly ha-ha movies he study at the university. He see this, and he want to go. For what? 'To see, Baba! To see! To see is to live, Baba!' What this mean? I no know. But I tell you I think he go. That is Ahmet. I no know how to stop him. He fight *me*! He and me, we be at war all the time, like enemy. And so—he no good boy.

"But *Mehmet*, he good boy like you. Once upon a time . . . Mehmet take the train all the way to Ankara. Alone. And now he tell me and Yonca he want to go to America. He and his friends, they like the American music. He like the American basketball. He love these things! He go to America one day, he say. I believe he go, too. Just like Ahmet go soon. Why they like to go so much? I think maybe because they see me move, move, move in my taxi, every day, every day, and they want to move, too. But I no go nowhere. I am still here. Ahmet want to go to Suriye! And he will go, too. I no can stop him."

Ramadan had been staring down at the floor of the cab, shying away from making eye contact with Emir. But at the mention of Ahmet's destination, which could have only one translation, he looked up.

"And Mehmet will go to America. That is my Mehmet. So you see, Ramadan?"

"See what?"

"Why I help you. If once upon a time, my Mehmet so stupid—like you—to be alone in a strange place, to be maybe in America—with no me, no Baba—I want someone help *him*. Like I help you. Now you see?"

"I see."

"And—it is *Ramadan*, Ramadan! I do good for you, Allah do good for me!"

Energized by his own generous spirit, Emir got out and sprinted around the car. "Come, come, come," he said, opening the door for Ramadan and grabbing his backpack.

"Thank you, Mr. Emir," Ramadan said, sliding out of the cab.

As they walked through the hotel entrance, they greeted the bellmen, and Emir put his arm around Ramadan's shoulder. When they had almost reached the check-in desk, Emir whispered, "I talk. I talk for you."

A young man behind the counter, Ozgur according to his name tag, greeted them, and Ramadan listened as Emir spoke casually in Turkish, his hands gesturing as if he were directing his own performance. Ozgur nodded, occasionally smiling at Ramadan. When Emir stopped talking, Ozgur said in flawless English, "So, young man, you will be staying with us for a few days while you await your father's arrival? Your identification and the credit card, please." And he began typing at his terminal.

Ramadan was so busy trying to process what Ozgur had just said that he didn't even realize there was no need for translation. Flustered by the clarity, he didn't respond until Emir touched his shoulder, prompting him to dig out his passport and American Express card. Ozgur looked these over, and continued checking him in.

"You are in luck, Mr. Ramsey. I have found something special for you."

As he completed the registration, he suggested Ramadan exchange some of his U.S. currency, which he had exposed during the search for his passport, into Turkish lira. Ramadan looked at Emir, who said, "Okay."

A few minutes later, they headed up to the tenth floor of the hotel. As they exited the elevator and approached room 1010, Emir said, "Ozgur say 'special.' We look with our own eye."

"You don't believe him?"

"Maybe. We see."

Emir's skepticism vanished the second they opened the door.

"Now I believe," he said.

Straight ahead, a series of wide floor-to-ceiling windows spanning nearly the entire back wall of the room, adorned with rust-colored silk drapes, revealed a majestic vista of Istanbul. Ramadan rushed into the room and pressed his hands and his face against the middle pane.

"Bosphorus," Emir said.

"Yes! We are in Europe and over there—that is Asia!"

Ramadan was mesmerized by the scene: a soccer stadium in the foreground to the left; a simple but gleaming mosque to the right, surrounded by patches of greenery; beyond that, a variety of ships—freighters, tugboats, cruise ships—streaming through the waterway. Farther out still, on the other side of the Bosphorus, a hilly landscape filled with what looked like village after village—houses, huts, churches, more mosques, fortresses even, for all he knew.

"Asia," he had said. But what he was really seeing was the entire map, which he knew well. The other side of world. All the way to the southeastern border of Turkey, all the way to Syria, to Aleppo.

"You like?" Emir asked.

Ramadan turned and said, "Yeah!"

Emir placed the backpack on the king-size bed and said, "Okay. I go now."

Reaching into his pocket, Ramadan went to Emir. "How much do I owe you?"

"Nothing."

"No, Mr. Emir!"

"Keep your money. You need new clothes for what you leave at the airport. Tomorrow I bring Mehmet. He good boy. He bring you shop. He show you Istanbul!"

Emir gestured out the window at the panorama of the city. Ramadan looked at it, and then back at Emir. "Okay."

Emir rushed out, saying, "I go home to dinner now." He pointed to the backpack. "Eat you chicken, Ramadan. Eat you chicken!"

A short time later, sitting at a small polished cherrywood desk, watching the light change on Istanbul's glittering strait, Ramadan did as Emir had commanded. When he finished eating, fatigue descended with the inevitability of, somewhere out of view, the sinking of the sun, and he succumbed to the rigors of his many hours of travel. It took all the energy left in him to rise from the chair and fling himself onto the bed. Sleep happened so fast he didn't even hear himself mumbling his own congratulatory words into the satiny duvet cover. "I did it . . . I did it . . . I did it . . ."

His breath circled back to him, wafting up his nostrils, and the vapors from his meal insinuated themselves into his unconsciousness, confusing his senses. He dreamed he could *see* the outside sounds that were bleeding into his room. The boats' horns blaring in from the Bosphorus took on the shapes of tubas, trumpets, and trombones. Later, the calls to prayer seemed to undulate to him from the minarets he'd seen out of his window, like sirens of blue ribbons. Near dawn, when a stubborn flake of cayenne-flavored crust dislodged itself from between his two front teeth and finally dissolved in his mouth, he dreamed he could taste, on the tip of his tongue, tomorrow.

12

THE MAGIC OF ISTANBUL

Ramadan awoke the next morning to the muffled sound of a text pinging his cell phone. He had slept on top of the bed covers, fully clothed, so he pulled his phone from his jeans pocket and read a one-word message from Clarissa: *Mustafa.*

"Mustafa," he murmured. "My father is Mustafa . . ."

Mentally, he jumped up and danced around the room. But still half-asleep, he just sank back into the pillows and pressed his phone to chest. He was dozing off again when the hotel telephone rang on the bedside table.

Groaning, he rolled over and picked up the receiver. "Hello?"

"Mr. Ramadan Ramsey, we are here!" It was a wide-awake and cheery Emir.

Ramadan sat up and stared out the window, thinking, *I am here, too.*

"Come, come, come!"

Judging from Emir's jolly mood, Ramadan figured he must have had a big breakfast. "I'll be right down!"

He got up and rushed into the bathroom, where he looked in the mirror and convinced himself he appeared more rested than rumpled. Besides, he didn't want to keep Emir waiting, so he just wiped his face with a damp towel and gargled with the hotel mouthwash. His hair, as naturally shaped as a head of hydrangea, warranted only a couple of palm pats. Then he fluffed his T-shirt a little and grabbed his backpack from the bedroom. When he exited room 1010—except for the Popeyes bag and a few creases in the bedding—it looked virtually the same as when he arrived.

The elevator trip to the lobby felt like a carnival ride, and he started laughing. Though plummeting, he was giddy from the sensation that he was also going up. He was on a roller coaster in the Ritz, or a Ferris wheel operated by Mr. Emir, rising higher than he'd gotten from the joint he'd hit with his cousins the night he was shot. His entire escape, improbable and fantastical, gave him the feeling he was levitating, above peril; that looking back or being afraid, like the ground, was beneath him.

The "ding" and the elevator doors opening almost brought him back down to earth. But after hustling through the lobby, he had to blink himself out of his lingering dreaminess, for the boy standing next to Emir had a single word emblazoned across his jersey, in sky-blue letters outlined in silver, that confounded Ramadan with its boldness: MAGIC. Centered below this dazzling noun was the number 15. Ramadan slowed his jog to a stilted, mechanical shuffle, and when close enough to the boy—Mehmet, of course—he noticed the tiny red-white-and-blue National Basketball Association logo near the left shoulder of the navy-blue pinstriped jersey. So not only was Mehmet an NBA fan, as Emir had said, but in particular, an admirer of a certain number 15 player for the Orlando franchise, whose nickname invoked enchantment.

"Ramadan!" Emir's voice helped steady him. Not since Mama Joon had anyone said his name in such an endearing and possessive tone.

More possessive still, Emir added, "This is my Mehmet!" and he shoved his lanky son forward. Dark-haired and winsome, Mehmet smirked at his father.

"Hello, Ramadan. I am *my* Mehmet, too. May I say I am happy to meet you!"

"Yes, you may," Ramadan said. "I'm happy to meet you, too." He wanted to tell Mehmet that in his front jeans pocket he had a card that was a perfect match for his jersey. They shook hands for so long Emir had to intervene. "Okay, okay, let's go!"

They went out to the taxi, Mehmet and Ramadan jumped in the backseat, and Emir drove off.

"Where'd you get your shirt?" Ramadan asked. "I want one!"

"Türkoglu!" Mehmet snapped his stretchy shoulder strap and showed Ramadan the name across his back. "You know him?"

"No."

"He is from Istanbul. He wore this one three years ago in the NBA Championships. You don't remember, Ramadan? He scored twenty-five points in the big Game Four. But I am sure you know the Magic lost in overtime to Los Angeles. Poor Orlando. You have to make the free throws. It is very important. Very important—if you want to be the world champion."

Then Mehmet lured Ramadan into his reality with a stream of devotional chatter—a litany of basketball begats and the promise of fairy-tale intrigue . . .

"The next year the Lakers beat the Boston Celtics. They had to do it because Boston beat them in 2008. Right? Right! And then last year the Dallas Mavericks beat the Miami Heat. Good for Dirk Nowitzki. But very bad for LeBron James. He left Cleveland—his home team, you know—to go to Miami. And this is not like Türkoglu leaving Istanbul to go to America—Türkoglu need to leave to make the money and to be famous and to have me wear his Orlando number fifteen. Of course he must leave. Right? Right! But LeBron James, he did not have to leave his home. And then he leaves . . . but only to lose. Very bad. That is what we think, no? Yes! But surprise! What happens this year? Miami beats Oklahoma! LeBron James, finally he wins the championship! Finally, the King is a king! Oh . . . it is a good story. A very good story. But what does this mean, Ramadan? You leave home because you want to win, but then you still lose? You leave home, you lose, but the next year you win? Maybe. And if you go back home, do you lose again? Or do you win when you go back home? What will happen if LeBron goes back home? What will happen next year? We do not know. This is why we watch. To see the story! To see the story! It is so great!"

Mehmet spoke as if he had been waiting his whole life for Ramadan or someone like him, to whom he could profess his passion. To Ramadan, sports had only ever been immediate and specific, and just for fun. Basketball was just basketball. But for Mehmet it was mythology, and *The Life of LeBron James* was an epic. *What will happen if LeBron goes back home?* As Ramadan, too, had just left home, he turned Mehmet's questions on himself. Would *he* win or would he lose? Would he ever go back home? What *would* happen next?

"Mr. Mehmet and Mr. Ramadan," Emir interrupted his passengers. "Where are you going?"

"Baba!" Mehmet yelled, pointing out the window. "Taksim! We get out here, Ramadan. Istiklal Caddesi."

"Isti . . . what?"

"Istiklal Caddesi . . . Independence Avenue," Mehmet translated. "We will find the things you need there."

Emir swerved to the right and stopped at the curb. "Okay. Is good idea. Ramadan, you stay close with Mehmet."

"Yes, sir," Ramadan said, as they got out of the cab.

Emir said something Ramadan couldn't understand. "What'd he say?"

"We meet him here at four o'clock. So we have all day!"

They sprinted across Taksim Square to Istiklal, where they walked in the street with the rest of the crowd. Mehmet gestured from one side of the street to the other. "Is great, no?"

"Yes," Ramadan said, comfortable on this touristy thoroughfare, which struck him as a combination of Bourbon and Canal streets back home.

"It is the best way to begin to see the city." Then Mehmet stopped and grabbed Ramadan's arm. "Oh! Now I know the plan. One, two, three, four. Four quarters! We will play a whole game today, Ramadan. You will see. Istiklal is the First Quarter. When we are finish, you will need to wash, to eat, and to sleep. Come, come, come!"

Less than a block up the street, they went into a sportswear shop where everyone knew Mehmet. One especially friendly salesman, a swarthy fellow with a scar above his left eye and a roguish manner, asked Ramadan, "Where are you from? New York? I think New York. They got a lot of chocolates in New York."

"Nedim!" Mehmet said, punching the young man on his arm.

Ramadan smiled at his proposed edibility. "No, New Orleans."

"New Orleans! Okay, okay," Nedim said, wagging his finger and winking at Ramadan. "New York, New Orleans—I can see there is something *new* about you."

Mehmet explained that Ramadan had lost his luggage and needed to buy some clothes, especially a jersey like his.

"Okay, okay." Nedim escorted them around the store, and Ramadan picked out a pair of Levi's, a few plain white T-shirts, and some socks.

As they went into the sportswear section, Mehmet asked, "Is this shop like the American shops, Ramadan?"

"Pretty close."

"One day I want to see the real thing," Mehmet said. "Not the pretty close. I want to see America!"

"I know."

"You know? How do you know?"

"Mr. Emir told me. And he said he believes you *will* come to America one day."

"What? Baba say this thing?"

"Mm hmm." Ramadan read doubt or confusion in the tilt of Mehmet's head.

They turned to face Nedim, who was holding up a white version of Mehmet's Orlando Magic jersey. "We don't have no more blue," he said. "Is this okay?"

The boys elbowed each other, and Ramadan said, "I wanna wear it now!"

"But of course." Nedim pulled off the price tag and tossed him the jersey. "Go over there. No one will see you." He was pointing to a spot near a wall of sneakers.

Nedim and Mehmet went over to the checkout area, while Ramadan stepped into the corner to change. Standing in front of a full-length mirror, he began pulling off his T-shirt, when it caught on the tape securing the bandage to his shoulder. The sensation of his healing wound being uncovered was more surprising than painful. Bringing the shirt back down, he glanced at the counter, where Mehmet was busy joking with Nedim. Ramadan grabbed the bandage through his t-shirt and bunched it into his fist. Then, in a single motion, he ripped the shirt off over his head. Stepping toward the mirror to examine his wound, he saw a slightly swollen scar come into focus. It was only the size of a large marble, purplish brown with flecks of pink, rising from the front slope of his shoulder. He watched with detachment as this other him in the mirror touched the bump. He ceded the horror of his injury—its original bloodiness, the treachery of its infliction—to this virtual Ramadan. All of it, if it had occurred at all, could have happened to someone else. In a way, so he convinced himself, it had.

And when he slipped the jersey on, the shoulder strap completely covered his scar. He turned and called to Mehmet, "How do I look?"

"Yes!" Mehmet rushed over and gave him a high five. "Ramadan— now we are on the same team!"

They left the store a few minutes later, each toting a bag of Ramadan's purchases. A slow-moving red-and-white tram coasted toward them on rails running along the middle of Istiklal Caddesi, and Ramadan had to shake himself off the streets of New Orleans, where such vehicles roamed like indigenous fauna. "A streetcar!"

"What?" Mehmet asked. "Street . . . car? But it is not a car. It is a train."

"Well, we call it a streetcar."

"Sometimes words do not say what they mean, no? How do you say? Makes no sense . . ." Mehmet touched a finger to his temple.

Ramadan shrugged and said, "Mehmet, sometimes *nothing* makes any sense."

As the tram rolled by, they exchanged a glance, a preternaturally articulate vow to commit mutual mischief. Their eyes darted from the streetcar and back to each other, and without speaking they ran after the tram. It only took five or six steps for Mehmet, who was fleeter than Ramadan, to catch the escaping train, and he jumped onto a semicircular piece of metal protruding from the back. He almost slipped, but he gripped the frame of the rear window and made a quick pivot.

"Come, Ramadan!"

With his shopping bag and backpack, Ramadan was huffing with every stride.

"You can do it!" Mehmet yelled.

The train was moving farther away, and Ramadan didn't think he'd make it. But then the tram began to slow down for its next stop, and he completed the same leap Mehmet had performed, landing on the opposite side of the makeshift platform.

"We did it!" Mehmet shouted.

"Yes!"

The tram started to move again, and Ramadan almost lost his footing, until Mehmet showed him the trick of holding on. They stood precariously on board, rejoicing on the back of the tram as Istiklal receded into the distance.

"Streetcar?" Mehmet returned to the nonsensical term. "It is a crazy name."

Ramadan shouted over the tram's clanging bells, "Let's call it something else!"

"But what, Ramadan?"

Ramadan looked back at the rails stretching all the way to Taksim Square. "The streettrain!" he said.

Mehmet leaned in and whispered conspiratorially, "It will be our secret. We are riding the Streettrain of Istiklal Caddesi."

"Okay," Ramadan said. "The Streettrain of Independence Avenue."

⋘⋙

THEY RODE THE tram to end of the line and walked along the streets of the Beyoglu section of town. "Okay, my friend," Mehmet said. "The second quarter. I race you!"

Mehmet burst into a sprint before Ramadan even knew he was in a competition. They had made several strides when a voice called out, "Mehmet . . . Mehmet!"

Mehmet and Ramadan slowed to a jog and turned around. A boy in a red T-shirt was waving, and they stopped to wait for him.

"Ibrahim!" Mehmet yelled to the boy, who came running over. Up close, Ramadan noticed that on the crest of Ibrahim's mound of his long brown curls, which were looping under the sides of his black-framed, nerdy-looking glasses, was a dark blue yarmulke.

"Ramadan, this is Ibrahim. We study at the same school." Mehmet spoke a couple of sentences in Turkish to Ibrahim, before returning to English. "Ramadan is my new American friend."

Ibrahim pointed to their matching jerseys. "Is good."

"We are shopping." Mehmet held up one of the bags. "I think I take Ramadan to the Grand Bazaar."

"Oof!" Ibrahim said. Then he made dismissive motions with his hands as he launched into what had to be a rant about Mehmet's plan, though Ramadan couldn't understand a word. Ibrahim's thick lenses magnified the outrage in his eyes, and he seemed willing to sacrifice his entire body to expressing his disapproval.

Mehmet said, "His father has leather shop at the Grand Bazaar. He don't like to go. He will have to work if his father sees him. And in that crazy red shirt, who would not see him—I said that, not Ibby."

Ibrahim started to say something else, but Mehmet cut him off. "Speak English, Ibrahim! For Ramadan."

"I hate it!" Ibrahim said. "The clothes smell like animal. They feel good, but smell bad. Why? I want the good feeling *and* the good smell. You understand, Ramadan?"

"Kinda," Ramadan said. "But we say in America, 'It's all good'— even when sometimes it's not."

"Huh?" Ibrahim's face was flushed.

Ramadan found his agitation humorous, and he knew he was about to upset Ibrahim even more. "It just means everything is okay. In the end, it's all good. So just be cool."

"I love it," Mehmet said. "It's all good! Just like we say on the streettrain."

"The street *what?*" Ibrahim asked.

"Sometimes words don't mean what they say," Mehmet continued. "Maybe it *is* all good, but we just do not understand."

"Exactly!" Ramadan agreed.

"You boys crazy!" Ibrahim said. "Change your shirts from Magic and Magic to Crazy and Crazy. It is not all good! I am the one who have to work in the shop. You no understand. And just right now, I leave the synagogue. Why? I have bar mitzvah Saturday. I do not want the bar mitzvah. Well—I want the party. But, Ramadan, you no understand Turkish. Right?"

"No—well, 'Istiklal' . . . and 'okay.'"

Ibrahim gave him a double take and said, "And I no understand the old talk. I want to tell the rabbi like you tell me, Mehmet—oh, he will be mad—'Speak English! Then maybe I understand you!' I do not want to talk the old talk. I want to talk the new! Like you, Ramadan. Like Jay-Z. Like Eminem. Like Drake. You know Drake?"

"Yeah. His music, I mean."

"Tamam—'okay' to the boy who knows two words in Turkish. My friends, Drake, he is Jewish, but he no rap in Hebrew!"

"Ibby!" Mehmet said. "I forget you have the bar mitzvah. I have the invitation. Is very funny picture of you!"

Mehmet laughed, and Ibrahim shoved him in the chest. "Tebrikler, Ibrahim! You are a man!"

"But I am no man. Leave me be a boy. Do you feel like a man, Mehmet?"

"Mmm . . . no."

"Okay. Then why I need to be a man and . . . follow the law?" Ibrahim removed his glasses and whirled them around. "I take this off, and I cannot *see* the law! I cannot see nothing! How do a boy or a man follow the law if he cannot *see* the law?" He was blinking, as if he were blind. "Is crazy!"

They laughed as Ibrahim put his glasses back on. He aimed his restored vision directly at Ramadan. "And you? Do you feel like a man?"

Ramadan tilted his head skyward. "Well . . . a little bit."

"Little bit? What is this, 'little bit'? Tell me—yes or no?"

Though recent events had pressed him for an answer to this question, he hadn't articulated a response until now. "Yes," he said, surprising himself.

Ibrahim frowned, and Mehmet rubbed his shoulder. "You are just afraid, but it's all good."

Ramadan said, "Think about it. Drake is a man. When you become a man, Ibrahim, you can speak whatever language you want."

Ibrahim stared at Ramadan, his eyes widening behind the glint of his lenses. "Hmm, yes. Yes. I have to become a man." He pulled the G on Ramadan's jersey and released it back into his chest with a polyester snap.

"Ramadan. The Magic Man. You, Mehmet—you the Magic Boy. Grow up!"

Then he hooked Mehmet's neck into the crook of his elbow, putting him in a fake chokehold. They all started punching one another, as if testing their mettle—probing for weakness or any verifiable virility. They tussled like this for a while, like kids, bouncing on and off the sidewalk and the street, straddling both the curb and the hurdles that lay between who they were today and soon would be.

Mehmet, sloughing off one last yank of his earlobe from Ibrahim, said, "Okay, we go now. Please come, Ibby!"

"No. No Grand Bazaar."

"We can go to a different place," Mehmet offered.

"Where?"

Mehmet stretched his arms high and leaped like a kid in a school-yard. "Everywhere! We will go everywhere!"

"You are such a little boy, Mehmet." Ibrahim shook his head. "You need the bar mitzvah very bad. Now your brother, Ahmet—he is a man!"

"Ahmet is crazy," said Mehmet, walking away with the other boys trailing.

"Why do you say that?" Ramadan asked.

"Why? Because—because he wants to go to the war. I don't like to talk about that. It makes me sad."

"Just like I say," Ibrahim gloated. "Ahmet is a man! He ride the motorcycle. The girls like him. And now, now he go to war. Ahmet is a man, Mehmet. What do you want him to do? Stay home and be sad like you?"

"He can stay home and be happy. Go to university. This makes him happy. And make his movies. This makes him happy, too."

Ibrahim pushed his glasses up on the bridge of his nose and struck an intellectual pose. "Maybe he want to make a movie *about* the war. A big movie. You think too small, Mehmet."

"You don't know what you talk about—"

Ramadan interrupted the squabble. "What war?" He just wanted to hear Mehmet say what Emir had said yesterday—*Suriye*.

But Mehmet didn't answer. He paused and then, as if someone had fired a starter's pistol, he took off in a full sprint. The street was sloping downward, so gravity helped him zip away. Ramadan and Ibrahim exchanged looks acknowledging that they were already beaten, but they bolted after Mehmet anyway, slapping at each other's arms, trying to leverage the slightest of advantages.

Old Istanbul was a blur. As they wound their way through narrow pathways and a dense mix of pedestrians, Ramadan heard snippets of at least five languages through the clatter and swoosh of their downhill plunge. With no idea where he was on a map, he looked up in casual wonder at this historic neighborhood. When he glanced back, an imposing brick medieval tower dominated the landscape. But the area was also marked with modernity. Blue-and-white Turkcell signs jutted from the façades of ancient buildings, reminders of the phone in his pocket, grounding him in his own century. With every stride, he submerged more deeply into the city, following Mehmet to wherever he was leading them.

They turned one last corner and left all of the buildings at their backs. Ramadan felt a fresh, misty breeze assault his face, as Mehmet's bobbing head came into view, silhouetted against the glimmering Bosphorus. Horns honked behind them as they made a final dash across the street to the water's edge. A sturdy metal railing absorbed their momentum. Mehmet slammed into it first, followed in quick secession by Ibrahim and Ramadan. The air was so sea-drenched that it simultaneously restored Ramadan's breath and quenched his thirst.

"There," Mehmet said through his own heavy panting, pointing straight ahead. Their eyes followed the line of his finger across the Bosphorus and beyond.

"What?" Ramadan asked.

"The war," Mehmet replied. "Suriye."

Ibrahim repeated his mantra of envy and adoration. "Ahmet is a man."

Ramadan's heart beat against the railing, and he brought his hand to his chest. It had occurred to him yesterday when he looked out his hotel room window that the thing he wanted most was close, but still beyond the Anatolian hills and their clusters of red rooftops, mosques, and greenery—beyond the beauty of Istanbul. But here on the ground, not ten stories up in a luxury hotel, his dreams seemed right over there, on the horizon.

"Syria!" he called out, trying to get its attention, to let it know he was here, *this close*, trying to summon it out of its invisibility.

THEY CAUGHT THE tram at the Karaköy station. During the ride, Ramadan consolidated the contents of his shopping bags into his backpack, while sneaking peeks at Mehmet. They got off at Sultanahmet Square and walked toward the Blue Mosque.

"I change the plan now," Mehmet said. "This is the second quarter." But he lacked the enthusiasm from earlier when he'd first envisioned their day as a game of hoops.

Ibrahim looked at the mosque with skepticism. "Is okay for me to go inside?"

"Now who is the boy, Ibrahim?" Mehmet asked. "You want to go to the Grand Bazaar instead?"

"This is my only two choice?" Ibrahim asked.

"Is good for Ramadan to see. You can wait here—if you are afraid."

Ramadan intervened. "Okay, okay. Let's just all go in together."

He draped his arms over their shoulders and drew them close to him. Holding them all together, but keeping Mehmet and Ibrahim apart, felt like a truce. As they passed under one of the archways leading into the rear courtyard of the Blue Mosque, he projected his own composure onto to others: maybe Mehmet had let go of his anxiety about Ahmet, which had turned him moody; maybe Ibrahim had beaten back his bar mitzvah blues. They joined the entrance line and shuffled forward. Near the doorway, they removed their sneakers, and as they stepped inside, their feet cushioned by a vast red carpet, the voice of a man singing with a mellifluous urgency filled the mosque.

"What's that?" Ramadan asked.

"It is noon," Mehmet said. "I pray."

He left them and joined the worshipers separating from the tourists and gathering on the floor, all facing the same direction. Ramadan and Ibrahim watched Mehmet and the others perform prayerful rituals. Their dexterity—squatting, kneeling, bowing, rising—fascinated Ramadan. Prayer, as he knew it, was about language—speech and thought that, on a good day, inspired feeling. Well, for him, sort of. Sure, you kneeled sometimes, especially in supplication. Or stood up to profess faith during mass, though Mama Joon had always had to tap him on the head when it was time to rise. But here, the body—and its positioning and motions—seemed as important as the words. The glorification of God was a physical act. Praise required muscle. Which made Ramadan wonder: were these practitioners also gaining bodily strength from their spiritual conditioning? Like athletes, but holier? Then he looked at Mehmet out on the floor with the others, as supremely prostrate as anyone. Mehmet, whose nonreligious actions had held him rapt all morning. Was there something, then, about the body, the thing that moved and prayed, no matter what it was doing or saying, or where it was doing or saying it, that was itself divine? Everything Mehmet had done today had made Ramadan want to follow him, all the way here. Maybe God, as religion instructed, really was everywhere. In a pantomimed jump shot. In the leap onto a tram. In a race to the water's edge. In a pouty confrontation with a friend. In this mosque. A breathy current blew by Ramadan's ear and grazed his cheek and, alarmed, he looked up sheepishly at the monumental, glowing tiled dome, concerned that daring to think his friend holy had elicited a reprimand from God. But then he realized it wasn't God—just Ibrahim, who was standing right next to him, entranced and huffing gently. Ramadan glanced at him, and saw that he was holding his hands at his chest, his fingers bending and arching with a balletic grace in concert with the congregants in the Blue Mosque, the place he had feared entering. It was as if Ibrahim were trying to master the choreography, memorize it, or reinvent it as his own.

⚜

AFTER THE NOON prayer, Mehmet seemed himself again—the team captain emerging from the locker room recharged, eager to play the second half. When they huddled outside, he said, "The third quarter!"

He pointed across the square at the Byzantine cluster of gray stone and terra-cotta structures, embellished with silvery, mountainous domes, surrounded by a quartet of minarets.

"Oh, no!" Ibrahim groaned.

"What's wrong?" Ramadan asked.

"No more church today!" he said.

"It is not a church," Mehmet said. "It is a museum. Ayasofya!"

"What is it?" Ramadan asked.

"Oh, man," Ibrahim said. He jerked the chain around Ramadan's neck. "Jesus boy, how you no know Ayasofya?"

"I don't know," Ramadan said, embarrassed.

"I cannot say in English," Ibrahim said.

"That is why we go there," Mehmet said. "For Ramadan to know."

Ramadan took out his phone. "How do you spell it?"

"Give me," Mehmet said, taking the phone. He typed into a Google search box, and handed the phone back to Ramadan, who read the Wikipedia entry as they walked.

Ibrahim whined, "What is happen to me? I go to temple, the Blue Mosque, and now this one, Ayasofya, all in one day."

Mehmet put his arm around Ibrahim. "Ibby, Allahu Akbar!"

"That is what I mean! Every god want me today. *My* god, *your* god, now *his* god. I am just one boy. One *almost* man. Is too much god for me!"

"It is okay," said Mehmet, amused.

"It is no okay," Ibrahim said. "Is *nokay!* Ramadan, you have this word in English? 'Nokay'?"

"No, we don't say 'nokay,' Ibrahim."

"Well, you should say it. You say, 'It's all good,' and I say, 'Nokay'!"

Ramadan laughed as he read his phone, which had never felt more modern, informing him about the ancient structure up ahead. Half-listening, half-reading, he processed only a few highlights: Hagia Sophia—Mehmet had spelled it differently from the way it sounded—meant "Holy Wisdom"; for almost a millennium it had been a church, a Greek Orthodox basilica, and then a Roman Catholic cathedral; for nearly five hundred years after, during the Ottoman Empire, it was a mosque. He skimmed words like fires and riots and earthquakes. The surviving building, as Mehmet had said, was a museum.

"Come, Ramadan!" Mehmet called to him. When he looked up, it took a few seconds to scan the scene—throngs of tourists, souvenir hawkers, a slow-moving police scooter. Mehmet and Ibrahim were on the right side of a dense part of the crowd, and he jogged over to them.

"Okay," Mehmet said. "My cousin Orhan is the guard over there. See?" At the main gate, Ramadan saw a tall, husky young man dressed in a dark blue uniform motioning for them to hurry. "Come, come, come."

Mehmet led them to Orhan. After the two of them whispered something to each other, Mehmet introduced everyone and explained the plan.

"See the boy over there, the one coming now? We buy the special tickets from him, and then Orhan will bring us to the front of the line."

"Okay. How much?" Ramadan asked.

"Twenty for all. Cheap, cheap. Thank you, Orhan!"

Orhan shook Ramadan's hand. "Allo, America," he said. When the boy with the tickets arrived, he had a simple exchange with Orhan. Ramadan didn't know if Mehmet meant American or Turkish currency, so he held up one of each. "Which one?"

"These one!" the boy said, swiping the American twenty. Then he pulled three tickets out of his worn green canvas satchel, handed them to Ramadan, and rushed off. Ramadan gave Ibrahim and Mehmet their tickets, Orhan escorted them past about fifty tourists, and they went through the entrance with ease.

Wikipedia had left Ramadan expecting more ruins than splendor, but inside the Hagia Sophia was so grand it seemed conscious of its own significance. Its saturation with history and religion gave the air a thickness, a humid wonder, that caught his "Ah!" in his throat. He raised his right hand and made the sign of the cross.

Mehmet pulled his other arm. "Come, Ramadan. Let's go see the beautiful from the top."

They started walking to the left side of the vast main nave and came to a wide walkway made of countless irregularly shaped pieces of stone, a mosaic cracked by both design and time. After they passed through a couple of doorways, Ramadan stopped. "Mehmet!"

Mehmet turned and said, "I am here."

"I know. But where's Ibrahim?"

Mehmet arched his neck and looked behind Ramadan. Shrugging with resignation, he said, "I don't know. Maybe he decided to wait outside. Too much god, he say. But Mr. Nokay is okay. We will find him later. Come on."

Ramadan adjusted his overstuffed backpack and trudged ahead. At first he felt as though he were regressing with each step. But after he reached Mehmet, he shifted gears—and they began walking up a cobblestone ramp, the dark, narrow, spiraling passage to the highest level of Hagia Sophia. It was a herky-jerky hike for Ramadan; a temporal glitch of a climb, wherein a five-year-old Ramadan (maybe in his dreams) was trotting up the ramps inside the Superdome, even as the twelve-year-old him was now ascending this surprisingly similar ramp. Dizzy with confusion, he stumbled on a gap between stones. He almost regained his balance, but the weight of his backpack toppled him over, and he landed in a heap.

"Are you okay?" Mehmet rushed over and kneeled beside him.

"Yes. My backpack is just kinda heavy. How much farther do we have to go?"

"Not very far. I take the bag for you."

"No, no. I got it. Let's just hurry up and get out of here."

Mehmet started walking again, and Ramadan stood and adjusted his backpack. Pressing his hand against the cool brick wall, he propelled himself into motion. As they wound their way up, the main light source in the dark space was sunshine angling in through small windows, and Ramadan noticed that Mehmet's face was lit with a subtler blush of his gloom from earlier.

"What's wrong, Mehmet?"

Mehmet kept climbing and tossed back, "My brother, he will leave us. When he goes, we will feel like Cleveland."

"Cleveland? *What?* Speak English!"

"'I am taking my talents to the South Beach.' That's what LeBron James say when he leave his home team, Cleveland. Remember, Ramadan?'"

Ramadan laughed. "Oh, boy . . ."

"Ahmet, he is take his talents to Suriye. He is the MVP of my family! You understand? If he leave, he might never come back. If he leave, we might always lose. This is why Baba do not want him to go. Me, too. We do not want to lose."

Ramadan groaned. Lugging his backpack was turning the climb up the ramp into a slog. Then, mocking his own feebleness, he had two visions: LeBron James soaring for a dunk; then, hoisting an NBA Championship trophy. "Mehmet, I'm going to talk to you in your language."

"Huh? You don't speak Turkish."

"No—and it's hard enough learning to speak Mehmet."

"What do you mean?"

"Don't you see? Ahmet *has* to go. He wants to play for something that matters. Something bigger, like Ibrahim said. He wants a chance to win the championship!"

Mehmet stopped and turned around. "This is true, Ramadan. This is true."

"It is?" He had surprised himself. Then something else flickered at him in the darkness of Hagia Sophia.

"Yes."

"It *is*," Ramadan agreed, and the other obvious truth hit him like a spotlight now. "Mehmet…"

"What?"

"I want to play for the championship, too!"

"What do you mean, Ramadan? *You* speak English!"

"I want to go with Ahmet."

Staring at Ramadan, Mehmet kept blinking his eyes, as if he were trying to translate Ramadan's words but was having no success. Then he turned and started walking up the ramp again.

"Ibrahim was right—you need the Crazy shirt!" His voice echoed. "Ahmet will not take you with him. You are a boy! I don't care how many smart things you say about Drake and the bar mitzvah. You cannot go to Suriye. You cannot go to the war. What do they teach you in America?"

"To be free," Ramadan said, following Mehmet closely. "That's how I made it all the way here."

"Free, free, free! I think this is why Ahmet is going to fight."

"I don't know how to fight."

"Why then you want to go to Suriye?"

"To free me—it's like I'm carrying this weight on my back."

"That is your backpack!"

"No!" Ramadan said. "I've been carrying it my whole life. It's bigger than a backpack."

"What is it then?"

"It's . . . a man."

"I no see him, this man on your back, Ramadan. No man is there! Maybe he is just in your head."

"Yes . . . I mean, *no*. He's real. *I think*. It's my father, Mehmet."

"Your father is called Mehmet?"

"No! *Mustafa*. He's in Syria. Aleppo. Until I find him, I'll never stop *thinking* about him."

"Like I say, he is in your head."

"You can't understand. You have Mr. Emir."

"Okay, okay, so you think your baba is in Syria?"

"I think so—and that means part of me is there, too."

There were only a few others climbing near them, a group of three up ahead and a couple several paces behind them. As they rounded the next dark turn, a tall, wide man taking up nearly half of the passageway appeared, heading down.

Mehmet was looking back at Ramadan and saying, "Part of you. But I can see all of you, Ramadan. You are right here!" when the bulk of the descending man caught them by surprise. Ramadan grabbed Mehmet's arm to save him from the full impact of the hulking presence, but the man's mass and momentum slammed them against the wall, and they tumbled sideways. Ramadan hit the floor first, and Mehmet landed on top of him.

"Ow!" Ramadan yelled.

"Oh!" said Mehmet, face-to-face with Ramadan. "Sorry."

Ramadan heard the people who were behind them whisper something in a language he didn't recognize as they stepped over them, continuing their ascent. His eyes widened as, over Mehmet's shoulder, the silhouette of the man moved toward them. Stopping at their feet, the broad-chested shadow bent forward.

"Whoa there, boys!"

His American accent was itself accented by a humor-filled rumble worthy of his girth. Looking back, he called out, "Marge! You got us goin' the wrong way. I just darn near killed these two lil fellas down here."

A woman's voice lilted in their direction. "Oh, my lord . . . what now, Ray? You're the one said, 'Let's go out the way we came in,' when anybody with eyes could tell wasn't nobody goin' down this way. This is fer up. All I did was point to the doorway—and now it's all my fault. Well, what isn't? That's what I wonder. What the *heck* isn't?"

An attractive, slender, fifty-something strawberry blond woman in a sky-blue magnolia-print sundress, Marge came around the corner and looked at Ramadan and Mehmet struggling to pull themselves up off the floor.

"Oh, my word," she said, putting her right hand over her heart. "Ray-ay!"

"There're all right, aintcha, fellas?" Ray took a half-step toward Ramadan and Mehmet. "Boys fall, Marge."

"Well, they darn sure do if you bowl 'em over."

"Oh, shoot," Ray said, disregarding her comment. "Come on, fellas, get up."

As Ramadan and Mehmet stood up, Marge said, "Oh, good," and clapped her hands. "Oh, good."

"Magic!" Ray said, pointing at their jerseys. "You boys from Orlando?"

Ramadan and Mehmet looked at each other, then at Ray, and shook their heads.

"We're from Tampa!" Ray said.

"Where're your folks?" Marge asked. "I want to apologize to them fer Ray almost mashing you to death in this dark itty-bitty ole tunnel."

After a brief pause, during which Ramadan and Mehmet offered only frightened-looking stares, Marge said to Ray, "Sweetie, I don't think they speak English."

"Course they do. They answered my question about Orlando."

"Not by speaking English, they didn't. All they did was shake their heads. Maybe that didn't have anything to do with what you asked 'em. For all you know, they coulda been just rejecting the very idea of you. That's been known to happen, hadn't it?"

Ray let a beat pass as Marge's remark simmered, and then he filled the small space with another of his big-barrel chuckles. After a quick cuddle, they resumed their wrong-way stroll down the ramp. "Take care, fellas," Ray said.

"They're cute as all get-out," Marge said. "Aren't they just as cute as all get-out?" She staggered a bit on the path and leaned into Ray's bulbous shoulder, either for support or just to sneak a snuggle in the dark. "You know, I always wanted twin boys. Just like them."

"You *did?*"

"Ray-ay, you know I did!" Her voice was dissipating but still drifted back up to Ramadan and Mehmet. "You *know* that!"

"We tried, Margie, we tried." They were out of sight now, but Ramadan heard Ray clear his throat and say, "Where the heck d'you think Fran and Jerry went off to?"

Ramadan and Mehmet gathered themselves and then circled up the last few steps to the top of the ramp. As they exited into the wide upper gallery, they both sighed, creating a warbling harmony that had the tremulousness of an organ. They giggled from the ticklish feeling, then put their arms on each other's shoulders, and walked straight ahead to a stony ledge, settling into a spot between two marble pillars. Leaning forward and resting their chins on their arms, they gazed out at the floor-to-ceiling panoramic view.

"Do you see the beautiful?" Mehmet asked.

Ramadan looked all around. *Did* he see the beauty? He didn't trust his uninitiated eyes, so he took out his iPhone and turned its camera on. Its one eye, he had learned, was often more observant than his two. Maybe it could decode the beauty of Hagia Sophia for him. The same way it translated his touches into miles of computer code, then back into a language he could understand: words, images, sounds. He snapped picture after picture—snippets of semidomes; halo-encircled mosaics of the Madonna and Child; rapturous gilded images of Christ and John the Baptist; wildly feathered angels; Islamic calligraphic discs suspended in a planetary orbit. Mehmet seemed to take his shutter-tapping as affirmation that Ramadan was bearing witness to "the beautiful," for he kept repeating, "Yes . . . yes . . . yes."

When Ramadan finished taking pictures, they huddled, gaping at the phone. Then they pressed their backs to the stone ledge, slid down, and sat on the floor scrolling through the photographs. Some of them were a blur. But others were majestic fragments of Hagia Sophia, accidental works of art, mini-masterpieces, incidentally cropped and lit into something new.

"Beautiful," Mehmet said. "You take beautiful photographs, Ramadan."

"Yes . . . ," Ramadan said, feeling the power of having created the digitized images he was holding in the palm of his hand.

He paused on a photograph of the mass of people milling about on the main floor. A hint of something recognizable had caught his eye, but he let it go. He was about to swipe to the next image *when—*

"Wait!" Mehmet said. He took the phone from Ramadan and spread-finger zoomed into the center of the crowd. A lone figure stood isolated in the middle of the frame. Hands raised. Arms spread wide.

Head leaning back, so that his face was ringed by a brim of curly locks. Black-framed eyes seemed to be staring up, directly into the camera. Or rather, they would have been—except they were closed, accentuating his enthrallment. It wasn't just any face, or course. *It was*—

"Ibrahim!" both Mehmet and Ramadan shouted.

They jumped up and leaned over the ledge, searching the crowd. Ramadan spied a red shirt, the crescent-like sliver of the front edge of a blue yarmulke, and Ibrahim's flapping arms. "There!"

Mehmet asked, "What is he *doing?*"

"I think he sees the beautiful," Ramadan said.

"With his eyes closed?"

"Maybe he just *feels* it."

Mehmet watched a bit longer and then whispered, "It is a very good dance."

Ramadan agreed. "The feel-the-beautiful dance."

He and Mehmet exchanged the same conspiratorial glance that had inspired them to chase down the tram on Istiklal Caddesi. Without saying a word, they bolted from the ledge and raced back to the ramp. Ramadan, slightly ahead, had to veer at the doorway to avoid bumping into three tourists on their way out.

"'Scuse me!" he said, starting the circuitous descent.

Mehmet was so close at his heels that Ramadan thought his foot might hit one of Mehmet's kneecaps. At every blind corner, they slowed down to avoid another incident. Unbeknownst to them, their shadows were gliding against the cloister-like walls lining the chamber. Their essences were cast into strange darts of darkness, ghostly semblances of them that ducked and dodged their way *up*, back into the bowels of Hagia Sophia, secreting themselves away somewhere, as if these phantoms intended to remain there and haunt the place long after their hosts had left the building.

Once they reached the main floor, they went swerving into the hallway, and charging toward the wide entrance to the central nave. Ramadan's heavy backpack was working against him now, and Mehmet rushed past him. Up ahead, in the middle of the crowd, he could see Ibrahim, still doing his little solo performance, and Mehmet, "Türkoglu" on his back, zigzagging toward him. Lagging behind, Ramadan saw the whole scene open up before him: Ibrahim flapping alone in the distance; Mehmet moving into the frame; Ibrahim, perhaps sensing Mehmet, opening his eyes (just a little, his lids drooping, making him appear high on Hagia Sophia), repositioning his glasses on his nose, but not stopping his dance; Mehmet goofily starting to flap his arms as well; museumgoers stopping to stare at them; Mehmet and Ibrahim looking Ramadan's way, motioning for him to join them.

Ramadan lumbered forward and, unable to resist the dance, started flapping his arms before he reached Ibrahim and Mehmet. Then he was in their midst, closing his eyes as he had seen Ibrahim and Mehmet do, the three of them forming a circle.

As more people turned to gawk, sounds of surprise rippled through the area. When Ramadan heard the murmuring, he peeked and saw that an audience was inching its way toward them from every direction. Some people were holding up their phones and taking pictures and videos. Strangers pressing in, trying to catch some of whatever they had, a feeling. But hadn't he and Mehmet looked down, seen Ibrahim doing his dance, and wanted to join in, too? Why had he just thought of these people, so coldly, as *strangers*? It was a question, like all sound in this holy cavern, with an echo—for there, shouldering their way to the front of the crowd were two strange, but familiar, faces.

"Whoo hoo!" Ramadan heard Marge's voice rise with femininity. "*Whoo hoo!*"

She was waving to him with one hand and holding Ray's arm with the other. Another couple was with them now, and Ramadan, letting the upsweep of his right hand gesture back to her, heard Marge say to the woman, "Aren't they just precious, Frannie? Cute as all get-out!"

"Y'all know 'em?" Fran asked.

"Sure do. Ray darn near killed 'em back there in the tunnel. Didn't you, Ray?"

"Sure did."

"'At's our boys out there!" Marge yelled, extending her hand toward Ramadan again, not so much waving this time as *reaching*, wiggling her fingers, as if trilling the notes on a keyboard to create something pretty, or simply to touch.

"'At's our—"

Then, just as Ramadan was about to close his eyes again to let the full effect of the feel-the-beautiful dance rush over him, he saw Marge start to tremble and, unable to finish her sentence, bury her reddening face in the ample refuge of Ray's chest. Ramadan couldn't hear Ray when he spoke, but because he had heard him comfort Marge earlier—because they were not, in fact, quite strangers—he could just read Ray's lips as he patted his wife's back. That was the last thing Ramadan saw before he closed his eyes and sank completely into the beautiful: *We tried, Margie, we tried.*

❧

LATER, WHEN THEY took a boat ride on the Bosphorus, Ramadan felt detached from the other boys—even as they stood close together leaning on the railing at the bow of the boat. He was haunted by Marge and Ray. Those cheery yet melancholy Floridians! *You have to try harder,* their disappointment said to him. Otherwise you wind up still wanting the thing you never got—whatever it is—long after it was much too late to get it. Calling "Whoo hoo" to some reflection of it, claiming it as yours, when you know in your broken heart it isn't.

"The fourth quarter!" he heard Mehmet proclaim this trip through the jugular of Istanbul, his voice so joyful it almost pulled Ramadan out of his meditative mood.

"Yes!" Ibrahim said. "And overtime will be Saturday—my bar mitzvah!"

"I will bring Ramadan," Mehmet said, "and we will do the feel-the-beautiful dance again."

They leaned into Ramadan, who was recalling their arm-flapping dance and imagining taking flight over the hills to the east. Like Marge, the world had denied him something crucial, primordial—and it was just over there. With Ibrahim on his left, Mehmet on his right, he felt strengthened in his devotion to his cause, to himself. But he understood now that he wasn't the only one like himself, the only one of these. *These.* Whoever they were. (He thought of them, including himself, as the lonely, though he really meant the dispossessed.) Marge was one. Something told him his aunt Clarissa was, too.

He listened to the loud hum of the old boat chugging along, glad the group had turned quiet. Looking down at the water, he sensed that if his were a darker soul, or merely a more impatient one, he might be tempted to jump. He had no real memory, of course, of that time when, as a baby, he had done just that, and plopped onto the muddy bank of the Mississippi River, wanting something he could not pronounce. If he could have remembered that early act of bravery and stupidity, he might have seen his future, even more clearly than Miss Bea—for everything in him, all that had happened to him, was about to make him take another leap of sorts, just as impetuously and far more absurdly, into the muck of the world.

13

MR. AMERICA COMES TO IFTAR

S o this is the Ramadan who came for Ramadan," said Yonca Adem, who was waiting for them outside the family's apartment building.

He had just watched her affectionately greet her son and husband, and now it was his turn. Yonca was so starkly compatible with Emir and Mehmet that Ramadan felt he could have picked her out of a group of a hundred women. "That's Mrs. Emir!" he would have blurted out once close enough to discern the contours of her character. "That's Mama Mehmet!"

In the last of the evening light, her bright orange hijab set her face aglow, and she patted his head and hugged him, just as she had Mehmet. Withdrawing reluctantly, Ramadan admired her light green eyes, which refracted the color of her shawl, and which, outlined with black pencil, seemed adorned to accentuate both beauty and bounty—his, not hers—as if being beheld by her was its own reward. As Yonca glided away from him, he noticed that her head cover was translucent; he could see the lines in his palm beneath it, for he had reached out to extend the embrace. He had to restrain himself from clasping a piece of her hijab and pulling her back to him—all because her warmth and kitcheny smell were making him swoon with a montage of Mama Joon memories. (*Mama*

Joon, one wintry afternoon, a rosy red scarf wrapped around her head—
not orange like Yonca's, but close—a "tignon," she called it, even though she
wasn't French, some vestigial thread of Creole woven into the fabric of her
private vernacular, swinging the screen door open to let him in after school,
standing on the porch with one hand on her hip, somehow knowing exactly
when he'd come racing home; Mama Joon's embosoming grasp, the defining
physical interaction of his life, which from the day he was born had given
him this urge to be held by women, like Yonca, who stood waiting for you
whenever you made it back to them; Mama Joon putting a ten-dollar bill in
his hand, sending him to the grocery store to buy a bag of flour, his staring at
the bill inked with gray-green coding, not translucent, covering the lines of his
palm, but still, like Yonca's shawl, inciting the inclination to clutch.)

But Yonca was not Mama Joon. She was Turkish, she was Muslim,
she had green eyes, she was not his—she was *alive*. Her hijab cascaded
over his hand, flowing away from him like the memories that had flashed
so vividly, going dormant again now, letting Yonca be Yonca, and letting
him be.

Then she whirled away, yelling something to them on her way back
into the building. Emir raised his hands in the air, mocking and surrendering, as he joined a group of men working on a car near where he had
parked his cab.

"Come on," Mehmet said. "We wait in my room until dinner."

He dashed off ahead, but Ramadan paused to look at the exterior
of the pale yellow four-story townhouse. A row of similar buildings,
all colorfully painted, stretched up the block; a pink one on the left,
a sky-blue one to the right. He knew neighborhoods like this from
home, where the houses shared walls or were set close together, separated by narrow walkways. But Istanbul was not New Orleans, just as
Yonca was not Mama Joon. And *he* was not . . . something he couldn't

quite figure out. Shrugging off his confusion, he was about to run in behind Mehmet, when someone called to him from above.

"Hey, you, Ramadan Ramsey—Mr. America!"

He looked up at a young man with long dark hair, leaning over the railing of a second-floor balcony. Even from this distance, Ramadan could see the man's greenish eyes glinting at him, and he knew he was looking at another Adem. Mehmet was Emir's son, but this one, at least physically, was more Yonca's. His voice had traces of his father's, but his face was a masculinized version of his mother's, a squarer chin the most distinguishing feature. Or maybe it was just the way he was jutting it forward, with the nonchalance of a magazine ad model, that was giving the jawline its prominence. His whole demeanor was stylized, as if his appearance on the balcony was, in part, a performance. One elbow rested on the railing, and his opposite hand was on his hip, a thumb loosely hooked in his jeans pocket, and his tucked-in, faded blue T-shirt bunched at his belted waistline. He looked like a rake or a rebel—or both, and, Ramadan thought, more like "Mr. America" than he ever would. Smiling, he stood up now and draped his hair behind his ears. It was hard to tell if he was just striking a different pose or preparing to hear the response to his transatlantic tease. Either way, Ramadan took the gesture as his cue, because there was no doubt who he was looking up at—and he knew exactly what he wanted to say to him.

"Ahmet! Ahmet!"

"Hello, Mr. America!" Ahmet was waving now.

Hearing the greeting again, Ramadan felt Ahmet was proposing some secret accord between them, a strategic alliance. He wanted his full attention—and something more. Maybe to verify that Ramadan was a genuine heir to the surname he'd bestowed upon him; or to test the validity of that family's fame. He must have been satisfied because now he truncated his wave and was angling a stiffened hand up to his forehead—*saluting* Ramadan! Ramadan put up two fingers and touched his forehead, sensing everything the act engendered: mutual respect, brotherhood, the esprit de corps necessary to a successful campaign. And then he raised both hands and shouted, with an implied global solidarity that belied his private motives, answering a question that had not been asked, accepting an invitation that had not been extended, "Yes, Ahmet, I want to go with you! I want to go with you to Syria!"

As he said this, Mehmet came running back outside and rushed over to him. "Ramadan—no!"

"Yes! I told you I want to go with Ahmet."

They looked back up at the balcony. There, a stone-faced, confused-looking Ahmet stood, his formerly saluting hand plunking onto the railing. His eyes, registering anxiety and fear, angled upward and beyond them. The boys turned, and a red-faced Emir, making quick, heavy strides, was heading their way, yelling and pointing at Ahmet.

"What is he saying?" Ramadan asked.

"*Leave Ramadan alone! You with your big ideas! You want to save the world? You cannot even clean up your room! You think you can save the world? Maybe you need to save yourself first!*"

Ramadan looked at the balcony. Ahmet's face had gone pale, and his eyes caught the fading light, which deepened them to a watery emerald hue. Ahmet shouted a retort, and his darting chin dotted the air with an exclamation point.

"What did he say?"

"*Maybe I can do both at the same time!*"

Emir started shouting again, and Mehmet put his arms up in opposite directions, one pointing at his father, the other toward Ahmet.

Translating his father and his brother, he had sounded to Ramadan like a play-by-play sportscaster; now he was a referee.

"Baba . . . Ahmet," he said, facing one riled-up relative and then the other. In the pause that followed, he raised his right hand, pointed skyward, and said, "Ramazan!"

Then a prayerful voice began to resound throughout the neighborhood, heralding the approach of darkness, and the few people still hanging out headed indoors. Yonca appeared on the balcony next to Ahmet, and she motioned for the group on the ground to come upstairs. Emir put his arms around the boys, and Ramadan felt him release some tension. He pressed down on their shoulders, using them as walking aids, canes or crutches. Had Mehmet's words calmed his father into this weighty surrender? Ramadan wondered. Or was it the voice of the singing man? Or weariness from a day's work? Up on the balcony he saw Yonca smile with satisfaction. Maybe it was that simple; the flap of her hand had made everything better.

But then Emir patted him on the shoulder as they entered the building and said, "Come, Ramadan, come. We make nice for you."

❦

"IF . . . TAR," RAMADAN repeated after Yonca, who was teaching him to say the word for the meal she had prepared and placed on the table before her family and their guest. "Iftar."

"Yes!" She applauded. "You say veddy good, Ramadan. You sure you no Muslim?"

"Well, my father is from Syria. I think he must be Muslim, and that's why my mama named me Ramadan. I don't know."

"You don't know?" Emir asked. He was sitting to Ramadan's right, and he paused as he was passing him a large bowl of rice. "This is the same father who come to meet you at the Ritz Hotel?"

Ramadan's shoulders went slack, and his head drooped. "Mr. Emir . . . ," he said, wanting to confess.

Emir palmed his head and moved it from side to side. "Is okay, boy. Is okay."

Ramadan sighed his way through a tremor of absolution, Emir having shaken away some of his shame. Instead of passing the bowl, Emir spooned a large helping of rice onto Ramadan's plate. Being served this way, he felt doubly forgiven, as he stared into the steam rising from the rice. The damp heat met the mistiness welling in his eyes, and the same meteorological quirk that kept rain from falling on a warm, cloud-ridden day occurred, sparing him the humiliation of weeping at his first iftar.

"This is a good time!" Yonca's sunny voice broke through his fog. "Eat, Ramadan, eat!"

His mouth watered as he admired the mound of plump grains—he realized now that he hadn't eaten all day—and the promise of being satiated lifted him as well. When he looked up, he saw a flurry of the Adem family's hands and arms passing and scooping, pouring and slicing, sharing the evening's meal, breaking their fast. On the table, in front of Ahmet, a dish in a white bowl—a stew of okra and peas—reminded him of Mama Joon's crowder peas and okra.

"Nohut? Chickpeas?" Ahmet asked, picking up the bowl and pressing it under his nose. The rich, savory smell turned his hunger urgent, and he heard his own soft "Wow..."

Holding the bowl, he could see that the peas and okra were comingled with glistening, beefy-looking slivers.

"What's the meat?" he asked.

"Lamb," Ahmet said.

From the far end of the table, seated next to his mother, Mehmet said, "That is also my favorite, Ramadan! You and me, *we* are the same!"

Ramadan heard longing in Mehmet's voice, a plea in his *we*. They'd spent the whole day becoming friends, getting close, but they were at opposite ends of the table. He felt like a traitor. First, he had said that thing outside. Now here he was fraternizing with Ahmet again, conspiring over a bowl of chickpeas. *Poor Mehmet.*

He looked around the table at the Adem family enjoying Yonca's meal. Emir had led them in prayer before the serving began, and he and Ahmet had eyed their apologies across the table. Watching them now, including Yonca (who had finally taken a seat and was humming as she nibbled the crusty edge of a slice of pizza-like flatbread covered with tomato sauce, black olives, and crumbles of feta cheese), Ramadan smiled and controlled his impulse to make the sign of the cross, just scratching his forehead instead. Then he picked up his fork and scooped up ample bits of rice, chickpeas, okra, and the succulent-looking lamb. When the flavors hit his tongue, they seemed redolent of the emotional complexity of the evening: the soulful neutrality of the rice was as necessary as the truce between Emir and Ahmet; Yonca's joy at delivering this meal burst out of the buttery center of every pea; the angst-ridden yank of Mehmet's *we* triumphed in the moist mélange, everything inextricably binding together, tethering Ramadan to Mehmet's entire family. In a single bite, he tasted the mood of the entire season. Acceptance, generosity, forgiveness—all of which he had received during his day with the Adems—melted in his mouth and dissolved in his blood.

His "Mmm!" was louder than intended, an exaggeration of the truth.

"Is good?" Yonca asked.

They all paused for his response, and his muffled "Mmm hmm!" competed with his nonstop chewing. Adem laughter rippled throughout the dining room, and Ramadan took a second forkful, humming another "Mmm hmm!"

The *Mmm hmm* was an answer to Yonca's question, but also a tuneful *Amen*, closure to the little prayer of grace he was chanting to himself. It began, "God is great, God is good," setting the table, as it were, for the most satisfying rhyme in the English language.

AFTER DINNER, EMIR sat dozing at the table, attempting, every few seconds, to blink himself awake. Ramadan and Mehmet nibbled on baklava, giggling at Emir's intermittent snoring. Ahmet had gone to his room, and Yonca was in the kitchen putting away the leftovers. Trying to rise from his chair, Emir made a couple groans that turned into a loud, wide yawn. He stretched his arms high and wide and in a weary tone said, "Okay, Ramadan . . . I take you back to hotel."

Yonca called something out from the kitchen and Mehmet responded, "Yes! Ramadan, you stay here tonight."

Emir, eyes still shut, grunted his approval. "Yes. Is good. Is good. And tomorrow, Ramadan . . . tomorrow I think we go . . . to the American Embassy."

"But—"

"No, no. I take you. I make everything okay." Emir's voice was fading into slumber as he added, "I must get you back home . . . *safe*."

Well, how long did he think Emir would let him drift through Istanbul as if such behavior were acceptable? How long could he participate in this business—help facilitate a twelve-year-old's questionable movements? Enable him, even? Possibly endangering him? *Safe*, he had said, emphasizing his adult responsibility to protect Ramadan, a boy who had somehow found his way into his care. Just how long was he supposed to tolerate Ramadan's little Turkish adventure? Apparently until he announced he wanted to go to a war-torn corner of the world with Emir's irresponsible son. Of course, Emir had concluded he had to consult with the authorities, get better answers than Ramadan's evasions. For all he knew, there was something truly wicked at the bottom of all of this. Ramadan watched Emir let out one loud snore after another. In repose, he didn't look like the wisest man, but behind those bushy eyebrows and that weathered forehead was a brain that had surmised the truth: something was very wrong here—someone might even have committed a crime. But what Emir had no way of deducing was a more frightening truth: the place Ramadan had left behind, and to which Emir vowed his return, was no safer for him than Syria.

❦

AT ABOUT ELEVEN thirty, Ramadan woke up with a familiar drive, the compulsion to move—to leap, *to run*. Mehmet was asleep next to him in the twin bed in this tiny bedroom just off the kitchen, a room so small it might have once been a pantry; Ramadan thought he smelled cinnamon spicing the air. Hung high on the wall at the foot of the bed was a poster of Hedo Türkoglu wearing his number 15 Magic jersey. He was holding a basketball, surrounded by a battalion of brown hands, NBA defenders, and as he drove down the lane, trying to make it to the basket, his face was grimacing with concentration and maybe fear. Like Türkoglu, like anyone determined to score, he had to keep moving. He looked down at the jersey he was still wearing, and he grinned at how

Mehmet's obsession had had its way with him, filling him with the anticipation of what could happen next.

His eyes drifted to the bedside table, where Ibrahim—glasses askew—was looking at him. Mehmet had left the invitation there after showing it to him before they went to sleep. Ramadan picked the card up and traced the embossed lettering with his finger. Leaving now meant he would miss the bar mitzvah, and there would be no reprise of the feel-the-beautiful dance. He sighed, put the invitation back, and slinked out of bed.

In its stealth, his body pulsed with its past successes at sneaking out and breaking away, adding an efficiency to his actions. He was fully dressed, backpack on his shoulder, and almost out the pantry-bedroom door before he decided to go back over to the bed. Mehmet, bliss on his face, was smacking his lips. Ramadan reached down and fingered a long, bristly lock behind his friend's ear. "Goodbye, Mehmet."

Mehmet mumbled a snippet of dreamy dialogue. "Take the shot . . . take the shot."

Just like Mr. Emir—talking in his sleep. Dreaming of basketball, maybe soccer. He shook his head at Mehmet's boyish ways. Then, as he walked away, Mehmet said more pointedly, "Take the shot, Ramadan."

He didn't turn around to see if his friend was asleep or awake, awake and encouraging him, coaching him. Adjusting his backpack, he stepped into the kitchen, and his hand was still gripping the doorknob when, across the room, he saw a shadowy presence creeping down the hall toward the top of the stairwell.

"Ahmet?" he whispered.

He tiptoed quickly through the kitchen, where he was distracted by a glass-covered cake dish on the table, filled with baklava. Yonca dusted her version of the pastry with sugary green pistachio crumbles, and they glowed in the dark, beckoning to him. Unable to resist, he rushed over, lifted the domed lid, and grabbed a fistful of the crusty, honey-drenched treats. Clinking the top back onto the bottom plate, he flinched. Then, after a pause, he rushed out to try to catch up with Ahmet.

But in the hall, he passed a room whose door was ajar. Hearing Emir's snores echoing, Ramadan, as with Mehmet, felt compelled to peek in for a goodbye look. When he nudged the door open, its hinges creaked dully, but he assumed if Yonca could sleep through Emir's honking, a squeaky door wouldn't disturb her. He balanced himself by gripping the doorknob with his right hand, the hand not holding the cache of baklava. Then, swerving his left shoulder into the room, he clamped his chin against the inside of the door, and he saw the husband and wife, side-by-side, elongated mounds under a white sheet. There was just enough moonlight coming through their window to see Yonca's long dark hair sprayed against her pillow. Like Emir, she was lying on her back, lips slightly parted; she could have been snoring, too, for all Ramadan knew, but he couldn't hear anything over her husband's rhythmic roars. He could just make out the outline of Emir's head, thrown back with fatigue, digging its density into his pillow. The curve of his mouth vibrating was the only movement in the room, as his lips trembled with every protracted exhalation. Each spouse's outer arm was flung against the ornately carved wooden headboard. Overcome with the sense that he was invading their privacy, he was about to leave when something moved, just an inch or so, on the headboard. The wood appeared to have throbbed, improbably, like a heart. Squinting at the raised spot, where someone might have carved a daisy or a dove, he saw a bulge that wasn't decorative at all—it was the intertwined fingers and hands of Yonca and Emir. Her left, his right. Ramadan, who had no real-life examples of marital affection, was so fascinated by the conjoined hands that he inhaled and waited in suspense for the notch of knuckles to twitch again, wanting to glimpse, one more time, romance come to life.

Gawking at this intimate scene, he was still holding his breath when five thick, fanned-out fingers—only inches from his face—came slicing into view. He would have screamed, but the would-be sound was muffled as the hand smashed into his mouth, covering it and his nose so thoroughly he feared suffocation. The tip of his tongue had darted out for the aborted yelp. Tapping a clammy palm, it met an unwelcome salinity, and recoiled with the swiftness of a lizard's. Would it be so horrible—Ramadan's shaken will proposed—to die here in Istanbul, to die now, having just seen true love? Just once? While waiting to see it again? He relaxed a little and tried to suck in some oxygen. His nostrils, flattened against his face, sniffed the air seeping between the splay of fingers pinning him to his captor's chest.

"Mr. America is *bad*." Ahmet's breath, whispery and accusatory, insinuated itself into his ear. The words—just contoured air, really—seeped through the pathways of understanding, and their meaning stung him, as did the notion, which he rejected, that they might be true. In violent denial, he attempted to shake his head, his entire body, or what of it he could move, trapped as he was in Ahmet's grasp. His *I was just saying goodbye* was an indecipherable mumble.

In turn, Ahmet's *Shhhhh* was a hiss, more gaseous than linguistic. There was something conspiratorial in the way Ahmet was urging him to be quiet—just as when he had called him *bad*, his tone had been congratulatory and clubby, as to say he was also not good—and pleased to welcome Ramadan into the fraternity of the mischievous. Sensing this collusion, Ramadan, feeling trustful, let his body go slack. When Ahmet caught his weight, he rejoiced, and Ahmet lifted him and carried

him into the hallway. He repeated his shushing sound, and then released him. Ramadan teetered but pressed one hand against the wall;
his other hand was stretched outward, forming a loose fist. He opened
it to the sparkle of pistachio sprinkles. Ahmet's eyes widened, and he
plucked one of the pastries, smashed but still intact, from Ramadan's
hand. He tossed it into his mouth and moaned. Then he started to
walk away, gesturing for Ramadan to follow—which he did, as he devoured the last two morsels of dessert.

14

"THE SULTAN OF SILENCE"

Ahmet and Ramadan crept to the door at the end of the hall. Shoving it open, Ahmet stepped inside and switched on the light. Ramadan stopped at the threshold of the only room in the apartment he hadn't seen yet. Although Ahmet's bedroom was three or four times the size of Mehmet's, it felt just as cramped: a messy desk to the left; jeans, shirts, and sneakers strewn about; and an imposing pair of disorganized floor-to-ceiling bookshelves. Centered between the bookcases was an unmade full-size bed, a tangle of sheets and pillows. Ahmet grabbed Ramadan's arm and pulled him all the way into the room. Ramadan heard the door close behind him and the sound of Ahmet rustling papers on his desk, but he didn't turn around. He *couldn't*—

A mesmerizing collage of posters—prints of various sizes and eye-catching colors—was pinned to the wall above the bed. Ramadan propped himself against the footboard and leaned forward for a closer look. His eyes settled on the large poster in the middle, from which all the others spiraled. He was staring at (and being stared back at in return by) a big-eyed, strange-looking man with a block of a chin and an almost girlish head of hair parted on the left side and swooping across his right brow.

He might have deemed the face unattractive, but the weird mix of masculine and feminine (pale streaks of eyeliner and a rosy touch of lipstick were also visible) tempered his judgment. This odd fellow of original mien and stylish manner appeared to be straddling a steel structure of some kind and, from the startled looked on his face, was in some way imperiled. His long-sleeved shirt was cuffed tight at the wrists and ballooned out along his arms, a puffiness that suggested flotation, if not flight. He seemed dressed to survive the implied swift motion (with the threat of catastrophe) that this colorized photograph conveyed. And his suspenseful pose gave the impression that, afforded a moment's animation, he would escape from the poster, come plunging off the wall and tumble onto Ahmet's bed. Or maybe he was contemplating a scheme of his own. (His eyes said he was.) What if, once he had landed on this messy mattress, he would reset himself in a crouching position? Then, aiming for Ramadan's chest, *willfully* pounce!

It took Ramadan a few seconds to break from the mutual stare and read the words printed below: *The General.* Then he looked up and saw, above the man's head, arching in gold letters: *Buster Keaton.*

As he scanned the other posters, he realized each was but a variation on Ahmet's centerpiece. And something else became clear: what Buster Keaton was straddling, riding like a horse, was actually a train. "Love, Locomotives & Laughs," one illustration promised. Another boasted: "one of the ten greatest films of all time"—and that's when Ramadan understood that all these artful placards were promoting a single movie, one unknown to him.

"You like Booster Keaton?"

Ahmet's voice startled him at first, but he relaxed, amused at how Ahmet had rhymed Buster with rooster. "Who is he?"

"Booster Keaton is my hero."

"Is he a . . . a general?"

"No—he is a genius!"

"I mean in the movie. Is he a general?"

"No. The train. That is the name of the train. You see?" He pointed at the illustration in the uppermost right corner of his wall collage. Ramadan saw GENERAL printed in white on the front of the purplish blue engine. In the cartoony artwork, Buster Keaton was holding a girl with big swirls of upswept blond hair and dark makeup around her eyes. Her hands were caressing his chin, and they were looking into each other's eyes as they rode atop the engine with an improbable nonchalance. *So this is the love in "Love, Locomotives & Laughs,"* he thought.

Ahmet said, "You see? The train is the General."

"I see."

"Do you? Do you, Ramadan? Well, really, the train is life. You jump on, and it takes you on the crazy ride."

Ramadan said, "Yeah, I get it."

"Hmm. I think maybe you do. You are bad boy, but you are smart boy."

They exchanged smiles, and Ahmet said, "I study cinema at university. I will make a great film one day. Then you will really see, Ramadan. The world will see. Baba will see."

Ahmet looked back over his shoulder. Then he went to the door and peeked into the hallway before shutting it again—locking it this time. "Sit, Ramadan."

Ramadan flopped onto the foot of the bed. Ahmet swiveled his desk chair around and sat down. A long lock of hair fell across his face, masking one of his eyes, and Ramadan wondered, *What does Ahmet have to hide?* Then, confirming the suspicion, he draped his hair behind his ears and said, "Ramadan—I tell you a secret."

"Okay."

"I am not going to fight in the war."

"But . . . I don't understand. Everybody's saying you are going."

"I know, I know. I let them think that. I said it once. Okay, maybe more than once." Ahmet smiled slyly, tongue lingering in the corner of his mouth. "I don't know. People believe what they want to believe. Don't you think?"

"I guess so."

"If you tell them the truth they no believe . . . or they think you crazy. So, yes, everybody believe I am going to fight in the war—but that is not the truth."

"What *is* the truth?" Ramadan felt his chance of going with Ahmet to Syria fading away, the improbability of it all being exposed by something as unavoidable and simple as the truth.

"Well, like I say, people believe what they want to believe. Even you. You are people, too, Mr. Ramadan."

Ramadan wished he could refute Ahmet. But Magic was just a word on a shirt. The Magician was just a card. He really was just a person— "people." "People" got taken to the American Embassy in the morning. "People" got sent back home before they were ready. Before they had a clue about what to do once there. That truth was bearing down on him with the intensity of Buster Keaton's glare, which he could feel even with his back to the wall.

"I know," he conceded.

Ahmet said, "The truth is . . . Well, I already tell you the truth. I tell the truth to anyone who come in my room. Look behind you—Booster Keaton. He is the truth!"

Ramadan turned around and saw Buster Keaton peering at him, poised to leap off the wall and further ransack Ahmet's untidy room. A man who could ride a train like that, or even *think* about doing that and then put it in a movie, *might* be able to break out of a two-dimensional state and come lunging right into your world. In a flash, Ramadan saw it: a pillow flipping high into the air, catapulted when Buster lands, the top sheet, floating almost to the ceiling, before landing on Ahmet's head, costuming him as a Halloween ghost; then Buster on all fours, scampering to a halt, stopping just in front of Ramadan, his face and Buster's but inches apart, both panting with fright at the implausibility of their encounter, and finally, simultaneously screaming: "*Ahhhhhhhh!*"

He shook off the fantasy and cleared his throat. Turning back to Ahmet, he shrugged. "*What?*"

"Don't you see, Ramadan? Is me! When you look at Booster Keaton, you look at me. I must be Booster Keaton!"

"I don't understand."

"How to say my story? In school . . . my marks, they are very bad. I no tell Baba. He will say, 'Your grades look like your room, Ahmet!' And, yes, this is correct. But I know this already. I no need him to tell me this thing. I know what I must do. My best professor, he tell me already. 'No worry, Ahmet. Do good with the thing you love. Make the high mark in your student film, and you will graduate.' So that is what I must do, Ramadan. You see? Make the best mark on my film. My film! I make my movie of *The General*. Only with my style. My story."

"But what does that have to do with people saying you are going to Syria, when you really are *not* going to Syria?"

"*Not* go to Suriye? Who say I am not going to Suriye?"

"But—" Ramadan scratched his head in his confusion. "But you just said—"

"I *am* going to Suriye! I must go back."

"Go . . . back?"

"Yes. I already go."

"Really?"

"Yes—two time!" Ahmet put a finger to his lips and shushed Ramadan. Then he whispered, "Baba no know. Mehmet no know."

"And you say *I'm* a bad boy."

Ahmet smiled. "Hmm—but I need to go one more time. Soon. Very soon. Before everything is destroy. Not everything. But almost. My English . . . I mean—before Aleppo is destroy. But I do not go to fight. I go to finish my film. You see, in the film, I am the main character. Like Booster Keaton in *The General*, I must ride into the war."

Ahmet pointed again at one of the posters, an illustration of Buster Keaton and his train in the foreground and a panoramic battlefield scene in the background. "When I write the script, I think . . . I need a war like Booster Keaton's war. Like the American Civil War. And then I look at the TV one day while I still write the film, and I see it on the news. Suriye! A civil war! I see the fighting on the internet. I watch all the refugees come here—*to my country*—to escape the war. It is only twelve hundred kilometers away. And I understand—this is *my* war. My movie war. My civil war!"

Istanbul to Aleppo—750 miles. Only 750 miles. Ramadan understood, and he mumbled, "It's my civil war, too."

"What?"

"Nothing. But, Ahmet, it is a *real* war."

"I know! Is terrible. But that is why it will be beautiful, for my film. Nobody in my class will have nothing so real as the war. So I write the story. Booster Keaton, he always say about the film story, you just need the beginning and the end. Everything in the middle will take care of itself. I believe I know what he mean. Film is like life. We born. We die. But in the middle—anything can happen!"

"Yes, I believe that!" Sitting here with Ahmet was proof enough for Ramadan.

"So I get footage before the war with me in Syria. Then I get footage from the internet after the bombing starts. I also make things happen with special effects. Nobody know but me. Like magic."

He tapped Ramadan's jersey for emphasis. "You know the CGI?"

"No."

"Computer-generated imagery."

"Do *you* know CGI?"

"Well . . . not really. But I can change some things to look real in the computer, in the digital film. Fake CGI. I have many, how you say, tricks." After a pause, he asked, "What time?"

Ramadan looked at his phone. "Almost midnight."

"Come, I show you. Quick, quick! I must go soon. I have to meet Nedim."

"Nedim? Nedim from Istiklal?"

"You know Nedim?" Ahmet pulled his chair to his desk and opened his laptop.

Ramadan sidled up beside him. "He sold me this jersey."

"Of course. Mehmet take you there."

"Yeah."

"Nedim is good friend," Ahmet said. "He will sell me something, too."

The computer lit this dark corner, and the desktop was a leaf-bed of loose pages—some plain white copy paper, some lined yellow sheets, all with scrawls of fine black ink or fuzzy gray pencil (none of it legible to Ramadan). Notebooks with fraying corners poked out in places, and pink and green Post-Its sprouted everywhere.

Ahmet pecked at his keyboard, and a program zipped open. At his commands, a series of videos played, one after another, as if to dazzle his audience of one. The images streamed forth with color and motion so bright and manic that Ramadan started with surprise—more so because at the center of the action was Ahmet, or rather Ahmet as the character he was portraying in his film. There was nothing distinctly different about him; he was wearing the exact same outfit he had on right now—a faded T-shirt, blue jeans, and black high-top sneakers. But a heightened quality of movement (even more evident than in his manner on the balcony) told Ramadan he was watching a performance. This Ahmet was *not* Ahmet.

"In my movie, I—how you say?—spoof three of the best Booster Keaton films. *The General*, of course, which is the greatest. But also *College*—because I am college student, you know? And then I put in a little bit of *Sherlock Jr.* Why that one? you ask me. *Ahh* . . . because my movie is just like the fantastic *Sherlock Jr.*, a mystery. Everything is a mystery, Ramadan."

Ramadan watched as Ahmet's finger traced movements the movie version of himself was making on the screen: running in slow motion through a tunnel while trying to dodge a spotlight that kept darting to where he had just been; kicking a soccer ball against a brick wall; falling asleep in a classroom, while watching a film.

"See . . . here I am in my real class, my eyes about to close . . . slowly . . . slowly . . . The professor is showing us *The General* on the screen in the background . . . there!"

Ahmet pointed to the upper right corner of his monitor, and Ramadan saw the real Buster Keaton in action for the first time. In the foreground, the movie-Ahmet was nodding off, head bobbing, as his eyes pantomimed drowsiness. He reminded Ramadan of Emir fending off sleep at the dinner table a few hours ago. "You look like your dad."

"No." Ahmet leaned in toward the screen and frowned. "Hmm . . . is strange. Is maybe the camera angle, I think."

"Who is filming you?" Ramadan asked.

"Kadir, my classmate. He is not so great. Just okay. He is the reason I must go back to Syria. He lost all of the footage from last time. Scenes on the streets of Aleppo near the Citadel. It is all a dream, you know. While I am—how you say?"—and Ahmet closed his eyes and made three quick snorts.

"Snoring!" Ramadan chimed in.

"Yes. Most of my film take place when I am snoring. I go back and forth between the snoring me and the *action* me. Why? Well, I am making the big, big symbol about how people sleep while the world fall down all around us, Ramadan. When I am big, big movie director, the critics, they will look at my little movie and say, 'Oh, that Ahmet Adem, he was already think big when he make his student film. You can see he is already on his way to be the great artist.'" Ahmet laughed, amused by his own daydreams.

"But . . . ," he said, "my movie will still be funny, you know, like Booster Keaton. You do not hear me snore, because it is a silent film, like Booster Keaton movies. What happen when we sleep is quiet. When the train sound blow, when the bomb go off, when people scream. Sleep make everything quiet. So my technique is good, I think."

"What's the name of your movie, Ahmet? And what's the mystery?"

"Okay . . . you ask very good questions, Ramadan. Very, very good. And the answer to these two questions is really the *same* thing! *The Sultan of Silence!*"

"*The Sultan of Silence*," Ramadan repeated. Then he looked, alternately, at the wall of posters and at the footage on the computer screen, paused on a close-up of the movie-Ahmet. Giving Ahmet a side-eyed look, he said, "That's a good title, but it's not a mystery. The Sultan of Silence . . . is Buster Keaton!"

Ahmet smiled. "That is what I thought. But that would be too easy."

Ramadan looked back at the image of Ahmet frozen on the screen and pointed to it. "Then it's you—you're the Sultan of Silence!"

Ahmet arched an eyebrow and shrugged. "Is this true? Maybe."

"It's you . . . I know it is! You're the Sultan of Silence."

"I do not think—besides, I do not look good in a turban." Chuckling, he added, "It is still a mystery. I am an artist, Ramadan. I look for the truth. We will see."

As Ahmet shut down his computer, a cell phone began vibrating and humming somewhere on the desk under the pile of papers. "Ahck!" he said, clearing away several pages. "Is Nedim . . . to tell me I am late."

When he finally uncovered the phone, he said, "This is why I came back . . . I forget my phone." He looked at the screen with surprise and answered. "Kadir?"

That was the only word Ramadan understood, but it became apparent from Ahmet's tone that he was unhappy with whatever Kadir was saying. After three or four contentious-sounding comments, Ahmet stood up and paced the narrow strip of floor between the desk and the bed, almost stepping on Ramadan's toes. At the end of the call, which lasted only a couple of minutes, he stood still in the middle of the room. He swung his hand back, and Ramadan had to duck to avoid an accidental blow.

"What happened?"

"Kadir, he tell me we cannot leave tomorrow. His family is going to their old village to celebrate Eid. He want us to go after that."

"When will that be?"

"Eid is Sunday."

"What's wrong with that?"

Ahmet faced him and heaved a long sigh. "Everything is wrong with that, Ramadan. It will be too late. You watch the news? Aleppo will be part of the war soon. I don't want to be there for no stupid war. Every day we wait will make the trip more dangerous. Even tomorrow was not the best time. The time to go is now. We should really leave tonight!"

Ramadan jumped up. "Then let's go tonight!"

"What?"

"I can help you. Let me be your cameraman. I take pictures all the time with my phone. I'm good—plus, sometimes lucky. But I can do it."

"Of course you can *do* it. Is easy. Even Kadir can do it. But you are just a boy. Is . . . crazy."

"I told you when I first saw you—I want to go with you. Remember? I need to go!"

"You *need* to go? But why? I no understand."

Ramadan pulled out his phone and scrolled through his camera roll. He showed Ahmet an image he had saved there. The Citadel: *The Love of Aleppo.*

"Why do you love Aleppo?"

"I don't know if I love it or not, but I want to see it. It's my father's home. I want to find—"

He almost said it. It would certainly have been the truth, or at least part of it. But "I want to find—" was all he could say. And yet, somehow this fragment was a complete thought: *I want to find!*

With that, he remembered something else—something he had already *found.* He gestured for Ahmet to hear him out. "And look," he said. "I found this . . ."

He picked up his backpack from the floor and dug frantically into an inner pocket. When his fingers touched the edge of it, he looked at Ahmet and said, "You said everything is a mystery."

"Yes. I believe it is. No—I *know* it is."

"Well, I don't know if everything is a mystery or not." Then Ramadan pulled out the letter and handed it to Ahmet. "But—I think this has something to do with mine."

Ahmet looked at the front of the envelope and read aloud. "'Adad Totah . . . Ram . . . part . . . Street . . .' Is someplace in America?"

"Yes. It's in my neighborhood. But turn it over," Ramadan instructed. "There is another address, I think. Only I can't read it."

Ahmet flipped the envelope over. "I see. It is Arabic."

"Can you read it?"

Ahmet slid the tip of his finger over the inky markings, tracing the script. He said with a half-smile, "A woman write this."

"You understand it?"

"Yes. Yes."

"What does it say?"

"It is address, like you say, in Suriye."

"I thought so."

"Ramadan . . . I . . . I know this street."

"You do?"

"Yes. Is near the university, the University of Halep . . . Aleppo. My friend Sami go to school there." Ahmet opened the envelope and slid the letter out. He flexed its folds, and read silently. "Is from this woman . . . to her husband. A letter of love. Where is the photograph she talk about?"

"Inside." Ramadan took the photograph out and gave it to Ahmet.

"Okay. I *see*. It is a very old picture." Then he went back to reading the letter. "Oh, no!" he said.

"*What?* What does it say?"

"Oh, man . . ." And then Ahmet read aloud, translating, "'Do not lose this photograph, the way you lose things. It is the only picture left from our special time in Cairo when we knew we would be together forever.'"

He shook his head and looked at Ramadan. "But then he lose the letter. What happen to this man, this Adad?"

"I don't know. There was a storm. A bad storm. I don't think he ever came back to the store—or if he did, he forgot the letter."

"But why do *you* have this letter, Ramadan? The letter of Adad and Zahirah?"

"Za-*who*?"

"Zahirah. His wife. The wife of Adad Totah. The one from Aleppo who send this letter to her husband in America. Is Adad and Zahirah in the photograph. In love. In Egypt. A long time ago. Is this your parents?"

"Uh . . . no. But I think they are my family. I'm not sure. But they know who my father is. And they can tell me *where* he is."

"You don't know where your father is?"

"Not really. Somewhere in Syria, I guess. But now with the war . . ."

"Ahck . . . Ramadan! Ramadan, Ramadan, Ramadan!"

"What—what, what?"

"Don't you see what this mean?"

"No . . . *what*?"

Ahmet waved the letter in his right hand and the photograph in his left. "This is a good, good story!"

"But it's not a story. It's real."

"Okay—it is a *real* good story."

"It is?"

"Oh, Ramadan, I forget—you have this letter, but you don't know what it say. If you understand Arabic, then you will understand everything that is happen to you."

"I *will?*"

"Yes. Well, you will *feel* it . . . in a different way. More deeper, I think. I explain. You see . . . Zahirah, she want this picture. Very, very much. It is from when she was young and beautiful and in love and there was no war in her country. And she knew her life would be great because of this day. Sometimes one day can change everything—who you are, what will happen, *everything*. This is the photograph of her dream. A dream that came true. Even if her husband—the dumb one, the dumb Adad—go back to her after the bad storm, he forget to bring back her dream. We know this, because here it is in my hand! Oh, I bet she scream at him when he come home with no photograph!"

Ramadan watched Ahmet tighten his face, contorting it, visibly transforming, somehow hardening and softening at the same time. Then he spoke in a higher pitched voice than his own, channeling femininity and scorn. "*Oh, Adad, you stand here in front of me, back from America without the picture I tell you not to lose, crying about the storm, but I now give you storm, too! It was our picture of love. Of love, I tell you! Do you know what this mean, Adad? This mean you do not love me like I love you! That is what it mean, Adad. That is what it mean! You leave the picture of our love to fade away in America—to wash away in the storm!*"

Now Ahmet put his entire body into his performance, raising his hands as if to shield himself, no, *herself*, from the imaginary Adad. "*No—no, do not touch me! Do not put your hands on the woman you do not love.*"

Ahmet began to laugh, as did Ramadan. "Oh, what a scene I know it was!" Ahmet's breathless voice was his again. "What a great scene! You see, Ramadan?"

"It's great!"

"And so now . . . now when you find Zahirah and give her back her letter, the old photograph of young love, she will give you something, too. She will give you what you want—*your father*. You see? What a story!"

"Yes!" Ramadan said. Ahmet had filled him with hope. "Yes! Let's bring it to her. Let's go!"

Ahmet's eyes had wandered during his performance, but now he looked at Ramadan. "Go where?" he asked, still catching his breath. "To Suriye? You and me?"

"Yes!"

Ahmet sighed. "But, Ramadan, what I say—that is just the way I talk, the way I think. Like the movies. I don't mean these things can really happen. What I say is not real. Is not real."

In the moment of quiet frustration that followed, Ramadan felt the presence of the bullish little boy who used to tramp the length of Mama Joon's house. His five-year-old self, his own private Buster Keaton, lunged at him from the wall of his anguish. And he recalled the last leap into Mama Joon's arms. The day he knew he couldn't pretend anymore. He *wasn't* pretend; he was real. The day he became himself. Ahmet had just said, "Sometimes one day can change everything—who you are, what will happen, *everything*." That was his day. And what he knew then, he knew now.

He reached out and pinched a corner of the photograph, which Ahmet was still holding, so that they were both in possession of it.

"But, Ahmet," he said. "This *is* real. Za . . ."

"Zahirah."

"Zahirah is real. Adad is real. My father is real . . ." He paused before saying it—"Because *I* am real!"

He saw himself reflected in Ahmet's glassy green eyes, validating what he'd said—but also flickering there like one of Ahmet's cinematic dreams.

Ahmet was about to speak, when his phone vibrated again on his desk. He handed the letter and the photograph to Ramadan. Then he picked up his phone and showed Ramadan the screen: NEDIM.

Answering, Ahmet spoke mostly in Turkish, although mingled into one of the sentences were two words Ramadan understood: Harley-Davidson. Then Ahmet's side of the conversation shifted into the diminishing tones of a goodbye. He was about to hang up, when he brought the phone back to his ear and shouted, "Nedim!"

Ramadan heard Nedim's tinny grunt of a reply.

"One more thing," Ahmet said in English. His eyes shot to Ramadan, who knew Ahmet was speaking to him now. "I decide—I decide to leave tonight."

❧

RAMADAN STOOD BEHIND Ahmet at his desk, watching him scribble on a sheet of notebook paper. "What are you gonna tell him?"

"The truth. We go to find your father in Halep. We will return before Bayram."

"Bayram?"

"Same as Eid. Sunday."

"Will we really be back?"

"Yes. One day to go there. One day visit. One day to come home. Then"—and here Ahmet threw up his hands in mock celebration—"Eid Mubarak!"

"Huh?"

"The end of Ramadan."

"What about your film?"

"Baba no need to know about that. He just need to know you are safe. That you and me, we did not go to fight in a war." He signed his name and said, "Finish."

Ramadan picked up the pen. "Can I write something, too?"

"Okay. Baba will like that. Mehmet will read it to him."

Under Ahmet's name he wrote, "Thank you for everything, Mr. Emir. Mehmet, maybe I will see you for overtime! *Ramadan.*"

"What does this mean?"

"Mehmet will know."

Ahmet folded the note in half. "Now, we go to Nedim."

Ahmet grabbed his backpack and motioned for Ramadan to do the same. They were about to leave, when Ahmet said, "No, wait!"

He squeezed past Ramadan, reached up to the top shelf of the left bookcase, and took down a small leather case. Ramadan watched him put it inside his backpack. Ahmet looked at Ramadan's curious face and said, "My camera."

"That little thing?"

"Hey, man," Ahmet said. "This is not Disney!"

✼

TO RAMADAN, THOUGH, everything did begin to feel like a movie—if not one with the lofty production values of a fabled studio, then with the raw appeal of Ahmet Adem's work, outtakes from *The Sultan of Silence,* scene after scene, spiriting them along.

Once Ahmet zipped his backpack, they were off in a montage of motion.

Ramadan's ordinary senses captured some of it. But his others— his sense of wonder, his sense of anticipation—these sixth and seventh alternative senses recorded the rest:

Ahmet slowly opening his parents' bedroom door, Ramadan looking over his shoulder, breathing into his ear this time;

Ahmet propping the goodbye note on a table near the door;

The two of them descending the dark stairwell, backpacks in tow, casting twinned Quasimodo shadows; coupled also on Ahmet's well-traveled silver Yamaha motorcycle, which they mount outside;

Then winding and bumping on a zippy twenty-minute ride, most of it, once they've left the narrow streets of the Adem neighborhood, along the Golden Horn down toward the Atatürk Bridge, which Ahmet takes to cross into Beyoglu;

Ramadan, arms wrapped tight around Ahmet's waist, pressing his head into the rough canvas of Ahmet's backpack, opening his eyes to that medieval tower near where he, Mehmet, and Ibrahim teased one another about who was or wasn't a boy;

"Ah!"

"You okay?" Eliciting a rub from Ramadan, whose shoulders shudder, and who can't be sure if the tears splashing from his eyes and whisked away by the breeze have in fact been caused by the wind or by a surge of nostalgia, the emotions of the day;

Ahmet swerving the motorcycle around the perimeter of a sleepy Taksim Square, passing only a few yellow taxis idling there and slowing down to avoid a smattering of touristy-looking pedestrians staggering their way out of Istiklal Caddesi;

Ahmet speeding up and veering the motorcycle down a dark little alley, the headlight spookily splotching the distressed walls rising up around them;

An arm waving up ahead—Nedim, who with his other hand is squeezing the nub of the cigarette he has been smoking while waiting, then plucking it away in a splatter of sparks on the sidewalk;

Ahmet screeching the bike to a dramatic halt at the curb;

Nedim rolling a shiny black-and-red Harley out of the tiny storage room at the back of his shop and into the alley;

Ahmet and Nedim huddling in the doorway, about to exchange keys and money, but pausing, an argument ensuing;

Ramadan appearing, reaching into his pocket—"How much?";

Nedim peeling two hundred American dollars from Ramadan's hand—smiling, telling him, "Wait right here," ducking into his storeroom and returning to present Ramadan with a gleaming silver-and-blue helmet;

Handshakes. Goodbyes.

Ahmet mounting the new motorcycle;

Ramadan, helmeted up, following suit;

Ahmet looking back, asking, "Ready?";

Ramadan answering with a tap to Ahmet's shoulder;

Ahmet, accepting that as a yes, replying, "Okay . . ."; revving the Harley, announcing their departure to the Istanbul night;

Vrooooooooom!

PART IV

THE OTHER SIDE OF THE WORLD

15

GET YOUR MOTOR RUNNIN'

Ramadan had slept almost all the way from New Orleans to Istanbul. Even during the changeover in Atlanta, escorted by an attendant, he'd been a virtual somnambulist. The numbing airplane groove had detached him from the distance he was traveling. So maybe it was the motorcycle—being this close to the ground and actually *feeling* his conveyance—that was firing his excitement. And, too, there was the anticipation of what he was moving *toward*, instead of relief from what he'd left behind. Fleeing the locus of his terror and plunging into an endless blue sky, a pale, magnetic nothingness, had felt like an unraveling, a coming undone. He'd had to vanish into all that emptiness, and trust there was salvation on the other side. Letting go of himself had been exhausting—no wonder he'd slept and slept and slept. But this torpedoing into the night, this rumbling charge from the edge of Europe into the Middle East, was an adrenal jolt. The back wheel was fanning swift circles at his ankles, and the axle facilitating its propulsive turns seemed to be pinning into him, too, pedaling him forward, making him feel, meter by meter, *rewound*. Well, who could sleep through that?

Holding on to Ahmet balanced him physically, of course, but emotionally as well; it felt like his arms were wrapped around his quest. Beneath the roar of the motorcycle, he tapped a private, percussive Morse code of desire against the back of his throat, a four-syllabic, close-mouthed cough: *I want to find—*

So no, he couldn't sleep now, not yet, not so early in this mad dash to do away with the dash.

AT DAWN, AHMET, who in Ramadan's opinion had steered the motorcycle all night with greater agility than Emir exhibited driving his cab through Istanbul, exited the highway. They dipped into a town twinkling with lights, and Ramadan squinted at the eastern horizon over Ahmet's shoulder, which was adorned by an orange swath of sunlight, like the stripe of an epaulet. Ahmet drove straight to a gas station for their second refill of the tank so far. At the first stop, remembering the money issue with Nedim, Ramadan had insisted upon paying, and he did so again now. Inside the convenience store, they stocked up on snacks, stuffing their backpacks with sandwiches, knickknacks, and bottles of water, and then went back out and settled onto the Harley.

They were about to speed away and merge back onto the highway when Ahmet did a double take at something to the right and veered in that direction, riding all the way into a wide pasture behind the store. He parked the bike, and they dismounted. Offering Ramadan only a sly smile, Ahmet dug into his backpack.

"We check the camera . . . and the cameraman." He handed the camera to Ramadan and gestured for him to film him riding through the open space. Ramadan fumbled with the camera at first, and Ahmet said, "I show you. It is easy."

He thought of Miss Bea. *It's so easy.* He had come all the way to Turkey alone, just on the faith that he could do it. Now he was on his way to Aleppo with Ahmet. Of course he could operate a camcorder! And he started laughing.

"What is funny?" Ahmet asked.

"This. How easy everything is."

"Really?" Ahmet pointed to a strip of crape myrtle trees heavy with white blossoms at the back of the field. "Aim the camera, boy. I show you easy. Action!"

He got on the bike and sped off toward the trees, as Ramadan lifted the camera and set him within its sights. At first, he recorded a few seconds of jittery motion, almost as if the camera were attached to the motorcycle and capturing its bumpy ride over uneven terrain. Then he bit his lip and steadied his hands as he followed the bike's movements. About ten feet before reaching the trees, Ahmet slowed down and made a wide sweeping turn, placing him in profile. As he came back toward the trees, he sped up, spraying a comet's tail of dust behind him.

"Ah!" Ramadan said. For a second, he wondered if his voice would ruin the take, but then he remembered that Ahmet was making a silent movie.

Before Ahmet passed the trees, he reared the Harley up to a near vertical position, doing a wheelie in front of the crape myrtles.

"Ah!" he said again, panning with Ahmet's motorized movement against the backdrop of pastoral beauty.

Having completed one track to the right, Ahmet retraced his path. A summer breeze blew counter to his advance now, and as Ramadan shot the scene, shards of snowflake-like blossoms cascaded behind Ahmet like an August blizzard. He finished his second pass and dropped the bike's front wheel. Then he rolled back to Ramadan, who kept recording.

"You still say everything is so easy?"

"Well, you made it look easy."

Ramadan lowered the camera, but Ahmet said, "No, do not stop."

Ramadan pointed the camera at Ahmet, who said, "This is the thing, Ramadan—in film and in life—make it look easy." Then he winked and said, "Okay. Finis."

Ramadan handed the camera to Ahmet, who rewound and played the footage. They stared at the little screen, watching Ahmet glide across the yard.

"Good work, Ramadan. Very good."

"I told you I could do it," Ramadan said. "And see—you make riding like that look easy."

"Whaaaah!" Ahmet's yelp startled Ramadan.

Then, to his surprise, Ahmet started laughing and waving the camera above his head like a trophy or a flag. Puzzled, Ramadan took a step back and watched the spectacle of the full-size, live Ahmet swinging the camera back and forth in the air, its screen still lit with the miniature, motorcycle-riding Ahmet.

"*Easy Rider!*" he shouted through his laughter. "*Easy Rider!*"

"What's so funny?" Ramadan asked.

"Peter Fonda . . . Dennis Hopper . . ."

"*Who?*"

"They make the movie *Easy Rider.*"

A movie, Ramadan thought—*of course*. Ahmet was as in love with film as Mehmet was with basketball. He didn't think he was that passionate about anything at all. Not yet anyway. But the Adem brothers sure made him want to be. "Okay . . . ," he said. But are they better than Buster Keaton?"

Ahmet, having composed himself, grew reflective. "Well, they are different. But they make a great film."

"So it's a comedy?"

"Oh, *no*."

"Then why did you laugh?" Ramadan asked.

"Oh, I laugh because in the movie Peter Fonda and Dennis Hopper, they ride the motorcycle, like we do now." He slapped his hand hard on the black leather seat in front of them. "And they go all the way from California . . . to *your* city!"

"New Orleans?"

"Yes. This is what I am telling you! You see? Funny."

"I guess so." For a second he wondered if Ahmet was making this story up. Just as he had done with Zahirah's letter and the fantasy ending he had spontaneously created for the road trip they were now actually on. "So what happens when they get to New Orleans?" he asked.

"Uh—a Mardi Gras parade . . . and then something with a gun."

Now it was Ramadan's turn for a quick laugh at irony. "Well, that can happen back at home," he said, with no inclination to say more.

"It can happen anywhere."

He turned back to Ahmet. "Is it a *true* story?"

"No, it's just a movie." Ahmet climbed on the bike. "Come on. Let's go."

Ramadan hopped on and settled in behind Ahmet, whose stomach he felt vibrate with more laughter. As they sped up the on-ramp and merged back onto the highway, he heard Ahmet shout above the motorcycle's thunder, "Ea-sy ri-der!"

⟡

SEVERAL HOURS LATER, when they reached the outskirts of a quaint port city on the northeastern shore of the Mediterranean Sea, Ramadan was finally growing weary. Maybe it was because Ahmet had brought up New Orleans earlier, but he felt the sensation of home. At this point in his journey, so far from his city, any town thrust as prominently as this one against a flashy body of water might have touched his New Orleans–bred, comfort-seeking heart. He twitched with homesickness as Ahmet motored them along the coastline. After almost twelve exhausting hours of riding, this quiver of nostalgia threatened to drain him of what little waking energy he had left. He forced his drooping eyelids open. The liquid beauty of the blue bay tickled his Mississippi River–loving core, the navel of his nature. How that river, ever pulsing but a dozen blocks from Mama Joon's, had beguiled him. Its curvaceous will had shaped the entire city's being, its character, so why not his? Slithery and serpentine, it had even predicted the cunning with which its enigmatic essence, from the first time he saw it, would insinuate itself into him. So fluidity had always set him reeling, left him wanting to dive back into whatever and wherever—there were no words for it—he had been before he was. No words for it, yet language had quietly written the rules of his infatuation. A river, a lake, a sea—"a body" of water. Of course—*a body*. Being near one never failed to force him out of his.

Entranced but fatigued, he kept bobbing his head to stay awake. "How far *now*? Where *are* we?" His shouts sounded more like whining.

"Iskenderun. We are very, very close. Only maybe two more hours."

Ramadan's drowsiness persisted, and his helmet bumped into Ahmet's shoulder.

"Huh?" Ahmet looked back and saw Ramadan's head sliding down the length of his arm. Elbowing him, he said, "Wake up, wake up!"

Ramadan didn't open his eyes but said, "I am awake . . ."

Ahmet pointed to a park up ahead. "Look there. We stop. We rest. Okay?"

"Okay . . ."

Ahmet guided the motorcycle onto a secluded patch of grass and parked in the shade of a lush palm. Out toward the bay, the verdant ground thinned in color, as green gave way to a carpet of sandy beach. Ahmet hopped off the bike, dumped his backpack, and ran toward the water. Ramadan watched him shrink into the sunlit terrain, disrobing along the way, as he dissolved into the blue.

Removing his helmet, Ramadan was assaulted by a breeze. The sweat coating his scalp and glistening his forehead helped stroke him down to a surprisingly cool temperature. For an instant, August was April. Another gust swept under the legs of his jeans, aerating his shins and thighs, rising up to his tacky briefs. Overwhelmed, he dropped his helmet. The wind and the expectation of more tactile pleasure made him raise his arms out at his sides, as if his body were craving an ascension. Earthbound but ecstatic, he began spinning around and around, a whirling weather vane of a boy. He had no frame of reference for this atmospheric change, other than the momentous passing of one season into another. Time travel, it was suddenly clear to him, was possible—no, *probable*. Yes! He was convinced. You could move minutes, months, centuries ahead, *or backwards*! He was sure of it. Its certainty was borne upon the winds of the Mediterranean, rising from his ankles to his crotch, flowing through his curls, caressing his skull. He trusted the message scrawling itself upon his skin. *August was April.* Summer was spring. No, Iskenderun was not New Orleans, and the Mediterranean was not the Mississippi. But now was forever!

When, in his dizziness and delirium, he started his fall, he was almost already asleep. Almost. His head was horizontal to the ground, cheek but inches from the thatch of grass about to cushion his landing. His eyes were open just enough to make out Ahmet on the beach, shoeless and shirtless, boyishly kicking up sheets of water. The last few frames before things went black: Ahmet facing in his direction, jumping up and down; arms straight up; acting—as always, posing for the camera. He knew Ahmet was hoping he was filming and, going under, he was thinking, *Don't worry, Ahmet, I am* . . .

∽✺∾

BOOM!

Ramadan woke to the sound of gunfire—or so it seemed, as one thunderous strike broke through his slumber. He cried out in a throaty whimper and clasped his right hand over his shoulder. The double-barrel combination of the boom and his exclamation roused Ahmet, who, lying beside Ramadan, propped himself up and in the universal inflection of *What happened?* mumbled, "Ne oldu?"

Ramadan cleared his eyes. The sun was setting on the Mediterranean, and the serenity of the waning light stood in contrast to his waking panic.

"I don't know," he said. "It sounded like a gun, a big gun. A cannon."

Ahmet sat up, stretched, and yawned. "It *was* a cannon. Ramadan cannon."

"*My* cannon?" Ramadan thought he was still dreaming, having a conversation that made no sense in the waking world. "I don't have a cannon."

Ahmet laughed. "No, boy. It is the big gun, to tell us the sun is going down. You forget—it is Ramadan, Ramadan."

He had, indeed, forgotten—and *yet again*, he had fasted the whole day. Sleeping through the last few hours had made the sacrifice endurable. Ahmet rummaged through his backpack. When he faced Ramadan, he was holding up a plastic bag of goodies, and they lounged together in the twilight of Iskenderun, preparing to break their fast.

"Iftar," Ramadan said.

Ahmet smiled at him and tugged his ear. "Allahu Akbar."

Ramadan was fixated on the sunset, as a plump date slid into view. The dark, dimpled oval fruit turned garnet with flecks of topaz and rose, bejeweled by the last of the evening light. Where Ahmet had placed it, brilliant as it was, it could have been the sun resurrected. Jittery with hunger, Ramadan was nearly cross-eyed as he pinched the date, inches from his face, and put it into his mouth.

Chewing and smacking, he said, "Amen!"

Ahmet placed the bag on the ground between them and motioned for Ramadan to take more, which he gladly did. The sweetness of the dried fruit, a pitted variety, was the only flavor that registered. Years from now, if you asked him what a date, eaten at dusk in Iskenderun for iftar, tasted like, he would say, "Cotton candy."

Ahmet pulled out a couple of bottles of water and two convenience-store sandwiches—pide bread filled with beef, cheese, diced green peppers, slivers of red onions, and parsley leaves—and he handed one of each to Ramadan. The horizon was flaming out, and they looked at the benevolent conflagration: oranges and reds blurring into golds and purples—and the Mediterranean bluing into black. Darkness engulfed them as they completed their meal.

"I am glad we will arrive at night," Ahmet said. "Halep is very beautiful at night. Will be good in the camera. The lights. The buildings. The trees. I shoot that myself."

"And the Citadel?"

"Yes. The Citadel will also look beautiful in my film. We will go there. Sami, he tell me that very soon it will be a real fortress of war again."

"Hmm," Ramadan said, trying to shrug off his sadness.

Ahmet looked at him and said, "I know. Is why we must hurry."

They gathered their waste, and Ramadan dropped it in a garbage can nearby. When he returned, Ahmet had put his shirt back on, along with a brighter disposition.

"But soon—happiness! Forget about the war right now, Ramadan. We find Zahirah and Adad. Then we find your father!"

They walked over to the motorcycle and strapped on their backpacks and helmets. "But how can you be so sure about everything?" Ramadan asked.

"What? You don't believe?"

"I don't know . . ."

"You don't know. Okay. When everything happen like I say, you will think, 'Oh, man, Ahmet told me this would happen.' And it will be like I tell your whole story. *Ramadan Ramsey* by Ahmet Adem. Is nice—I like how this sound. You will see. But first thing—get on the motorcycle."

Ramadan got on, wondering who he was in Ahmet's storytelling mind. Peter Fonda or Dennis Hopper? And once they got where they were going, was something going to happen with a gun? Then Ahmet started the engine. "Now say, 'Forget about the war!'"

"Forget about the war!" Ramadan yelled.

Ahmet revved the bike, and sped off. "To Halep!"

"To Aleppo!"

16

THE POET OF REFUGEE ROAD

B ut of course, wars, if nothing else, are unforgettable. That might be
their only redemption. Ahmet couldn't even forget Buster Keaton's
cinematic war—and that was only historical fiction. Were it not for
his obsession, he and Ramadan wouldn't have been zipping along the
southeastern edge of Turkey, searching for an obscure entry into Syria.
And if forgetting an invented war was impossible, the idea of forgetting
a real, present-day one would soon prove a delusion.

Not long after leaving Iskenderun, they were cruising past a sprawling industrial complex, an oil refinery or a chemical factory, when
Ahmet shouted, "This is it!"

At the first opportunity, he steered the bike off the main highway
onto a dirt trail, pausing there. "Sami tell me we must go this way."

"Why?"

"No checkpoint."

"You sure?" Ramadan asked warily.

Ahmet reset himself on the seat and guided them toward the unas-
suming road. "Is ea-sy!"

But it soon became apparent that this "ea-sy" way—at least this stretch of it—was also dark and bumpy. Only about twenty feet wide, the road was lined with overgrown trees, whose branches occasionally encroached into their pathway. With the motorcycle headlight brightening only ten feet or so in front of them, they sometimes had to duck at the last minute when limbs reached out with a predatory aggression. They made the best of things at first and were making good time, until a particularly animalistic branch swiped Ramadan's right shoulder, throwing the bike off balance.

"Whoa!" he shouted, tightening his grip on Ahmet.

After that, Ahmet slowed down—which was fortunate, because only a few minutes later a parade of shadowy figures darted out just a few feet in front of them. To steer clear of this jaunty line of scrambling silhouettes, eight or nine in total, he had to bring the motorcycle to a skidding, sideways stop, spraying a fountain of dirt from the rear wheel. Ramadan heard several high-pitched cries being swallowed by the bike's idling gurgles. *Children.* The headlight was pointing into the wooded area lining the road, but it also spilled onto the path, allowing him to see the last scampering movements of a hunched-over man and, tagging along behind him, holding his hand, a young girl. When she glanced back, the headlight illuminated her face. She was eleven or twelve years old, roughly Ramadan's age. Her eyes, locked in their own high-beam alert, must have been twice their normal size. Was she peering straight at him? She was searching, he thought, for the dangers that lurk in the dark—and yet her anxiety had more resignation than fear, which he understood: when forced to run, you can't imagine that where you're heading is worse than what you've left behind. You don't mind, especially once you're safely across the road—or an ocean, for the matter—the uncertainties of the journey, the occasional scares, the things that jump out at you when you least expect them. A Harley. A big man from Tampa named Ray. And the worst of it was the best of it—not knowing what would happen next. Then he saw the girl, exultant at this latest moment of survival, move into the cover of the foliage, which started closing behind her like the entrance to a secret passage. Through the dusty mist lingering in the air, he saw, disappearing into the brush, her back leg and her shoe—a tattered, once-white sneaker bronzed with grime.

Above the hum of the motorcycle, Ahmet, technically shouting, but somehow achieving the intimacy of a whisper, said, "Refugees."

Yes. *Refugees.* The word itself sneaked through Ramadan, seeking some place of comfort in his memories, safe harbor in his heart. "I ain't no gotdam *refugee!*" he had once heard Mama Joon, sitting in the motel room in Houston after the storm, yell into her phone. "That's for foreigners!" *Evacuee,* he had deduced, had a respectability, an Americanness, even, that "refugee" did not. An "evacuee" had escaped the uncontrollable forces of nature—a Gulf Coast hurricane, a California wildfire; "refugee" connoted shame. But Ramadan felt a kinship to the people crossing the road. Theirs was a migration inspired by the same impulse that had brought him here to witness their escape. That he was running *to* where they were running *from* made him feel even closer to them. New Orleans had been ravaged by the storm, but it had been revived; Syria could come back. He hoped so, for their sakes. Because soon enough—he knew this from the time he and Mama Joon had spent away—the place the Syrians had left would start to feel like the only true sanctuary in the world. Maybe if their nightmare could be his refuge right now, then one day it could be theirs again, too.

"Okay," Ahmet said, steering the bike back into the forward position. The amber-lit passage ahead was still grainy with dust particles, making for a moody visual effect. "Is nice. I can use. Now is when we need GoPro! Get the camera—film over my shoulder."

Ramadan reached into Ahmet's backpack, which throughout their

journey had served alternately as a makeshift pillow and an unacknowl-
edged buffer of decency.

"Ready?" Ahmet asked.

"Almost." Ramadan lifted the camera and craned his neck up so that
he could rest his chin on Ahmet's shoulder. "Go slow. Let me focus."

He pressed record and watched evocative images—movement, night,
mysteriousness—pass into the lens.

"Is okay?" Ahmet asked.

"Yes."

"Is beautiful?"

Smiling behind the camera, Ramadan said, "I think so . . ."

"Good. See how the road turns here?" Ahmet guided the motorcycle
through a couple of tight S curves.

"Yes."

"I want this scene because I am not sure where one country end and
the other country begin."

"You mean you don't know when we will cross into Syria?"

"I know we are close. Very, very close. But no—I no know. Could be
here . . . could be here . . . could be right here!"

As Ahmet crept the motorcycle along and teased with his non-
committal narration of their arrival into Syria, Ramadan kept filming.
Coming at him this way, through the lens, this fluid, nameless, grayish
brown strip of land—the end of Turkey, the beginning of Syria—felt as
if it was not just being recorded by the camera, but by *him*; dissolving
into him, and he into it.

A few kilometers later, after they had picked up speed, the motorcycle hit another bump and skidded a little, and Ahmet slowed down
again, almost to a halt. He hunched his right shoulder, Ramadan's tri-
pod, and said, "Okay, that is enough film."

"Let me finish this last shot."

He leaned back as far as he could, making sure Ahmet's head was in the frame. Moonlight, gliding along the fiberglass surface of his helmet, added a lustrous stroke, and Ramadan thought Ahmet would be pleased with this image of himself haloing into the night. He was about to put the camera away when the right edge of the frame went dark and atmospheric. For an instant, he believed it was a serendipitous intrusion, more leafy branches extending into the trail—a physical nuisance, but a visual enhancement. But then the curving road began to straighten, and the black patch in the camera gained definition into two shapes, two vertical forms—*two men*—standing in the middle of the road. Unlike the other refugees, who at the sight of the motorcycle had rushed fearfully out of the way, these men had stopped and turned to face the light, to face them. And it became clearer with every slow revolution of the wheels, drawing them nearer, the men were proposing a confrontation. Indeed, crouching and stiffening their bodies, they looked like goalies or, worse, linebackers, staunch defenders, stalkers determined to make a tackle—or create a turnover.

Ramadan wanted to lower the camera and stop recording, but the tension had turned his arm rigid. And his own paralysis augmented his terror, as the menacing figures he had isolated in the frame were coming closer, growing larger.

"Ohhh . . ." Ahmet brought the bike to a complete stop, and Ramadan relaxed his arm and rested the camera on top of the backpack. The men appeared to accept this pause as an overture of engagement, for they took one step forward, rose up on the balls of their feet, and began to rock from side to side.

Ahmet whispered, "Hold on, Ramadan," and he pressed the gearshift with his left heel. Ramadan let the camera drop into the backpack and locked his arms around Ahmet's waist tighter than he had during the entire trip.

"They want the bike," he mouthed so softly that it may not have qualified as an utterance. At any rate, it was as superfluous as yelling "it's raining" in a downpour—and surely inaudible to Ahmet, who couldn't have heard anything Ramadan said, not above the motorcycle's screeching, not above the primal scream he had let fly: "Ahckkkkkk!"

He leaned forward, tensed his arms, and rose from the seat. Ramadan, holding on as instructed, was jerked forward, sliding into the spot where Ahmet had sat all the way from Istanbul. The Harley revved loudly, resisting the sudden demand for its maximum r.p.m., and the rear wheel spun violently and ineffectually for a few seconds. When the bike finally lurched forward, Ramadan's face smashed into Ahmet's backpack. He heard the commotion of gravel and dust spewing behind them and, more frighteningly, shrieks of attack from the men. The grunts and growls quickly eclipsed all the other sounds, and Ramadan opened his eyes to the stark vision of one of the marauders, whose snarling face was but inches from his. In an instant, Ramadan's expression of stoic dismay transformed into a warrior's mask, mirroring the monstrous face in front of him: his eyebrows arched; his mouth drew back, exposing his teeth; his nostrils flared and pulsed; and he heard himself screaming. The man flinched, frightened or repulsed by what was essentially his own reflection, but he recovered his criminal will just as the bike had moved past him, and he reached out and latched on to Ramadan's arm, peeling it from around Ahmet's waist. Still holding Ahmet with his left arm, Ramadan struggled to win his release, but the man's grip, though hot and human, had the strength of a metallic vice. He turned and shouted, "Ahmet!" but he saw out of the corner of his eye that his friend was locked in a battle of his own. The other robber had grabbed the left side of the handlebars, and the counterweight of his attempt to wrestle command of the bike from

Ahmet was the only thing preventing the motorcycle from spinning out of control.

This four-headed moto-man of a contraption sputtered along the dirt road in the Turko-Syrian night for only a few seconds more, a beast at war with itself—a life-form mercifully too horrid to be sustained. In simultaneous instances of inspired distress, Ahmet lifted his left leg and applied a thumping kick to the chest of his rival, who went flying forward, which suddenly seemed backward as the bike regained some of its intended speed; meanwhile, Ramadan reached into Ahmet's backpack with his free hand, removed the camera, and repurposed it into a weapon, slamming its steely back plate against the boniest part of his assailant's wrist, and the man's fist released Ramadan's arm like a handcuff submitting to a key.

Ahmet looked back over his left shoulder, and Ramadan over his right. Perhaps an owl witnessed the completion of their escape, but the human eye saw only night. Their forceful exhalations—the huffing residue of the skirmish—mingled with blasts of Harley exhaust, boosting their getaway with a lung-powered thrust. The motorcycle regained its form and, with the grace of a steed, spirited them safely on their way.

Ramadan examined the camera for damage and found it intact. He sighed, relieved that his survival hadn't required destroying the instrument of Ahmet's art. As he put the camera inside the backpack, Ahmet asked, "You okay?"

"Yeah. You?"

"Yes. But I wish Sami had told me we would be riding on Refugee Road!"

For a while after that, they moved along a smooth, straight stretch, and in the calm Ramadan, despite recent trials—or maybe because of them—again appreciated the advantages of motorcycle transport.

The immediacy of it. The tactile thrill. The sensuality of distance being conquered by time. Entering Syria through this backwoods artery,
a path so secluded and underground that refugees were using it, had
heightened his awareness of the secretive nature of their journey. Ahmet
hadn't mentioned they would be taking such a route—sneaking in,
essentially—until they'd left Iskenderun. Not that it would have mattered. But at least he could have prepared himself, in his way, for what
might lie ahead. He would have consulted his talismans. Tapped his
iPhone and checked in with Mama Joon. Rubbed the Magician for a
little luck. Kissed his mother's crucifix. And since they hadn't yet made
it safely off this road, all the way to Aleppo, he figured it wasn't too late
to say a quick prayer just in case. *In the name of the Father . . . the Son . . .
and the Holy—*

He was about to say "Spirit," when, at the side of the road, he saw
something that, indeed, looked spectral. Ahmet had just come around a
sharp turn, and he must have seen it, too, because he swerved to the right
edge of the road, surely trying to avoid hitting the haunting form on
the opposite embankment. Ramadan looked back and saw the silhouette shrinking and swelling, and what might have been an amorphous,
horror-movie blob or some large wild animal, gradually humanized. A
head stuck up—a man?—seemingly as surprised by them as they were
by it—by *him*. The white underside of the brim of his flat-billed baseball
cap flashed, removing the last trace of Ramadan's fear that they were en-
countering an apparition. No ghost would wear a snapback, he thought,
as the bike skidded to a stop in a shallow ditch.

"What was that?" Ahmet asked, guiding them back onto the road.

"A man," Ramadan said.

"Another one?"

A faint whimpering or just a gentle dry heaving came their way, emanating from where the man, shrouded in darkness, was crouching. "Listen . . . don't you hear him?"

"Yes," Ahmet said. The man was saying something in staccato bursts, and Ramadan thought he might be calling out for his mother. "Ma-un . . . Ma . . ."

"What is he saying? Is he okay?"

"He is asking for water."

Ahmet looked back at Ramadan and arched an eyebrow into a question mark. Ramadan said, "We have water!"

"But maybe he wants the motorcycle, like the bad men back there."

"But, Ahmet . . . it's Ramadan."

Ahmet sighed. "Is true. You are a bad boy, Ramadan—but a good boy, too."

Ahmet turned the bike around, and the headlight illuminated the man, his back rising and falling as he gasped for air. Ramadan jumped off the bike while it was still coasting and rushed over to the man. Squatting, he unzipped his backpack and pulled out a bottle of water. Before he offered it, the man snatched it from him, twisted off the top, and started chugging. The thrust of his chin skyward popped his baseball cap off, and it somersaulted down his back to the ground. Ramadan picked it up, a worn navy-blue body with a once-white, but now beige NY embroidered on the front. He looked up as the man took his last gulp.

"Ramadan!" Ahmet called from behind, out on the road.

Removing his helmet, he turned, raising one hand to block the glare of the motorcycle headlight.

"Ramadan!" the man chimed in.

"Hmph?" Ramadan responded—but the man, if he'd heard him at all, ignored him. Instead he began speaking in Arabic and making gestures. His voice sounded eerie but soothing to Ramadan, who understood only his final words, spoken as he pointed to the sky. "Allahu Akbar!" Then he smiled and patted Ramadan on the back.

Ahmet had finished parking the bike and was walking over to join them, laughing. "He said, uh, something like, 'It is hard to be a refugee during Ramadan—the hunger, the thirst—Allah should make sure there is war only when men can eat and drink like winners!'"

Ramadan said, "But I don't understand. Is he a refugee . . . or a fighter?"

Ahmet's face went quizzical. "Good question. I ask." He looked at the man and spoke so stiffly that Ramadan assumed he must be stuttering in Arabic.

The man paused, then rattled off an answer that made both him and Ahmet laugh.

Ramadan waited for them to regain their composure and translate for him. Ahmet began, "He say—" but the man cut him off.

"I *said* . . ." He paused to look apologetically at Ahmet. Then in a formal voice, more British than American, "Forgive me . . . ," extending his open hand, leadingly.

"Ahmet."

"Forgive me, Ahmet, but my English is better than your Arabic." Then he put his arm around Ramadan. "I said, 'Sometimes, my friend, it is possible to be both.'"

"A refugee and a fighter?" Ramadan asked.

"Well, or a fighter *and* a refugee—it works both ways."

"I don't know," Ramadan said.

"Of course you don't. You're too young. I am thirty-three years old. Yesterday I was a fighter. Today I am a refugee."

"And?"

"I must tell you, in the best of worlds, *tomorrow* I should like to be neither!"

With that, the man stood up and stretched. Ramadan rose, handed him his cap, and asked, "Where are you going now?"

The man sighed, rubbed the bill of his cap, tracing the NY with his finger, and said, "I am on my way to tomorrow—wherever that is."

He and Ramadan exchanged smiles. "I am Isa," he added, putting his cap on.

"Ramadan."

"Oh! Now I understand—Ahmet was calling out to you. Well, you live up to the season and to your name. Thank you for the water, Mr. Ramadan . . ." Again, Isa did his "tell me more" hand motion, soliciting additional information about Ramadan's identity.

"Ramsey. Ramadan Ramsey."

"Ah, Mr. Ramadan Ramsey! Very nice indeed. *Ramadan Ramsey.* Your parents must have been blessed—blessed with the spirit of poetry. Your mother must have looked down at you when you were born and said to your father, 'Look, our son, he is a song.' And your father replied, 'Yes, we should name him so that when the world calls to him it is liberated from its prison of prose—but also, so that it is commanded to sing the duet of our love.' Yes! Yes! Every poet is a dictator *and* a liberator. You know? They force us, whether we want to or not, to submit to the tyranny of their idea of beauty. But, at the same time, they *free* us to hear the beauty, to sing, if we choose, their melody, their *poetry*, which is always a form . . . of liberty."

Ahmet interrupted, "You don't speak like a fighter *or* a refugee."

"I don't? And how does a fighter speak, Ahmet? Does he only shout the angry words of war, or can a warrior strike out against an ever-present enemy, one as dark as the night surrounding us now—

ignorance—with the powerful weapon of wisdom, with the saber of enlightenment? And what is the language of the refugee? Is he doomed only to call out for assistance, to beg in murmurs for water from the side of the road? Or might he repay such generosity as Ramadan's with an offering of his own, imagination and wit, perhaps his only possessions, substances as modest yet as priceless as water itself—but that, too, can quench a thirst?"

Isa turned to Ramadan, placed both hands over his heart in dramatic fashion, and said, "Ah, Ramadan Ramsey, your poetic parents, they inspire me! They make me cry!"

Ramadan mimicked Isa's pose and said, "Me, too!"

Isa touched his hand to Ramadan's cheek. "Well . . ." Then he turned back to Ahmet, who looked stunned and starry-eyed, and said, "Ahmet, Ramadan, it has been a pleasure. Thank you again. Now I disappear back into the night. And you, you go wherever you are going."

Ahmet cleared his throat and said, "We are going—"

Isa put up his hand in a halting gesture. "I do not need to know. It is not my affair." He began to walk away.

Ahmet jogged over to Ramadan. "Isa, we are on our way to Halep!"

"Aleppo!" Ramadan said.

Isa walked slowly back to them with a concerned look. "Why are you going to Aleppo?"

Ahmet said, "Well, as a poet—and you *are* a poet—you will maybe understand. We are going there to find . . . *The Sultan of Silence.*"

"The Sultan . . . of . . . Silence?" Isa repeated the words, his face registering befuddlement. "Who is this Sultan of Silence?"

"To tell you the truth, we don't know either!" Ahmet laughed, and he turned to Ramadan, who joined him in a moment of private amusement. Isa folded his arms across his chest and stared at them.

"No, no, no . . . I make a joke," Ahmet said. "Ramadan, show Isa the letter."

"Okay." Ramadan dug into his backpack.

Ahmet continued, "We must deliver this letter—do you know Halep, Isa?"

"All too well."

"Is it still safe?"

Before Isa could answer, Ramadan was shoving Zahirah's letter into his hands. "We're taking it to the address on the back."

Isa turned the envelope over, and his eyes widened.

"You know this place?" Ahmet asked. "I think it is near the university."

"It is, indeed," Isa said. "This is in my old neighborhood. I was a professor at the university, until I left to join the fight in Damascus. When I came back—"

"Yes—finally the truth!" Ahmet yelled. "I knew you could not be a real fighter!"

"Well, I certainly was a real fighter. But if you mean to say I was a bad fighter, then you are correct. A very bad fighter, to be sure. That I survive to confess my ineptitude is a miracle. But it would not have made a difference if I were a good one. My country is in a battle against history—and history is too strong. History wants to be made. History is a *blitzkrieg*. History is undefeated. It always wins. I was hoping to help stop the war from coming to my beloved Aleppo, but now it is clear that is not possible. This is why I am leaving. Like a very bad storm, gentlemen, history approaches."

Ramadan said, "So you had to evacuate."

"Yes, Ramadan."

Ahmet said, "Isa, you say history *approaches*. You mean, it is not there yet, right? Halep is still okay?"

"Yes, most of Aleppo is still safe. The government has one side of the city, the rebels have the other. Things are relatively calm now—but not for long, my friends."

"Then we need hurry."

"You are almost there. But do not stay long—not even one day."

"We will not."

"But tell me, what is so special about this letter that you would venture into such uncertainty?"

"Someone left it in America, and Ramadan is bringing it back to them."

"Hmmm. It is widely accepted that the global postal service is some-what unreliable, but—why are *you* bringing this letter back to them?"

"It is a very beautiful story, Isa. Not silly like my joke. You will like it. Tell him, Ramadan. Isa will understand."

"Uh, well, because . . . the people the letter belongs to—" He paused, wanting to use words worthy of Isa's hearing them. "They know who I am."

Isa looked Ramadan up and down, and then their eyes met. "And you do not know who you are?"

Ramadan scratched his right temple, and he heard himself reply-ing, "No. I don't." He had never said this before. All this time he'd been telling himself he was searching for someone else.

"Well . . . ," Isa sighed, "then this is a very important letter indeed." He handed the envelope back to Ramadan. "You've brought it this far. Now return it to its rightful owners, Ramadan, and by all means, re-trieve your ransom!"

After they'd said their goodbyes, Isa came rushing back to them. "Take the right turn about one kilometer up ahead. It will lead you into the city from the north."

"Thank you, Isa!" Ahmet said, revving the motorcycle.

Isa glanced at Ramadan, and his eyes angled down to the crucifix shimmering at his sternum. Ramadan noticed and tucked it inside his jersey. "You know, Ramadan, my ancient homeland has been touched by all faiths. Tortured by them, too. Abraham—beloved father to Jews, Christians, *and* Muslims—once milked his sheep on the hill of the Citadel in Aleppo. Did you know this?"

"No."

"Well, it is true. It is a famous story. I suppose, in a way, everything, as they say, has been all downhill from there."

17

THE HOUSE OF TOTAH

B efore they heard it or felt it, they *saw* the first explosion. It was almost ten o'clock, and they were riding literally downhill—as opposed to making Isa's figurative descent—into Aleppo proper. The splotch of bright orange faded in the distance, and the delayed sound was but a muted rumble. Still, Ramadan's chest quivered. If he'd been unaware of the city's precarious state, he might have wondered if they were arriving just in time for a firework show celebrating the holy season. After a second eruption in the same area, he braced himself for another round of spooky, man-made thunder.

"Don't worry—the university is on the other side of town," Ahmet said, and he made a right turn onto a street leading away from the disturbance.

Ramadan's anxiety waned as they cruised into the center of the city. At first it was all black, gray, and beige—various shades of nocturnal gloom—but soon a welcoming metropolis emerged, lit by a rainbow of pale accent colors. Greens, golds, and reds dotted the cityscape in asymmetrical rays shining up from ground level or flooding down from balconies. Through the open door of a late-night coffee shop he heard the rhythms and melodic urging of live dance music, the plinking of a stringed instrument, the propulsive beats of a drum. Framed in the large window of another café, blurred in his vision as the motorcycle zipped by, two men were in animated conversation, their heads and shoulders set against a sepia interior. The older man wore a plaid patchwork cap and was smoking a hookah pipe; he was gesturing with both hands, doing most of the talking. The younger man, maybe a son or a nephew, was looking in the direction of the street, beyond the café, beyond the moment.

Staring at them, Ramadan remembered going for a late-night walk in the French Quarter shortly after Mama Joon died. He had just drifted along, block after block, even wandering through Jackson Square past Miss Bea's vacant spot. His aimless stroll led him by a couple sitting near the open window of a bar at Chartres and Dumaine streets. The woman had a wizened, old-lady look about her, thinning hair and dark, wrinkly skin around her eyes. When she sipped her drink, ash from her cigarette flicked onto the windowsill. She had smiled "hello" as he passed but, preoccupied with his solitude and grief, he looked away, though she had just offered him what he was looking for, a human connection in a moment of despair.

Now he found himself waving at the man in the window, the one looking for something, as the older man spoke. About what? The job the young man should have? The war? The bill? Ahmet made a left turn and Ramadan craned his neck to see if he'd made the young man acknowledge a fellow traveler, therein redeeming himself for ignoring the old woman back home, all because something in her face—her loneliness and his—had repelled him. And just before they swept around the corner, he saw the man's fingers wiggling out the window.

Affixed to the wall of the building that wiped the flailing hand from view were four vertically stacked signs, rust-colored backgrounds with bold, white bilingual messaging—trilingual, counting the universal icons. Ahmet was driving so fast now that Ramadan had time to read only the bottom sign—ALEPPO CITADEL.

"Ah!" He pointed at the wall, where a directional arrow told him they were heading *away* from the landmark.

Ahmet said, "I know. We will come back. First we find Zahirah and Adad!"

⟋⊁⟍

THEY TURNED ONTO a bleak-looking street, and Ahmet leaned back and grumbled, "I need to stop and check the address."

He pulled the bike over to the sidewalk and parked under a streetlamp. Ramadan peeled off his backpack and removed the letter, while staring at a graffiti-sprayed wall to the right. Red and white squiggles artfully surrounded a line of black Arabic writing, all above one big English word written in green paint: FREEDOM.

"What does it say?"

"What you mean? It say 'freedom.'"

"No. At the top."

Ahmet looked again. "Oh. 'Fight today. Cry tomorrow.'"

As he said this, there was a long whistling sound, and a glittering arch of fireballs streaked the sky. A few miles away, somewhere on the outskirts of town, a dull explosion quaked. Ramadan's arm, extending the envelope to Ahmet, trembled from the jolt.

"You know, Ramadan," Ahmet said with a little nervous laugh, "I start to think maybe we ride into the middle of the war."

Accepting the letter, he mumbled some numbers, then, "Fatih Sultan Mehamed Avenue . . . yes, we are near the address."

He handed the envelope back to Ramadan and looked around. "This was a nice area last time I come, but something is happen. Something is change. Let's go."

They hopped back on the motorcycle and cruised along for a couple of minutes before a group of institutional-looking buildings appeared on their right.

"The university!" Ahmet yelled. "We are close."

Ramadan saw the main street entering the campus, where there was a light but steady flow of students coming and going on foot, bicycles, and scooters. Flying atop its pole in the grassy median that stretched toward an impressive administrative building was the Syrian flag flapping in a gentle breeze. He had seen this image many times in photographs of protesters marching through the streets; but also in his dreams, mirages that morphed his desire for paternal intimacy into its surrogate, patriotism. The three horizontal stripes of red, white, and black (with two green stars stamped on the middle white panel) struck an emotional chord in him—ethnic or nationalistic, genetic or acquired. Or was it simply the satisfaction of having a crucial matter settled? Marked by a country's expressed faith, *his* faith, in the power of symbol, he knew for sure, at last, he was here.

Ahmet turned onto Fatih Sultan Mehamed Avenue, and there was almost no traffic on the wide thoroughfare. They passed a few hotels, a shopping area, and office buildings, but soon the neighborhood began to look more residential. Ahmet slowed the motorcycle, and it jerked and sputtered.

"We should stop over there for gas," he said, pointing to a small filling station and convenience store up ahead.

"Okay," Ramadan said. "And we can ask where the address is." He fanned the envelope in front of Ahmet's eyes.

"Okay, okay," Ahmet acquiesced.

They parked the bike next to a pump and went into the store. The dark-haired man behind the checkout counter had his head down reading a magazine. He appeared to be in his mid-thirties, and he was wearing glasses. He smirked noticeably when the door chimed, as if disappointed he had to engage with customers, and seconds later, his strained smile confirmed that they were interrupting his leisure. At the counter, Ramadan saw that the man wasn't reading a magazine, but some kind of a comic book. The speech and thought bubbles, which he couldn't make out from the upside-down perspective, except for a big POW!, were written in English. Ahmet stuttered his way through an Arabic request for directions, and Ramadan watched as the man somewhat grudgingly snapped his glasses from his face. The exchange was brief, consisting mostly of Ahmet's stilted talk and a couple of grunts from the shopkeeper, after which Ahmet said to Ramadan, "Show him the letter."

Ramadan slid the envelope onto the counter, between the pages of the man's comic book. Placing his glasses back onto the bridge of his nose, the man picked it up and looked at it closely. His eyebrows arched, as if he were absorbing something more than the details of an address, something that, like the comic book he'd been forced to put down, was telling an engrossing story, one to which even he, a would-be disinterested shopkeeper, could personally relate. His eyes, moving slowly as he read, started to twinkle, or so it seemed to Ramadan, who wondered if that was because they were catching the overhead light or—and this he intuited was more likely, as a tiny fleck of moisture gathered on the man's lower left lash—if it was because his eyes had, for whatever reason, grown steamy and reflective. Ramadan and Ahmet stared at the man as he continued to examine the envelope, almost forensically, holding it with the tips of his fingers, turning it from front to back, before flipping it over again. His movements had all been slow but then, in a flash, his attention ratcheted to them. His eyes darted above the top frame of his glasses, peering first at Ahmet, then Ramadan, before his focus, laced with wariness, panned again to Ahmet.

"Who are you?" he asked in English, his voice clipped with suspicion. "Where did you get this?"

"We want to find the people in the photograph," Ahmet said.

"What photograph?" The man opened the envelope.

"Yes, it's inside," Ramadan said. "We are looking for Zahirah and Adad."

The man glared at him again, looking him over. When the picture slid out onto the counter, he picked it up and stared at it for a moment. Then he swallowed visibly, expelling, at the end, a little cough. He muttered, "My father . . . is dead."

Ahmet and Ramadan stared at each other for a moment. Then, facing the man again, they saw that while he was still holding the photograph in his left hand, he was reaching under the counter with his right, letting it rest there, suggestively. "And why are you looking for my mother?"

A few elongated seconds ticked away during which neither Ramadan nor Ahmet moved or managed to reply. They regained some rudimentary skills of vocalization and animation—however primal and stop-motion jittery—when the man pulled out a large shiny silver pistol and pointed it at them, his arm stiff with tension, his index finger crooked around the trigger with intent. The gasps from Ahmet and Ramadan, as throaty and alarmist as the squawks of crows, matched their hands-up, finger-feathered poses.

The last things Ramadan saw and heard with any real clarity were the gun pointing at him and the man's gruff, repeated inquiry, "Who are you? *Who are you?*"

After that, his vision blurred, and he experienced a dizziness he hadn't felt since the day he was shot. Having a gun aimed at him— actually *seeing* the weapon this time—he revisited, in an instant, his complete trauma. It was as though he had never really stopped feeling it. The sting; the burn; the sensation of his blood rivering coolly down the length of his arm, puddling in his palm; the wooziness; and, perhaps most distressing, the hurt of it all, not the physical pain, but the ache of betrayal—not by anyone in particular (that would come later)—just the awful understanding, as he fell to the ground, presumably slain, that life, in general, had let him down. Then, after the initial panic, a subsidence of anguish, an acceptance, a *pleasure* even, the sleep that in spite of life's wonders, he'd always secretly craved—*the ultimate silence.* Now his knees were buckling, and he was crashing to the floor in this little Aleppo convenience store, about to black out completely, when he heard what must have been Ahmet's voice warbling with fear. "*Please . . .*"

Ahmet . . . , he wanted to say, but his paralysis had rendered him as mute as the essence of the very idea he wanted to express. *I know who the Sultan of Silence is. The Sultan of Silence is D—*

⚭

THOUGH RAMADAN COULDN'T understand the words the feminine voice was murmuring, its tones of consolation coaxed him from the depths. Maternal caresses broke through the barriers of language and unconsciousness, and he awakened in a state of sublime comfort.

"Ah . . . ," the woman staring down at him said.

"Ramadan, we are here." Ahmet was somewhere in the room. "This is Zahirah."

Zahirah's celestial blue garment heightened the holiness with which a dazed Ramadan was endowing her. Gaining awareness, he realized he was lying across her lap, and his torso was draped in the folds of the azure fabric covering her from head to foot. His legs were stretched out on the small sofa holding them both as snuggly as she was cradling him. Lying here in the care of this woman, who was treating him as if he were hers, it struck him as odd that he had willed himself around the world in search of a man he didn't know, *a man*, in pursuit of a hazy, elusive, unfelt-before, father-feeling—when here was the thing he knew best, the thing in which he had almost always been able to trust. Yes, his aunt Clarissa's cruelty had blemished the sanctity of womanhood for him, swinging the pendulum of his heart toward the pole of masculinity. But still, after Mama Joon's passing, wouldn't making a daring effort to discover another version of this affection, which all his life had been his saving grace—the nurturing warmth of a mother figure—wouldn't making a frantic run for that, *for this*, have been a far more sensible goal? Why had he wanted, why did he *still* want Mustafa? Had he come all this way under false pretenses? What if, in the end, there was nothing greater than *this*?

"Bae-bae is wake," Zahirah said, dabbing a thin glaze of sweat from his forehead with a fistful of her garment, adding, with this pampering, more gravity to his self-doubt. Her dark, expressive eyes beamed down, asking about his well-being with far more depth than her English permitted. "Is okay?"

Ramadan sat up and put his feet on the floor, breaking the contentment he'd felt while in her arms. She scooched closer and took his face in her hands. "I see Malik, when he was a boy."

"Ma-ma . . . ," Malik said from across the room.

"I am the mother," she said, still looking at Ramadan. "I know. You have just one thing different—American color."

"And that curly hair!" Malik shouted. "Boy—you could be a comic-book character!"

"No, no. Adad father, he have this hair—how you say—*kully?* But change the color and the kully, comedy hair, and I am looking at the young you." Her voice lost its wistfulness when she added, "And you show the boy the gun, Malik! Is like you show the gun against you-self! The war—it make men crazy."

Zahirah let her fingers disappear into Ramadan's curls. "Yes, you look like the Totah boys."

"But he is *not* a Totah boy, Mama."

"I know this! I just say he look like Totah boys. The eye. The nose. The mouth. Is very strange . . ." Then she yelled something in Arabic.

Malik responded, sounding to Ramadan as though he might be cursing. After a pause, he said, "She just likes you because you bring her that picture of her and Baba."

"Yes," she said. "Thank you . . . thank you!"

Distracted by the idea that he looked like a Totah, he'd forgotten all about the letter. Now he felt certain his father was related to these people, that *he* was, too. But whatever Ahmet had told them, he must not have mentioned anything about Mustafa.

Zahirah picked up the photograph from the coffee table. If Malik had handled the letter like someone wanting to know everything about it, she held the picture as if it knew everything about her. "This day!" Her voice was filled with nostalgia. Then she added, almost inaudibly, "My secret . . ."

"What secret, Mama?"

Ignoring the question, she continued, "Look, Malik—" She showed him the image. "Baba is so young. He look like Totah boy, too! But he was a man . . ."

She cackled, and Malik shrugged, averting his eyes.

Ramadan looked at Ahmet, who motioned for him to say something. But he shook his head. What if, like Adad, Mustafa . . . was . . . ?

"Ramadan . . . ," Ahmet said.

"Allahu Akbar," Zahirah and Malik said together.

"No," Ahmet said, pointing to Ramadan. "*Him.* He wants to ask you something."

"Oh, yes, Ramadan." Zahirah rubbed his hand. "Is *you.*"

"Uh," Ramadan began. "I was wondering . . . what happened to Mr. Adad?"

Zahirah pointed her chin toward the ceiling and sighed, but Malik stepped forward. "The big storm. You are from New Orleans, but maybe you are too young to remember."

"No, I remember. I was there."

"Okay. I was there, too. Me, Baba, and my brother, Jamil. We should stay in the store that night, near the high ground. But instead we go home to the parish, past the Ninth Ward. St. Bernard. We have never been through a storm before. We do not know the smart place to be. We do not know what will happen."

Ramadan said, "Nobody knew."

"This is true, Ramadan. Well, we think while we sleep in the night, Baba must decide to go back to the store. Maybe for the computer. Jamil left it in the office. The whole business was in the laptop. No backup nowhere. Stupid, you know. So maybe that was why he went back out, but we don't know. The levee must break when he leave. Too much water. Water everywhere. *Everywhere.* We wake up and the neighborhood is like the ocean. And Baba, he cannot swim. He always say he hate the water. That night—the water hate him, too."

"No!" Zahirah objected. "He did not hate the water. He like a good bath. And he like the river! See here, in the picture. We ride in a boat on the Nile!"

"Okay, Mama!" Malik heaved a sigh before continuing. "So then, next day, after the crazy night, is water everywhere. Me and Jamil, we must swim to be safe. And while we stop to rest on the roof of a mechanic shop, we see a little boat come to us. Is like a dream. So much of what happen is like a dream. I look at Jamil, and Jamil look at me. We don't believe it. But if he see the boat and I see the boat, it must to be true. 'Allahu Akbar,' I say. 'Allahu Akbar,' Jamil say. And then we get in the little boat—and we go to look for Baba in the city." He paused and chuckled. "Mama, is like we float on the Nile, the Nile of the Ninth Ward."

Zahirah's body vibrated with complicated laughter. Ramadan saw the corners of her eyes twinkle the way Malik's had when he had pored over the letter in the store.

"But then the police, they stop us. They think we are bad Arab men. We try to explain about how we search for Baba, but we do not find him. But with no Baba and the whole city destroy, nobody believe us. The police do not believe. They point the guns at me and Jamil—like I do to you, Ramadan. Is what people do when they do not understand, when they do not put them self in the place of the other man. And then . . . and then we go to jail! And then they move us to Texas. And then we deport. Boom, boom, boom. Just like this. Is crazy but true." Malik raised his hands in surrender.

Zahirah said, "And one day, more than *two years* after the storm— government letter. Official papers of death. Adad Totah, dead, drown.

It make me think how my Adad die. Alone. In this Nile of the Ninth Ward. In the water he sometime love, sometime hate. Was he afraid? Do he think about me? I wish to know what happen. But the government letter do not tell me nothing. It do not tell me what happen at the end. The *end* end. Who know that? The government do not know. Even if I am there with Adad, I do not know. Only Allah know. Only Allah . . ."

Where did all this water come from? Adad wondered. So much, so fast! Streaming into the old Ford that carried him and the boys to the store every day and home every night. A minute ago the truck was still just a truck, rolling on the dark, slick road, skidding a little, shifting in the wind, pelted by the rain, but nevertheless rolling, as it was meant to do, as he rushed back to the store. And then—whoosh—the truck was a boat. Out of the stormy blackness of this last stretch of the Lower Ninth Ward right before he reached the Industrial Canal—this crazy current had lifted the vehicle off the ground, set it afloat, set him adrift. The engine had choked up, then gone silent; the headlights and the dashboard had blinked off; and the steering wheel had locked. Rudderless, the truck-boat had spun around and around, out of his control. Those first few seconds of the Ford canoeing in the water had felt almost magical. Like experiencing the impossible. Or maybe it felt more like a dream, because in this case he was in the middle of the magic. In the middle of a thing becoming a thing it was not. And if a truck could become a boat, then what could this dream make of him? What would he, part of this becoming, become? The dreaminess of the situation proposed promising possibilities. Meet Admiral Adad Totah, the naval commander, at the helm of a vessel on the high seas, leading a flotilla of other truck-boats, charging toward an unsuspecting shore, one deserving of being conquered, doing the bidding of a worthy king. Or, more modestly, but no less purposefully, the crusty old angler Adad, a fisherman alone at sea in a tempest, out early, before dawn, line cast, awaiting the weighty tug, the challenge and the satisfaction of reeling in the first catch of the day. Either way, an Adad who was up to this task. An Adad perfectly compatible with this: the magical floating Ford. His dream boat.

And it had been a dream that had brought him here, waking him up in the middle of the night. A happy dream at first. Just ticking off in his slumber the events of the day before they meandered into meaning—oh, yes, the surprise of seeing the young one, Mustafa's boy. The little Totah. He had been dreaming about the boy. How things like this happen, there's no way to know. If the boy had not run out of the store. If the old woman, his grandma, no doubt, had not called after him. If Adad did not owe her change! If there were no such thing as change! Thank you, Allah, for change!

"Today I saw your boy!" he had said to Mustafa. "They call him 'Ramadan'! Can you believe this? What a blessing! What a blessing!" And how happy Mustafa had sounded. Which should have reminded Adad. He had still been at the store when he had placed the call home. Malik and Jamil had not yet finished outside with their rushed, haphazard hammering, boarding up the building. (They had been so flustered by the preparations for disaster. Later, after the rain had already started, Malik had poked his head into Adad's bedroom and muttered, "Jamil forgot the computer.") Adad could have just walked into the office—oh, he would have seen the laptop, too!—opened the desk drawer, and found the letter, the photograph.

Yes, during the call, it had not been too late to remember.

"What about Alicia?" Mustafa had asked.

"She wasn't with them. Just the boy and the grandmother. But isn't it a blessing?"

"Yes, yes!" Mustafa had said, sounding to Adad as excitable, as frisky as the nineteen-year-old he had been in America years before, getting into trouble with all that bad business, the business that—in spite of everything, judging by the boy with the Totah eyes—had turned out pretty good. "What a blessing!"

Yes, the joy in Mustafa's voice should have reminded him. It should have brought him back to when he himself was young, and he had first known he was going to be a father—when Zahirah had told him she was pregnant with Malik! Even before they were married. Before their time on the boat. On the Nile. Before the photograph in which she and he had been captured in the resplendence of their sin!

But no. He had not remembered until he was in bed asleep. Muttering to himself about Jamil leaving the laptop, he had dropped off quickly. Sighing, thinking how it could be replaced—everything could be replaced—if the hurricane damaged the store. He was counting his blessings . . .

Then later, through the sounds of the storm, which was rattling his bedroom window, he had heard Mustafa ask about the girl when he had called him about his son—"What about Alicia?"—only in his dreams, where things become things they are not, Adad had heard a different question. "What about Zahirah?"

Zahirah!

And only then did he remember. What time was it? What difference did that make? He had peeked out the window. Wild winds and rain. This was why he worked indoors! Who needed such misery! He had to go back. If he hurried, he could drive to the store and get the photograph before the worst of the storm arrived, before the boys were even awake. They would think he went back for the laptop. Yes, that was what he would tell them in the morning, in the light of day. Not for the picture of him and their mother—which he could not explain—not to rescue the resplendence of sin. You can't explain why the bad business, even to a good businessman like him, was, in the end, all that really mattered.

It was almost a straight shot up Claiborne Avenue to the canal, then over to St. Claude Avenue . . . he could do this in his sleep!

And the truck-boat was being tossed into the branches of a tree, more water sloshing inside. More water than air now. The air becoming water. He couldn't blame his lungs for their confusion. All because he'd seen the boy and the woman. Called Mustafa. Remembered too late. Dreamed.

What was this death, his death, worth? he wondered. What commodity could it buy? Surely Allah knew the precise value of things. All things. He would not ask for too much or too little. What Allah took—in this instance Adad himself—was just what was needed to cover the cost of something, the cost of whatever Adad had extracted from the world. Yes, Adad knew this. He was paying for his life with his life. What a perfect transaction! There would be no need for Allah to fumble around with paper or coins. No counting change. No shutting the drawer. Just a smile. A thanks. A "Next!"

And Adad could feel the truck-boat, now filled with air-water, becoming something else. A womb. A womb welcoming him—at long last—home.

"And now," Malik said, "all these years later, you, American boy, you come into my store, in my country, my *home*, with another letter. Like I say, I do not understand. I think back to the storm, Baba, the police, how America push us out. When I see you, I see all of this. So I show you the gun! And, you know, I still do not understand, Ramadan. I am confuse. I am *confuse* . . ."

Malik began to cry, and Zahirah rushed over to console him.

"I'm sorry," Ramadan said. He frowned as he squeezed the bridge of his nose. Ahmet sat next to him and put his arm around him.

"Speak, Ramadan." He looked at Ahmet, who whispered again, "Speak."

They stood up together, and Ahmet placed his hand on Ramadan's back and pressed him forward. Ramadan looked at Zahirah and Malik and said, "What happened to Mustafa?"

The mother and son stared at him and asked, in unison, "Mustafa?"

"Yes, Mustafa."

"Mustafa Totah?" Zahirah alone asked.

"Yes . . ." *Mustafa Totah.* So there was such a man, and Zahirah knew him! "Malik, did he get deported with you?"

"No . . ."

"Well . . . was he with Mr. Adad in the storm?" He couldn't bring himself to ask what he was wondering.

Malik's face looked even more confused than a moment before. "No . . ."

Relieved but unsatisfied, Ramadan persisted, "Well, then . . . what happened to him? What happened to *Mustafa Totah—*"

Startled, he interrupted his inquiry—the unanswered question of his life—for the most ghostly of figures, springing from behind Zahirah, suddenly entered the room. Had it been there all along? This queer silhouette had an almost supernatural presence, and the timing of its arrival (just as he had uttered, for the first time, his father's full name), made him feel he had somehow conjured it into being. *Mustafa?* Was *this* Mustafa Totah? Had his ardent pleas for the spirit of his father finally projected before him what had loomed so long only in his mind? If, defying all laws of probability and reason, that same passion had transported him (and surely it had) across thousands of miles into the living room of his would-be relatives, then what couldn't it do? But no—of course, this was *not* Mustafa, or his ghost. Dressed like Zahirah, roughly the same height, the form was proclaiming its gender. And when it—*she*, Ramadan understood now—was about to walk past a corner table, she suddenly stopped, and the hem of her garment swept from the floor, whipping up so far it slapped knee-high against Zahirah. The lamplight behind them revealed that whereas Zahirah was a vision in blue, this woman was a billow of black.

"*Mustafa?*" Zahirah and Malik had harmonized his father's name, but for the dark lady it was a solo, her melody to perform—hers and hers alone.

Ramadan staggered backwards, bumping into Ahmet's chest.

"What do you want with *my* Mustafa?" the woman asked, verbalizing the claim her manner had already asserted.

Overwhelmed by her presence, Ramadan couldn't speak, and judging from the wordless huffing at his back, neither could Ahmet.

Zahirah stepped forward and delivered a fast-talking Arabic explanation of the situation, gesturing to the visitors. Ramadan heard his name, and Zahirah finished her account by pointing to the photograph. As she spoke, the other woman did not move, though her coloring altered. Her face, mostly hidden in the shadows of her shawl, had originally been pale, but now Ramadan saw her cheeks dappled with the red of a fresh bruise, adding to her formidability a simmering heat.

"You come from America—and you want my Mustafa! *Again?* When he come home, he was never the same. America take my Mustafa away from me!"

Ramadan was focused on her *my.*

"No, Rana." Zahirah made an apologetic bow to Ahmet and Ramadan.

"Mama . . . ," Malik said, trying to press his way between his mother and aunt, but Zahirah warded him off with a stiff left arm.

"Is time to speak the truth," she said. "Speak the truth, Rana. Is time we all speak the truth. Me, too. America did not take Mustafa from you. *You* take Mustafa from you! You and Adad! This is why Mustafa was never the same."

Rana clasped her hands over her ears.

"Is true," Malik said, stepping forward, turning and speaking more to Ramadan and Ahmet. "Mustafa tell me. One day after I open my store, he come and he say, 'Malik, I am very proud of you.' This make me feel good, you know. It was hard to do this alone. My brother, he move away years ago. And Mustafa say, 'Malik, this place make me think about your father and his store in New Orleans, but your store is not so good as that one.' And we laugh and laugh."

"Is not true," Rana said. "Mustafa never laugh!" She stuck her chin out smugly.

"I know. But Mustafa laugh when we talk about that time. And when we talk, he walk around my store like he walk in his memory. He touch things—the food, the drink, candy, gum—and he smile. And, yes, he talk about the American girl, the one who call him the funny name. Me and Jamil, we make a joke about it."

Malik stared at the ceiling. "Mustafa say to me that is when he fall in love with the girl, when she call him the name. Then he say, 'Malik, it was the best time of my life.'" He eyed everyone in the room. "And after he say that, he no laugh no more."

Ramadan and Ahmet stood together watching Rana glare at Malik. Zahirah extended the photograph to Rana, who turned her head away.

"Look at this picture." She showed it to the whole room. "Look at me! I am like the American girl Mustafa leave behind. Malik, you are in this picture, too!"

"Mama!" Malik said.

"Is true. This is why me and Adad marry. This is my truth."

A flash of light angled in through the windows, and the room trembled. Rana dropped her hands, and Zahirah showed her the photograph again. "This is the picture of what you and Adad destroy."

Another missile went shrieking outside and thudded somewhere in the distance. This time the lamp in the corner flickered twice before it regained full power. Zahirah looked at Ramadan and Ahmet. "Rana kill love like the men outside destroy the country. Now soon Halep. Bad men destroy the world!"

Rana inhaled and then began screaming at Zahirah.

"What is she saying?" Ramadan asked Ahmet.

Ahmet paused, grimacing. "I don't know. I do not speak this language."

Zahirah covered her mouth with one hand, her eyes tearing up. With her other hand, she poked the photograph at Rana, as if it were a smoking gun of proof. Rana flinched with every jab of the picture near her face. The whistling sound from a third missile whizzing overhead entered the room, and with impressive speed and a purposeful trajectory, Rana's hand shot out from her sleeve and launched at its target—snatching the photograph from Zahirah's grasp so fast that Ramadan didn't see it move until Rana had started ripping it apart.

In her destructiveness, she exhibited the precision of her profession, only in reverse, a seamstress committed to disassembling, beyond repair, the fabric of Zahirah's memories. As she shredded the faded image, she kept yelling the same words Ahmet could not translate, perhaps some patois of fury spoken only in this household. At first visibly upset, Zahirah looked on stoically now, only a glimmer of emotion buried in the crease of the raised right corner of her mouth. It might have been a wince—or a restrained smile, an impossible-to-contain self-satisfaction.

Rana flung the confetti-like remains of the portrait into the air, and one shard landed on Zahirah's lower lip. She spat it out with a loud puff in Rana's general direction. This jagged remnant of her past floated up and away. When it finally landed, in a lower fold of her garment, no one even noticed. She rushed out, into the darkness of the hall, and Malik followed. "Ma-ma . . . Ma-ma . . ."

Rana moved in that direction as well, but when the black cape of her back was all Ramadan could see, she stopped. Her head angled down to the right, toward the corner table, and her robe fluttered, as if, birdlike, she was testing the expanse of a wing. With a swooping pirouette, she spun to face Ahmet and Ramadan. Where a feathery appendage might have flapped, her hand stuck out from her robe, brandishing Malik's gun.

"Now—why do you want Mustafa?"

"I . . . I . . . ," Ramadan stuttered. But looking at the same weapon Malik had drawn on him, he felt a calming familiarity. His inability to form a sentence had more to do with *who* was pointing the gun at him.

"Speak like a man, boy! You behind the boy, speak! You the bad Americans Adad tell me about? The family of the girl? You want to make Mustafa pay for her? You want to take my Mustafa, like you steal candy from Adad?"

Ramadan again felt Ahmet's warm breath at his back, and those rhythmic pants, like a wordless mantra, stroked him to an even deeper equanimity.

"I am not afraid!" Rana shouted, though the gun wavering in her jittery hand belied such valor. "Zahirah say I kill love. Maybe she is true. But only to save Mustafa."

She alternated her aim from Ahmet to Ramadan. "And if I kill love to save my son, then I kill you, too!"

"No!" Ahmet said, followed by a whisper—"Tell her, Ramadan . . ."

"I kill you!" Rana yelled again, pointing at Ramadan, steadying her hand.

Finally, Ramadan said, "If you kill me, you kill Mustafa."

Her face went quizzical, and her lips moved, mouthing his words. After a pause, she said, "Speak English, boy! *Who are you?*"

Her stare was ravenous with yearning—the need to know—

reminding Ramadan of himself. She looked the way he had felt the day Clarissa had told him he had a father, made him aware of just how little he knew and just how hungry he was for more knowledge. But now that he knew, he no longer felt the sting of his ignorance—of all ignorance, really—*shame*. Maybe in answering Rana he would be returning something to her more precious than Zahirah's photograph, if just as fragile, assuming you ever find it, ever possess it at all. When he spoke, he did so as if he were delivering a gift, the same one he'd received since entering this house, the thing that comes with knowing—dignity.

I am Ramadan.

Ramadan Ramsey.

My mother is Alicia Ramsey, the American girl.

The one Mustafa loved.

Adad is my uncle.

Zahirah is my aunt.

Malik is my cousin.

Mustafa Totah . . . is my father.

You—

Perhaps it was the rare nature of their relationship, as revelatory to him as it must have been to her, that muted him, for he was face-to-face with Mama Joon's only equal. Rana, his one surviving grandmother, could have pulled the trigger and not caused in him a more extreme adrenal surge. Can you kill someone as you are resurrecting him? Unlikely. Rana had fired one of the biological bullets that had bled him into the world, but she wouldn't pull *this* trigger. And what was that flickering in her eyes? What had set her lashes aflutter? A wish to behold him as clearly as possible—and for the first time—as *hers*?

When, instead of rushing to him, Rana started to collapse, he thought, I know the feeling. Malik had been pointing the gun at him when he had fainted—and yelling, "*Who are you?*" This time, Rana had aimed at him and asked the same thing. He had just answered the question, for them and himself, with similar results. When she hit the floor, the gun dislodged from her hand and skidded across the room, stopping when it hit Ramadan's right sneaker. Squatting to pick it up, he wondered: Is there something about that question—no matter how carefully you answer it—that can lead to a fall?

"I KNEW THIS! I knew this! I knew you Totah!" Zahirah came running down the hall and strode over the black splay of Rana to get to Ramadan.

She took his face in her hands and kissed both his cheeks. As she held him, he saw Malik stooping beside Rana, patting her face, trying to revive her, and she started moaning into consciousness. Ahmet was stepping forward to help but paused when Malik looked up with a half-grimace and said, "Ramadan, come."

Zahirah released him, and he went to his grandmother's side. Her mumbling began again as they lifted her and, with Ramadan backpedaling, shuffled over to the sofa. She was much lighter than he expected, and it was strange to him that this woman, who seemed so densely packed with anger, should feel like this in arms, a deflated blow-up doll, slack and wanting for air. The backs of his calves rubbed the sofa's edge, and Malik slid his arms along Rana's legs, which put Ramadan in the solo position of holding her torso. This shift tipped him back and forced him to sit down with a plop. Malik swayed Rana's feet to the far end of the sofa and stepped away, leaving Ramadan alone, cradling his grandmother. Bounding onto the cushion helped revive Rana, and he looked down at her the way Zahirah, when he awoke earlier, had been looking at him. Her lashes performed, to reverse effect, the same fluttering motion as before she fainted. Then, as she stared at him, he felt an affection he hadn't experienced since Mama Joon's eyes had closed for the last time.

"Mustafa!" Rana said. Did she think he was Mustafa? he wondered. Did he look that much like his father?

"No," he attempted to correct her. "I'm Ramadan."

Rana reached up and caressed his cheek. "I know who you are." She propped herself up on her elbows. Then, reacquiring her toughness, she said, "I am not crazy. Mustafa—we must call Mustafa!"

She lifted herself from Ramadan's lap and rattled off an Arabic command, which dispatched Malik back down the hall. Her manner went soft again when she turned and stared at her grandson.

Ramadan sat still, his face blank with astonishment. Somewhere Mama Joon was smiling at the medium of this miracle—his father was but a phone call away. Petrified, he experienced a numbness worthy of his posture, and though his lips were parted, he was breathless. Odd—on the precipice of tapping into, of virtually touching his origins, he should become this effigy of himself. A bloodless boy. On the verge of conversing with the one who had given him life, he had lost the powers of animation, lost full access to the state that had facilitated his inquiry in the first place.

Rana reached up and, just as Zahirah had done, stroked his curls. A tingling swept across his scalp like a brushfire, lighting the wicks of his senses. The deep breath he took felt like his first. Rana's scent, a blend of something feminine and edible, incited a hunger so atavistic that for a second he sucked his tongue. Blurrily, he saw Malik rushing back into the room, extending his hand to Rana. The sudden movement of metal cooled Ramadan's palm, as Ahmet sat beside him and slid Malik's gun, which he was unaware he was still holding, from his hand. The unmistakable sound of cell phone dial tones added music to the moment, but nothing was as melodious as what he heard Rana say.

"Mustafa?" She was speaking into a small flip phone. "Mustafa . . ." She closed her eyes and began to shiver. Through tears, she stammered out sentence after sobbing sentence, none of which Ramadan could understand—except for the last word, his name.

Then she handed him the phone, and he pressed it to his ear.

"*Ramadan?*" Mustafa, even in his tentativeness, spoke the name as if he'd been waiting for this call.

Ramadan had regained all of his senses now, but not the ability to speak, at least not to his father.

"Ramadan?" Mustafa said again. "Is this . . . *my* Ramadan?"

Another missile passed overhead and, only seconds later, the boom of a blast, not outside, but through the phone, near wherever Mustafa was. Was his father really as close to him as these sounds of war were making it seem?

"Allahu Akbar!" Mustafa said. Ramadan couldn't tell if he was expressing gratitude for his own life or—could it be?—for Ramadan's.

With a spontaneity he had never exhibited when saying the phrase, Ramadan responded, "Allahu Akbar!"

"Allahu Akbar, Ramadan," Mustafa said.

They exchanged amused sighs. Ramadan looked around and saw everyone in the room reacting. Malik stood mouthing the holy chant to himself. Rana got up and embraced Zahirah. Ahmet looked on with more fascination than when he had first read Zahirah's letter, appearing stricken with both happiness for Ramadan and disbelief at the realization of his own prophecy.

Ramadan asked, "Are you okay?"

"I am okay," Mustafa said. "Are *you* okay?"

"I'm okay," Ramadan said. "Where *are* you?"

The sound of another explosion came through the phone. They exchanged a second round of *Allahu Akbar*, and Mustafa said, "I am in the war. We fight—we fight for freedom." After a brief pause, he continued, "Ramadan . . . I wrote you a letter one time—a long time ago—but it came back to me."

"You did?"

"Yes. The day before that big storm in New Orleans, Uncle Adad called to tell me he saw you."

"He did?"

"Yes. He saw you and your grandmother at his store. He say you run out of the store because you hear music in the street, and she chased you and call, 'Ramadan! Ramadan!' Uncle Adad tell me this was when he know you was my boy. He say he can see me in you. I tell you that was a happy day! It made me remember my dream. It made me feel like I could still have what I wished for the most. The thing I thought I lost forever the day I come back to Aleppo. It is hard to live with no dream. But hearing about you, you know, that gave me hope. I never know before then that you was alive. That you was real. It was like to me that was the day you was born! I know it sound crazy, but it is true."

"No, it's not crazy. Guess what . . ."

"Huh?"

"That was the first day I ever heard about you, too! Just like your uncle told you about me, my aunt told me about *you*. That same day."

Ramadan saw himself, after Clarissa had told him about Mustafa. Five years old. Throwing the tantrum of his life. Screaming like a baby. Finally, alive.

"I got so mad, so angry."

"But why, Ramadan? When I hear about you, it make me happy. Why when you hear about me it make you angry?"

"Because I didn't know you, didn't have you, because I . . . I wanted you! Ever since then, I've never stopped thinking about you, never stopped trying to find you."

"So your mama—she never talk about me?"

And Ramadan realized—Mustafa did not know about Alicia. How could he? "Well, she . . . I—"

"Huh?"

"Nothing..."

"I see. I understand. I don't blame her. The way I leave her. I try to forget. Try to make myself forget. Maybe I was *her* dream. She must try to forget, too. Is okay."

After a few seconds of silence, Mustafa said, "So the day after Uncle Adad tell me about you, I write to you and your mama. But the storm stop the mail, I think. Like it stop everything. Like it stop Uncle Adad. And then the letter come back to me."

"What did it say?"

"The letter?"

"Yes."

"That one day . . . I will come to you. My American boy. My American girl! So I keep my English good. I keep think how freedom is good. I make myself ready for you to love me when I come to you." Mustafa sighed. "Aye . . . but so much happen so fast . . . the storm, death, time pass . . . now the war. And I never do what I say in the letter, Ramadan. I never do. I am sorry."

"It's okay," Ramadan said. "But now I've come to you!"

"Yes—but how? I no understand? Who is with you? Your mama? No, she no come."

"No."

"Then how did you come here all the way from America? How did you do this?"

He heard the incredulity in his father's voice. How *had* he done this? He closed his eyes, and his actions played out in his mind: *the leap from Mama Joon's front porch,* just days ago; the getaway at dawn in Miss Bea's station wagon; the flights; the cab ride from Atatürk Airport, Popeyes on his breath, with Mr. Emir, hungry and in a huff; the streettrain on Istiklal Caddesi with Mehmet; the boat ride on the Bosphorus; his journey through Turkey on the Ahmet Express; the detour on Refugee Road and the descent into Aleppo; and, albeit out of sequence, *that other leap off Mama Joon's porch,* seven years earlier—scampering through the night, hopping over the shadow of St. Augustine's cross, breaking into Adad's store, grabbing the laptop (only there, he knew now, because Jamil had forgotten it!) and snatching Zahirah's letter—a random bit of thievery, but also a reclamation on behalf of his family, leading him to where he sat now, talking, however remotely, to his father.

How did you do this?

It had taken all that and much more, but it all came down to—

"I jumped," he answered. "I jumped off the porch—and here I am!"

"Amazing. There you are."

Another muffled but explosive thud, followed by general clamor, in-terrupted their conversation. "Where *are* you?" Ramadan asked again, over Mustafa's heavy breathing.

"A big fight is come soon. Very, very big. We will face the enemy here for the first time. Near the great fortress."

"The Citadel?"

"Yes. You know? On the other side of Halep from where you are."

"I know where the Citadel is!"

"You do?"

"Yes."

"With the war, is like this place is a different country from where you are."

"I will come to you!"

"No. You cannot! Is too dangerous!"

"Then you come here."

"I wish—but it is not possible. I cannot leave my men. It is our first battle. This is the most important time."

"Then I am coming to you!"

"No. It is crazy."

"I can do it! I can make it to you. It's easy!"

"But this town will soon be more dangerous than any place you ever know. If you go down the wrong street, you can be killed."

Ramadan felt the heat of metal tearing into him. "You can get killed on any street!"

"No!"

"Yes!"

"Ramadan, go home! Go back to America! Go back to your mama!"

"I can't."

"Why? *Why?*"

"Because . . . my mama is dead!"

"What?"

"She . . . she died."

"*What . . .*"

"A long time ago, when I was still a baby." Everyone in the room had gasped at his revelation, and he heard his father cursing in Arabic with such ferocious clarity he felt he understood the pointed vulgarity of every word. Then he had to hold the phone away from his ear to withstand the clamorous rat-a-tat-tatting of an automatic weapon firing an incalculable number of rounds.

"I'm sorry! I'm sorry!" he shouted. "I didn't know how to tell you." Though he didn't think Mustafa could hear him over the racket he was apparently making with his own gun, Ramadan screamed, "Daddy! Daddy! Daddy!"

When he stopped, the shooting ended, too. Pressing the phone back to his ear, he heard a sound more penetrating than gunfire, his father's whimpering. "Daddy, it's okay. I'm sorry."

"Ramadan . . . Ramadan . . ."

His father weeping his name saturated him with emotion as well—but he didn't cry. "Yes?"

"If I let you come to me, will you go back to America, where you will be safe?"

Ramadan was slow to answer. Mustafa hadn't so much asked him a question as presented him with a riddle. If he went back to America, the place where he was almost killed, how could he really be safe?

"Promise me!"

Still brooding, he stalled. "Promise you what? That I will be safe?"

"Promise me you will go back home."

Ramadan sighed. To be united with his father, he had to agree to be separated from him again. Then there was the sordid complication of the condition that he return home. He didn't dare tell Mustafa what he'd escaped. Somehow, it was too personal a matter—his own battle to fight, one that could only be resolved on the turf of the Ramseys. It didn't concern the Totahs at all. These two factions, it seemed, had nothing in common except him.

"*Promise me,*" Mustafa pleaded.

Ramadan weighed the worst thing that could happen if he agreed to Mustafa's demand, against his not meeting his father at all. He could make this pact with Mustafa—and be granted the privilege of seeing

him. Then yes, of course, he would have to keep his vow to return to
New Orleans—where the worst might happen. But at least he would
have met Mustafa. If the price of meeting and obeying his father was
death, he would pay it. Besides—yes, this was possible, the optimist in
him said—once Mustafa saw him, maybe he would change his mind.
He might not want him to leave!

So he was smiling as he accepted his latest challenge. "Okay. If you
let me come to you . . . I will go home. I promise."

❧

"TAKE THE GUN."

Rana was sneaking Malik's pistol to Ramadan as he settled onto
the back of the motorcycle. The silvery butt of the gun flashed up at
him. Malik and Ahmet were distracted upfront, reviewing the directions Mustafa had given them to a secluded spot near the Citadel. Bits
of their conversation drifted back to Ramadan . . . *Mehamed Avenue . . .
Omar Bin Abdel Aziz . . . then Hawl Al Qalaa Street . . .*

A missile flared across the night sky, attracting everyone's gaze.
After it passed, Ahmet and Malik went back to their planning, and
Rana gave Ramadan a grandmother-knows-best stare.

"Take it!" she said again, lifting his jersey and shoving the pistol inside the waistline of his jeans, where the cool metal tickled his skin. His
giggle elicited a smile from her, and she hugged him and kissed him on
both cheeks. "Beautiful," she whispered. And he blushed—no one, not
even Mama Joon, had ever called him that.

Zahirah came running out of the house with a bag, yelling, "Food,
food!" Ramadan thanked her and put the bag in Ahmet's backpack. He
was hungry, but he knew he couldn't eat anything. Not until he had
made it to Mustafa.

He put his helmet on, and amid a flurry of farewells—*Wadaa'an, Goodbye, Ma'a salama*—Ahmet revved the motorcycle and set them on their way. Ramadan turned and waved to the Totah clan.

"Say goodbye to your family," Ahmet said. "Goodbye to your aunt, your cousin—and your grandmother who almost killed you!"

18

ALMIGHTY FATHER

Mustafa had directed Ahmet to a series of palm trees near the bridge to the Citadel.

"Seven palm trees, your father say!" Ahmet shouted after they'd been riding for about fifteen minutes. "A mosque on the right—and then seven palm trees."

"Okay," Ramadan said. "I'm looking out! And then what?"

"You stand by the middle tree and wait."

"What about you?"

"No me. Just you." Ahmet laughed. "You know, he scream at me for bring you here. 'Too much danger!' he say. 'Why you bring my son into the war?' I want to make a joke and tell him, 'Booster Keaton made me do it!' But I do not think I can make this man laugh."

"What happens after I stand by the middle tree?"

"A light will flash, three times, from the place where he is hide."

"And then do I go to him or will he come to me?"

"Uh . . . well, I do not know."

"You don't know?"

"He did not say. Maybe you must go to him, like you have come so far. Just look for the light."

"Okay."

As they cruised along, Ramadan noticed that the intermittent shelling had subsided. Mustafa had warned him about a coming battle, but the quiet, starry midnight sky was the picture of peace. His eyes drifted back down to the sparsely populated streets and the dimly lit vistas of apartment buildings and shuttered storefronts. With each passing mosque, he sharpened his vision, scanning the landscape for a septet of palms. "One, two, three . . . ," he'd counted several times without reaching that luckiest of numbers. He had just been teased by a conspicuous quintet, when he saw it rising up in the distance, lighting the horizon and proving to him its existence—the ancient fortress.

He had first seen it on Adad's laptop and subsequently, after countless internet searches, in hundreds of other digital images that had stoked his dreams. With its lore thousands of years in the making, he knew the Citadel was supposed to be real, not merely two-dimensional and virtual. And for the most part, he had believed in it, though he had also remained slightly suspicious. Wasn't there a chance it might not be real? Couldn't it be just a communal mirage? Something everyone agreed to say they'd all seen—because wouldn't it be a supreme comfort if it really *did* exist? Wouldn't it make everyone feel much safer? How reassuring it would be to know there was a vast zone up on high from which a great force could oversee the proceedings, and make sure everything was all right. Part of him had questioned it as one questions heaven—which for him in a way it was, inseparably tied to a father who, in his absence and invisibility, also had the characteristics of an illusion.

But there was no denying it now. The Citadel was real—and it was just over there. "Ahmet!"

"Yes, I see it!" Ahmet said.

The landmark was getting closer and closer. Ramadan's mind was toggling back and forth between the screensaver vision of it and the real thing in front of him. Surging forward, he saw all around him, however peripherally, the rest of Aleppo streaking by. Up ahead on its hill, its crests surrounded by golden lights, the Citadel looked like a crown—a gem-encrusted piece in a larger-than-life game of checkers—kinging the entire city. His eyes made a slow-motion, lazy-lidded blink, and when he stared out again, he was confronted with a larger and more intimate view. Coming to it after all these years of fantasizing, he saw more than a majestic monument to Aleppo, it essence, and its stature as a special place that knew it needed protecting. The Citadel also had the thrust of personal fulfillment. He saw his memories and aspirations, in essence, himself.

Looking at the fortress—he almost didn't see *them*. The palms came slicing through his focus, their fronds swiping at the radiant Citadel beyond them like the feathers of dusters. The motorcycle had just passed the sixth tree when Ramadan spotted the last one up ahead, and the inner abacus that had been tallying palms slid one more bead into place.

"Ahmet! Seven palms! Seven palms!"

"Yes?" Ahmet said, slowing down. Then he looked at the road behind them. "Yes! And back there—we pass the mosque, too."

"This is it!" Ramadan said.

Ahmet performed a shaky U-turn and drove back toward their destination. Coasting, he steered the motorcycle to the opposite side of the road from the trees, idling for a moment before turning the engine off. On their side, set back about twenty feet, was an apartment complex, which looked recently abandoned. A few stray pieces of clothing hung from lines between upper windows, laundry either forgotten in the rush to depart or intentionally left behind as territorial markings. A long-sleeved denim shirt pinned at one cuff caught a breeze; it looked to Ramadan like the torso of a ghost trying to flee because he had discovered its presence. He saw a toppled tricycle in the courtyard and thought of the children back on Refugee Road. He saw the girl's face again, frightful but defiant, and he was glad she was gone.

Ahmet elbowed him out of his daze and said, "Yes, this is it."

Ramadan turned around, gladly putting behind him a place that looked as abandoned as, until now, his heart had felt.

"Take off your helmet, and leave your backpack," Ahmet said, as if directing the scene. "Go to him with nothing but you."

Ramadan hopped off the bike, peeled off his backpack, and tossed it to the ground beside the front wheel, raising a puff of dust. He coughed as he removed his helmet and handed it to Ahmet. Then he stared across the deserted street. The Citadel was to the left, beyond the darkness on the other side of the palms. He surveyed the hidden terrain and wondered if it was as dusty and desolate as this side of the street. Was it another row of abandoned apartments? Acres of dunes? A desert? *What was over there?*

"Don't be afraid," Ahmet said, though his own voice sounded apprehensive. He rummaged through his backpack and pulled out his camera.

"I'm not afraid," Ramadan asserted. He lifted his jersey and pulled out the gun Rana had given him. Gripping it by the barrel for maximum leverage, he turned and threw the pistol at the apartments. It disappeared into the night, and several seconds later the sound of shattering glass chimed their way. Ahmet nodded his approval, and Ramadan started to walk away. When he reached the middle of the road, he stopped. What if he somehow convinced his father to let him stay? What if this was goodbye?

He turned around and said, "Thank you, Ahmet."

Ahmet lowered his camera, which had been pointing at Ramadan. "No," he said. "Thank *you*, Ramadan. You make me believe I can tell any story—and make it true."

A noisy helicopter streaked the sky with orange and red, and they followed its flight for a moment.

"I must hurry," Ahmet said. "While you are with your father, I ride to the Citadel and get the film I need. I will be here when you return."

Ramadan turned to finish crossing the street, wondering if Ahmet was filming him again. But then behind him he heard the motorcycle engine start and the sound of Ahmet revving it up.

⌒✖⌒

HIS FIRST STEP onto the other side was into a shallow swale. His right foot dipped into the sloping, sandy ground, and he stumbled forward, bracing himself against the trunk of the middle palm tree. Regaining his balance, he held on to the tall, sturdy column, his hands gripping knobby bits of bark. As he caught his breath and circled around to the dark side of the palm, he drew in the fresh earthiness of the plant, which soothed him. He heard the growls of the motorcycle dissipating, Ahmet riding off on his own mission, and it occurred to him, standing here, his back against this tree, that other than the night at the hotel, this was the only time since leaving home that he'd been alone.

As Mustafa had instructed, he waited under the palm, whose trunk had a diameter greater than the width of his frame. He would be shielded from the view of anyone spying in this direction from the opposite side of the street on this desolate strip of Aleppo. A breeze rustled the fronds above, and when he looked up at the umbrella of foliage the anxiety of his isolation faded. Maybe, he thought, Mustafa had directed him here because he knew the tree would give him this sense of serenity, the feeling that he was covered.

You'd think the solace of safety would induce a more enduring patience but—and, really, it was this simple fact, as much as anything else, that had brought Ramadan here—a boy is a curiously restless being. Only seconds passed before his comfort incited boredom. A fit of the fidgets. A nose scratch. A tug of the ear. An arch of his neck to the left, then the right. Useless squinting, trying to see through the impenetrable darkness. In his immediate vicinity, there was just enough starry luminescence and ambient urban luster for him to notice, when he idly looked down, that his sneakers were covered with sand. He lifted his right foot and wiggled away most of the beigey grit, revealing the shoe's white rubbery toe. And it was then, bending to rub away a stubborn splotch of grime, that, out of the corner of his eye, he glimpsed the flashes of light.

About fifty feet away, three laser-like rays of red had striped and strobed the blackness, in the meandering motion of searchlights, but also with the beckoning pulsations of airport landing lights, at once exploratory and invitational. The source of the redness was looking for him as much as he was looking for it. Then the light appeared again, blinking three times, more pointedly in his direction now, the last flash not a flash at all, sustained, a ray hitting the trunk of the palm just inches above his head. Stricken with surprise, a rigid Ramadan, standing fully upright, felt the glow begin to warm his forehead and glide down farther, gradually flooding and blushing his entire face. His eyes were open, but all he could see was the red. It was pale to start, as diffuse as a sunset, but then it began to change, growing richer with each second. As the device aimed at him came closer, the watercolor hue intensified into a rosiness.

And now, accompanying the increasing saturation of color, he began to hear footsteps, slow and faint at first, but quickening to the patter of a jog, trembling the ground with the rhythmic force of thuds. Ahmet had guessed he would need to go to the light, but no—it was coming to him.

Before Ramadan could decide if he should run or cry out, he felt the relentless beam sweep away from his face. Temporarily blinded, all he could see was a residual ruddiness, blackened by the sudden, relative darkness of night—the color of blood.

Instinctively, he raised his hands to protect himself, almost flailing, bracing for an impending impact with this swiftly approaching stranger. He sighed with panic as the unseen, unknown heavy breather (he could now hear grunting) continued to sprint toward him.

Then—now—a likely but unverifiable whisper: *"Don't be afraid . . ."*

The man's voice—one whose tone (if a muffled murmur could be said to have a tone) Ramadan accepted as familiar to him from the phone call—delivered this message so close to him that he could feel Mustafa's lips strum the ridges and loops of his ear. Even if the words were not really audible, Ramadan somehow read for meaning the movement of the lips as they skimmed his skin, in a sort of interactive form of braille. Indeed, it was hard to be sure if anything had actually been spoken at all, or if in fact what had been pressed into his ear, planted upon Ramadan, was not an utterance, but rather the gesture that speaks volumes—a kiss.

"I've got you!" he heard now—this time for certain—as Mustafa placed one arm around the small of his back and the other in the crook of his knees and swept Ramadan up into his arms. Swirling around, Mustafa began running back in the direction from which he had come. Ramadan wrapped his arms around Mustafa's torso and shoulder, but the rest of his body went limp. His legs dangled and his head drooped until his face smooshed into the sheltering nook of Mustafa's neck. Once nestled there, being physically transported, Ramadan was emotionally transported as well. Whereas years ago, he'd had to leap to another species in his quest for this very comfort, swaddled in his father's arms for the first time, he was now being whisked away, backwards and deeper, into the distant but apparently accessible impulses of his true origins. Ageless but decidedly infantile, he couldn't stop his lips from puckering, couldn't avoid the awkward exhibition of a primordial, mammalian thirst. Finding no nipple, but instead a thick tendon, his mouth, of its own volition, squeezed and kneaded at this tough, stubbly strip of Mustafa's muscularity. If Mustafa noticed this preternatural pecking at all, it only inspired him to hold his son tighter (which Ramadan felt him do) and to run faster, as if the boy, with his touch, were capable of controlling the movements of the man. Just as the woody smell of the tree trunk had quelled Ramadan's anxiety earlier, Mustafa's scent—the pungent cologne of manliness commingled with his minty breath—sedated Ramadan into a dreamlike state of surrender. When, without stopping his run through the darkness toward whatever zone of safety they were presumably headed, Mustafa uttered "Bae-bae," Ramadan's submersion in the waters of parental bliss, the pool of an alternate childhood—the one he'd missed—was complete. Embarrassed by his vulnerability to Mustafa's strength and feeling smothered by his submission, he summoned just enough access to the particulars of his journey to poke his head out of all this liquidity and take a deep breath. He felt the fortitude of his personality rising—the gumption that had carried him all the way here, the chutzpah pumping in and out of his heart, which was thumping madly through his Magic jersey, tapping against his father's chest. Oh, it was a prideful, valiant attempt to reassert his independence and regain some sense of composure. But a second later, when he released the breath, it vacated his body as a prolonged sigh of fatigue fusing with shudder after shudder of relief, exhaustion meeting elation, a warm draft colliding with the coolest thing he'd ever felt, precipitating a hail of tears.

⋘⋙

MUSTAFA'S RUN FELT timeless to Ramadan, who, with every stride, bounced up and down in his father's arms. So then, after either a minute or an eternity, they entered the bunker and Ramadan lifted his head and sniffled himself into wide-eyed vigilance. At first, the darkness was even starker than outside. Mustafa's pace slowed, and he wound them through a couple of sharp left turns. After he veered once more, this time to the right, Ramadan saw a speck of light in the distance. They continued straight ahead, down this narrow, foyer-like chute, and the brightness began to widen and sharpen. Soon Mustafa was carrying him into what seemed the main den of this cave. Ramadan couldn't tell where the light was coming from, but the entire cavernous space was awash in a dusty, golden luminescence. He was able to make out six or seven huddles of men—all clad in some form of warrior gear, more ragtag than uniform, and all with weapons. Two rifle-toting, fatigue-wearing soldiers rushed over and offered to help Mustafa carry him. One was shirtless but draped in a camouflage, multi-pocketed vest accessorized with a red, white, and green bandana tied around his neck; the other was wearing a bright red T-shirt, sporting a khaki bucket hat, the underside of its brim haloing his head. Mustafa shooed them away, but both men smiled greetings to Ramadan as they parted to clear the path. Their welcoming faces made Ramadan realize he had yet to see Mustafa's. Angling his eyes upward, he traced the tanned, bony jawline as it disappeared into a long, black goatee that pointed out, divining the way forward. Following its direction, Ramadan saw a worn but luxurious sofa at the back wall of the cave, looking bizarrely out-of-place. Its curvaceous, baroquely carved wood frame held cushions covered with a tattered gilt brocade woven into a rich, velvety brown fabric, and it reminded him of furniture that, in its more hopeful days, could have been in the lobby of a Ritz-Carlton Hotel. Rushing toward it, Mustafa yelled something in Arabic, and the two young soldiers reclining there jumped out of their leisurely poses. The slower and clumsier of the two, who was smoking a cigarette, had to go back to retrieve his rifle, and when he turned to them, like the other men, he smiled at Ramadan. His face stiffened, though, when he looked up at Mustafa, to whom he made an obsequious-sounding remark, offering a quick, apologetic bow, before scampering away.

"Here," Mustafa said, lowering Ramadan onto the sofa's still-dimpled middle cushion. Agitated or preoccupied, he added, "I come right back."

Mustafa swerved away in gallant strides, leaving before Ramadan had seen his face in full. The untucked tail of his long dark green shirt flapped behind him, brushing against the wrinkly folds of his camouflage pants. Ramadan watched his father take a few steps into relative darkness, his black military boots imprinting the dusty floor with their geometrically designed soles. Mustafa called out to a group of soldiers on the opposite side of the lair. One of them dashed off, out of sight, having been plainly ordered to do so, returning within seconds, running over to Mustafa with a canvas tote bag and a leather satchel. He handed these to Mustafa, who was clearly the commander of this regiment, then started to duck away, waving to Ramadan as he departed in a backward shuffle. Ramadan was waving back as his father's shadowy form pivoted first in his direction and then whipped around to face the retreating soldier, who darted out of sight. Mustafa wielded power here with nothing more than a look, and his hypervigilance and casual superiority sent a shiver of caution through Ramadan. Sensing he was breaking some kind of protocol by fraternizing with this man of lesser rank, he put his hand down and swallowed hard. Then he sat up straight and prepared to meet his father.

Gliding toward him, Mustafa's silhouette grew incrementally larger. This spooky embodiment of Ramadan's most ardent dreams crept into the softly lit sofa nook, casting a shadow upon the floor. Nervous and shy, Ramadan focused on the projection, not the man, and his father's outline moved toward him like a benevolent fog. Soon the forehead met and enveloped the toe of his right foot, the whole head swallowing his sneaker, lace by lace, past his ankle. As the shadow climbed up his shin, knee, and thigh, it broadened and was soon coloring the entire width of his body with its shade, pressing its way up his stomach and over his chest. That character-defining sensation—who would he be, after all, without having felt it—of diving into Mama Joon, came back to him with an uncanny clarity, and it released him from its grasp. All he had ever wanted was this, to be in this presence. And then his father's shadow went invisible. Its head reached Ramadan's, encasing his entire face in the manner of a veil, "forehead" to forehead, "ear" to ear, "nose" to nose, "mouth" to mouth. Ramadan closed his sightless eyes and made a promise—if he ever had a child, he would be more to him than a ghost.

"Are you hungry?"

Mustafa stepped into the light and, as the other men had done, gave Ramadan a smile, only brighter. If his shadow had become a mask, Ramadan now felt he was staring into a mirror, being beheld by his own eyes. Zahirah had been right—the resemblance was unmistakable. If his hopelessly smooth chin could sprout a beard like

Mustafa's—which he suddenly wanted to happen more than anything else—and if they were the same age, they could be the Romeo and Julius of Aleppo. Mustafa walked over to the sofa, extending the tote bag. Sitting next to Ramadan, he put the bag on the ground and placed the satchel on the sofa. He stared at his son, mouth agape, as if in search of something he'd lost, or in wonder at something he'd just found.

"What?" Ramadan asked, assuming his father was appreciating their similarities.

"Is like," Mustafa said, his eyes moistening, "is like for the first time in many years . . . I see your mother."

Ramadan saw himself blurrily reflecting on the watery surfaces of his father's eyes. It was only when a tear rolled down his cheek that Mustafa looked away. Reaching for the bag, he cleared his throat and said, "Come, let's eat. We must hurry. I want you to be safe. You must go soon, before the battle begins."

"But—"

"No." Mustafa cut him off. His voice was not gruff, just authoritative, emphatic.

"Now take this."

Mustafa lifted the lid from a plastic bowl he had removed from the bag, revealing a mouthwatering mound of dates. Ramadan's hunger erupted but, distracted by wanting to protest Mustafa's insistence that he leave, all he did was sigh.

"Take!" Mustafa said, plucking a date out of the bowl. He brought it to Ramadan's lips and pressed it into his mouth, onto his tongue.

The sweet pulp, chased by the salinity of his father's finger, had the potency of something distilled, brewed, aged. Dizzy with satisfaction, he chewed and moaned.

"Ah! I knew you was hungry. Eat, boy! You skinny, just like I was. Skinny Israel."

Ramadan scrunched his face with confusion. Too hungry to ask what his father meant, he accepted the bowl, grabbed a fistful of dates, and ate as Mustafa had directed.

Mustafa pulled out a colorful bag and ripped it open. "You like potato chips?"

"Mmm hmm," Ramadan hummed, his mouth full of dates.

"They are my favorite." Mustafa took out a single chip and crunched it loudly. "The best!"

For a couple of minutes, father and son sat eating together without speaking, each reaching into the other's supply of munchies at will, blending the salty and the sweet, alternately crunching and smacking. Then Mustafa paused and, massaging his beard, said, "You know, Ramadan, I was only in America for five or six months. Very small time. But it was a very big time. For me. The best days of my life. You understand?"

Ramadan said, "Today is the best day of *my* life."

Smiling, Mustafa quipped, "Okay, then you stay here—and I go back to America!"

He tousled Ramadan's hair, and they laughed together for the first time. After a moment, Ramadan, basking in the naturalness of their intimacy, asked, "Why did you carry me?"

"Huh?"

"Outside, under the tree . . . why did you pick me up and carry me?"

"Oh—because I see you look tired."

"I *did?*"

"Yes. Very, very tired. And . . . because I wish I can carry you your whole life."

The reverse of this desire—wanting to be carried by Mustafa—surged through Ramadan and, uncontrollably, he leaned into his father's body, spilling the dates on the floor, crushing the chips between them, burying his face in Mustafa's chest.

"I don't want to go! I want to stay with you!"

"Ramadan . . . my boy." Mustafa patted Ramadan's back with one hand and held his head with the other. "Is okay. I make you promise. And this time I make it true."

Ramadan sniffled. "What?"

"One day, when all this is over, this crazy war, my crazy life in this place, under the ground, I will come to you."

"I don't believe you."

"No? You do not believe your father?"

Flushed with guilt, Ramadan hedged his doubt. "But *how?*"

"The same way you come to me. That is how. *How?* I ask myself when my mother call and tell me you are there. How is this possible? I keep thinking this while I wait for you to come here to me. How this boy, my son, come all the way from America? *How? How? How?* Then, when I see you stand there under the tree, that is when I know."

"How?" Ramadan asked.

"Allahu akbar, Ramadan. Allahu akbar."

And for the first time, Ramadan marveled at his achievement. All along he had told himself it had been easy. But had it? Or was that just what he had had to tell himself in order to accomplish something so seemingly impossible, something so hard? And he wasn't even done yet, because he'd already lost this fight with his father—no contest. What would happen next? He tried to channel Miss Bea, who could somehow see what others could not. He tried to think like Ahmet, who in his way could, too. So he would ride with Ahmet back to Istanbul. Say his goodbyes to the Adems. Then, okay, return to America, to New Orleans, where he would have to negotiate some kind of a truce, make peace in his own civil war with his aunt Clarissa and his cousins. But *how? How? How?* he asked, sounding to himself like Mustafa. And he, too, heard only: *Allahu Akbar!*

And, yes, he would wait, and wait, and wait for Mustafa.

"Allahu Akbar!" Mustafa repeated.

He had barely finished professing his faith, when the ominous sound of fighter planes whistled aboveground, several passing in quick succession, inciting a mood of general agitation throughout the bunker. Like a chorus, the voices of the soldiers, which had been just ambient sound before, reverberated throughout the chamber: "Allahu Akbar . . . Allahu Akbar . . . Allahu Akbar!" Mustafa looked around, and Ramadan watched his face as he observed the activity the jets had caused: rifles clanking; feet shuffling; voices grumbling and mingling, oddly, with yawns. Someone aimed a shout into their cozy corner, and Mustafa stood up and yelled something back.

Then he turned to Ramadan with a half-smile and said, "Okay. Is time for you to go meet your friend. Tariq over there will take you back outside, and he will show your friend the safe way to the border. Everything will be okay. *You believe me.*"

Mustafa spoke this as a command.

"Yes," Ramadan said. "I believe you."

Mustafa kneeled on the floor at the edge of the sofa and reached for the satchel. "Before you go, I have something for you."

"You do?"

As he unfastened the crackly brown leather strap, he winked at Ramadan, who was filled with the anticipation of a much younger kid on Christmas morning. Mustafa lifted the top flap and as he reached inside the satchel, said, "My mother gave me this before I go to America. She was so worry about me . . . the same way I worry about you right now. She told me it will keep me safe. But it did much more than that. It gave me your mother—and it gave us you."

Ramadan's eyes widened as Mustafa pulled out an object encased in a golden silk cloth cover. "Open your hands," he said, which Ramadan did.

"The Quran." Mustafa placed the book in his son's hands. "It belonged to my father." He slowly unzipped the case and added, "My mother make this cover. Is beautiful, no?"

"Yes."

"She likes beautiful things." Then Mustafa flipped the pages, which looked almost new to Ramadan, who stared at the Arabic script as his father thumbed the book.

"No worry," Mustafa said, side-eyeing Ramadan. "It is okay if you cannot read it now. Keep it with you. It will make you strong, like the light of the sun. Like a good thing you remember. Like today."

He zipped the case, handed the Quran back to Ramadan, and patted his shoulder.

"Thank you." Ramadan furrowed his brow.

"What?" Mustafa asked. "You don't like?"

"I love it. But I . . . I don't have—" He was trying to say he didn't have anything for his father in return, when the soldier who had waved to him earlier reappeared, cleared his throat, and pointed to his watchless wrist. Mustafa acknowledged him by pointing one finger in the air, after which the man departed.

"That is Tariq. He is ready to take you away from me—I hate Tariq!"

Then Mustafa, still kneeling, reached out and pulled Ramadan to him in a move so sudden and crushing that it forced the breath out of Ramadan, smashing and squeezing his relatively slight frame into his father's solid chest. As he was trying to wiggle himself into a position of comfort worthy of this last embrace, he felt something press into his sternum, a thing that had come between them, perhaps a metal button on Mustafa's vest or a spare bullet in one of his breast pockets. But a second passed, and Ramadan knew.

"*Daddy*," he whispered.

Mustafa released him, and as they separated they were both panting.

"I have something for you, too," Ramadan said through his heavy breathing. He raised his right hand to his neck and clasped both lines of silver hanging there. Then he dug down the front inside of his jersey. The force of his father's hug had stuck it to his sweaty chest, so he had to peel it away from his skin. In one quick motion, he looped the chain from around his neck and ducked his head through its lasso.

"What is it?" Mustafa asked.

"Open *your* hands," Ramadan said, clinching the surprise in his fist, and this time his father obeyed him.

In a spiraling pattern, he lowered the chain onto the seam where his father's palms met, forming a lopsided little pedestal, on top of which he rested the crucifix. He watched as Mustafa's eyes moistened again, just as when he had taken his first long look at Ramadan, that look of recognition and recovery.

Ramadan sensed there was no need to explain, but he said, "It belonged to—"

"*Alicia* . . . ," Mustafa said, staring down at the crucifix, as his tears fell around it, trickling between the silver strands of the necklace. "The love of my life," he said. "The love of my life . . ." A casual observer might have thought him in worship, which perhaps he was.

"Mustafa!" Tariq had returned, though he kept his distance.

Mustafa snapped his right hand into a fist over his gift, and then he pounded his fist against his chest and said, "Thank you, my son."

"Thank you."

"Is time."

"I know," Ramadan said, picking up the Quran, holding it in his lap.

Mustafa rose from his knees and put the chain around his neck. Ramadan stood up, too, holding the Holy Book at his side, looking at once studious and learned—and resigned to his departure. They turned to face Tariq, and Mustafa draped his arm around Ramadan's shoulder.

Then he spoke in English, more, it seemed, for his son's understanding than his comrade's, or perhaps for the convenient translation of anyone close enough to hear the sound of his voice. "Ramadan is ready!"

⚭

RAMADAN HEARD, UNDERSTOOD, and took his father's words to heart. He had felt Mustafa not only wanted him to remember what he said, but also wanted to be remembered as the one who had said it.

In the coming days—the few that would press him homeward, the many plotting the course of his life—he would return, one way or another, consciously and not, to this pronouncement again and again, having added it to his little secret list of gospels.

Mama Joon's commandment. *Everything depends on how hungry you are.*

Miss Bea's psalm. *It's so easy.*

Ahmet's verse. *Everything is a mystery.*

But it was Mustafa's declaration, spoken in a cave but as if from a mountaintop, that mattered most. *Ramadan is ready.*

It emboldened him when, upon returning to Istanbul, he had stepped forward in the Adem dining room and interrupted Ahmet's rambling-sounding Turkish explanation. "Mr. Emir, I told you I was here to meet my father. I wasn't lying! You drove me to the hotel. Mehmet brought me here to your house. Ahmet just took me the rest of the way."

Emir had slumped in his chair, his rage defused.

And that evening, *Ramadan is ready* had quickened his smartphone finger-tapping as he bought his plane ticket back to New Orleans, and kept his voice from cracking when he told Mr. Emir he would be leaving on Monday, the day after Eid.

"I just need you to check me in at the airport."

"Of course. But why?"

"They say I'm too young to go alone."

"They don't know you."

⚜

WHEN MEHMET TOOK him to the Grand Bazaar the next day, Mustafa's expressed confidence in him had informed his purchase of a leather-bound notebook for Ibrahim at his father's shop. He inscribed it:

To Ibrahim,
Now you can speak any language you want.
Happy Bar Mitzvah!
Love,
Ramadan

There was even affirmation the next day, when the DJ, as Ibrahim requested, played Drake's "Take Care," and after they'd finished the feel-the-beautiful dance, Mehmet and Ibrahim agreed—Ramadan's moves were the best.

❧

ONE DAY LATER, the first day of Eid-al-Fitr, he felt the confusion of himself with the season become, at last, a clarification. As he witnessed the communal revelry marking the end of Ramadan, he privately celebrated a beginning.

❧

"WHY DID YOU do it?" he asked Clarissa, when, bolstered by his readiness, he had called last night to tell her he was coming home.

"I found a letter . . . from my . . . from your grandfather."

She didn't say anything else, but Ramadan could hear her sobbing. A letter? Mama Joon's deathbed mutterings came back to him. His *grandfather*? Maybe everything really was a mystery. He was curious about the details, of course, but he didn't ask. Anyway, Clarissa was too busy having a good cry to answer. So this all had something to do with his mother's father. Clarissa's father. He was aware of what such relationships could do to you and what they could make you do. Things that if you didn't do them could make you feel crazy. Things that if you did, could make you *seem* crazy.

"It's okay," he said, trying to sound consoling. Even if he wasn't sure he could trust her, he still loved her. "We'll talk about it when I get home." And he really wanted to go home now. In fact, nothing could keep him away—he had to read that letter.

❧

THEN, AT THE airport earlier today, when it was boarding time and Mr. Emir asked, "Are you ready, Ramadan?"—all he could do was laugh.

❧

BUT RECLINING ON the plane, cruising somewhere over the Atlantic, he woke up in his window seat in the middle of the night. Still drowsy but restless, he rolled onto his side and was shocked by what he saw reflected in the pane. It didn't look like someone who had in him what he was so convinced he had in him now. It wasn't reminiscent of any man, not even Mustafa. It was the face of a child.

ACKNOWLEDGMENTS

My gratitude to the following, for making this novel and its author possible:

Joy Harris, who not only finds homes for books, but who once, during the great evacuation of 2005, even found a home for me.

Patrik Bass at Amistad for seeing and believing—and conjuring, out of digital dust, *Ramadan Ramsey* into being.

George Wein and my festival family. Especially Quint Davis, who called me one day in 2012 and asked, "Lou, you wanna go to Istanbul?" E.J. Encalarde, who, when I told her about the character I was writing, said, with an oracular clarity, "He's blessed." George Wright, who for years patiently listened to more of Ramadan's story than anyone else— and who is no doubt as relieved as I am that it's finally done. Nalini Jones, my twin in balancing literature, festivals, and life—which she's accomplished with enviable grace. Reginald Toussaint, for insisting, despite my occasional misfortune, that I remain "Lucky Lou." My brothers, Matthew Goldman and David Foster. And my sister, the late Susan Mock, who in our decades as inseparable colleagues always treated me like an artist.

Defne Akman, whose charm, intelligence and generosity in guiding me around Istanbul and answering questions, helped turn a boat ride on the Bosphorus into a mission.

Dear friends, who have encouraged and nourished me with laughter and wisdom: Denise Turbinton, Darren Jackson, Dwayne Aaron, Gwen Richard, and Joshua Feigenbaum.

Alexa Birdsong, without whom I suspect I'd become, like this book, a work of fiction.

And finally, Mama and Bea—our little trinity of Faye, Marla, and Louis has always made me feel as if I'm part of something holy.

ABOUT THE AUTHOR

The Guggenheim Fellowship and Whiting Award–winning Louis Edwards has published three acclaimed novels, including *Ten Seconds*, *N*, and *Oscar Wilde Discovers America*. His fourth novel, *Ramadan Ramsey*, is his eagerly anticipated comeback.

Born and raised in Lake Charles, Louisiana, Edwards attended Louisiana State University in Baton Rouge and Hunter College in New York City. After graduating from LSU with a BA in journalism, he moved to New Orleans, where he has had a decades-long career as a producer of music festivals and other special events. He is currently the chief creative officer and chief marketing officer of Festival Productions, Inc.-New Orleans, which produces the world-famous New Orleans Jazz & Heritage Festival (aka Jazz Fest).

Over the past thirty-five years, Edwards has worked on countless events, including the JVC Jazz Festival-New York and the Essence Music Festival, as well as festivals in Philadelphia; Washington, DC; Los Angeles; Houston; Newport; and elsewhere. He lives in New Orleans.